Clearwater Run

Clearwater Run was previously published by HardShell Word Factory under the title ***Death Row Defender***

PRAISE for *Death Row Defender (AKA Clearwater Run)*

"…the depth of Dix's treatment of the criminal appeals process makes this novel more than a murder mystery. *Death Row Defender* is clearly written by an author who has first-hand experience in defending criminal cases, and it showcases Ray Dix's expertise as a writer."

The Florida Bar Journal, February 2006, Vol. 80, No.2

"…a page turner…compelling…crisp and fast…captures the stress, the frustration and the excitement that accompanies the defending of a capital case through the courts."

William McLain, capital appeals attorney, Tallahassee, FL

"DEATH ROW DEFENDER . . . is as interesting a legal detective story as one will find . . . it has everything." "Bravo!"

Jaye Dee Tyrack, reviewer, Gotta Write Network

AWARDS for *Death Row Defender* (AKA *Clearwater Run)*

The Electronically Published Internet Connection, EPIC, awarded *Death Row Defender,* the 2006 EPPIE for BEST MYSTERY of 2005 published in electronic format

The Maryland Writers Association awarded the at-the-time unpublished *Death Row Defender* SECOND PRIZE in the Mystery/Suspense/Thriller category in the 2003 Novel Contest

Authorlink, in association with the Harriette Austin Writers Conference, awarded the at-the-time unpublished novel, then known as ***Clearwater Run,*** THIRD PLACE /Mystery in the Year 2000 International New Author Awards Competition.

OTHER BOOKS BY RAY DIX

Tampa Bay Blues, © July 2012

Praise for *Tampa Bay Blues*

"Attorney author Ray Dix gives lawyers the benefit of the doubt in *Tampa Bay Blues*, a morality tale tightly wrapped in a murder mystery. A shark with a heart, Capt. Woody Thomas navigates Florida's court system with a persistent sense of duty to his criminal clients and his profession, and just enough recovering alcoholic to run himself aground in every summer squall. One adventurous investigation and fast-paced trial later, Thomas proves that good guys are not all good, bad guys are not all bad, and lawyers are not all liars."

- Cindy Lane, reporter/columnist, *Anna Maria Island Sun*

"Another surefire winner from the author of *Death Row Defender*. Dix's legal expertise and passion for justice shine through on every page. In Woody Thomas, readers are treated to a hero for our times - flawed, reluctant, but committed to doing what's right despite the personal cost. Don't miss this white-knuckled journey into the darkest reaches of our judicial system."

- Jackie Minniti, author of the award winning book, *Project June Bug*, and columnist for *The Island Reporter*

Clearwater Run

By

Ray Dix

COPYRIGHT

DEDICATION

This novel is
dedicated to my brother,
Elwood Thomas Dix
8/30/40 to 5/19/95
He lived his life with grace, style, and compassion.
I miss his wisdom and his sense of humor
and wish he were here to share even one more day.

ACKNOWLEDGMENTS

This book would not exist without the encouragement and loving support of my wife, Cindy. She is my heart's inspiration.

Special thanks to our close friends and prayer partners, Reverend Larry and Paula Schneider. Their faith and encouragement prodded a reluctant writer of creative non-fiction (legal briefs) to follow his heart's desire.

To my dear friends: Dr. Marion Neil and Dr. Ruth Glass, thank you for suffering through and editing the earliest drafts. You are angels of the highest order.

Thank you to my final editor, Larisa Vann, for her good work—yes—but even more, thank you for your patience with a reluctant author.

Special thanks to Susan and Bruce Bingham, Bill McLain, Kathryn Hathaway, Terry Carley, and Frances McVay—as fine a flock of friends as a man can find—for their unwavering support, advice, and encouragement.

To Edyth James of Saffron's (inspirational food and atmosphere!), my friends and neighbors in the Gulfport Marina Neighborhood, my neighbors in Americana Cove, and all the other wonderful people who have encouraged me and loved the book... Thank You.

Table of Contents

Clearwater Run

Chapter 1 — Florida State Prison

"I DIDN'T RAPE that girl, and I didn't kill her. In fact, I never even saw that girl before in my life. I know you've heard this from every client you've represented, but...I'm innocent." Jon Clayton took a breath, leaned forward and looking me straight in the eye said, "Mr. Thomas...I swear to God...I...didn't...do it."

"Well, Jon, you're wrong. I don't hear that from every client." I shrugged and added, "A lot of them, yes, but not every one. So my question is, if you didn't kill her, how'd you end up here?"

"I don't know, sir. I went to trial. I got convicted. All I know for sure is I didn't do it," he said, shaking his head. His gaze never wavering, he sighed and said, "My attorney said it was the bullet that convicted me. They said the bullet they found in the girl matched the gun I was arrested with."

"Any ideas how that might've happened?" I asked, knowing prisoners have plenty of time to think of answers to such questions.

"Either someone else used the pistol and put it back in my car, or the cops got the pistols mixed up, or maybe they just plain lied about it...I don't know," he said, "but I swear to God I didn't shoot that girl. I didn't kill her."

Good stock answers. We criminal lawyers call it the SODDI defense—Some Other Dude Did It. Somehow, it was always someone else. However, innocence is rarely a question after all direct appeals have run, and not after five years on death row. I wrote what Clayton told me on a yellow legal pad, and decided I might as well start with the penalty phase, and why he was sentenced to death.

Just because a person is convicted of a capital crime does not mean he is automatically sentenced to die. The nature of the crime and the prior life of the defendant are considered. Then the jury recommends, and the judge imposes, the sentence. I needed to know about Clayton's background, his life—the good he had done, the pain he had suffered. Maybe I could at least keep him alive.

I leaned my chair back, hitting the wall before it balanced and said, "Jon, I need to know about you, about your life before your arrest. Tell me about yourself. What do you remember about your childhood?"

"Wait a minute, Mr. Thomas," he said. "You don't believe me, do you? You think I killed her."

"It doesn't matter what I think. I don't care if you are guilty or not. What matters to me is that you're alive, and I'd like to keep you that way. I'll go over the trial. But what I need from you is not in the trial records. I need to know you from the day you were born."

"You mean you want to overturn my sentence, but you aren't interested in overturning my conviction."

"Not so—"

"Listen, I didn't do it," he said.

Clayton's voice had deepened and there was a cold edge to his words. His eyes narrowed. He leaned toward me over the table and said, "I'm innocent, but I'd rather be dead than rot in a cage the rest of my life. Do you understand what I'm saying?"

"Yes, I—"

"Do you have any idea how I feel?"

We sat staring at one another for a moment. I could hear his breathing. I could feel a slight ache in my left arm as my blood pressure rose.

I believed I understood how he felt. I had heard it before and often wondered what I would do were I in his situation. Convicted and waiting to be executed versus life with no chance of release, guilty or innocent. No chance to sail, to walk beaches, to see sunsets. Would I choose to go to my death quietly—perhaps a form of suicide? No…each time I'd considered the question, I had chosen life. But if actually faced with a caged life, with absolutely no hope of freedom, I'm not sure I would make the same choice.

We sat silently a moment more before I sighed and said, "Jon, I think I understand how you feel and what you want. Now you understand this..."

Jon started to interrupt, but I formed a "T" for timeout with my hands.

"Hear me out," I said loudly. Then more softly, "Please."

Jon leaned back, sighed, then nodded as I began.

"I intend to talk with everyone you know, everyone who knows you, everyone involved in the case—relatives, friends, cops, enemies, whatever. I'm gonna talk with 'em. Maybe, just maybe, someone has heard something or knows something that can help you. You're innocent, right?"

He nodded.

"Well, maybe they can help me find who really killed the girl. I don't know what I can do at this point, but you've got to help me first. Okay?"

THAT MORNING, WHEN I arrived at the prison just before my 10:30 a.m. appointment, I found the guards had been up to their old tricks. Jon Clayton had been put in a holding cage at eight a.m. to wait for me, even though the prison knew I would not arrive for two-and-a-half hours. The holding cage was the width of a telephone booth, but only half as deep. It was impossible to sit down, so prisoners were forced to stand during the entire wait, their hands cuffed behind them. Some of the guards did this to get the prisoners agitated, hoping to make them not want to see their attorneys. Often it worked, but not this time, not this prisoner.

When the guard ushered Clayton into the eight-foot by eight-foot conference room where we could talk privately, his presence surprised me. As the guard moved his manacles to the front, Clayton's eyes were quiet and gentle. There was a serenity about him the guards' games could not dispel. So he would not be distracted, I had him sit with his back to the door, which had the only window in the room. I sat in the other gray metal chair across the small gray metal table from him, my back against the twelve-foot high, tan concrete wall.

NOW CLAYTON APPEARED to relax. Maybe he believed me, or maybe he simply accepted that he couldn't change me. It didn't matter; I could still do my job.

He looked down at his manacled hands, sighed, and said, "Okay."

Then he looked me in the eye and said, "I'm sorry, it's just...you're the last chance I have, and I'm...I'm scared." He looked gentle and peaceful again, as though the storm of anger I just witnessed had never happened.

"I understand, and I suspect you've met some of my former clients."

"Yes, sir, and they say you're pretty good, and that you will listen, but..."

"But they're still here."

He smiled again as he nodded and said, "Exactly." Then he leaned back in his chair and said, "Mr. Thomas, I'm sorry...and truly, I do appreciate you taking my case."

"I'm your attorney now, only if you want me to be," I said. "Are you willing to work with me?" Before he could answer, I added, "Take a moment to think, and remember, 'No' is an answer, even 'No' without explanation. Take a deep breath, and think about it."

I watched quietly as Clayton closed his eyes and took a breath like I had suggested. He was six-feet tall, but eighty pounds lighter than I am. In fact, he was downright thin. To me, he did not look like a killer, but killers often look like everyday people. Other than the momentary agitation, he had shown no madness, no anger. He appeared to be just a skinny, blond-haired kid in an orange jumpsuit as he looked up at the ceiling and took another deep breath—almost a sigh.

After he said he was satisfied with my explanation of what I would be doing for him, we made small talk about the conditions at the prison, mainly to get the rhythm started as I ask questions, and he answers them. Finally, I asked him to just tell me what he thought I should know about his life. He started by telling me he had lost both parents when he was nineteen years old.

"My parents died the summer I graduated from high school. Dad wiped out the old station wagon. My brother, Bill, was six years older than me and married. He tried to take care of me, but I was dumb. I forced him to sell

Mom and Dad's house, made him give me half the money, and I went surfin'."

"You what?"

"I went surfin'. I bought an old Dodge van, threw a mattress in the back, took my surfboard, and headed out along the coast. I worked when I wanted...bummed when I could. Man...I had a blast. Did the Atlantic Coast, then California, Malibu, shot Huntington Pier, the works."

"And you came back to Florida?"

"I called Bill and his wife every couple of weeks like he got me to promise. I'd been gone a little over two years when I called Bill one night. His wife—her name's Jean—she answered and said Bill had been shot during a robbery. She told me to come quick if I wanted to see him alive. I sold my board and van for airfare and... flew from San Diego...but I got there too late." Then his voice cracked. "I didn't get to tell him I loved him, or even say goodbye." Clayton looked down at the table and choked back a sob.

I waited for Clayton to regain composure and asked, "What did you do then?"

He took a breath, looked up and said, "Well, sir, Bill and Jean had bought a little bar in Clearwater. They named it Billy Jean's. That's where the robbery was. They had a couple of girls working there, and after the robbery, things were pretty tight. I figured Jean probably couldn't go back in the place for the first couple-a months, so I just kinda moved in and started helping out. Finally, Jean came back to work. She started trying to fill her life with work. You know how some folks are. She was there all the time."

"So you helped her run the bar?"

"Yeah. Well, actually, I cleaned and cooked more than anything. I moved into the storage room upstairs. So I was there all the time, too, until I got busted."

"For the murder?"

"No, before that." Clayton shrugged. "I got in a fight with a customer, some biker dude. He was bigger than me, so I kinda cut him down to size with a two-by-four."

"Cut him down to size?" I asked.

"Yes, sir. I busted his nuts and broke his legs. I got arrested and had to plea out 'cause I couldn't afford to go to trial."

This is a normal problem faced by the poor, and seen at the PD office every week. Even if innocent, they can't afford to go to trial because they're living from paycheck to paycheck. So they plead out in exchange for probation. "What did you get on the plea?"

"It was a good deal—six months in jail, suspended if I could complete five years' probation. Bummer was...I was on probation when they accused me of the murder. They used the biker thing against me to get the jury to sentence me to death. Said I'd committed a prior violent felony."

Great, just great, I thought. *Probably aggravated assault with a deadly weapon, and on probation for it at the time of the murder.* I decided that he might look gentle, but Jon Clayton was trouble.

"I hear you had an alibi at the time of the murder. Tell me about it," I said, flipping to a fresh page on the yellow tablet. "Where were you when the murder occurred?"

Jon looked away as he spoke. "I spent the night with a lady friend. She testified at trial, but really couldn't say what she wanted to."

"What did she want to say?"

"That I couldn't have raped the girl."

I noticed a little red in his pale cheeks.

"Why is that?" I asked. "Why couldn't she say what she wanted to say?"

His eyes met mine again as he said, "I think you need to ask Fawn about that. I would rather you hear it from her. She'll tell you. Hatfield said it wouldn't have helped me, but I think it might have."

"Jake Hatfield was your trial attorney?"

"Yes, sir."

I already knew that Jake Hatfield, a private attorney, had been appointed by the court to represent Clayton because the Public Defender had a conflict of some kind. I knew enough about Hatfield to know there was a good chance he had made serious mistakes; he was lazy and a drunk. We could discuss Hatfield later. For now, I wanted Jon to continue telling me his story.

"Fawn. Is that her real name? Fawn what? Do you know the rest of her name or how I can get up with her?"

"I only knew her by Fawn," said Clayton. "Her last name was Lee, I think. She used to dance at a place called Delicto's. It's a show bar in Clearwater. I hear she left there a while back. The head bouncer was a biker named Tiny. Huge, hairy dude. Kinda scary, but real friendly. He ran the place. I hear he's still there and he'll probably be able to put you in touch with her. Talk to her. Fawn'll tell you I couldn't do it, 'cause I was with her all night."

"Okay, so you were convicted of a felony for the assault at Billy Jean's, right?"

He nodded.

"Then you were arrested with a pistol in your possession, the one linked to the murder. I think you also plead to possession of a firearm by a convicted felon for that. Right?"

"Yeah. The prosecutor offered me a good deal—two years' jail time for the plea or else he'd ask for five straight time." He shrugged his shoulders and said, "Heck, I had the pistol, no doubt about it. They caught me fair and square."

"Had you been charged with the murder when you plead on that?"

"No. They'd asked me about it, but I didn't know anything. Hatfield said it was a good deal. And it was at least a week before they filed charges on the murder."

"Hatfield was your attorney for this also?"

"Yeah, he handled all my problems."

I realized the prosecutor had most likely decided to charge the murder before he negotiated the plea. With the second felony conviction on a weapons charge, he knew he'd have a better chance at getting the death penalty on the murder.

"Why were you carrying the pistol?"

"I wasn't carrying it. I just had it in the car."

"Okay, so...why?"

"I was afraid. That guy I busted up was one mean biker and his friends said they'd get me."

"Where'd you get it?"

"Tiny gave it to me. He knew the bikers. Said they might try something, so he gave me the pistol."

"Tiny...the bouncer?"

"Yes, sir. It was free. He said he found it...someone had left it at Delicto's a few weeks before. He said it was a good one, but he wouldn't take any money for it."

The only stupid question is the one not asked, I thought. So I asked, "Did he give you the pistol before or after the murder happened?"

"I think it was the last weekend in April, a week or so before I went to court and pled out to the assault."

"So you weren't convicted on the biker thing when you got the pistol, but you did have it when the murder was committed, right?"

"Yeah, 'fraid so," he replied. "But I never fired the damn thing. I'd never even held a pistol before. I don't even know for sure if it worked. I was just going to wave it around...try and scare the bikers if they came after me. I didn't know it was illegal for me to have it."

"It wasn't when you first got it, but it became illegal after you were convicted."

Okay, I thought, *so I need to find a biker who was a bouncer five years ago. Worse yet, a biker who gave my client a murder weapon.* I was getting a bad feeling about this case. Jon's execution would probably happen as scheduled.

Clayton gave me his sister-in-law's address. He said Jean occasionally came to visit, and gave me permission to talk to her about any part of his case. He said he "trusted her with his life." He didn't say that about me, but then, she's a relative and a friend, and I'm just a court-appointed lawyer. He hadn't had much luck with court-appointed lawyers.

I watched as Jon Clayton shuffled down the corridor in his oversized orange coveralls and prison issue, rubber flip-flops. I had filled seven pages of the yellow legal tablet with notes and had promised to return with more questions after I read the trial transcripts.

As I was being escorted out of the prison, my senses were assaulted by the nature of confinement. It was always like this. There was the constant noise of bars clanging, people yelling, the sound of every footfall echoing along the corridors. I recognized again, the ugly cleanliness of the place: the dark gray floors, flesh-tan walls, and tan painted bars all shining in an unnatural light. The smell bothered me the most. The odor of armpit, crotch, and buttocks, but not like a locker-room and not just sweat. It was the musty, foul odor of anger, violence, and most of all, of fear. Fear gives off a smell that permeates everything in prison.

Even I felt fear in this place—standing in the cage formed by separate sets of electric gates, fully at the mercy of a person I did not trust. The fear lessened when, after checking the black light stamp on the back of my hand, the guard said, "Yep, you can go. Have a nice day." In a stage whisper, he added the word "ponytail" and something else I couldn't quite hear.

It felt wonderful to step into sunshine and to breathe the warm, moist air. It was early May, 1996, and I was in Starke, Florida. Outside the prison building, I still had to cross fifty feet of free-fire zone, then pass through two gates of razor wire set in the twenty-two-foot tall fences. While waiting for the outer gate to open, I looked up and waved at the guard in the tower. I think he made an obscene gesture. Here, guards control every move. Visitors, inmates, it didn't matter, the guards were in control.

"Here" was Florida State Prison, better known simply as F.S.P., the only prison in the state. The rest of Florida's Department of Corrections are known as "correctional institutes."

The legislature has made it clear there is no rehabilitation in the system, only punishment. At F.S.P., over three hundred and twenty people live on Death Row waiting to die in Old Sparky, Florida's electric chair. Standing between the tall fences and roll after roll of razor wire sparkling in the noonday sun, I thought over my new case: The State of Florida versus Jon Clayton.

I had spent well over an hour talking with Jon Clayton. I had taken his case just a few days before and had only read a short statement of the case, a synopsis which had been written for his original, or first, appeal. I had not even received the trial transcripts, but since I was in the area on other business, I had decided to visit my new client. There were forms to fill out, of course, but mostly, I had just wanted a chance for us to get to know each other.

Clayton's case had what we in criminal defense called "bad facts." It was an apparently random murder. The victim was an attractive young woman. Her car had broken down on the way to work and she was picked up by a man in a large, black car. She never made it to work. The next day her body was found several miles away. She had been raped and murdered—shot once in the back of the head, execution style.

Clayton's alibi was worse than weak. That he'd been with a hooker until sunrise on the day of the murder was the "good" part of his alibi. He had also stopped for breakfast on the way home—at a restaurant only a mile from where the victim was abducted. Worse yet, the route to Clayton's home from the restaurant would have taken him past where the victim's car was found, at the time she disappeared.

If that was not damning enough, Clayton was caught speeding in a large, black car about a week later. A pistol found in his car at the time was positively identified as the one which fired the bullet found in Donella Nash's head. That was a bad fact—a seriously bad fact.

Based on those facts, the jury convicted Clayton of kidnapping, rape, and murder, and recommended by a seven-to-five majority he be sentenced to death. Based on the facts, they had good reason to find him guilty and probably to recommend death. My job was to review the entire case for anything *other* than that which had already been considered on appeal. This was what was known as post-conviction review, and I was to zealously represent my client's interest if I found anything amiss. It would be his last chance.

It was springtime in an interim election year, and it was common knowledge the governor intended to sign one death warrant a month until November. Although his office wasn't up for grabs, his party wanted to look tough on crime.

Clayton's direct appeals had ended. His warrant was scheduled to be signed in September, the execution scheduled in October. Innocent or not, Jon Clayton's time was running out.

TIME! I REALIZED I had been standing between the fences for at least five minutes waiting for the outer gate to open. The noon sun burned hot on my shoulders and head. Sweat rolled down my neck, back and legs. I probably would have been standing there longer if one of the prison staff had not wanted to enter the compound. When the outer fence finally rolled open, I walked out quickly.

Sometimes it's hard to tell the difference between the keepers and the kept, I thought.

I looked forward to getting home to Marathon, back on board my *Defender*. But first, a little detour would be in order.

Chapter 2 — Flagrant Delicto's

I WAS IN northeast Florida, but wanted to be six hundred miles away in the Keys, south of South Florida. My choices were Interstate 95, which I hated, or Interstate 75, which I just didn't like. Both were major arteries with serious clogging—heavy traffic, constant construction, road rage, occasional snipers, and kids tossing concrete blocks off bridges onto cars.

Two things drew me to I-75, the western-most route. First, a preference for the west coast of Florida—it's less congested. Second, it would take me near the scene of the crime. I could stay the night in Clearwater, visit Delicto's and find out how to contact Tiny and Fawn Lee, or at least go to Billy Jean's and meet Jean Clayton.

I was especially interested in meeting Fawn Lee. Clayton had said she had more to tell than what the jury heard at trial, and I needed to find out from her what it was. He also told me he had heard she was thirty-nine years old, but that she looked nineteen. She was an exotic dancer, she moved like a cat, and she had a sideline as a hooker. Since Clayton said Tiny knew how to reach her, a conversation with Tiny was high on my new to-do list.

I-75 is not on anyone's list of Great-Roads-to-Travel. I joined the high speed traffic, roaring past horse and cattle pastures, and hundreds of billboards, while bypassing the few large towns. I made good time and stopped at a great little barbeque restaurant near Ocala for a late lunch. Before I ate, I changed out of the white shirt, tie, wing-tipped shoes, and pinstripe suit into comfortable traveling clothes. Then I ate far too much smoked beef with hot sauce, sweet barbeque beans, and Texas toast.

Back on I-75, I knew there was no way I would fall asleep at the wheel because my stomach was churning in total revolt. I slipped off my Birkenstock sandals, hit the cruise control button at eighty-four miles an hour, leaned back, and let the steel-belted tires sing their cruising song.

Even with a quarter-million miles on the odometer, Vicky, my faithful '85 Ford Crown Victoria two-door, loved fast runs on cruise control. She wasn't one of those new suppository-shaped cars. Like me, Vicky was big and square and showing her age, but comfortable and reliable. Like me, she could be very intimidating in tight quarters and yet, cleaned up well. Most important for my many long trips, Vicky's cassette player could blast out the music I liked: Jimmy Buffett's brand of Gulf and Western, country and western, and old-time rock and roll.

At four in the afternoon, I rolled west across Tampa Bay on the Courtney Campbell Causeway. The sunshine on my shoulder, the palm trees, and sparkling blue water all brought joy to my spirit. I sang along with songs about Banana Republics, faded love, and broken dreams. Life was good, very good indeed.

STRANGE HOW FLORIDA'S legislature raises hell about, and even bans, dirty song lyrics, yet when you drive down almost any large city's main streets you'll see signs for all nude dancers and gentlemen's clubs. Delicto's show bar was one of those clubs.

Delicto's was in northern Clearwater and easy to find—I just followed the signs, all of which portrayed the same beautiful, young woman wearing a lacy negligee. She had high cheekbones, dark eyes, and straight, raven-black hair. She looked very exotic, almost oriental. With her head held high and smiling, the woman on the signs looked happy and self-assured, not wounded, submissive, and afraid like the women most show bars choose to use on their signs. They were all just some sign painter's male fantasy, or so I thought.

The building was painted hot pink, with red-purple and yellow-green trim in paint and neon. These are colors that do not exist in nature—except on poisonous rainforest frogs and a few tropical fish. As with the frogs and fish, Delicto's colors warn sensible creatures to stay away. Naturally, some male humans are attracted by such warnings.

It was a weekday afternoon and not even four-thirty, yet Delicto's parking lot was already half-filled with the usual pickup trucks and motorcycles. Surprisingly, there were far more than the usual number of Mercedes, BMWs, Volvos and Infinitis. The place had an interesting clientele.

They must serve good food, or something, I thought. Then I noticed the sign over the door and knew what that "something" might be.

The full name of the place was *Flagrante Delictos,* Latin, which translates roughly to "in the very act of committing the crimes." Only the neon pink F of Flagrante and the letters spelling Delicto's were lighted, hence, the name, F. Delicto's.

The place was warm and moist, and smelled of cigarettes, alcohol, and sweat. The music was loud and very rhythmic—an insistent, driving, sexual beat. Young women, warm, moist, and probably smelling of cigarettes, alcohol, and sweat, "danced" provocatively to the beat on a raised stage. In the semi-dark, I could see about forty men sitting, watching attentively, some in groups of three or four, some alone.

I was dressed in white slacks and a bright yellow Hawaiian shirt. While the other patrons tried to be invisible, my clothes seemed to glow in the darkened atmosphere of the club. I felt like I had a neon sign over my head flashing: *rob this fool*! The bottles behind the bar—the smell and the music—they all told me Delicto's was a place I did not belong—except on business. *I'm here on business*, I thought, feeling my saliva turn to dust. *Only on business.*

The man behind the bar was a little less than six-feet tall, baldheaded, and lean. He wore a tight, black, short-sleeve shirt which showed off a muscular chest and huge, hairy arms. I approached him and said, "I'm looking for a guy named Tiny. Used to bounce for this place."

"He's not here."

"I'm told he still comes here almost every afternoon. Mind if I wait?" I asked. I had no idea, but it was worth a try.

"Grab a table, big fella. Maybe you'll get lucky," he said, turning and walking away.

I found a table off to one side where I could watch the door. I had a solid wall behind me—a habit that had started in the military and never went away. I've always had trouble sitting with my back exposed, especially when it felt like I was about to be ambushed.

An attractive young woman with haystack blonde hair sauntered from the bar toward my table. She looked straight at me as she walked. She appeared to be eighteen or nineteen, younger than my daughters, and naked but for a G-string and a little lace negligee that covered none of her abundant charms. She placed her hands on the table, leaned forward allowing her breasts to swing down in front of me, and asked, "What's your pleasure, honey?"

I had quit drinking alcohol and found my way into AA a few years prior. For work I had to occasionally venture into bars and clubs—only when the job required it, of course. And, while not a monk or even a prude, I was doing my best to look her in the eye as I ordered, "Coke."

She glanced to my right. Following her glance, I noticed a packet of white powder and a mirror on the table next to mine and blurted out, "No, make that Pepsi!"

The waitress giggled and wiggled toward the bar.

So much for trying to blend in with the crowd, I thought as I watched her heart-shaped butt jiggle and sway.

A few moments later, two other young women came over from the direction of the bar and asked if they could do anything special for me. They were dressed like the waitress—nearly naked.

"How 'bout a lap dance, honey?" asked the pale-skinned, red-haired girl with too-firm, extra-large breasts.

I pretended not to know what she was talking about. "That's a new one on me, babe. What's a lap dance?"

The younger looking girl—slim, modestly proportioned, her smooth skin the color of Suisse Mocha coffee—smiled and pointed across the room.

There, another young woman was... well, she was...sort of sitting in a man's lap and wiggling in very suggestive manner. It looked like magnificent torture. The customer was fully clothed and I knew he was not allowed to touch the dancer with his hands. Somehow, I just never really wanted to try it, at least not in public with a stranger.

"Thanks for the offer, babe, but I'm on duty." Bad choice of words, I realized instantly.

"Are you a cop?" asked the coffee-skinned girl.

"Nope," I answered as the girls sat down close on either side of me.

"Are you a narc?" asked the red-head, her too-firm breast pressed against my arm.

"Hell, no! I just have business with Tiny."

My drink arrived, and as I reached for it, I noticed the table was bolted to the floor. I was trapped between two naked women and an immovable object. Things were looking up.

IT WAS NEARLY five p.m. and I was still watching the girls doing things, both on stage and at the tables that I had rarely imagined, or perhaps had forgotten. Twice, one or the other of my two companions had gotten up, only to be replaced by another half-naked woman-child. My coffee-skinned friend had just returned from dancing when the light from the open door to the street went dark.

The hulk of a huge man filled the door. He was at least six-feet, five-inches tall and two hundred and sixty pounds, with a mane of wild, long, dark hair, a bushy beard and wearing black leather and dark glasses. I hoped it was not Tiny, then I noticed everyone at the bar pointing in my direction.

At six-two and two-twenty-five pounds, I am not easily intimidated, but suddenly the term "dead meat" took on a new and deeply personal meaning.

When the man walked toward my table, I started to rise and greet him, but a hand on each leg held me firmly to the seat. The girls were doing their job.

"You lookin' for me?"

"Are you Tiny?" *Oh God, does that ever sound stupid*, I thought, as I looked up at the mountain of a man.

"Depends. Who wants to know, asshole?"

"I'm an attorney working for the State of Florida." I liked to sound official. It added weight to my presence. "I represent Jon Clayton."

"Whatcha mean, asshole? You work for the state or you represent Clayton?" The man placed his hands on the table and leaned his massive head down toward me. "Well? Which is it? You his attorney or the state's attorney?"

"I'm his court-appointed defender. The state's paying me to try and get him off death row, and I need your help." *Not totally true*, I thought, *but close enough.*

It had become quiet in the bar. The music had stopped and the dancers no longer gyrated on stage or in laps. A few of the girls and a couple of bikers stood nearby. I sensed they were waiting to do whatever Tiny needed or suggested. Some of the clientele were beating a hasty retreat out the door, others to the other side of the room. My knees would have been knocking together if the girls on either side had not been holding them so tightly.

"Hot damn! This guy is trying to help Clayton," Tiny yelled toward the bar. "Anything he wants, he gets!"

I said a silent prayer of thanks and breathed a deep sigh of relief. The music and dancing started again and one of the naked girls kissed me on the cheek and got up. Tiny sat down next to me where she had been—though not as close—and asked, "What's your pleasure, brother? You name it, it's yours." Somehow, I believed him as the coffee-colored girl sipped my Pepsi, rubbed her small, warm breast against my arm and winked.

Tiny turned out to be Timothy Jacobs. He appeared to be in charge of the club and his leather clothing with Harley Davidson patches and chains made him appear to be a biker. However, several things about him caused me to wonder if he was a real biker—gang member or otherwise. His leathers and boots were too clean—he had obviously not been riding a motorcycle. He wore a Rolex, which seemed unusual for a biker. And I noticed a tattoo on the back of his left wrist; a human skull with a knife in its teeth and wearing a black beret. Under it was written Team 1 in large letters, with more words written above it I couldn't read.

I decided to inquire about Tiny's tattoo since I suspected we had military service in common. My job was to find out what I could about Clayton and find Fawn Lee, and the best way to do that was to be a friend to those who could help me.

"Were you a SEAL?" I asked.

Tiny grinned and pulled up his sleeve exposing the rest of the tattoo. "You bet your sweet ass. Six years."

The words above the tattoo read, "Some kill for money, some kill for fun, SEALS kill for money and fun." I recognized the slogan from a deadly place far away in both distance and time, if not in mind.

"You do 'Nam?" I asked.

"Bigger than shit, bro. You?"

"No, 'fraid not. I enlisted. Did four years Army. Military Intelligence," I said. "I volunteered for the big bash, ended up in Korea for the Pueblo mess instead, and spent the rest of the time stateside. Still developed a few nasty habits my V.A. counselor said were related." Guilt, alcohol, and suicidal thoughts had been my closest and most constant companions for years. "Survivor's syndrome" my vet counselor called it.

Tiny nodded his head knowingly, looked away and said, "Hey, bad shit, bro. 'Least I got to shoot back."

"Yeah, no shit." I felt the twinge of guilt I always felt around combat vets.

"You in 'Nam when Bob Kerry was there?" I asked, remembering that Nebraska's Senator Kerry had been in Vietnam and was the first SEAL to get the Congressional Medal of Honor. Unlike the Senator Kerry from New England, Bob Kerry was neither anti-war nor was he a high-profile politician. Still, I suspected another SEAL would know who he was.

"Damn right. He was Team 1, too. I got there a couple of days before he got the big ticket home, but never met him."

"Yeah. He paid a hell of a price. See much action?"

"Shit yeah, bro. Too much. And I was only in-country for sixty days."

"Sixty days? No shit? What happened?" I asked.

"SEALS jump out of moving choppers into water, right?"

"Yeah, fall from the sky like bird-shit and fools," I said, regretting the joke the instant it left my lips.

"Damn right." Tiny laughed and raised his hand as though in a toast. "All the way!" Then he got serious again as he told his story.

"Hey, man...it was pitch black," he said. "I jump out of this chopper at thirty miles an hour, thirty maybe forty feet up, and I hit the water—splat!" Tiny smacked the table for emphasis, and continued, "My legs and back were wasted. Screwed me up big time, bro."

"Sorry to hear that. What happened next?"

"We were on an insertion, and it became a rescue—of my sorry ass. One guy stayed with me, the other guys wasted a village, then came back for us. I spent three months in Japan before they'd ship me back to the States." He stopped and took a drink of the beer which had just been brought to him, then continued. "Spent two years in VA hospitals learning to walk again. The VA tossed me out in the street with lots o' pain killers and a ten percent disability. I ended up real angry, with a hell of a habit."

"Drugs?"

Tiny nodded as he sipped more beer.

"You clean now?"

"Yeah, bro. Been clean 'bout six years. Still have a little anger problem." He grinned as he said, "Yes, *sir*! I's clean...but I's mean."

"Tiny, listen, man, I really need your help with this Clayton thing. What do you remember about him?" I knew we could probably swap stories all night and that it was time to get to the business at hand.

"Hey, I liked Clayton," Tiny said with a slight shrug. "He was a good kid. He wasn't an asshole like a lot of the younger shits who come in here," he continued, nodding toward a table of four yuppie types yelling and occasionally pawing at the dancers. "He never gave nobody no trouble. Not me, not the girls, and especially not Fawn. Clayton had the hots for her bad. It was funny. She cost way too much for a kid like him."

"What do you mean, cost way too much?"

Tiny leaned toward me and lowered his voice, as though he were telling me a secret. "Fawn hooked. Okay?"

"Yeah. I heard that was her sideline."

"Well, she was very expensive," he said, still leaning toward me and talking low. "I mean *very*. She had about five or six Johns she serviced, and that's all. I mean these boys were loaded, well-heeled heels. Business men, even a lawyer, a judge, I think. They'd take her to parties, take her to dinner. She even took a two-week cruise with one of 'em. But she didn't work the riffraff, you know. Just did her stuff with the high rollers."

"Would you say Clayton was riffraff?"

"No, bro, he wasn't trash. He was all right…just poor. He helped his brother's widow run a bar over near the beach. Just didn't have the kind of money Fawn required, that's all. Dig?"

I nodded and asked, "Fawn danced here, right?"

"Yeah, about four hours a day. That was how she kept in shape...and what a shape," he said smiling. "She was our calling card. You see those signs along the highway?"

I nodded.

"That's Fawn! She had them done herself."

"You're shittin' me. That's really her?"

"Yep, in the flesh...or at least on the sign."

"You said she had the signs done? You mean the owner paid her to do 'em, right?"

"She *was* the owner, bro! At least up until a year or so ago when I bought her out."

Now, I really wanted to meet this woman. A true entrepreneur! She was beautiful and apparently had money, and she might hold the key to Clayton's case. I asked Tiny where I could find her.

"She lives up in New Port Richey, but right now she's caring for a sick relative or a friend...out in Hawaii. Should be home this weekend. I'll get her number for you and you can leave a message on her machine. She's good about returning calls. Professional habit. You know what I mean?"

Caring for a sick friend, maybe a relative. Right! And in Hawaii at that, I thought. I talked a while longer with Tiny and learned a little more about Jon, his brother Bill, and Bill's widow, Jean. When I felt I'd learned all I could, I decided to take a chance with a loaded question.

"One last question," I said, wishing Tiny had removed his dark glasses.

"Shoot," he said, then raised his beer to his lips.

How appropriate, I thought as I asked, "Do you have any idea where Clayton got the pistol he was arrested with?"

Tiny pulled the beer bottle from his mouth and held it as though reading the label for a moment, then he took a deep breath and said, "Yeah...I'm afraid that was my fault. I gave the damn thing to him. And even worse, you know that assault charge?"

"Yeah, what about it?"

"It's sorta my fault, too."

"How so? You send the guy over there to shut down the competition or something?"

"Fuck no, bro, I don' work that way," he said waving the empty bottle before setting it on the table. "It was that asshole-biker...all the time harassing my girls. I threw his ass out and tol' him to go somewhere else. Next night, Clayton had to break the asshole's legs. Bad scene. I'm really sorry it happened."

The girl with the overly-firm breasts came to the table and whispered something to Tiny, then leaned back and showed him a hand mark on her left breast. He turned to me and said, "Those tits are expensive. I've got to toss some asshole out...might take a couple minutes."

"It's time for me to go anyway," I said. "And thanks for your help."

Tiny gave a wave over his shoulder without turning around as he followed the girl across the room.

I had almost reached Vicky, when I heard loud voices and looked back toward the entrance. Tiny was having an animated conversation with the four yuppies. The bartender and two other men appeared at the door. Suddenly, Tiny placed his hand on one man's shoulder, close to the neck. It was not a friendly gesture—the man's feet were hardly touching the ground as they moved into the parking lot.

I turned, got in my car and drove away. Some battles you not only stay out of, some you don't even watch. Besides, I was hungry and I had one more person I wanted to meet before the night was over. There was a little restaurant I wanted to visit in Clearwater where I could do both.

Chapter 3 — Billy Jean's

I LEFT DELICTO'S just before sundown. My time there had been productive, enlightening, and more than a little titillating.

Crossing the causeway from Clearwater to Clearwater Beach, I enjoyed another beautiful, brilliant Florida sunset—gold, pink, and aqua streaks and swirls on a turquoise sky. I had no choice but to enjoy it—I was driving directly toward it.

Sunset accidents most often involve people who are blinded by the light of sunset, or simply chose to watch it instead of where they are going. I wove through the remnants of one such accident within three-hundred yards of the beach. It contained a representative mix of Florida drivers. A Cadillac had rammed a red and orange Jeep driven by a young man in a swimsuit. A tiny, white-haired lady standing beside the Sedan Deville was loudly questioning the intelligence and pedigree of the jeep driver. As I drove by, he replied with a raised middle finger. Several other drivers were already out of their cars.

Welcome to Paradise, I thought as I turned toward Billy Jeans.

I had learned Clayton's sister-in-law, Jean, still ran the bar. However, the bar was now more of a restaurant than a bar. The place was on the water near one of the few marinas left standing by Clearwater's condo commandos. Jon had told me Jean still worked twelve to fourteen-hour days, five or six days a week. Tiny had said the food was excellent. With luck, Jean Clayton would be working that night. However, I wanted to freshen up before supper—I could still smell the stench of Delictos' smoke and sweat in my hair and clothing.

Since it was a weekday night in late spring, I thought I'd be able to find a nice Gulf-view room. If I couldn't, my old friends, Dr. Noah Raphael and his wife, Mitzi, owned a turn-key condo nearby. I hated to drop in unannounced, but had done it before. I'd met Noah and Mitzi Raphael during a hurricane in Antigua, when we'd shared an anchorage, food, and water, and became close friends. I had always felt safe and happy, whether sleeping on their floor or on their yacht.

The Raphaels owned a big, beautiful fifty-foot Hinckley Sou'wester,

The Rx, which, like so many other big, beautiful boats, spent most of her life docked behind her owner's condo. The condo also had a spare boat slip where I had often docked *Defender* in *The Rx's* shadow. While I really wanted to spend time with Noah and Mitzi, this was business and I felt it only fair to try at least one or two motels before I bothered them.

Unfortunately, I found a room at the first place I tried. Pink and blue, plastic and glass, it was a chain motel that gave me a state discount based on my old state employee business card. My schedule was simple; first to the pool, then the shower, into clothing that didn't smell like a bar, and then off to Billy Jean's Bar and Grill for an informative late supper.

I RECOGNIZED BILLY JEAN'S from years before when the building had housed a restaurant called Tuna's, with a dock master's office above it. There were still a few boats there, but the marina was closed and the building had become a bar and restaurant favored by the locals.

Physically, it hadn't changed much, except for the weathered boards placed on end across the front windows. Someone had tried to make the white concrete block and stucco building look like a wooden boathouse. A ripped fishnet with green-and-pink plastic fish hung over a corner of the building. A six-foot tall, old style anchor was planted by the door with a light mounted on the cross-tree. The sand parking lot was half-filled with domestic and lower priced foreign cars—not a Mercedes in sight.

Inside, I was impressed. Even in the low lighting, Billy Jean's was so spotless it shone. It had a clean restaurant smell, no smoke and no alcohol odor. The juke box played Dr. John, A.J. Croce, and other New Orleans' style white-boy blues. Four waitresses dressed in black hustled beer and food, and a man and woman were behind the bar. Jean Clayton had not only remained in business for at least five years, she had found a niche and prospered.

Since I was hungry and cannot think clearly on an empty stomach, I decided to eat first. I found the only available booth overlooking the docks and ordered supper. Again, I was favorably impressed.

The food was served on heavy white china plates with metal utensils. The Amberjack sandwich was fresh and not overcooked. The skin-on French fries, fresh and hot, were cooked in peanut oil, and the tall glass of sweet tea was pure south Georgia. With my mind cleared of hunger, I was ready to interview Jean Clayton. When my waitress, Lucy, brought the check, I asked to see the owner.

"That's her behind the bar," she replied, pointing.

I really couldn't see much because of the distance, just big hair, brunette, moving fast. "Jean Clayton?" I asked.

"Yes, it is."

Realizing Lucy seemed to think in very literal terms, I decided I had best ask her for exactly what I wanted.

"Could you.... Would you tell Ms. Clayton a friend of Jon Clayton's wishes to speak to her? Please."

There was no reaction from the waitress. She just took my money to the register and spoke to Jean. Jean reacted, taking my check from the waitress and immediately leaving the bar in the hands of the other bartender. I watched her cross the room, stopping at almost every table, working hard, making sure everyone was happy with the food and service. I liked her already.

Jean Clayton was five feet six inches tall, medium build, an attractive figure with a flat stomach and wide hips—designed more for having babies than modeling. She appeared to be a woman in her early thirties, but with a lot of wear and tear. She was dressed for the job: black short-sleeved top, short black skirt over black stockings, and black hiking shoes.

"You wanted to see me about Jon?" Her voice was deep and pleasant, with just a slight edge to it.

"Are you Jean Clayton?" I asked.

"Yes, I am. And who might you be?"

"I'm Woody Thomas. I'm an attorney, and I've been hired to do what might be Jon's final appeal."

Jean Clayton slipped into the seat across from me and smiled a tight smile. I noticed lines on her forehead and at the corners of her mouth… the kind of lines that come more with worry than age.

"I heard someone was asking about him at Delicto's. Was that you?"

"Yeah, earlier tonight."

"I'm really glad to get to meet you, Mr. Thomas. What can I do to help?" The edge was gone from her voice.

"First, the food was great and your staff wonderful. Please call me Woody. Everyone else does."

"Okay...Woody. So, like I said, how can I help?"

"I need to know everything you know about Jon, from his past up through his conviction and anything you've heard about him or his case since."

Jean leaned back in the booth. Her eyes glazed. "Kind of overkill, don't you think?"

Overkill. Right, I thought, and said, "But, since you are working tonight, let's start with some specifics. Is this where Jon got in the fight with the biker?"

"Yes, but the fight wasn't his fault." She leaned forward on her elbows and looked me in the eyes. "He did it for me."

"What do you mean, he did it for you?" I asked. "You didn't sic him on the other guy, did you?"

"No, of course not," she said, smiling tightly. "Let me start back before the fight, when he first came back."

Before she could continue, the waitress returned with two cups of coffee and a question on her face which Jean answered. "It's okay, Lucy, he's a friend."

Lucy smiled and left.

"I like that," I said. "She was looking out for you, wasn't she?"

Jean lit a cigarette and, while using the saucer for an ashtray, answered, "Yeah, and that's what Jon was doing. After Bill died, Jon moved in upstairs. It was a mess. We'd used it for storage. He made it livable and spent every day working here. I was hurtin' bad and he knew it, so he took over 'til I was ready to come back."

"When was this?" I asked, grateful she blew the cigarette smoke straight up into an air intake.

"Bill died January 19th, 1991 and Jon arrived the next day. He moved in after Bill's funeral, sometime in late January. Everything's a little fuzzy from that period after Bill died."

"And he just started working?"

"Yeah. He called up the waitresses and opened the place up again the first day of February."

"How did he get paid?"

"He paid himself. He took over the books. I put his name on the bank accounts. He caught our old bartender skimming profits and fired him. Then he hired J.R., the guy behind the bar now. Hired him away from Delicto's. That all happened in February, '91."

"Did he do a good job?"

"Yeah, he did." After a pause she added, "I had the books audited after Jon was arrested. He had only been paying himself about four bucks an hour. He and J.R. had worked their butts off and this place had really begun to turn a profit. They even got a projection TV and a satellite dish so we could do sports specials."

"When did you get back to work?"

"March—three months and one week after Bill's death. I had sunk deeper and deeper, until I couldn't stand being alone and crying anymore. One day, Jon stopped by my house and suggested it was time for me to come back to work. He made me feel needed and I knew he was right. I've been doing okay ever since."

"Can you tell me about Bill's death, how it happened?" I asked, leaning back in the seat.

"It was just after closing, on Saturday, the week after New Year's. I was hauling trash out the back. Two men grabbed me at the back door and forced me back inside. Bill was still counting the final till in the back room. It was a good night, 'round eight thousand on the table."

"You had that much on hand?"

Jean nodded. "Well, we didn't let anyone else do the counting or bank runs, just Bill and myself. That night, we were short-handed and hadn't been able to make our early evening drop. It was over twice what we normally kept on hand."

"What happened next?"

"The younger of the two held a pistol to my head. The other made Bill bag the money and give it to him. He struck Bill in the face with a pistol as he took the bag." Her voice began to quiver and she looked out the window.

I leaned forward and said, "Listen, you don't have to go through this now."

"It's okay...really." She drank the rest of her coffee, and continued. As she spoke, her eyes focused somewhere down and in back of me, somewhere in the past.

"They were taking me out the door with them, dragging me by the neck. I was scared. The older guy kept screaming, 'Waste the bitch.' And then Bill was there. Later I figured out he had run through the bar and struck the alarm button. He ran out the front and circled 'round the back to surprise the bastards.

"Bill was bleeding and crazy. He wasn't armed. He just grabbed the gun away from my head and blasted the guy who had been holding me. Shot him in the face with his own pistol. Killed him instantly. The other guy shot Bill twice in the chest and ran off. The police were here within minutes and air-lifted Bill from the parking lot. He died two weeks later."

"Did they ever catch the man who shot him?" I asked.

"Oh, yeah. Bill got one shot off and hit him in the stomach. He showed up at the same hospital later that night. I saw him come into the emergency room and went hysterical. The bastard was arrested on the spot. You know what really hurts?"

"No, what?"

"He got life, and Jon was sentenced to die. Why? I just want to know, why?"

"It happens that way sometimes. The justice system is often neither just nor much of a system." I regretted getting sidetracked by the story of the robbery, but was pleased her story had matched what Clayton and Tiny had told me, with details they could not have known. She lit another cigarette.

"If you're up to it, tell me what happened with Jon. Can you tell me about the fight with the biker, the one he got convicted on?" I asked.

Jean leaned on her elbows and started looking at that place behind me again. I recognized the look. It's called the thousand-yard stare. It comes with Post-Traumatic Stress Disorder, when life has dealt a hand too painful to play. It comes from going to that place in the past too often. She sighed deeply as she started talking. Her voice became a little deeper and sad.

"I had been back to work about a month. The night it happened, Jon was cooking. J.R. was behind the bar when one of the customers, a biker, started getting loud and foul. He was irritating the other customers, so I went over and told him to leave. He said, 'Okay, I'll leave, but you're coming with me, bitch.' Then he grabbed me, threw me over his shoulder and headed for the door. J.R. jumped the bar and ran toward us, but this guy's friends stomped him. He was hurting me and I was screaming.

"Jon had just stepped out back to take a break and heard my screams. He came running 'round the corner of the building, and faced off against the guy. The biker dropped me on my back and they went at it. This biker guy was almost as big as Tiny over at Delicto's. You met him earlier, right?"

I nodded. "Definitely one big dude."

"Well, this guy was that big, and Jon wasn't doing so well. I mean that biker was pounding the crap out of him. Then Jon grabbed a chunk of two-by-four, a broken board from the dock. The biker was standing over him and Jon brought that board up between his legs. When that biker hit the ground, Jon was on him in a flash. He struck him twice more and broke both his shin bones."

"That sounds sorta like self-defense to me. How'd Jon get convicted for that?" I asked.

"The prosecutor wouldn't deal and Jon didn't want to go to trial. They said he didn't qualify for a public defender and it was going to cost more than we could afford, so Jon took a plea bargain. He got a six-month suspended jail sentence and five years' probation."

I now knew this wasn't just a conviction for a prior violent felony…the murder had actually occurred during the time Jon would have been in jail if the sentence had not been suspended. I suspected the prosecutor had argued that Clayton committed murder when he should have been in jail for a violent felony. Only by reading the transcript and record of the trial would I know for sure.

Jean was open and friendly, but her cigarette smoke finally overpowered me. Besides, she needed to get back to work. We agreed to get together again later.

As Jean got up from the table she laid the money I'd given the waitress on the table, held up the check and said, "This one's on the house."

I thanked her, and left a hefty tip for the waitress.

THE INTERVIEW WITH Jean had been intense. To relax, I rolled down Vicky's big windows, popped in a cassette, and cruised down Gulf Boulevard to Indian Rocks Beach. Jimmy Buffett sang about trying to reason with hurricane season, as the soft, salty, warm evening air soothed my soul.

It was the middle of May in Florida and hurricane season would soon arrive. It had been many years since a big blow had hit the Tampa Bay area directly. I reasoned it would be wise to bring *Defender* up from the Keys to Clearwater. I could write the trip off as a business expense since the investigation would be centered here.

Back at the motel I called my friend Noah Raphael. His son, Peter, answered and told me his parents had left the week before. Noah, Mitzi, and another couple were taking *The Prescription*, as Peter called the yacht, to the

Chesapeake Bay for the summer. Peter was sure they would be happy for me to use *The Rx's* slip, including water, electricity, and the telephone. The only conditions would be no long distance calls, and I was to look after the condo while Peter stayed in Gainesville with his girlfriend.

It appeared I had a safe harbor for free, but appearances are deceiving and nothing is free.

Chapter 4 — Just The Files, Ma'am

I AWOKE, SHAKING and sweating, my heart pounding. I lay on the queen-size bed and tried to remember the details of the dream.

In the dream it was dark, and something even darker was after me. A red beam of light glowed. I knew if the light touched me I would die. I threw my hands in front of myself for protection. There was a flash. That's when I awoke. That was all I could remember. That and the fact I'd had this nightmare before.

Even when I was drinking heavily, my dreams were vivid and colorful, and some would reoccur. I learned to pay attention to them and to accept them as a gift—often they warned of dangers to come. Several times, what I learned from them had given me a little edge, that extra split-second that had meant the difference between life and death.

Other than the nightmare, I had slept well. It was still very early when I said my morning prayers and took my morning walk—two miles over the bridge to Sand Key County Park and back. By eight o'clock, I had checked out of the motel and was headed for the Pinellas County Criminal Justice Center.

Far from the classic old Pinellas County Courthouse in concept and distance, the new Justice Center included all the trappings of a modern criminal justice system: courthouse, jail, juvenile detention, sheriff's office, guns, guard towers, and bad dogs all rolled into one. It looked like a big mall, with the multi-story Florida-modern, pink, fake-stucco courthouse being the anchor store, Justice R Us.

Good things do not happen in there, I thought as I walked across the packed parking lot.

As if to punctuate my thought, the main walkway from the parking lot to the courthouse was carefully strewn with three-foot-in-diameter concrete balls. I decided the scattering of giant balls was either an architect's misconception of how to stop a car-bomb, or a warning to the men who would be tried there as to what to expect at sentencing. The four-foot tall, phallic shaped light fixtures that lined the walk reinforced the latter impression.

Though hardly old, the courthouse was in the throes of reconstruction. I was stopped at the metal detector by security and sent back across the six-lane highway to a low-profile warehouse with a bright blue metal roof—temporary quarters for the Clerk of the Court. They had been displaced by construction crews.

The Clerk of the Court's office is responsible for all trial records. The transcript of trial testimony was to have been sent to my floating "office" earlier in the week. However, I had called and told them I wanted to see the actual exhibits and files—not just undecipherable copies of photos and objects.

The clerks, like everyone else at the courthouse, treated me well—until they found out I was defending a murderer in his final appeal. At that point they became, at best, pliable.

A quick scan of his computer told the man at the counter that the records were there. A quick scan of the room told me that they had received my records request. The file boxes were clearly marked, sitting beside a desk no more than fifteen feet away.

I was allowed to sit on a worn, wobbly, gray typing chair at an old gray metal table in a corner of the clerk's main office. There I went through two cartons of exhibits and records.

After a cursory look at the pictures of the crime scene, maps, and medical examiner's reports, I asked for copies of everything, and said, "Yes, I'll wait here for the copies."

During the half-hour wait, I realized a lot was missing from the evidence file—like the murder weapon itself. I was told it wasn't kept there, but they could "probably" find it within a week or two. Meanwhile, I should try the State's Attorney's office, back across the highway, through the metal detector.

My reception at the clerk's office had been indifferent, but at the state attorney's office I was met with outright, frigid hostility. Handing the receptionist my card, I smiled, and said, "I wrote your office last week about the Clayton file."

"What Clayton file?" she asked.

"Jon Clayton. First Degree Murder, a death case, tried in December, 1991."

"Oh, that Clayton file. Mr. Conchman is not in now."

"I didn't ask to see Mr. Conchman. I want to review the Clayton file. I filed a Rule 119 request under the Sunshine Law, and I was told it was available."

"I'll get his secretary. Have a seat over there," said the receptionist pointing to a pair of chairs by the door.

Conchman's secretary appeared to be in her late '20s, pale and soft, with fake, flame-red hair. She looked like an inverted Christmas tree: lean of hip and large of bosom, with bright red lipstick, red nail polish, and red buttons on her ankle-length green dress. Even her eyes appeared to be the wrong color, a bright green that comes from wearing yellow contact lenses over blue eyes.

When I introduced myself, she neither shook hands nor told me her name, only that she was Mis-ta Conchman's secretary. She spoke with a Southern accent, slowly, as though she were talking to a young child. I assumed she had her orders about how to handle this matter, part of which I felt sure, was to make me feel uncomfortable. I decided her nickname should be "Red."

"Mis-ta Thomas, Mis-ta Conchman said you may look through the file, but I'm to watch you. He tol' me not to leave the room while you looked at the file. Is that understood, sir?"

Yes, I understood. They were afraid I would take something or tamper with the file. I understood I was the enemy—I represented a convicted murderer. Still, I often wondered if the real reason behind this treatment was that the state was hiding something.

"That's fine." I replied. "In fact, I'd appreciate your staying with me. And I'll need copies of some—"

"No, sir! I'm not gonna make any copies for you. If you want copies, make 'em yourself."

"That's fine. You will let me use a copier, won't you?"

"You'll be charged for 'em. Ten-cents a copy, paid before you leave this office."

"Of course. No problem. This is being paid for by the county anyway, ma'am, so I don't mind at all."

As Red led me through the State Attorney's office, many workers stopped talking and stared at me. Some turned over the folders on their desks as though they thought I was a spy. I felt like a leper. I wanted to hold my hands over my head and cry out, "Unclean! Unclean!"

"My reputation precedes me," I said.

"We know who and what you are," was Red's reply.

I was ushered into a small room with two copy machines. Red left and returned with an open file box labeled J. Clayton, Murder 1, and the case number.

I noted the box was also marked "1 of 2" and smiled as I asked for the other box. I knew she couldn't leave me alone with the file, and wondered how she would get it. A few seconds later a man arrived with box "2 of 2." He was dressed in a white shirt, dark tan tie, dark tan slacks and dark tan shoulder holster with a coal-black automatic pistol. He obviously was not happy hauling boxes and shoved the box into my arms while saying something under his breath. It didn't sound pleasant. I let it pass.

To save time, I copied everything in the boxes without reading it. I tried to copy a yellow legal tablet of trial notes, but Red spotted it and grabbed it from my hand saying, "You know better than that. That's work product."

She was trained well. Original notes are not discoverable under the rules. But anything I find and copy is...discovered. While Red was busy hiding the legal pad, I "discovered" and copied several sheets of a phone message pad.

I was surprised to see two copies of the June 2, 1991 *St. Petersburg Times*, Section B. Even more surprising was the fact there were two different front pages. Hurriedly, I copied both sides of both pages, stapling the sets together.

In the bottom of box "2 of 2," I found an open evidence bag with the clear impression of a man's shoe sole. Then I looked inside the bag at the remains of a rape kit—crushed glass vials, a couple balls of cotton, and what looked like cigarette ashes. I suspected the shoe print and contamination were not an accident. Clayton would not be exonerated by DNA testing.

Red leaned against the side of the doorway, her back to me. "Excuse me," I said. When she turned around, I showed her the bag and asked, "What do you make of this?"

"Oh my, looks like someone stepped on the evidence. Good thing I was here, otherwise we'd just have to blame it on you," she said with a smile.

I copied the bag on the darken image mode so the foot print was visible on the copy.

Red counted every page I had copied, but she wasn't careful enough to notice the notes and phone messages. I wrote a check for the copies, asked for a receipt, and gladly left Red behind. The two cartons of files translated into one carton filled with copies. It grew heavy long before I finished carrying it across the parking lot to Vicky's trunk.

Next stop was the public defender's office. It had been in the courthouse up until a few weeks before. Due to the reconstruction, the PD's office was also relocated across the highway, temporarily housed in another warehouse with a blue metal roof.

The PD had contacted the firm where Clayton's specially-appointed attorney, Jake Hatfield, had worked at the time of the trial, and had obtained his entire trial file. My good friend, Elsa Salvadora, met me at the reception area and handed me a copy of Hatfield's file. It was less than an inch thick, yet it supposedly contained all of Hatfield's notes as well as all the information released to him by the state. Elsa told me to follow her through the catacombs of cubicles to her little office so we could talk. I did so with pleasure.

Elsa Garcia de Ramirez de la Salvadora was a Senior Assistant Public Defender and head of the capital crimes division for her circuit. By her twenty-first birthday, she had finished high school, college, and law school, and been admitted to the bar. All this and she spoke three languages.

She was also beautiful. Slim, almost too slim despite ample feminine endowment, Elsa stood five-feet-four-inches tall in heels. She had shoulder-length, fluffy, brunette hair with gold highlights...and now some silver. Her dark, deeply-set eyes still flashed, though they looked tired. Her lips, once full, were drawn thin. This day, she wore a gray pinstripe skirt-suit and comfortable, old, flat shoes she always kept for use in the office.

Elsa had the heart of a public defender. She could have made a fortune in the private sector, but she chose to stay where she believed she could do the most good. As a new attorney, she had interned with me. We had worked together for several years, and she was still a close and trusted friend. She'd had *this* public defender's heart for a while—and still possessed a piece of it.

I closed the door as we entered her office, and noted three sets of trial shoes in a shoe hanger on the back of the door, all with three-inch heels. Elsa's office window opened to a view of the parking lot. Posters of Caribbean beaches covered the walls. Boxes of files were stacked behind her next to two file cabinets. A six-inch stack of correspondence sat next to her computer.

She leaned back in her chair, feet resting in the bottom drawer of her desk, and watched silently as I flipped through Hatfield's file.

"This is it?" I asked.

"Um-humm. I've never seen so little preparation for a capital trial." There was a note of sadness in her voice.

I could tell she had already reviewed the file and felt Hatfield should have done more for his client.

"How are the girls?" I asked with a sigh, laying the file at my feet. "How old are they now?"

Her eyes brightened and she smiled like any proud mother as she said, "The girls are great. Electra is fourteen. Starts high school this Fall. Alexandra's thirteen going on twenty, thinks she must run the world. She's just like her mom." She sat up and turned the only two pictures on her desk so I could see them. Both girls were blessed with their mother's beautiful dark intensity.

"And Emile? Is he still with that big securities firm?"

Elsa's eyes darkened as though a light, turned on at mention of her daughters, had been turned off. She leaned back in her chair and sighed.

"I don't know how he is," she said. "You didn't know we were separated?"

Emile had interned two years after Elsa, and I had watched with envy as she fell in love with him. I thought they were a good match—both considered themselves Cuban, although he was born in Miami, and she in New York. They both had fiery spirits and were excellent trial attorneys.

"I'm sorry. Want to talk about it?" I asked.

"Maybe later. It's been almost a year. There's nothing left," she said with a shrug. "I've got a couple of big trials next week and I don't need to get all sappy. In fact, I've got a depo in twenty minutes. Damn. Woody, I'd love to talk...maybe sometime soon. Sorry there isn't more in that file," she said as I picked up Hatfield's file and stood to leave.

"Hey, it's not your fault if it's all there is. Pretty damn slim. I do appreciate your getting it for me."

"No problem, Woody. The chief okayed it since the case is out of Clearwater. You bringing your boat up?" she asked, walking around the desk toward me.

"Yeah. I'm heading down to Marathon today. Should be back up before Memorial Day," I said, fighting the urge to touch her as she came near.

"Must be nice having a floating office to work out of. I want to go sailing again when you get it up here."

We were standing by the door. I started to open it, but Elsa put her hand on mine, stopping me and causing my heart to skip a beat. She handed me her business card with other numbers hand-written on the front.

"Listen, Woody, you may have some problems on this case. If you do...well, those are my home and direct phone numbers. I also put both my home and office e-mail addresses on there, just in case," she said and smiled. "You can call, or write, anytime."

"I appreciate it. I like it when women give me their phone numbers without asking." She blushed a little and started to say something, but I continued, "What kind of problems you think I'll have? Anything special about this case?"

Elsa leaned against the door, her arms crossed in front of her. She looked toward the window as she said, "It was a high-profile case, bad timing, lots of press. Clancy Flynt was the chief investigator. He and Mikel Conchman, the prosecutor, still work together. Flynt is a bully. His sidekick, Nigel Hedeon, is at least as bad. He's physically intimidating, not just huge, but huge and scary." She stopped and looked up at me, then added, "People who cross them seem to get busted for something or have accidents. You get the picture?"

I nodded.

"There have been charges filed against them," she continued, "but nothing ever proven." She hesitated and touched my arm as she said, "Be careful. I don't want you hurt."

We hugged and I enjoyed the warmth and fragrance of her. It stirred memories of dancing on the beach, of sunset sails, of what might have been. As we separated, I tried to look into her eyes to see if, maybe, just maybe, she felt something, but she turned back to her desk quickly. There wasn't much else to be said. I thanked her, turned, and walked away.

I thought of Elsa as I headed Vicky south over the Skyway Bridge. Fifteen years ago, the thirteen year age difference had been too much. Now, maybe it wasn't.

Chapter 5 — Lee Shore

I DON'T KNOW when my watch died. I had lived in the Keys for about three months when I noticed that it always read 12:30. I took it off and never bothered with another one. It's been several years and I've learned to live on Island Time, where close is good enough. Driving south, I realized again that only the angle of the sun mattered and that I was truly happy for the first time in weeks.

Another strange thing about Florida, is the farther south you go, the farther north you end up. Clearwater is really Canada. St. Pete is Michigan and Wisconsin. Naples is Chicago. Fort Lauderdale is Pennsylvania and New Jersey. Until you reach Miami, where it's New York, Boston, with a taste of Havana and San Juan, all rolled into one huge city. At least, that's what it seems like if you look at the license plates on the cars and listen to the accents of the people.

South of Miami, in the saw grass sea, you turn east at Florida City and hit the two-lane road to Key Largo where things change again. Marathon is at mile marker fifty, almost exactly halfway between Key Largo, a transplanted New Jersey seashore resort, and Key West, a sleazy, raw, Caribbean town. Just south of Marathon is a special point where you suddenly realize you are no longer in the U.S. You have arrived in The Islands.

Vicky rolled into the Pigeon Key Marina at supper time. Since, like most live-aboards, I couldn't afford the prices of the seafood restaurant at the marina, I had stopped at Winn-Dixie and stocked up on provisions for supper and the trip to Clearwater. As I walked down the dock, a young female voice called out behind me.

"Hey, Big Woody, 'bout time you got back. You been land sharkin' again?"

Blonde, green-eyed, petite, tan, and twenty-three years old, Angela Osburn was impossibly cute and lively as a kitten. She lived alone on her own thirty-six-foot Gulfstar motor-sailer, aptly named *Wild One*. We became friends because we both live aboard Gulfstar sailboats. Angela had been caring for *Defender* for the previous three weeks and, I suspected, she had also been partying aboard. She liked the larger boat, but not the staggering difference in expense. Angela was wearing my "Mother, Mother Ocean" T-shirt from Jimmy Buffet's Caribbean Soul T-shirt company with only a string bikini bottom underneath.

"Hey yourself, you sexy wench. You're wearing my T-shirt!" I said. "It looks better on you than it does me, but I want it back."

Angela behaved like a little sister. She borrowed my clothes, my car, my boat. She was fun to be around and I could trust her to take care of everything, including the car and boat. She grabbed one of the grocery bags from me and started going through it as we walked down the dock.

"I had to borrow it. Ran out of clean clothes," she said. "But I've washed all of yours with mine. All right! A pineapple and ripe mangos!"

I noticed Angela had added pieces of rubber hose to my dock lines to prevent the lines from chafing due to the wave motion in the marina. When we were just about to board, I saw a head pop out of *Defender's* hatch and duck back in as though trying not to be seen. It was Victor, another live-aboard and Angela's sometimes boyfriend.

"What the hell are you doing on my boat? Police! Help!" I yelled.

Victor Armanno greeted us with a wide, toothy grin as he placed a full brown paper bag on the dock with a clank. He was a deputy sheriff, and a good friend.

Tall, lean, and darkly handsome with clear brown eyes, Victor came to the Keys from Chicago for a winter vacation with his wife three years ago. He fell in love with the Caribbean feeling, but his wife didn't. She went back to Chicago alone, just in time for one of the worst blizzards of the decade. They were divorced a year later with no regrets. Victor then bought an older wooden sloop of no known lineage and became our *de facto* security guard. Angela named his boat *Centurion*, for his job and his Roman good looks. He named *Wild One* after Angela's appetites.

"Hey, old man. Welcome home," Victor said, his Chicago accent intact.

He held a bottle of spray cleaner in one hand and a sponge in the other and had just set a second grocery bag of empty beer cans on the dock. I was not pleased by the cans, but as we stepped aboard, I saw *Defender* was spotless. Even the teak cockpit trim had been oiled.

"I hope you turned the mattress," I said.

"Yep," said Victor.

"And put on clean sheets," added Angela.

Victor and Angela enjoyed the queen-size berth in the aft cabin. Neither of their boats had anything as comfortable for them to sleep on—at least not together. Whenever I was out of town for an extended period, they moved aboard *Defender* and took care of her for me.

It felt good to climb back into the safety of my home-a-float, to see the teak and holly trim on white cabinetry, set off by the dark green upholstery emblazoned with bright red and yellow parrots. A white cardboard box on the cabin sole, in the entrance to the forward cabin, told me the transcript of Clayton's trial had arrived.

BY THE NEXT day, *Defender's* water tanks were filled, holding tanks for the heads were pumped, and all systems were checked out. I always kept her fuel tanks full to prevent contamination of the fuel by condensation. Still, I had to drain sludge from the bottom of the tanks and clean the two big Racor fuel filters. Finally, I ran the old diesel for a half-hour as I finished checking items on my offshore cruise checklist.

I could easily handle a boat *Defender's* size alone, but I wanted a crew for this trip so I could read the trial transcript at sea. I got the best crew I could imagine.

Angela had been born at sea while her parents sailed around the world and she was the best helmsperson and finest navigator I knew. Like many of us who live in the Keys, she worked only when necessary. Angela had found her calling as a marine calligrapher, painting names and graphics on boats. She earned enough working forty hours per month to live well, by her standards. Freedom was the most important part of her life, and she was free to sail with me.

Victor had a lot of vacation coming to him, but the sheriff's department wanted him back on duty Memorial Day, which meant we had to leave right away. He was a good sailor with a lot of experience racing E-scows on the Great Lakes. E-scows are basically twenty-eight-foot sailboards with a cloud of sails, fast and unforgiving. From those, Victor had become a master at sail handling. He was also a decent helmsman, and he had great physical strength and stamina.

Victor—Deputy Armanno when in uniform—had to work one last shift before he could leave. We agreed to pick him up in Key West. Angela had already planned the trip and navigation as she came aboard *Defender* a little after sunset. She spoke to me through the main hatch as she stowed their personal life jackets in the cockpit hatch.

"Woody, I've been up to the dock master's officer and checked the weather," she said. "There's a tropical wave off Africa. It may become a hurricane, but we'll have at least eight to ten days before it affects us."

"You call your mom?"

"Yeah. She'll meet us in Clearwater. She wants to meet the infamous Captain Woody."

I looked up from checking the forward bilge pump and was greeted with the sight of Angela's beautiful bare bottom as she climbed down the ladder into the main cabin.

"Will you please put some clothes on your body?" I said, even as I noticed the absence of tan lines.

"Ooh, testy, aren't we? Morning high tide is at oh-seven-fifteen. What time you want to leave?"

"I want to be in Hawk Channel before high tide. How about six?"

"You're on. I'll sleep on board tonight. Okay?"

"But of course, my li'l chickadee," I replied raising an eyebrow lecherously. I couldn't say no. She was already dragging her duffle bag through the hatch, her bare butt still showing. We'd shared the boat before. Angela would take the V-berth forward; I'd sleep in the queen-size main berth in the aft cabin—alone.

Even without an alarm clock, we were only fifteen minutes late as we motored out of Marathon, heading south to Key West, the southernmost city in the continental United States.

We arrived in the late afternoon to find Victor waiting at the marina, accompanied by four other uniformed deputies. What probably looked like a drug bust to onlookers was only friends waiting to greet Angela, Cap'n Woody, and *Defender*.

The other officers were on duty and couldn't take their shoes off to board the boat. Since we all were hungry, we piled into their patrol cars and headed to our favorite Cuban deli, at the Laundromat on White Street. Angela, Victor, and I walked back to *Defender* in time to watch sunset from the deck.

THE FOLLOWING MORNING was just another day in paradise—eighty degrees at five a.m., when we left the dock. Bob Marley and the Wailers sang "I Shot the Sheriff," from the cockpit speakers as two deputies danced around the dock and tossed us the dock lines.

We looked pretty normal, perhaps even tame, for Key West. Deeply-tanned Victor wore a white-and-purple flowered lava-lava and a smile. Angela was dressed in her normal string bikini bottom and a T-shirt, cut off just below her breasts. I wore long white cotton pants with a purple sash, a long-sleeved white cotton shirt, and a wide-brimmed straw hat with a purple flowered band. Once out of sight of land, Victor and Angela completely lost their inhibitions—and their clothing—opting instead for a good layer of SPF-30 sunscreen.

We raised the sails as the sky began to lighten. With the engine off, the music was changed to a steel drum CD, perfect for sailing. The joy of the trip and the beat of the music had all three of us swaying and singing. The sea was calm and the wind ten knots aft of the beam. Angela was at the wheel, and Victor napped in the cockpit, his hand resting on her leg. Less than an hour from the dock and the rhythm of the cruise was already established.

I felt secure enough in their hands to turn my full attention to Jon Clayton. I hooked large steel clips to the folders, with strings tied to the hand rails, just in case the wind suddenly breezed up, or I dozed off. In a lounge chair on the aft deck, ten miles from the nearest land, I began to read.

The briefs from Clayton's direct appeal told me that the trial had been pretty clean. What problems there were, for the most part, had not been preserved. To preserve an error, the trial attorney must make an objection on the record, and there had been none. Since no trial is perfect, the lack of objections was *not* a good sign.

This had been the last case Jake Hatfield had tried as a defense attorney. The day after he filed Clayton's notice of appeal, he went to work for the State Attorney as a prosecutor. I was certain he had been offered the job before the trial.

After the appeal was denied, Hatfield was called ineffective in a motion for extraordinary relief under Florida Rule of Criminal Procedure 3.850. The trial court, considering the motion, ruled that, "Mr. Hatfield did just fine, especially with what he had to work with." Furthermore, the court found "no evidence of a conflict of interest concerning Mr. Hatfield's move to the side of the prosecution."

The Florida Supreme Court reviewed the trial court's decision and agreed Hatfield's representation of Clayton was not below the level expected of an attorney. From what they allowed to pass as effective representation, I felt they had a low opinion of defense attorneys.

I wanted to talk to Hatfield about the case, but doubted I would find him. He had been fired by the state attorney's office before a year had passed and could not get a job with any firm in the state. His reputation and his penchant for showing up to work drunk, or with a hangover, were well-known. The last anyone heard, Jake Hatfield was somewhere in Texas, where he had developed a taste for cocaine and young boys.

In trial transcripts, the judge is referred to as "The Court," and in this case The Court was Richard Harris, III. This was Harris' last murder trial prior to retirement. A crusty, old buzzard, short and rotund with a thinning shock of white hair, Harris was known for his sharp tongue, dry sense of humor, and harsh sentences. He seemed to take pleasure in forcing defendants to take unsavory plea bargains, and made it clear if they chose trial and lost, he would sentence them to the maximum allowed by the law, or more. Among trial attorneys, such semi-coerced pleas were known as Harrisments.

The prosecutor, Mikel Conchman, was young, new, and apparently out to make a name for himself on this, his first murder case. He had done a workmanlike job, tied all the loose ends together, and put on a good show for the jury. I heard he now headed a special prosecution section dealing with vice, but knew little else about him.

The review of the black-and-white, unemotional, printed testimony was critical. This transcript would tell me the who, what, when, and where—the facts of the case. I had been in enough trials, and knew enough of the players in this one, that it would come alive for me.

PROSECUTOR CONCHMAN STARTED with the body being found. It got the jury's attention and told them why they were there.

On June 3, 1991, Lenny Larson, a twelve year old boy from Oldsmar, was riding his mini-bike with a friend and found the body in an abandoned development. When asked to describe the body, Lenny was graphic, as only twelve-year-old boys can be. "Well, there was blood all over her neck, and a mess of it on the ground, and flies and fire ants. You know? She just looked dead, but I poked her with a stick a few times to make sure, you know? She smelled horrible."

Lenny and his friend rode the mini-bike back to Lenny's house and told Lenny's father, Hans. The three went back to the scene, then returned home and called the police. It was through Hans Larson that the prosecutor first introduced photographs of the body and the place where she was found.

Hans testified he regretted getting involved because he became a suspect. If it had not been for his ex-wife and her fiancé, a state-trooper, vouching for him, he thought he might have been charged. Luckily for Hans Larson, he had opened up the church hall and helped cook at his church's homecoming. He had been there from five-thirty a.m. until noon the morning of the murder.

There was no cross-examination of either of the Larsons by the defense. After all, there was no doubt the victim was dead and Clayton's defense was that someone else did the crime. I put Hans Larson's name on a lowest priority list of persons I might wish to learn more about.

The police testimony generally reflected what Lenny and Hans had already told the jury. The local police called in the sheriff's department, which did the actual investigation. The body was found in Pinellas County, one of the most populated counties in the state, yet with plenty of open spaces to dump a corpse—palmettos, saw grass, sink-holes, and salt marshes. It was not quite a jungle, but not far removed.

THE WIND FRESHENED out of the west. We made it through Gordon Pass into Naples late in the day. I was determined this would be an easy sail—short runs and sleeping in port at night.

The fragrance of fresh ginger root, lime juice, and cilantro filled the cabin. I was cooking a vegetarian, Caribbean-style stew made with cabbage and sweet potatoes. We ate fresh mango and pineapple covered with chopped coconut for dessert, while watching a bright orange sunset and listening to steel drums on the stereo. The breeze blowing from the west kept the bugs away as the waves gently rocked *Defender*. Sleep came easy.

Morning brought a troubled sky. We shook off the night with fruit and cereal, orange juice and strong black coffee. I took the first watch, and steered *Defender* back through the pass and into the Gulf. There was more wind than the day before, and it now came from the northwest. The sea was no longer calm. We knew it would be a fast sail—cool and probably wet. In preparation we had laid out sweat shirts, long pants, rain gear, and deck shoes.

Close-hauled, the sails pulled in tight, we headed into the wind. We were sailing fast and the ride was wet—more so than could be called comfortable. *Defender* is no toy—she weighs twenty-two thousand pounds, eight thousand of which is lead ballast in a long, deep keel. Still, even with the sails reefed, we were heeled to starboard fifteen degrees. Florida was now a lee shore, and the wind kept trying to push us toward the beach. The land we called home had become our enemy.

Two miles off Sanibel Island, conditions began deteriorating rapidly—the temperature was dropping and the wind increasing. To ward off the chill, we put on hooded rain jackets, long pants, and deck shoes. Still, the wind drove salt spray back to the cockpit, stinging our eyes and exposed skin. We decided to continue to Boca Grande Pass, hoping for peace in the Peace River. It was a constant battle as we punched into the seas. Four hours later we made the turn east, flew through the pass on a broad reach, and swung north into Gasparilla Sound.

We were protected behind Gasparilla Island in a safe anchorage near Placida. There were condos in the distance, and less than fifty feet away, dolphins and manatees swam in *Defender's* shadow. We rested, listening to the surf beyond the barrier island and the wind in the rigging.

It had been nine hours since we had eaten breakfast. To keep our energy up, we had eaten only turbo-gorp—Good Ole Raisins and Peanuts, turbo-charged with chocolate candy. Victor cooked a very early supper of conch chowder and toasted Cuban bread. The chowder had been precooked and frozen several days before, and the fragrance of conch, salt pork, garlic, and onions was wonderful.

The late afternoon was spent napping and reading, then the discussion turned to my new case. Victor and Angela wanted to know what I was finding. After I told them about the victim and how the body was found, Angela went forward to check on the anchor line and watch for manatees. She didn't return. She was tired and didn't want to hear about a murder involving a woman her own age.

Victor was a good cop…he knew the law and he was honest. He often listened and talked through cases with me. It was a process that always helped me do a better job. He also knew one of the players in this case—and it was someone he didn't like.

Chapter 6 — Bad Facts

VICTOR POURED US each a tall, cold glass of fruit punch and leaned back on the deck chair.

"So, a couple of kids found the body. What's the rest of the story?" he asked.

"After the Larson kid found the body, the police were called in. Investigator Clancy Flynt had swapped shifts with another officer that morning and was at a—"

"Wait a minute. Did you say Clancy Flynt?" asked Victor. "Like in six-feet tall, dirty yellow hair, dark eyes, gaunt face, broken nose? Flynt from New York City? The one who came down to Florida ten or fifteen years back? Clancy Flynt of repeated brutality complaints?"

"Sounds like the same guy. Why? You sound like you know him and don't exactly like him."

"We've met," he said, with a frown. "Flynt is supposed to be some kinda super cop. I was at a training seminar where he was teaching take-down techniques. He broke an officer's shoulder. It was an accident, of course...but not really. It was payback over comments the guy had made about Flynt's investigative methods. He's not well-liked. Not even inside The Club." Victor often referred to law enforcement as The Club.

"Well, he was the investigator on this case. Did a pretty good job of tying all the loose ends together. Seems my boy Clayton had shacked up with a hooker the night before. From Flynt's testimony, apparently Clayton's path crossed the victim's on his way home. Her car broke down and he gave her a ride."

"Someone saw that?" Victor asked.

"More or less. An elderly Russian lady saw the victim get out of her car and make a phone call. Then Clayton pulled in...well, actually, scratch that. A black, four-door car like Clayton's, pulled up and she got in. Other than the killer, the old lady was apparently the last person to see the victim alive."

"So what's the clincher? Lots of folks drive black four-door cars."

"Well, the girl was killed with a .38 caliber pistol. On a hunch, Flynt put out a notice to be on the lookout for anyone arrested with a .38. Over the next few weeks he went and talked to a couple of dozen suspects. Clayton and one other guy were busted with .38s, the right ammo, and weak alibis. When

Clayton's pistol was tested, the bullet came back as a match for the one found in the victim."

"He drives a car like the one she was last seen in, and he was caught with the murder weapon in his possession. He got convicted. What's the problem?"

"Clayton swears he didn't do it."

"Like I said, what's the problem? Don't they all?" Victor asked. "Was there any other evidence?"

"Yes and no. Three Florida Department of Law Enforcement experts testified."

"Any question about chain of custody?" asked Victor.

"No objections. I had questions about it, until I read the testimony of the FDLE witnesses. Jane Candy was the hair and fiber specialist. She compared samples of Clayton's hair with unknown samples found on the victim, and found no matches. No hair mixed in her pubic hair, or in her underwear, which could be attributed to Clayton."

"What about Clayton? Was any of the girl's hair found on him or in his skivvies?"

"No, but he was arrested over a week after the murder. He didn't even have any dirty laundry left."

"You say your boy got convicted of raping the victim. How'd that happen? And why did the state put on Candy? Doesn't sound like she had any evidence against him."

"Tactics," I replied. "The prosecutor wanted the jury to feel that the state was being totally up front and honest with them. By bringing it out himself, the prosecutor defused the evidence. Also, some of the jurors would only remember there was hair found on the victim, but not whose hair it was."

"So, how'd they get the rape conviction?"

AT FORTY, PAT Hurley, the state's serology expert, was an old hand at prosecutions.

Hurley looked like everyone's favorite uncle. He was about five-eight and plump, like a teddy bear. His light brown hair had gray at the temples and his slightly red, jowly cheeks always appeared freshly shaven. His eyes were gray-blue and twinkled as though he was constantly thinking of a joke. He carried an air of respectability about him and would frown and look hurt if you questioned his expertise too harshly.

I had cross-examined him several times, and had been very careful to treat him with respect, lest the jurors be offended. However, from my experience, I knew he could—and would—warp his testimony enough to help the state. Hurley was law enforcement first, expert second.

Clayton's trial attorney, Hatfield, was at a serious disadvantage against Hurley. First, it was apparent from his questions that Hatfield knew little about serology, not even enough to recognize serious problems with Hurley's testimony. Second, as was pointed out in the first 3.850 motion alleging ineffectiveness of counsel, Hatfield had never received his copy of the expert's depositions. He had gone to trial unprepared.

Hatfield had stipulated to the chain of custody of the evidence and expertise of the witness. After all, the defense was that Some Other Dude Did It.

The main thrust of Hurley's testimony was to show that the victim had been raped and Clayton either was, or at least could be, the rapist. The medical examiner's report indicated semen was found in the fluids in the victim's vaginal cavity. That meant that someone had had sex with her. Hurley told the truth, but the truth didn't mean anything. DNA identification was not developed to the point where it could be used in court at the time, so the case revolved around blood typing and the antigens found in the blood.

I was surprised to see Conchman did not do the direct examination of Hurley. Senior States Attorney, and Conchman's immediate supervisor at the time, Todd Soldier was an old hand at murder cases and an expert at handling experts. He handled this one well for his protégé.

Soldier was an ex-Marine, and like most Marines, the "ex" never really applied. He still wore the same short haircut he'd received in basic, a haircut so short on the side it resembled white-wall tires. His posture was ramrod straight, a fact which earned him the nickname, Todd the Rod.

Soldier always conducted his examination of witnesses in the same manner: one page of notes and one hand on the podium, standing tall. His questions were usually clear, unless he wanted to draw attention to an issue. Then he would ask something blatantly objectionable, something which didn't actually matter. The defense attorney would jump up and object, waking the jury. Then Soldier, knowing he had the jury's attention, would ask his real question.

Hurley would look at Soldier during the questions, then look at the jury, making eye contact with as many jurors as possible, during each answer. Soldier would watch the jury during the answer to see if they were receiving the information. The two worked well together.

At Clayton's trial, Hurley told the jury how the victim, Donella Nash, was what was known as a secretor of her blood type. That meant if you tested her saliva or vaginal fluid, you would be able to type her blood, which was O. He next told them how the defendant, Jon Clayton, also had type O blood, but was not a secretor. He explained that meant Clayton's blood could not be typed through his semen or saliva. This was all very basic, and totally correct.

Then Hurley told how he tested the fluid found in the victim's vaginal cavity, and found both seminal fluid and spermatozoa. He said he couldn't separate the two, but tested the mix and it indicated type O blood.

Hurley was a good witness. He always referred to Donella Nash as the victim, and always called the act either rape or sexual assault. Perhaps that's what swayed the jury in the end. That and his expert opinion.

SOLDIER TURNED TOWARD the jury. He had picked out a couple who seemed impressed with the testimony and concentrated on looking at them as he asked the next question. His deep voice became just a little louder. He wanted to impress upon the jury that this was important—*Now Hear This*!

"Officer Hurley, based on your expertise in your field, and your experience over the past fifteen years, were you able to draw any conclusions regarding your findings relative to the fluid, seminal fluid, and spermatozoa found in Donella Nash's vaginal cavity?"

Hurley answered Soldier directly, not turning toward the jury. "Yes, sir, I have formed certain conclusions on this matter."

Soldier's voice was lower, though not as loud, as he asked the only question that really mattered. "Will you please share those conclusions with the jury, sir?"

Hurley turned toward the jury. He straightened his back and rose slightly in his seat. His face, usually gentle and friendly, took on a more serious appearance. He wrinkled his brow as though he were pained by what he must say. His voice deepened a little and he spoke slightly slower.

"Having determined the secretor status of both the murdered victim, Donella Nash, and the defendant, Jon Clayton, and having determined that the vaginal swab carrying vaginal fluid, seminal fluid and spermatozoa demonstrated O type blood, I am able to make a determination that the defendant, Jon Clayton, falls into the male population that could have sexually assaulted or raped the victim, Donella Nash.

Sometimes juries convict because they are simply dazed and confused. What Hurley said was long and convoluted—one sentence, and intentionally hard to follow.

The test showed only O positive, which it would have shown even if there were no semen present. Clayton was, in fact, one of the males on planet Earth who could have left the semen in the victim: Clayton, or any other man who was not a secretor, or any man who was a secretor but was also O positive. That accounted for seventy-five percent of the male population of the planet.

The only line that mattered, and the only one the jury really heard was, "could have sexually assaulted the victim." The jury heard Hurley say Clayton could have been the rapist, and translated it to he was the rapist. And after all, there were hair samples....

For someone trying his first murder, Conchman was using some extremely advanced techniques. Even if he did not get a conviction for the rape, the jurors themselves would feel abused and raped, and would be more likely to vote guilty on the murder charge.

IT WAS GETTING late in the evening and I decided to skip to the closing statement to see how Conchman argued this particular evidence to the jury. I was not surprised to see he played up the DNA results when he argued, "Mr. Hurley told you that he typed the semen in Donella Nash's body. The sperm that was found in her vagina...when he typed that sperm…was consistent with Jon Clayton's blood type. That test could have, once and for all, proven Clayton's innocence—*if* the sperm did not match. But it was consistent. Jon Clayton raped Donella Nash. Then Jon Clayton murdered her to cover his crime."

"WHAT ABOUT DNA?" Victor asked. "Nowadays all kinds of cases are being overturned...."

"No can do. The evidence was destroyed," I said. I told him about the footprint on the rape kit, and that it wasn't the first time I'd seen evidence destroyed.

Victor was visibly upset by the fact the rape conviction was based on so little evidence. He started to join Angela on the foredeck, but changed his mind. He sat down, looked at me with distress on his face, and said, "Please tell me the evidence on the murder is better than that."

"Well, the bullet in the victim's head did match the weapon in Clayton's possession, and he admitted it was his pistol."

"Was there a decent expert? And none of this circumstantial crap."

"How 'bout Drew Pearson from FDLE?"

"You've got a problem. They don't come any better. He's the top cop in firearms ID nationwide."

"Yeah, how well I know. Clayton thinks someone swapped weapons on him. But, there'd have to be a reason. And whoever swapped it would have to be in the system and have the real murder weapon. I just can't see it."

"If he admits it's his weapon and Pearson says it's the murder weapon, your boy is S.O.L.," Victor said. He looked relieved as he got up and walked forward to join Angela.

I understood his relief. He's a cop and the prosecutor is a cop. Victor is as honest as they get, and like most good cops, he doesn't like to see the system soiled by dirty tactics and bad busts. He also felt that, even if the rape conviction were wrong, so what. The murder would stick. At least for Victor, that made it okay. It was one of those fine points of the law on which we didn't agree.

I COOKED BREAKFAST the next morning well before sunrise. We shared eggs scrambled with shrimp, Vidalia onion, red and green peppers, and Caribbean spices. Ice cold orange juice, hot Jamaican coffee, and a stash of iced sweet buns rounded off the meal. It would be a long day. We were going to sail the rest of the way to Clearwater.

We sailed out of Gasparilla Sound through the pass that pirates, such as the legendary José Gaspar, had used for decades. For the occasion, I flew the Jolly Roger from the port spreader. *Pirates are we all, each in our own way,*

I thought, as I turned *Defender* northward.

At sunset, still a mile offshore, we sailed past the twin yellow peaks of the Sunshine Skyway. We had decided, since all three of us had sailed these waters before, arriving in the dark was, "No problem, Mon!" By ten p.m., *Defender* was tied securely in the main slip at Noah and Mitzi Raphael's condo.

Angela's mother, Gale, tall, red-haired, freckled, and strikingly attractive, was waiting at the dock when we arrived. Gale had invited Victor to spend a few days with her and Angela at her home in Holiday. The three of us would get back together and drive down to Marathon before Memorial Day so Victor could get to work and I could bring Vicky back to the city.

It was late, we were tired, and they left quickly. I was alone again, but in a very familiar environment, my home-afloat, *Defender*. I was ready to begin the investigation, to meet and question the players.

Chapter 7 — Memento

SLEEPING IN A beach resort like Clearwater, even off-season, was not as pleasant as sleeping in the Keys. Its carnival atmosphere had gone late into the night. Even with *Defender's* water-cooled central air conditioner on and all the hatches closed, the level of noise had been irritating.

It was now eight a.m. and I had already walked four miles, eaten at a nearby pancake house, and was connecting the shore-side water and electrical lines when Peter Raphael arrived in his old diesel Mercedes 240-D. I hadn't seen my friend's son in a couple of years. With his new beard, I didn't recognize him until he called out, "Hey, Captain Woody! Welcome back."

Peter had called and gotten approval to do what we had already agreed to do and more. Not only could I keep *Defender* at the dock, I also had unlimited use of the condo.

"I guess you want to borrow a car," Peter said.

I eyed Noah's shiny white Jaguar XJ-12 sedan. "Sure would. But just for a few days until I can get my own up here."

Peter tossed the keys to the house and the Mercedes to me, as he slid into the Jag.

"You know the routine," he said. "Dad says for me to take the Jag. He can't afford to let you drive it again."

"Hey, it wasn't my fault. She backed into me!"

The door to the Jag was closed and the engine snarled to life. *So much for negotiating*, I thought. Actually, I was pleased to have any wheels, since there was much to be done and little time in which to do it. I had a list of persons with whom I wanted to talk about the case, and first on that list was Behrooz Caspari, the County Medical Examiner.

I called the medical examiner's office just after nine a.m. and spoke to Dr. Caspari. He seemed quite cordial. We agreed to meet at his private office near the old Clearwater Courthouse at two p.m. Meanwhile, I reviewed his testimony and compared it with the medical records I had received from the two attorneys and the clerk. I like to know what to expect before talking to witnesses; it allows me to better focus my questions.

Behrooz Caspari had testified in almost every case I had encountered from Pinellas County. I knew he did not often bend the facts, but I considered him to be just another cop—he wasn't in the business of trying to help my clients. Often his opinions, while based on the facts, were, at best, suspect.

Caspari's credentials were all from medical schools in the Middle East and Caribbean. Hatfield had wisely stipulated to his expertise rather than allow the state to parade all the impressive-sounding foreign degrees before the jury. As the county medical examiner, he testified about his findings—the normal gruesome details of the autopsy. Then, the prosecutor asked the first question which went directly to the core of the case.

"WOULD YOU PLEASE share with the jury what your findings and conclusions were as to the time and cause of death?"

Caspari nodded, then turned toward the jury and said, "I fix time of death between six-thirty and seven-thirty a.m., June second, approximately twenty-four hours before the victim's body was found."

His voice was rather high-pitched and, combined with his thick Middle Eastern accent, was about as pleasant as fingernails on a chalkboard. He raised his bushy eyebrows causing his eyes to protrude more than usual, as he continued, "The victim, Mrs. Nash, was shot in the back of the head one time with a small caliber firearm. It appears she was kneeling at the time. The barrel of the weapon was placed close to the base of the skull, in such a position that the projectile would cut the medulla oblongata and enter the cavity of the cranium. Death was instantaneous."

"Doctor, were you able to determine if Donella Nash had been raped?"

"Yes, I believe she was sexually assaulted."

"What led you to that conclusion, Doctor?"

"There were marks on her arms and breasts which had been placed there shortly before the murder. They had not yet formed bruises when she died. The marks appeared consistent with someone squeezing or pinching her breasts and holding her arms extremely tight.

"There was also semen found in the victim, and her husband denied having sex with her that morning. I conclude she was sexually assaulted shortly before she died."

I WAS NOT impressed with Caspari's logic. The victim could have had sex without it being rape or assault, or with her husband. Eddy Nash, the victim's husband, was already on the list of persons to whom I would be talking, no matter what his testimony was. Now, I had another question for him.

Caspari testified he had collected evidence during the autopsy: hair, vaginal swabs, and the bullet from the victim's brain.

"What, if anything, did you do with these items?" asked Conchman.

"I gave the pictures to you. The hair samples and vaginal swabs were packaged and sealed and I gave them to Investigator Flynt. I also removed the bullet from the victim's brain, packaged it, and gave it to Investigator Flynt."

Caspari also testified that the victim had been killed on the spot where she was found. He said the blood had settled to the lower part of the body, in such a manner that it indicated she had not been moved since she was shot.

Defense attorney, Jake Hatfield, refused to honor the doctor's credentials by calling him Doctor. Refusing to bestow honor through addressing the witness by his title was a good method when dealing with police officers, but it could backfire when dealing with a doctor. The jurors sometimes took offense. Hatfield had only one line of questioning for Caspari, but it was a good one.

"MR. CASPARI, YOU testified that, in your opinion, the victim had been sexually assaulted and murdered, correct?"

"Yes, that is correct," said Caspari. He took his time answering because he was never sure what defense attorneys would ask him.

"And in your opinion, was she murdered immediately, or at least shortly, after being sexually assaulted?"

"I believe she was."

"What was the state of her clothing when she was found?"

"What state? I do not understand your question."

"Was any of her clothing torn or ripped?"

"No...not that I recall."

"Was she wearing all of her clothing?"

"Yes. Yes, she was...fully dressed."

"Including her underwear?"

"Yes. Yes, she was wearing her underwear."

IN HIS CLOSING arguments, Hatfield had told the jury that it would be unusual for a rapist to let the victim get dressed before murdering her. He'd also argued it was inconsistent with sexual assault, a crime of violence, for no clothing to be torn, and that the semen, and even the marks on her body, could have come from consensual sex.

The prosecutor had countered with the argument that the sexual assault probably took place several miles away or in Clayton's car, then the victim was transported and murdered.

To me, both were logical explanations and sequences of events. However, the jury believed the prosecutor.

CASPARI'S OFFICE WAS a second-floor walk-up with a small reception area furnished with two plastic chairs. A single open door led to a dark paneled room behind the receptionist. I arrived ten minutes early.

Layla, his twenty-something, gum-chewing, bleached-blonde receptionist, confirmed this was Caspari's legal/medical office. He knew I was coming, but he was not there, and he would not be coming in. However, he did leave the file on the Nash murder with instructions to allow me to review and copy anything I might need.

I had wanted to discuss the case with Caspari, but this would be a good start. Layla handed me the file and turned her attention to typing letters, a single earpiece leading from her right ear to the dictation recorder.

I found the original of Caspari's report. It appeared to be the same report I had seen copied in the files of the prosecutor, defense attorney, and the court clerk. All were typed and dated June 6, 1991, four days after the murder.

I also found a handwritten report listing each item of clothing, dated June 3, 1991, the day the body was found. I had seen no copies of the handwritten report, but the list of clothing matched one found in the prosecutor's typed discovery file released to Hatfield.

Then I found a second handwritten list, identical to the others, except for one item. At the end of the list was added: single earring from the right ear of victim. Obviously, either Caspari failed to tell the police, or the police failed to review the file. Nowhere else had I seen an earring mentioned. I realized Caspari may have been the only person who knew of its existence.

The file contained dozens of pictures of the body and the autopsy, both black-and-white and color, all of which I copied. Even if I had copies from the other files, I wanted copies of everything in this file so I could compare the items.

Loose at the back of the file, I found two color photographs of an earring lying next to a 6-inch ruler on a white sheet of paper with Clayton's case number written on it. The pictures were clipped to a handwritten note, signed by Caspari and dated June 4, 1991. *Single earring given to husband at time of identification. He will make available for police.*

The pictures showed a hook type earring made for pierced ears. A gold wire formed the hook, with a blue bead hung where it would fall just below the earlobe. Below that hung a half-inch piece of grayish rock. It wasn't exactly my style—I preferred a diamond stud myself—but it was a nice earring.

Layla allowed me to take the two color photographs to a nearby copy shop where she said I could get good color copies. "Just bring them back today," she said as I left.

Color copying is a cheap and quick way to reproduce photographs without negatives. I enlarged one set to two hundred percent and was surprised to see streaks of sparkling matter in the gray rock. Enlarged, the stone was beautiful, like a gray sky with the stars of the Milky Way spread across it. I suspected the stone contained crystals of some type, like fool's gold.

I thanked Layla profusely for her help and for allowing me to take the pictures out of the office. Years before, I'd realized receptionists and clerks have the ability to help or hinder an investigation beyond belief.

As I turned to go, she said, "I'm sorry Doc wouldn't meet with you. He's just got a problem with defense attorneys who wanna talk off-record."

That told me two things. One was that Caspari could have met with me, but chose not to. Second, if I wanted to discuss anything with “Doc,” I would have to do so in front of a court reporter.

“Thanks again...I’ll keep that in mind,” I said, heading out into the afternoon heat.

The human brain is an amazing piece of equipment. Often, when you need an answer to something, if you just quit thinking about it, the subconscious brain will make the connections you need. Before I was halfway to the car, I recalled reading that the victim had been seen using a pay telephone the morning of her death, just before her last ride.

I wondered if she took off her earring to use the phone, and where it ended up.

Chapter 8 — The Empty Chamber

THE PUBLIC BEACH at Sand Key County Park is a wonderful place where the sand is pure white and the blue water sparkles with diamonds of light. The constant sea breeze moderates the sun's heat. Tourists run rampant. What bikinis had been in the '60s, thongs were now. The only real difference—both men and women wear thongs.

I settled under Mitzi Raphael's red-and-white beach umbrella to review my notes and read a little more trial transcript. The sound of the surf, the smell of the coconut oil coating the sun worshipers, and the sun and salt on my own skin, made my work quite pleasant.

My notes were terse. The state had a dead woman who'd obviously been murdered. It's hard to shoot oneself in the back of the head. The state's evidence of rape was unimpressive—the prosecutor was simply creating an aggravating circumstance, a reason to impose the death penalty. I wondered if the evidence connecting Jon Clayton to the murder was as twisted as the evidence of rape. I felt a chill go through my heart as I considered the possibility. Fighting for justice was often fun, unless it involved the life of someone who was actually innocent.

With the testimony of Clearwater Police Officer Tracey Sanders, who'd arrested Clayton two weeks after the murder, the trial took a definite turn for the worse.

Sanders had spent twenty years as a police officer and, while a corporal, was still basically a patrolman. It was five in the afternoon and he had been radar man in a speed trap on the Memorial Causeway, just west of the Clearwater Bay Bridge. There he clocked and stopped a black, 1985 Chevy Caprice four-door, cresting the bridge at forty-eight miles an hour, thirteen miles-per-hour over the speed limit.

When Sanders walked up to the car to get the driver's license and registration, he noticed what appeared to be the butt of a pistol under a red T-shirt on the passenger seat. He asked the driver to step out of the car for "officer safety." He wanted to separate the man from the gun. Sanders called for a license check and found that the driver, Jon Clayton, was a convicted felon.

He asked Clayton if there was a pistol on the front seat of his car, and Clayton readily admitted there was, and that it was his pistol. It turned out to be a .38 caliber Smith and Wesson six-shot revolver in a holster, loaded with five live rounds and an empty chamber under the hammer. Sanders arrested Jon Clayton for "possession of a firearm by a convicted felon," a crime which was a new and separate felony.

The state played its hand well. The jury was never told about the reason for the arrest, just that Clayton had been arrested and that he'd had a pistol in his possession at that time. If the state had slipped in evidence of the prior crime of battery at this point, it would have been grounds for a mistrial.

"OFFICER SANDERS, WOULD you recognize the weapon seized from the defendant that afternoon, if you were to see it again?" asked Conchman.

"I believe I would. Yes, sir," said Sanders.

"I have here a pistol...which... yes, it is not loaded. May I approach the witness, Your Honor?"

"You may," Judge Harris replied. Harris sat forward on the bench, raising himself up so as to observe a little better. It was his way of signaling to the jury that this was important testimony and they should pay attention.

Conchman handed the pistol to Officer Sanders, stepped back a few feet and turned toward the jury as he asked, "Would you look at this weapon and see if you can identify it, Officer Sanders?"

Conchman then stood off to one side, out of the line of vision of the jury, but blocking the view of the defense attorney. He expected Hatfield would want to observe the witness and object, a simple tactic to pique the jury's interest even more. But Hatfield did nothing. After all, the defense was that someone else committed the murder.

Sanders turned the pistol in his hands, then held it up so the jury could see it. "Sir, this is a .38 caliber Smith and Wesson, six-shot revolver. It appears to be the same weapon I retrieved from the defendant on the afternoon of June 15th of this year."

"Officer, is there...what, if anything, is special about this particular pistol? From examining the pistol, can you say for certain this is the pistol you took from the defendant.?"

"Yes, sir. It still has a tag affixed to the trigger guard which I placed there before I turned it into the evidence technician. Also...well, there are several other tags and a couple of marks, but here on the handle, I scratched my initials, TS." Sanders held the pistol for the jury to see and pointed to the butt of the handle where his initials were scratched.

"Officer, is there any doubt in your mind that the pistol in your hands is the weapon you took from the defendant, Jon Clayton, on June 15th, 1991?"

"No, sir. This is my mark. This is my tag. This is his weapon."

"Officer Sanders, the pistol is not loaded now, but was it loaded at the time you found it in the possession of Jon Clayton, the defendant?"

"Yes, sir, it was. There were five unspent cartridges, or live rounds, in the pistol. One chamber was empty."

"One chamber out of six was empty. Thank you, officer, no further questions."

Tracey Sanders came across, even in black-and-white, as straightforward and honest, just a man trying to do his job. He was competent and his testimony concerning the pistol was pretty much plain vanilla. No smoking gun, just an empty chamber.

Realizing the jury would assume the empty chamber carried the murder bullet, Hatfield asked Sanders why someone might leave an empty chamber under the hammer. Sanders answered that, with older pistols, some people considered it to be an extra safety precaution to make sure the weapon did not fire accidentally.

Conchman was obviously unhappy with Sanders' explanation, and on redirect he chose to disarm Hatfield's success.

Standing near the jury, Conchman held the pistol up in the air and raised his voice just slightly. "The empty chamber could've held a cartridge, could it not?"

"It could've held a cartridge, yes, sir."

"And that cartridge could've been fired and not replaced?"

"It could have. Yes, sir."

"It could've been the bullet found in Donella Nash's brain, could it—"

Hatfield objected to the question, stating that any answer the officer gave would be speculation. It was a good objection, and the court sustained it.

The state asked no further questions. It didn't have to. By asking the question, Conchman had planted the seed of guilt in the jury's consciousness. Now, all he needed to do was prove the bullet in Donella Nash came from Clayton's pistol.

BACK ABOARD *DEFENDER*, I called the dozen or so Tracey and T. Sanders in the telephone book. Finally I reached the right one in Tarpon Springs, a town several miles north of Clearwater. Sanders' wife answered and told me he was out on the Gulf helping on her father's fishing boat. Mrs. Sanders said they would be at the boat yard for a few days after they got back in, painting the bottom and doing minor repairs. She promised to have Tracey call me when they returned.

I had been messing around in boats all my life, and still enjoyed it. Knowing I would go up to see Sanders soon, I loaded some old clothes and a few tools in the Mercedes' trunk. I hoped Sanders would need my help. I needed his.

Chapter 9 — A Good Ole Harvard Boy

HAVING PLACED THE weapon in Clayton's possession, the State needed to prove it was the murder weapon. I was not surprised to find the next witness was Drew Pearson, an expert in firearms identification from FDLE, the Florida Department of Law Enforcement.

I called FDLE in Tallahassee around four p.m., right after I had spoken with Tracey Sanders's wife. I correctly guessed Pearson would be unavailable. Like most professionals, he would want the chance to review his file before talking about it, especially since it involved a five-year-old murder case.

I set an appointment to call Pearson two days later and gave his secretary the telephone number at the dock, just in case they had a problem finding the case. Using the Rafael's telephone for local calls and incoming calls saved me a lot of money.

Before she hung up, the secretary asked, "By the way, are you in the St. Petersburg area?"

"Pretty close," I replied. "I'm twenty minutes north of there."

"Well, Mr. Pearson is teaching a firearms safety class down there tomorrow. You could probably talk to him after the class."

She wouldn't give me a number where I could reach him, just the name and number of the gun shop where the class was to be held.

An hour later the young man behind the counter at the gun shop took my check and handed me a brown folder containing the necessary paperwork to apply for a concealed weapons permit.

"You're in luck two ways, mister," he said.

"How's that," I asked.

"We thought we were going to have to cancel this class because the state attorney who normally teaches it is tied up in court. Turns out a friend of his from Tallahassee is in town, and is *the* expert on firearms. It should be a great class. See you a little before five tomorrow afternoon."

DREW PEARSON HAD been with FDLE for only ten years. Georgia born and Harvard educated, he'd received training from the FBI and the Bureau of Alcohol, Tobacco, and Firearms—the ATF. He had taught criminology at Duke, University of Florida, and Florida State University. In Florida, such credentials gave Pearson instant credibility. A Southern boy, who met the Yankees on their own turf, then came home to share what he had learned. In addition, he had written several textbooks, including the standard reference on firearms identification.

We had sailed, shot targets, and lunched together dozens of times over the years. It was a strange relationship, born of respect. In the courtroom we were at war, but outside the courtroom we were friends.

In court, Pearson always wore a light tan suit and an off-white shirt, to go with his maroon tie bearing the Harvard shield. He had a handsome gentleness about him, and a way of looking at you that made you feel you should trust him.

PEARSON BEGAN BY explaining how his work differed from ballistics. "Ballistics is the study of projectiles either in motion or within the barrel of a firearm. My specialty, firearms identification, is the science of identifying what weapon fired a particular projectile. Each particular firearm leaves certain marks on the casing and the bullet. Much like fingerprints, each set of marks is different, and can be made by only one weapon."

Conchman got right to the core of his case quickly with Pearson. "Investigator, I have here two exhibits that I would like you to examine and tell the jury if you recognize them." He handed the exhibits to Pearson.

Pearson looked over the items carefully, giving Conchman time to return to the podium before answering. "Yes, I do. This small package contains a projectile. It and this pistol were both sent to me for testing by Investigator Clancy Flynt of the Pinellas County State Attorney's Office."

"Are the items in substantially the same condition as when you received them?"

Pearson took a second to review the packets before answering. "Well, the items themselves seem to be, however, when I received them, each was in a packet which was sealed with evidence tape. I broke the seals and removed them from the packages myself, and then I examined and tested the items."

Conchman stayed behind the podium, always looking at Pearson. He did not want to distract the jury's attention from Pearson's testimony.

"How do you mean you examined the items? Would you describe for the jury what was done?"

"Well, the projectile was weighed and photographed from several angles through a high magnification lens."

Pearson's testimony was of the standard tests and standard results. He used the gun in question to fire ammunition similar to the subject bullet—the one now in evidence. Then he carefully compared the marks on the test bullets with those on the subject bullet. The tooling marks matched. After all, if the tests did not show evidence of guilt, he would not be on the stand.

After ten minutes of technical jargon, complete with photographs and charts, Conchman knew it was time to wake the jury. He took a full minute to look at his notes, then stepped out from behind the podium. The silence and the sudden movement were calculated to get the jury's attention.

Conchman raised the volume and lowered the tone of his voice perceptibly as he continued his questioning. "Investigator Pearson, you examined this bullet...this bullet found in the brain of Donella Nash. And you examined this pistol, found in the possession of the defendant. Based on your extensive experience in the field of ballistics...excuse me, firearms identification, were you able to make any determinations regarding these items?"

"Yes, I was."

"Investigator, would you share those determinations with the jury?"

Pearson held the bullet in one hand, the pistol in his other. He turned and looked at the jury, trying to catch each person's eyes as he spoke. "Based on my examinations and comparisons, I have determined, with a high degree of scientific probability, that this bullet was fired from this pistol."

"So the bullet found in the brain of Donella Nash came from Jon Clayton's pistol?"

"*This* bullet was fired from *this* pistol," replied Pearson.

Even though he knew it was coming, Clayton was unable to stop himself from sobbing out loud and saying, "God, no. I didn't shoot anyone. I swear to—"

"*Order*!" Judge Harris' booming baritone overwhelmed Clayton and the courtroom as he yelled. Then he said to Hatfield, "Counsel, control your client. Another outburst and he will be removed from the courtroom. Continue."

Clayton had done exactly what Conchman had hoped for—he made sure the jury was awake, and very aware of the testimony.

I ADMIRED PEARSON. It would have been so easy to have just answered, "Yes," but he was totally honest. He had only compared a bullet and a pistol, and he had no idea where they came from. He spent less time on the witness stand than anyone else. Still, it was his testimony, and the inferences drawn from it, that convicted Jon Clayton.

However, I saw a major hole in the evidence. Neither Tracey Sanders nor Drew Pearson had mentioned the serial number of the murder weapon. The typewritten police report the state gave Hatfield during discovery condensed Tracey Sanders's testimony into a short paragraph listing a Smith and Wesson Model 10, six-shot revolver. The police report was signed by Flynt, and neither signed nor witnessed by Sanders. While it is not unusual for only the senior officer to sign such documents, it was one more loose end to tie up. Pearson's report, which did list the serial number of the pistol tested, was never entered into evidence—never given to the jury to take back with them during deliberations. As with Sanders' testimony, only a summary of Pearson's testimony had been released to Hatfield. The actual lab report had never been released, nor was it requested by Hatfield.

What had been done at trial was not unusual. Still, I wanted to talk to Sanders and Pearson. I had to be sure the pistol found and the one tested were the same.

SOME NIGHTS I fall asleep as soon as my head hits the pillow and sleep through the night. Many were like this one. After ten minutes, I awoke and could not go back to sleep. I lay there until four in the morning doing the mullet flop, tossing and turning. Memories I didn't want to recall ran through my mind....Suddenly, I found myself awakening from the same bad dream, exhausted. I did my morning back exercises and took a two-mile walk. It was not even eight in the morning and it had already been a long day.

At nine a.m. the dockside phone rang. I grabbed it assuming it could only be Peter Raphael, Elsa Salvadora, a telephone solicitor, or a wrong number.

"Woody Thomas, may I help you?"

I was surprised to hear a slow, deep, Georgia drawl asking, "Is this *the* Woody Thomas?"

"Speaking."

"This is Pearson. What are you up to, you old coot? I heard you were *re*-tired. Thought I could rest, and here you are harassing me again. Can't even rest at the beach."

"Drew Pearson! I didn't expect to hear from you so soon," I said. Actually, I hadn't expected him to call me at all. "Gimme a minute to grab some papers, and I won't take much of your time."

I slipped into my Tidewater Virginia accent and told him I had gone over the testimony and his report.

He said he wasn't surprised, "Checkin' every T and I, right, boy?"

I took no offense. From him, it was a compliment he felt I was doing a good job. "Yep, and I've only got one question. You never mentioned the serial number of the pistol at trial. Why not?"

"I knew darn well that's why you were a-calling. I didn't even have to look it up in the file."

I was surprised. I had assumed this one was just another case in his legion of cases, but apparently it wasn't.

Pearson continued, "You know, boy, that pistol the girl was murdered with had a history. When I ran that sucker through NCIC—you know...the National Crime Information Center—well, by golly, the serial number came up from a murder two years before this one, in Pasco County, right up the road."

"The Pasco County murder…you don't think it was the same guy, do you?" I asked. My stomach tightened as I thought, *Maybe Clayton hadn't been surfing after all.*

"Oh, heck no. The boy who did that one is doing three consecutive lifes. No, Woody...problem is...that pistol was supposed to have been destroyed. It was stolen from an evidence locker with about thirty other weapons, less'n a year before this murder. They were all supposed to have been melted down and made into manhole covers, but it didn't happen."

I realized the prosecutor might have wanted to tell the jury about the stolen weapon. It would certainly have made my client look even worse. "So, why wasn't the jury told in this case?" I asked.

"Well," Pearson said, talking even slower. "I told that young prosecutor, Conchman, about the pistol's history, and he made a tactical decision. Ole boy said it might just confuse the jury...tellin' 'em about the pistol being stolen. And worse, it might cause a mistrial to mention another murder.

"You know how I am. I try to work with these boys...even when I think they lost their brains in law school. Anyway, he tol' me if the questions were asked, answer them. If not, we weren't gonna talk about it. And, well, you probably already know, nobody asked."

"Matter of fact," I said. "You did right, ole buddy. That's what you're supposed to do." He knew it and so did I. Pearson was a cop and a professional witness. He never volunteered anything on the witness stand.

"Yeah, yeah, I know. But it's bothered me ever since. I feel better now, just talkin' to you about it. I don't think it really matters, but it wasn't completely honest, and that always bothers me. Now, the burden's on you, ole buddy."

The old, Georgia Cracker had earned his reputation for being fair and honest. I felt he was telling me to look into the matter further.

"Listen," I said, "some other things came up at the trial that I want your opinion on."

"Sure, just don't quote me on it," he said and chuckled.

"How 'bout we get together this evening?"

"I don't know. I'm going to be tied up until...oh, seven o'clock," he said. "I'm returning a favor for a friend…gonna teach a gun class."

"I know. I signed up for it," I said.

PEARSON STARTED THE class at exactly five p.m. in front of a packed room in the back of the gun shop. In addition to how weapons worked, the difference in weapons, and the law as applied to possession of firearms, Pearson stressed safety on every level.

"Never point your weapon at anything you do not wish to kill or maim. Why?" He hesitated and turned toward me, saying, "Mr. Thomas?"

I answered, "Because there's no such thing as an unloaded gun?"

"Correct," he said. "Use common sense. Keep the muzzle pointed in a safe direction."

Pearson picked up a large, black semiautomatic and, looking around the room asked, "Anybody know what's on the other side of these walls?"

Some of us shook our heads. "No."

"Neither do I. This much I can tell you, if this .45 caliber pistol were to discharge, the bullet would do one of two things. If the walls are concrete it'll probably ricochet and could injure someone in this room. If the walls are anything less than concrete block, the bullet would most likely go through the wall." He hesitated and then added, "And still have enough velocity to kill someone on the other side. Common sense, folks. Ya gotta use it."

Shortly after six, the class adjourned and all sixteen of us followed Pearson in a caravan to an indoor pistol range in south St. Petersburg. In the nondescript, beige concrete building with a two-foot square sign designating it as the Outta Sight Pistol Range, we each received ear and eye protection, and waited our turn.

Even with the double doors between us and the shooters, several weapons were extremely loud. I could watch through the bullet-resistant glass and hear the bang...bang...bang of my classmates firing a six-shot, .38 caliber revolver. Punctuation was provided by a teenage girl and her father, apparently in competition, blasting away with large-caliber semiautomatics, each shot rattling the glass and doors.

I went last, stuffing the plugs in my ears, entering the range, surprised as always by the acrid smoke, and flinching the first couple times the big guns fired. I could feel the blasts more than hear them.

Pearson was putting a fresh target in the hook, and smiled as I walked up.

"Are you the last one?"

"Yep, just you, me and the target makes three."

"Six rounds, twenty-five feet," he said as he loaded the weapon. "If someone is further than that from you they're not a threat. Ready?

I nodded and he laid the pistol on the shelf in front of me aimed down range. The barrel appeared to be only three inches, on a lightweight frame. I laid my right hand on top of it, gripping the handle with my index finger straight beyond the trigger.

"Thank you," he said, as I picked up the pistol. "Only four out of sixteen of you actually remembered not to touch the trigger. You may fire when ready."

I placed my right leg back slightly, straightened my right arm down range, wrapped my left hand around my right in a two-handed, police-type grip, and fired the first shot. There was almost no kick at all, just a four-inch ball of fire and a bang.

"Slightly high and left," Pearson said.

"I see it, Drew." I took a couple of deep breaths, then fired five more rounds in rapid succession. All six rounds were high and to the left, in a pattern which could be covered with a quarter.

"The sights are off. You're shooting fine," Pearson said. "Want to go again?"

I adjusted my aim for the sighting error, and the next eighteen rounds went through the center ring of the target leaving one hole the size of a half-dollar. We were out of ammo when I set the empty weapon on the counter.

Pearson pulled the target in and handed it to me saying with a grin. "Not bad. I guess I'll have to pass you."

After the firing range, Pearson and I drove back north to the Hot-Rod Burger and Barbeque restaurant on 49th Street. I could smell the beef cooking two blocks away. It was Pearson's favorite place, where the food, cars, and waitresses were hot.

"So, you're gonna get a permit to carry?" asked Pearson eyeing the petite, dark-haired waitress with the bare midriff and short-shorts as she leaned over the next table.

"I'm thinking about it," I replied. "If nothing else, the class and range were an excellent refresher course."

"Hell, fill out the paperwork and get the permit," he said. "You don't have to use it, but if you get caught carrying without it…well, it won't be nice. You in the market for a decent weapon?"

"Not really," I replied. "I dropped my Mariner 12-gauge overboard off Trinidad, but I've got a new, stainless steel .357 Magnum."

The waitress had been about to deliver our food and overheard my last words. As she set the food on the table, she whispered, "No guns in here boys...please. We don't need the trouble."

Pearson flipped out a badge and winked at her. As she left, he said, "Speaking of trouble, you had some questions you wanted to ask me."

"Yeah, on the Clayton case, the one we talked about on the phone."

"Off the record...what can I do for you?"

"There were only five cartridges in the pistol when Clayton was arrested with it. The arresting officer mentioned something about leaving an empty chamber under the hammer for safety. Do you have any idea what he was talking about?"

As he answered, Pearson's accent deepened, and he spoke like he was teaching a young nephew. "Yep, matter of fact I do. As I recall this was a real old Smith and Wesson." He took a bite of fries and continued, "A lot a guys believe that the older, single-action revolvers, especially some early Colts, but also old Smith and Wessons, and even some early double-action ones, always need t'be carried with an empty chamber under the hammer. They think if the hammer is either struck or the pistol gets dropped, even if it don't land on the hammer, it can go off."

"Is that true?"

"Well...yes and no, depending on who you ask," he said.

"What do you say?"

"You know my collection of old Colts, the single actions from the 1870's?"

"The ones in the wooden cases?"

"Yeah. Those I *always* carry with an empty round under the hammer because some single actions *could* fire accidentally, and some early double actions had a non-rebounding hammer and *could*...possibly fire accidentally. In fact, with most any pistol made from 1870 to 1930, I recommend people use the five-round carry if they want to keep them loaded, just in case."

"Is that because you're an old-timer?"

Pearson shook a french fry at me as he said, "Don't sass the help." Then, with the fry in his mouth, he said, "It's because the pistols are old-timers, and even the best built guns...and people...show some wear after a while…smart-ass."

Grabbing another fry he continued, "But there was another problem. A company in Spain made cheap knock-offs, which look just like the real Smith and Wesson...even had ".38 Cal. Smith & Wesson" written on the barrel, with little, tiny letters saying Spain on the lower side-plate. The metal in those things was so cheap...well, they were just plain dangerous...and some of them are still out there. Most folks don't know the difference, and some seem to have forgotten about it, if they ever knew. Which is why I recommend the five-round carry for older pistols."

As Pearson stopped and took a bite of burger, cheese and grease dripping into the paper lined basket that served as his plate, I said, "Are there a lot of these older weapons still in use?"

"Yep. Ya gotta remember, Woody, that particular model has been around since the turn of the last century, over a hundred years. The modern ones look almost exactly like the earlier ones. There've been several million of them made, literally. Most folks jus' don't realize what th' heck they're a-holdin' onto," he said, waving his double cheeseburger around in a circle.

Pearson bit and chewed slowly. I started to speak, but decided to wait. He looked deep in thought. His eyes were focused far away, missing the waitress who bent over the next table showing off her assets.

Pearson laid the burger down, folded his hands over the plastic basket of food and continued. "The more modern pistols, especially the double-action ones, have a thing called a hammer block which holds the hammer back off of the cartridge unless the trigger's been pulled. Still—" He nodded and raised an eyebrow. "—carrying the weapon with an empty chamber under the hammer is the safest way to go."

We talked pistols and exchanged a few more pleasantries and barbs, then, while waiting for the check, I thought of one last question. "Listen, old buddy, one more thing you might be able to help me with. Whatcha know about Clancy Flynt?"

"Damn Yankee carpetbagger. Hard-ass, but otherwise...he's a real good cop. Closes a lot of cases, but a real hard-ass."

"I know that much…what else can you tell me? Stuff I might want to know."

"Oh, you want state secrets!" He laughed. "Well, he was a flatfoot in

New York City, a street cop. He was in some kinda trouble, being investigated, an internal. Then somebody torched his house. His wife and son died in the fire, right in the middle of the newsprint trial. You know what I mean?"

"Oh, yeah. Trial by press, and they love a tragedy. Anything come of the investigation?"

"Nope. No charges. But he never went back to work up there after the fire. He showed up down here and got on board as an investigator with the Pinellas sheriff. Now he's assigned to the State Attorney's office."

"How 'bout the incident where he broke some kid's arm? You know anything about that?"

"Yeah," said Pearson as I noticed a flash of anger cross his face. "The kid was a rookie from Jacksonville. He was a smart-ass, bad-mouthing Flynt during a training session. Flynt let his Irish temper get the best of him. But he didn't break the kid's arm."

"Oh no? Well, that's good."

"No, not good! He ripped the kid's arm right out of the socket. It'll never be right again. There was a bit of a stink about it, but most everyone said it was an accident. If he wasn't such a damn good investigator, his butt would've been in a bind...I tell you it would!

"Hey, guess you also want to know about his sidekick, don't you?" he continued. "Now I can tell you something about that Hedeon boy."

"Well, yeah, if you've got the time. I know you're a busy man."

The check arrived and I tossed a twenty to the waitress.

"Short version of a long story," he said. "Okay?" He didn't wait for me to answer. "Hedeon's nickname is Bear, 'cause he's big and likes everyone to know his grand folks were Russians, maybe related to the Czar—some such mess.

"He's from here—St. Pete that is—and you know St. Pete was founded by Russian folks. Well, Bear took criminology up home at Florida State. His daddy's a cop, and I was one of Bear's professors, and that's how come I was at the game."

"Hold it. You lost me. What game?" I asked. Instantly, I realized I had just been suckered into one of Pearson's good ole boy stories.

"Boy, I'm glad you asked. Let me tell you 'bout the game! Bear was a lineman for the 'Noles. It was his senior year, and the game was 'Noles versus Gators in Gainesville, back in the days before the Swamp. Bear's daddy and a bunch of other law enforcement types, including me, had gotten seats together to watch the game. You with me, son?"

I nodded, but he would have continued anyway.

"It was the end of the third quarter, a half minute left on the clock. 'Noles just hadn't been fired up at all, and the Gators were a-leading. The ball was on the Gator twenty-yard line. At the snap, ole Bear jumped straight up and landed on top of the Gator defense. He ran over them, straight for the quarterback. He had that big, ole, bear-paw of a hand wrapped around the ball before the quarterback could toss it. Then Bear did the play of a lifetime."

"Okay. So tell me, what happened next?"

"Well, Bear couldn't claw the ball from the quarterback and neither one would let go. So ole Bear just reached down, grabbed that Gator-boy by the cup, and hefted him up over his head. By God, you should've seen it. Ole Bear holding that Gator over his head like he was pressing weights...and then running with him! He ran into the end zone, spiked the ball *and* the quarterback. Then he commenced to do his bear dance. It was wonderful."

"Pearson...you wouldn't be making this up, would you?"

"No way, ole buddy. It really happened. Neither ole Bear or that quarterback ever played again." He hesitated and shook his head, saying, "That was the bad part, but it really happened. You know I wouldn't lie to you."

We laughed and swapped more stories, some true, some stretched just a little. Pearson made me promise to go to the pistol range with him the next time I was in Tallahassee. A half-hour and twelve miles later, I was alone and sitting in *Defender's* cockpit, grinning while trying not to think about dancing bears.

I was glad to know more about Flynt and company, but was not pleased with what Pearson had told me about the pistol. I now had another item for my to-do list: ask Tiny Jacobs where he got the gun. I already had bad feelings about the big biker, and this gave me new, grave concerns.

I was also concerned that Clayton knew enough about pistols to keep an empty chamber under the hammer on that particular weapon. He told me he knew nothing about pistols beyond the very basics, and he denied ever firing the pistol. Jon Clayton had some explaining to do as soon as I got back to F.S.P.

Chapter 10 — A Hard Case

I SAT IN the cockpit in the shade of *Defender's* Bimini top, and reviewed more of the transcript, Hatfield's file and his personal notes, and the personal notes on the players given to me by Elsa Salvadora.

Elsa wrote that Clancy Flynt was known as a hard line cop. I knew he liked to work undercover and that his yellow/gray hair hung over his collar, but she noted it was his deep-set, hungry, dark gray eyes that caught your attention. They didn't sparkle and they seemed to look into your soul.

Flynt had trained at the FBI academy in Quantico, Virginia, and was assigned as a special investigator with the Pinellas County State Attorney's Office two years before Clayton's trial. He was known to be thorough, and had solved a lot of supposedly unsolvable cases, often by following his well-honed intuition. He would be in the right place at the right time, often for no apparent reason. He lived up to his reputation as the state's key player at Jon Clayton's trial. It was Flynt who laid out the case through precisely crafted testimony recounting his investigation.

CONCHMAN KNEW HIS investigator well. They had gone over the testimony several times and worked out exactly what needed to be said, and perhaps not said. Flynt had great presence on the witness stand. He knew how to dress, how to sit, and how to deliver the information. He even wore tinted glasses to hide the mean look in his eyes, lest he scare the jurors.

"Investigator Flynt, how did you come to be involved with this case?"

"I was on duty the morning Ms. Nash's body was found. I'd taken the shift of another officer so he could spend the weekend with his family. When the call came in, I happened to be sharing coffee and donuts with some other officers—it was early and some of us do drink coffee and eat donuts. Anyway...I was at the Countryside police station."

"When you say the call came in, do you mean the 911 call?"

"No, sir. Officer Lopez—Tito Lopez—radioed that he needed a crime scene team and an investigator because a body had been found and it appeared to be a homicide. I was the ranking investigator on duty, so I went to the scene."

Flynt next told of the collection of evidence and the removal of the body to the morgue for the medical examiner. His explanation was fairly detailed, yet shed no real light on the case, except that his description of the young woman's condition was excessively grim. He described the scene in graphic detail, including what the fire ants and sun had done to the body.

The excessively vivid description was intended to anger the jurors; to make them want to convict *somebody*. It was a good prosecution tactic, legal and quite effective. Conchman may have been young and lacking experience, but he was good at his job.

Flynt continued, "The medical examiner informed our department that the victim appeared to have been killed with a .38 caliber wad-cutter or dum-dum type of bullet. I sent a notice around to all of the departments in the area to be on the lookout—we call it a BOLO—and asked to be personally notified of anyone arrested with a .38 caliber weapon, especially if it was loaded with that kind of bullet—wad cutters or dum-dums."

"Is that a normal procedure for this type of crime?"

"Sometimes, but...actually, no. This time, I had a feeling—a hunch if you will—that the killer would still be out there hunting anoth—"

"Just generally, what is special about a...wad cutter, did you say, or a dum-dum type of bullet?"

Conchman cut Flynt off in the middle of his answer, quickly enough to prevent an objection, but with enough said to place the concept of someone "hunting" another victim in the minds of the jury.

Flynt continued with non-technical answers. His job was to teach the jury. "Wad-cutters and dum-dums are lead bullets, flat-faced slugs of lead, blunt like the front of an old Mack truck. They are made to do as much damage as possible on impact...to destroy...to kill...not to maim."

"You said you had a hunch the weapon might show up. Did your hunch pan out? Was anyone called to your attention because of the notices?"

"Yes, as a matter of fact. Fifteen people were arrested in the Tampa Bay area with .38 caliber pistols in their possession over the next two weeks. Five had weapons loaded with similar ammunition."

Flynt told the jury how he had interviewed each person arrested with a .38 caliber pistol in their possession, including Jon Clayton. Based on his investigation, he sent two pistols to be checked by firearms identification experts at the FDLE lab in Tallahassee. Those pistols belonged to two people whom he felt did not have solid alibis for the morning Donella Nash was murdered.

The bullet found in Donella Nash's brain came from the pistol found in Jon Clayton's possession, and that pistol was loaded with wad-cutter ammunition.

While Flynt had not made a tape recording of Clayton's conversations, he wove them into his testimony. Conchman stayed behind the podium and let Flynt tell his story with little prompting.

"Mr. Clayton indicated he had been at Delicto's show bar until around eleven p.m. Delicto's is near the intersection of U.S. 19 and Countryside

Boulevard—"

"Excuse me, Investigator Flynt, would it help you to explain this if we used a map?"

He marked Delicto's and other sites on the map for the jury, and as he did, he related the story told him by Jon Clayton concerning the night before, and the morning of, the murder.

"Mr. Clayton indicated he left Delicto's around eleven p.m. with a young woman. She was a dancer at the club. They went to her room off Philippe Parkway near Main. Clayton told me that he stayed the night with the young woman, leaving about sunrise to drive to his residence on Clearwater Beach."

"And where did Mr. Clayton tell you he lived?"

He told me he lived at Billy Jean's Bar and Grill in Clearwater. I confirmed that he, indeed, lived in a room over the bar."

"Did the defendant indicate at what time he arrived at his home...the bar?"

"He told me that he stopped at Angelo D's on Sunset Point Road for breakfast and arrived home sometime after nine a.m. I was unable to confirm either place or time."

"Investigator, you say the defendant left his lady friend's house at about sunrise. Do you have any knowledge of what time the sun rose in Clearwater on June second?"

"I have no personal knowledge of that, but I have a copy of the *St. Petersburg Times* for the second of June, and Section B of the paper lists times for sunrise and sunset that day."

"Will the court take judicial notice that the *St. Petersburg Times* is a newspaper and, while we may not all agree to the truth of that which is printed in it, the times given for sunrise and sunset are correct and accurate for Clearwater as well as St. Petersburg?"

Judge Harris smiled and nodded. "Defense, do you wish to address this?"

Hatfield stood, his hair mussed, his suit a little wrinkled, and said, "Your Honor, as I told the state before trial, the defense will stipulate to the time of sunrise for June second, as printed in the June second *St. Petersburg Times*."

Conchman addressed the court. "Your Honor, this copy has already been marked as State's Exhibit BB for identification."

Harris nodded and Conchman continued. "Investigator Flynt, what time is given for sunrise on June 2nd, 1991?"

"Six-thirty-five a.m."

"So, by your calculations, how long a period of time was involved between when the defendant told you he left this woman's house, and when he said he arrived at the bar where he lived?"

"At least two-and-a-half, perhaps three hours."

"Investigator Flynt, in your investigation, did you find out how long it takes to drive from the woman's house, where the defendant spent the night, to the bar where he lived?"

"In my investigation, I drove from the woman's house to Mr. Clayton's residence several times. I've found that it normally takes between thirty and forty minutes. Using the route he told me he took, excluding the stop at the restaurant, it took forty minutes in traffic, driving at the speed limit."

"Investigator Flynt, did you happen to try driving the route a little faster than the speed limit?"

"Yes, I did. I was able to make the trip in just under twenty-five minutes without exceeding the speed limit by more than ten miles an hour at eight a.m. on a Sunday morning."

"You say that the defendant told you what route he took. What route was that? Would you indicate it on the map for the jury?"

Tracing the route with a yellow marker, Flynt testified, "The defendant told me that he left the woman's house here on Philippe Parkway, turned left on Main Street, took that to Countryside Boulevard, to Belcher. Here, he turned off Belcher onto Sunset, to Angelo D's, here on the map."

"And he said he ate breakfast there?"

"Yes, sir."

"Where did he go next?"

Flynt pointed at the map as he replied, "He told me he took Sunset Point Road to Edgewater Drive—"

"No, that's not what I said," Jon Clayton cried out. "That's not right."

Judge Harris slammed his palm on the bench and yelled, "Counsel, this is definitely the last time. Control your client or he will be expelled from this courtroom." Harris' face was red as he added, "Is that clear?"

Harris had tried several murder cases without the defendant in the courtroom, and at least one with the defendant present, but bound and gagged.

As Clayton whimpered, "But, Judge..." Hatfield pressed his hand on his client's shoulder and stood up slowly, replying, "Yes, Your Honor, he'll remain quiet."

Clayton may have been upset and outraged, and maybe Flynt was lying, but his outburst did not play well before the jury. They now saw him as a man who slept with a stripper, lived in a bar, and could not control himself in the courtroom.

Flynt testified that Clayton had admitted he had gone right to the very area from which the victim had disappeared. To drive from where Clayton spent the night to where the victim's car was found took eight to twelve minutes. If Clayton told a different story now, it would appear that he had recently fabricated it.

Flynt continued telling the jury the who, what, and when of his investigation, marking the map as he testified. At the end of Flynt's testimony, Conchman requested the newspaper page showing the time of sunrise, be entered into evidence. There was no objection from Hatfield, but Judge Harris asked to see it first.

"Let's break for fifteen minutes," Harris said. "Before I admit this into evidence, I think defense counsel should review it carefully. We wouldn't want a mistrial, now would we, Mr. Conchman?"

When court reconvened, Hatfield objected and the state withdrew the newspaper.

I WONDERED WHY and, digging through the state attorney's file, found the two newspaper sections I had copied. Hatfield had underestimated Conchman.

Both newspaper pages were the first page of Section B, "Tampa Bay and State" of *the St. Petersburg Times*. Both were dated June 2, 1991, the day of the murder. However, the *Times* is a state-wide newspaper, and Section B is regional news—slightly different for each region serviced.

What I had copied were two different regional sections. Page two of each was the same: weather, tides, and, of course, sunrise at 6:35 a.m. However, it was on the first page, the reverse side of the page being entered into evidence, that Judge Harris had seen a problem.

The main headline of both read, "Suspect in serial killings has long, troubled past." The story told of Aileen Wuornos, the only suspect in the murder of seven men.

I suddenly understood why Flynt had started to make the comment about the killer in this case still hunting another victim, the comment which Conchman had interrupted. If Conchman had gotten the paper into evidence, that comment, combined with the Wuornos article, would have raised the specter of Clayton as a possible serial killer. Trials are as much about emotions as they are about truth. Jurors are human, and can be misled more easily than anyone wants to believe. And, as in marketing, the *subliminal* message often works best. Flynt's testimony was well-planned, but that wasn't the only surprise.

In the upper right corner of page B2 of one issue was a sticker labeled "BB," indicating it was the page the state actually attempted to place into evidence. I turned it over and found it had a different first page than the issue I'd already read. It still had the Wuornos story on the left, but the right hand headline had changed. Instead of a story about a defiant doctor losing his license, the headline read "Woman raped in Hyde Park." The story on *this* regional section was about a serial rapist, and Jon Clayton was charged with rape. Conviction of the rape would mean the murder was committed to get rid of a witness—the victim—or committed in the course of a capitol felony—the rape itself. Either would be reasons to impose the death penalty. Thus, making sure Clayton was convicted of the separate crime of rape was important to the prosecution.

Conchman had chosen his evidence well, right down to which regional edition of the newspaper to place into evidence to show the time for sunrise on the day of the murder—he chose the edition most likely to prejudice the jury against the defendant. He was very good at his job, perhaps too good, willing to do whatever it took to assure a conviction.

I looked up from the transcripts to see a great blue heron standing on a nearby finger pier. I watched as he tried to swallow a fish half the size of his body. The great bird's neck was stretched straight and distended by its burden. The bird danced from side to side as the fish's tail flopped back and forth. The fish was being swallowed head first and, because of the spines in its dorsal fin, the heron could not disgorge it, not even if it choked to death. There was no turning back.

When I thought how Conchman was handling the case, my throat tightened up. I suddenly felt that I had taken on more than I could handle. Still, like my feathered neighbor, I knew I couldn't stop now.

I went below deck and packed up the transcript, a couple of note pads, and my old, reliable Olympus OM-G camera with the huge 80 to 200-mm telephoto lens. I wanted to see the crime scenes with my own eyes—to compare them with Flynt's testimony.

When I came back on deck, the great bird was walking slowly down the dock with a belly full of fish. I hoped I'd be so lucky.

Chapter 11 — The Tailor

PEOPLE OFTEN GET upset when they learn I'm investigating a murder, but they never seem to mind when they think I'm a bird watcher. I can sit and watch a house for hours, even take photos, and they just treat me like another eccentric nut: a little off-center, but harmless.

I showered in the condo and put on my bird watcher's outfit—fatigue pants, jungle shirt, leather deck shoes, and floppy hat. It was a good disguise and went well with my 35-mm single-lens-reflex camera and large telephoto lens. Just to add to the appearance if somebody challenged me, I threw a couple of bird identification books into the back seat of the Mercedes, courtesy of the library of Mitzi, Noah Raphael's petite, blue-gray haired wife of 30 years. She and I had often taken her pink Cadillac to the game refuges in search of rare birds. From her, I'd learned the bird-watching techniques that I now used as a cover.

The 240D smoked and banged to life and I headed off in traffic to the nearest crime scene, the last home of Donella Nash. Flynt's testimony and map led me "just off Sunset Point Road on Stevenson Creek."

Late May in Central Florida at ten-thirty in the morning and it was already ninety-one degrees and humid. Even the salty sea breeze carried the heat like weight, reminding me why I did not like the old 240D. Its air conditioner had not worked in years.

I rolled the windows down and headed across the causeway toward downtown Clearwater. The eighty-foot Royal palms and their shorter, bushy cousins that line the causeway had survived both man's automotive onslaught and nature's hurricanes. I felt joy just looking at them. The park beside the causeway was populated with happy fishermen and sun worshipers. Two forty-foot sailboats raced through the sparkling blue-green water of Clearwater Harbor. I thought to myself, *There could be worse places to investigate a murder.*

Turning into the neighborhood where Donella Nash had lived, I discovered a quaint community of small, wood frame houses. They were quite different from the cement-block and stucco variety I had come to expect. Most were cute, woodsy cottages with nicely kept yards, flowers, and occasional palm trees. Donella and Eddy Nash's home appeared to be a rental property. The yard was shabby. The little, two-tone brown house was plain and in dire need of fresh paint. In a neighborhood of joyful cottage homes, the Nash home looked sad and unloved.

It had a garage of sorts to one side, more like a small shed with a wide pair of doors sprung open. Automotive and motorcycle parts were piled in the shed and on the ground around it. Behind the house, and probably the donor of the automotive parts, hid a silver early-80s Chevy Cavalier. It had a tropical tan; the paint had been burned off all horizontal surfaces by the sun, leaving rust and red primer.

The house looked abandoned. All the window shades were drawn, and the sand driveway showed no recent tire marks. I had not yet checked on Eddy Nash's address and wondered where he lived now, if he still lived in the area, or if he was even still alive.

Before I left, I popped the camera out the window and got close-up pictures of the house, the car and the yard. Through the big lens, I could tell the left front tire of the little Chevy was flat, the rim touching the ground. I also noticed that the grass in back of the house was mashed down, which meant someone lived there or was at least using the place. I knew then that I would be back.

Following what Flynt had marked as Donella Nash's route, I drove to the Sunset Square Shopping Center on Sunset Point Road. Donella Nash's car was found there two days after the murder. An officer had received a complaint of an abandoned vehicle. He checked the license plate number to find the owner, and called Flynt to the scene when the tag came back registered to Donella Nash. The car was found only a mile from Angelo D's, where Clayton said he had eaten breakfast.

I arrived at Angelo D's only to find it was now known as The Flamingo restaurant—Island Cooking at its Best. The bad news was that it had been five years since the crime, and no one at The Flamingo had worked at Angelo D's, or had even heard of Angelo D's. It had been The Flamingo for four years.

The good news was they had a Jerk chicken special for lunch, with a side of Caribbean yellow rice and pigeon peas covered with spicy mango salsa, and iced tea. Lots of strong, cold iced tea. I enjoyed an early lunch as I read the testimony of Yalena Levkaska, the last known person to see Donella Nash alive.

I have great respect for the average citizen who is called as a witness, who saw something and is willing to come forward, or at least admit they know something which might help solve a crime. It is so much easier and safer not to get involved, especially when the crime is murder.

Yalena Levkaska was one of those special persons. She was apparently elderly, though it was hard to tell from the transcripts. She testified that she and her husband came to the U.S. from Russia to escape the Soviets and started a tailoring shop in the same building they were in at the time of the murder. She was the person who called the police to complain about the victim's abandoned car.

CONCHMAN LED MRS. Levkaska though the introductions, then gently got down to business, "You told us that you called the police to report an abandoned car on your parking lot. Were you there, or did you see the car at the time it was abandoned?"

"Da...Yes," she answered.

"Did you see who was driving the car when it was left on your lot?"

"Yes. A young woman. Very small. Very pretty."

"When did this happen? What time of day?"

"It was early...forty minutes after six, in morning...Sunday, the second day of June, this year. We—Nicolai, my husband and I—live upstairs over the shop. Every day, I do the same thing. The paper arrives. I walk down the stairs. I pick it up. It is always six-forty in the morning."

"The paper arrives at six-forty a.m.?"

"No. It is there already. I pick it up, walk back up the stairs, and it is six-forty."

Conchman asked his questions, laying the facts out before the jury. "Please tell the jury what happened on that particular morning."

"That morning...that morning, I walked down to get the paper. A little car drove into the parking lot. It stopped. A girl got out. There was white smoke coming out from everywhere in her car. She left the car in front of the shop. When she did not come get her car the next day, I called police. It took three calls and the whole day to get the police to come. They finally come and suddenly police were everywhere."

"Now let me see if I have this straight. The car was left Sunday, you called the police on Monday, and they came on Tuesday, June 4th. Is that what you are saying?"

"Yes. Then the police were everywhere."

"What do you mean, the police were everywhere?" Conchman asked.

"Many policemen came. They asked things like what did you see, what do you know, what this, what that. They talked about a murdered girl and a murderer in my parking lot. They made me very frightened."

Conchman stepped up to the witness stand and handed an exhibit, a photograph, to the witness, asking, "Do you recognize the woman in this picture?"

"Oh, yes. That is her. That is the girl who drove the car. I think she is the one the police say died?" It was a question.

"Yes, she is the girl who was murdered," answered Conchman, then he asked, "Can you tell us what this young woman did after she stopped her car in front of your shop that Sunday?"

"She got out of the little car. Then she went to the pay telephone. Then some man came in a big, black car and she got in the car with him."

"Would you recognize the man if you saw him?"

"No, I could not see him. The windows of the car were dark. I could tell it was a man. It was not a woman."

"You say it was a large, black car. Do you know what kind of car the man was driving? Would you recognize it if you saw the car again?"

"No. I do not think so. It was a big, black car. I do not drive. We do not own a car. I do not know cars. It was not small. It was not a truck. It was a big, black car," she replied.

"Mrs. Levkaska, do you remember if the car had four doors or two doors?"

"Four doors? I saw two on the side I saw."

"Two? And they were on the same side of the car as you were standing?"

"Yes. That is how I saw them."

CONCHMAN NEVER ASKED her to identify a picture of Clayton's car, but, unless she was sure, she probably would not have identified it. From her testimony, Yalena Levkaska was honest and feisty. I wanted to talk with her. Maybe she would remember something else.

From the Flamingo Restaurant, it took less than five minutes to drive to the shopping center, which was really a strip mall added to an old brick building. The brick building was two stories tall and appeared to have been there much longer than the new glass-and-concrete shopping center. It was only about thirty feet wide and seventy feet deep, with two large windows facing the parking lot and the only door between them. Windows high across the front and halfway down the side appeared to be for a second-floor apartment, apparently where Mrs. Levkaska and her husband lived. The rest of the windows down the side were twelve feet tall, composed of one foot square panes of glass, with opening sections at the top and bottom.

I was greeted by the ringing of a cow bell brushed by the door. It was a relief not to hear the electronic ding-dong of modern entry warnings.

Standing at the counter, I could smell wool and cotton, the musty fragrance of many years' accumulation of fabric dust. In the back, I could hear only a couple of sewing machines. The tailor shop apparently had once been a large operation, but that was long ago.

A young man's voice called out from behind the wall saying, "Just a minute." I hoped that Mrs. Levkaska was still connected with the shop. It had been five years.

A man in his mid-twenties, dark hair, tall and lean, came from the back and asked cheerfully, "How may I help you today, sir?"

"I am looking for Yalena Levkaska. She used to work here."

His smile disappeared, as he frowned at me and my birding costume, asking, "Who are you and what do you want with Mrs. Levkaska?"

I explained who I was, what I was doing, and that it was important I ask her if she remembered anything else about the day the murdered girl left her car in front of the shop. I noticed that the noise of the second sewing machine had stopped while I was talking.

The young man started to turn away, his face a dark scowl. "Go away. She is not here, and if she was—"

"Yasha! Shame! I am here. Do not lie about me," a woman said in a husky voice. As she came through the door, I knew it had to be Yalena Levkaska. She was a little over five feet tall and almost three feet around from her shoulders down. She wore a gray dress which matched her hair and her complexion, and in the midst of all the gray, her eyes shone a brilliant blue.

Mrs. Levkaska spoke with a heavy Russian accent. "Please forgive my grandson. It is his wish to protect me from people who ask about the murder." She smiled. "You are not a policeman? You represent the young man who was convicted?" I nodded yes and she asked, "What can I tell you?"

As Yasha, still frowning, turned to leave, I said, "No, wait. You shouldn't lie, but to protect your grandmother...I'd have done the same."

I stuck my hand out to shake his, and Yasha's smile returned. I noticed he had the same brilliant blue eyes and long, thin nose as his grandmother. He suggested we sit in the back and asked, "Vodka? Coffee? What may I get you, Mr. Thomas?"

I asked for ice water and explained I had an illness that prevented me from drinking alcohol. Many of my Russian and Ukrainian friends took offense if I did not drink with them; at least until they learned I could not drink. Yasha did not ask what to get his grandmother…they just exchanged a glance and a smile. They were family, familiar with one another's ways.

Yalena Levkaska and I sat in old, green, padded dinette chairs around a worn wooden table. I had finished explaining what I was doing and had just started to discuss Yalena's testimony when Yasha returned, carrying a tray with a tall, cut crystal glass of ice water, a bottle of vodka, and two shot glasses. We toasted to life, and both Yalena and Yasha appeared to relax as they tossed down their shots of vodka.

Yalena Levkaska had no intention of ever retiring. Mr. Levkaska had finally succumbed to cigars and alcohol about two years after the trial, and now Yasha was helping his grandmother three days a week, his sister helping two days. The shop had made custom business suits for years, but since her husband's death, Yelena had turned to making theatrical costumes. We talked for over an hour before we approached the subject of the murder again.

"So, Mr. Thomas, you are here for a reason. What do you need to know?" asked Yalena.

We discussed her testimony, more so she would know I had actually read it than anything else. Then I asked, "When the young woman went to the pay phone, did she only make one call?"

"Yasha, I think this one has a brain!" Yalena said almost laughing.

I sensed I had asked the right question.

"She did not make any calls. The telephone was broken. It was always broken. She just walked to it. She picked it up. She put it to her ear and the car arrived." She was speaking loudly, her face only inches from mine.

It may have been her answer or the alcohol on her breath, but I felt a slight rush...or nausea. Her blue eyes sparkled as she continued, "Young punks had broken the wires. No one could use the telephone. I told the police, but the police did not listen."

"Why do you say the police didn't listen?"

"I answered the questions at trial. Then, after I finished, the judge said I can go or stay. Nicolai, God bless him, Nicolai said, 'Yalena, we must stay. This is like on television.' So we stayed and listened to the rest of the trial.

"That boy, your client, he is a bum. He slept with that woman, the dancer. He lived in a bar. But that prosecutor, he is a bum also. He told the jury the dead girl had used this phone to call where she worked. But she did not use this telephone. I told the policeman, Flynt. I told him, 'No, she did not make a telephone call.' Yalena's eyes had narrowed and her face reddened as she spoke. "The prosecutor lied when he told the jury she called from that telephone."

"Did you ever tell anyone else what the prosecutor said was not true?"

"I tried. I went to the judge the next day. His secretary said she would tell him. I do not think she did. I went to the boy's other attorney, Mr. Hatefilled. He refused to talk to me. Nicolai said, 'Do not go to the police.' He was upset I talked to the police. Nicolai told me to remember how, in Russia, people would disappear if they talk to the police. Nicolai's father was an artist. Police came to his house one night and he disappeared. He never returned. Nicolai remembered and he was afraid."

"It was good you tried to tell the judge and the attorney. And Nicolai was probably right about talking to the police. Most are good honest people, but some are not. Tell me, can you think of anything else that the girl did, or anything about the car she left in, or the driver of that car?"

Yalena stopped talking. Her eyes closed and I heard her breathing slow. I realized she was meditating, trying hard to remember, to see the girl again. I looked at Yasha, he smiled and nodded.

Moments later Yalena opened her eyes and smiled. "Yes, there is one thing. The girl, when she was walking to the telephone, she took off her earring as she walked." Then she looked straight into my eyes. "The left earring. The girl had it in her hand when she was at the telephone. I did not see her put it back in her ear before she got in the car."

I had intentionally not mentioned the earring and was surprised she remembered it. "Did you tell the police about the earring?"

"No, I did not think about it until you asked me. Not until now. The police ask questions, but they ask you what they want you to answer." Her brow wrinkled and she leaned forward, touching my hand as she spoke. "I did not really remember it back then. Do you think it is important? Such a little thing?"

"I don't know. I doubt it, but I'm glad you remembered, even now. Do you know if the police ever found an earring, or if anyone found one here in the parking lot?"

"I do not know. But the police told me nothing. He just asked me what I saw. He showed me her picture." She looked sad as she answered, the sparkle gone from her eyes for a moment. "She was so young."

"You say the police, but refer to them as he. Was there one policeman or more than one that asked questions?"

"One. Flynt. That was his name. He asked the questions. He was...hard. Not nice. The other policeman, Hedeon, made Nicolai remember the bad times. Do you know Hedeon?" she asked, then continued immediately, not waiting for an answer. "He is a big man. He has a square head, black hair, a black moustache. He wants to look like Joseph Stalin."

I told her I had not met Hedeon, but promised not to trust him when I did.

We talked for another half hour, about Yasha and Nicolai, and about vodka. I was really glad I had not accepted their offer of the vodka, and not just because I can't drink. Yasha had made the vodka himself and it was close to two-hundred-proof. My mouth watered at the thought of it. However, two-hundred-proof vodka, combined with the ninety-five degree temperature and hundred percent humidity I found when I left the shop, would have probably killed me. The long pants and long-sleeved shirt of my bird-watcher outfit were soaked with sweat before I reached the car.

I parked a block away in the shade of several palm trees, and made notes of what I had just learned, while it was still fresh in my mind. I liked Yalena's mispronunciation of Hatfield's name—Hatefilled. I felt it fitted his handling of the case.

I was surprised Conchman had argued to the jury that the victim had used the pay phone, especially if he knew she hadn't. Normally, I would assume there had been a lack of communication between him and the police, but after what I had already discovered, I wondered if it was another tactical decision.

Chapter 12 — Bad Scenes

FLYNT HAD TESTIFIED that Donella Nash was abducted while on her way to work at the Super Mini-Market. From the tailor shop, I drove three-quarters of a mile east on Sunset, then north for four blocks. It was a total of almost exactly a mile, parking lot to parking lot.

H.A.L.T. is the acronym for Hungry, Angry, Lonely, Tired. While these are natural functions of humans, my alcoholic mind tended to try and ignore them, often with disastrous results. I was getting hungry and a little tired, two out of four, so I took a ten minute nap in the hard bucket seat of the 240D, then returned to The Flamingo, where I drank Cuban coffee and tried their Key lime pie.

Key lime pie is one of the great blessings of life, if it is done right, but this one wasn't. The pie was yellow, sweet-sour, and they gave me a huge piece, but it contained flour, corn starch, and shredded lime skin. I sent half of it back with my favorite recipe written on the back of my business card.

Finishing my coffee, I read the transcript of Randy James, Donella Nash's boss at the mini-mart. Most trial transcript is dry, dead, just black-on-white words. A little imagination usually helps, but not in the case of Randy James.

CONCHMAN KNEW RANDY James was, as usual, a little high. He also realized the jury would just think James was mentally challenged, which was more or less true. Conchman distanced himself from his witness by remaining behind the podium. He spoke slowly and distinctly to James, as to a child. "Mr. James, did Donella Nash work for you at the Super Mini-Market?"

"Yeah."

"How long had she held that position?"

James looked puzzled, "Ya mean how long had she worked there? Right?"

"Yes, sir. How long had Donella Nash worked at the mini-market?"

"Two weeks the day she disappeared."

"June second, the day she disappeared, did you receive a phone call from Donella Nash?" asked Conchman.

"Yeah, I did."

"Can you tell us the essence of her conversation?"

"Tell you what?" asked James, looking confused again.

"Why did she call you? Do you know?"

"Oh, she was going to be late," answered James with a smile.

"What time was she supposed to be at work?"

"Seven o'clock...in the morning."

"What time did she call that morning?"

"I marked it on the note pad...six-forty-five."

I LOOKED AT the map. Donella Nash's car was found less than a mile from where she worked. The average person can walk three-miles-an-hour, which is twenty-minutes-a-mile. At six-forty in the morning, she still had twenty minutes to get to work. She could have made it on time if she had walked.

I wondered why she caught a ride if she were so close, and where she was when she called her boss to tell him she was going to be late. Or why she was going to be late in the first place. People are not always rational in their decisions or actions, but Nash's actions puzzled me. She might still be alive if she had walked.

At trial, the prosecutor had argued that the call occurred at six-forty, and came from the pay phone at the tailor shop, but that didn't happen—the payphone was broken. Randy James testified that he received the call at six-forty-five, not six-forty as indicated by Mrs. Levkaska's testimony, but clocks are not synchronized in the real world. Donella Nash had called her boss from someplace, walking or not. The question remained: If not from the payphone, from where?

There was only a slim chance I would learn more from Donella's boss than what was in the transcript, but I would not feel comfortable with my work if I didn't talk to him.

I arrived at the Super Mini-Market at four-thirty in the afternoon and, though Randy James was not there, I was in luck. The owner of the mini-mart was there and remembered James well. He had fired James four years before for drinking on the job, and yet James still used him as a reference for new jobs.

James' ex-boss said he had received a call within the last three months from a place where James had applied for a job. He sent me looking for a no-name used tire shop, "somewhere on Route 60 near 19." I found three off-brand tire shops in the area.

The last shop I found had a sign that said simply, "Tires." It sold used tires only, and Randy James worked there, but had gone to get sodas. His co-workers said Randy would be right back, so I found a spot to sit in the shade of the building. As I smelled the acrid aroma of old tires, oil, the hot black-top parking lot, and exhaust fumes from the nearby traffic, I remembered, *Even with sparkling blue waters, beautiful beaches, and palm trees, Clearwater, in many ways, is just another big city.*

Randy James returned with a case of cold beer, not soda. I was told the place closed at five p.m., then he could talk, but it was four-fifty, and the four workers were killing off the case of beer quickly. Promptly at five, James wandered over to the 240D with his last beer in his left hand, stuck out a blackened and greasy right hand and said, “What can I do you for, Pop?”

I never turn down a handshake, no matter what. The contact of two humans is special. It indicates a bond of trust. I suspected he was testing me. Afterwards, when he grinned as he offered me a clean rag from his hip pocket, I was sure of it.

I introduced myself and told him what I was doing. He remembered the murder well, too well.

“I guess I kinda lost it after Donella was killed. I really liked that girl. She was cute, kind of like an elf, liked to play jokes. And then...she was just gone. Just fuckin’ gone, man. It got to me, man. It got t’ me big time. Grass wasn’t enough. Booze wasn’t enough. I started doin’ hard stuff, lost my job...I guess I haven’t stopped drinking, tokin’ and losing jobs since,” James said, his eyes never focusing on mine.

“Do you remember if she had any friends or enemies? Anyone who ever stopped in the store? Did she ever mention anyone?” I was fishing, but it seemed a good place to start.

“No. She was married to a real dip, Eddy the motor head. Fixed cars in his back yard, ’cept hers. I don’t think he really worked at all. But she never mentioned anyone else. I wanted to get in her pants, but she wouldn’t play. She was kinda sad. Sometimes she’d get real down.”

James drank the last of the beer and lit up a generic brand cigarette which reeked more of sea grass than tobacco. My stomach began to get queasy from the smell.

“How about booze and drugs?” I asked. “Did she drink or do dope?”

He laughed and said, “Oh, yeah, she did weed. She talked about it anyway. I never saw her toke, stoned, or wasted. She made it to work on time every day, ’cept that last one....” His voice trailed off and he took a deep drag on his cigarette.

“Mr. James, you testified she called you on that last morning and you were sure of the time. Do you remember the actual call?”

“Oh, yeah, sure. I was a pretty good manager, maybe even a little anal. I covered my ass all the time and wrote everything down. Besides, I remember her voice.” He belched and I almost gagged from the odor of the beer and cigarette on his breath.

“Did you tell the police she called you from a payphone that morning?” I asked.

“No, man, I never said that. She might have…I don’t know. I mean, it was a phone call, but I never said it was from a payphone. How would I know?”

“Do you remember anything special about the call? Maybe traffic noise or people in the background?"

"There was a little noise, some damned elevator music. But I didn't hear any traffic and no voices, just that limp ass, long hair shit. You know, violins and no words."

Now I knew where the phone call did *not* come from, and that wherever she was, they were playing elevator music. It was another fact that did not get to the jury. For now, it meant nothing, but it would go into my notebook as soon as I got back to the 240D.

"One last thing, Mr. James. When you hired her, did Donella give you any references, anywhere she had worked before?"

"No, man. She said this was her first job. Imagine, twenty years old and finally getting your first-ever job. And she'd not been in college either. Ain't that some shit?"

"Yeah, sounds like she had a good life, up 'til it ended."

I thanked James for his time and got away from the tire lot as quickly as I could, driving fast, windows down, looking for clean air. I was not happy.

It had been a long day, with several surprises, and surprises this early in an investigation tend to be a bad omen. Still, I had learned nothing which would have affected the verdict in Clayton's favor, nothing that pointed to innocence, just unconnected facts.

I was hot and tired, but the drive back along the palm-lined causeway was refreshing. I drove all the way to the beach, got out and walked for a full hour along the water's edge. The surf hissed. The sand squeaked beneath my feet. Seagulls whirled and dove, squawking and fighting. The gulf was so alive it made the air smell like iodine. I walked north, not stopping to rest until I passed the last house built on Clearwater Beach.

I had not realized how tense I had become during the afternoon, until I tried to sit down on the sand and my back refused to bend. A few stretches, and I began the long, slow walk back to the car, followed by an easy drive home to *Defender* for a light supper and hopefully, a good night's sleep. By sunset, the temperature had already dropped to the mid-seventies. It would be a great night to sleep on board.

I reviewed the rest of Flynt's testimony before I went to sleep, dreamed of Russian vodka and Cossack dances with friends long ago, and awoke at six-thirty to the roar of twin, V-8 Caterpillar diesel engines warming up fifteen feet away from my head.

Harrison 'Dread' Smith, the U.S. born, Jamaican skipper of *Rambunctious*, a Hatteras sport fishing boat, was preparing for a day of hunting black-fin tuna and marlin. I had slept with the hatches open and now the sweet stench of diesel smoke drifted straight down the aft hatch into my face. I jumped up and slammed the hatch.

Just after dawn I put on a swimsuit and my Converse high-tops, stretched, and walked four miles on the beach. I showered, meditated, ate a little yogurt and fruit, put on a clean birding outfit, and headed out again, all before the ungodly hour of seven in the morning. I felt good, and strangely excited about the case.

If yesterday could yield such surprises, what will I find today? I wondered.

I was in the car no more than ten minutes when the electric motor in the driver's side window of the 240D died with the window only open two inches! I longed for Vicky's ice-cold AC, and hoped the day would be cool.

As I headed toward Oldsmar, about twelve miles east, the morning did not get better. I baked in the sun in a traffic jam on the causeway when the bridge jammed, and then crawled through street work on Countryside Boulevard. My route took me by Delicto's and the Countryside Mall, past the police station where Investigator Flynt had eaten donuts the morning of the murder, and within a hundred yards of the condo where Fawn Lee lived.

Once across the bridge over Safety Harbor, I may as well have been in southwestern New Jersey. It was definitely blue collar, road construction, factories, factory outlets, and warehouses.

Not far beyond the huge flea market, I found the abandoned housing development. It smelled of industry, exhaust fumes, tires, and plastics. There were no signs, just two trios of palm trees, with a hard surface road between them leading into what appeared to be a stunted pine forest. The palm trees were all that indicated this was not southern New Jersey in the summer.

Several turns later, I found myself in the exact middle of nowhere. I noticed a weathered wooden cross standing in the edge of the palmettos, and presumed I had found the correct place—the scene of the crime. A check of the photographs from the trial proved me correct. Dead live oaks change very slowly and there were several nearby which matched the photographs.

The road was a form of blacktop, but instead of stone and tar, it was composed of shells, shell fragments and tar, something very familiar to me from my native Chesapeake Bay. There were also dozens of large sand mounds, home to thousands of fire ants. The stings of the well-named little beasts burn like fire and raise pustules which remain for weeks. Enough stings will kill even a healthy person. Knowing what they can do from first-hand experience, and seeing the place swarming with them, I hoped Donella Nash had died instantly.

Stepping from the car, I was struck by a solid wall of heat. The Florida sun was broiling hot as I walked to the old wooden cross. It had one word carved into it: "Donella." Someone had cared. I pulled out the crime scene photos and found that, except for the cross, little had changed in five years.

In the distance to my east, in a skeletal, dead, live oak tree, sat three buzzards, watching me, waiting. Five years after the murder, my eyes would tell me nothing. I closed my eyes and tried to feel the place though my other senses. I heard the hiss of a gentle breeze in the pine trees, punctuated by the nervous rustle of the palmettos and palms. I smelled the warm fragrance of the sandy soil, felt the sun broil my body and even more heat rise from the road. I sensed the fire ants watching me, an intruder. It yielded no secrets. It was a good place to commit murder.

I wondered what the murderer told Donella Nash to get her to come to this desolate place, or if he gave her a choice. Whoever it was knew this place existed before the murder because they were not likely to stumble on the entrance by accident. I had a map, knew what to look for, and still almost missed it.

Clayton had only been back in town four months, but he had spent his youth in nearby Palm Harbor. He may have known this place existed. I was seven miles northeast of the place where he had supposedly eaten breakfast that morning five years before, and only two-and-a-half miles away from where he lay with a hooker the night before.

Everything fell into a corridor less than twelve miles long and a mile wide. It was a corridor which had plenty of easy access roads, which began at Billy Jean's and ended here, where Donella Nash's body was found.

I remembered hearing a theory that a murderer would probably leave the victim as far from his home as possible. I looked at the twelve mile corridor I had marked on the map. The spot where Donella Nash's body was found was the farthermost point from where Clayton lived. Yet, to kidnap her and bring her to where her body was found, Clayton had to drive right past the house where he had just spent the night. It bothered me. It was not rational. But then, murder rarely is.

In his closing argument, Conchman, the prosecutor, had used Flynt's map to show the relationship of the places, and used the times to show his theory about how the murder occurred. Clayton picked up a woman at a bar, spent the night with her. He left her, saw Donella Nash walking from her steaming car a few minutes later, and instead of having breakfast, he took her out in the woods and raped her. Then he shot her in the head, turned around and drove home. It was all circumstantial evidence…all except the bullet from Donella Nash's head and the pistol in Clayton's car.

Just past noon I returned to *Defender*. The temperature had reached ninety-nine degrees and I took refuge in the condo where it was always seventy-four. I raided the refrigerator and tried to nap on the sofa, but awoke feeling anxious. My mind churned over the evidence from trial and the new facts I had learned. My intuition told me there was more to be found.

Noah's big leather chair and ottoman was the perfect place to finish learning about the trial. With James Taylor singing on the stereo, and iced tea by my side, I read on.

THE LAST WITNESS called by the state was Eddy Nash, the victim's husband. His testimony was interrupted several times by his crying, a total lack of control that had to be heartrending to the jury. Which was exactly why he was chosen to be the last witness for the state. His distress was what the jury would remember most.

Nash had the least to add to the information already before the jury. His wife left their home a little before six-thirty a.m. on Sunday. She was going to work a little early because she had only been on the job a couple of weeks and wanted to make a good impression. He never saw her again after that morning. Her boss had called Nash when Donella did not show up at work. Nash called the police, but they refused to take a missing person's report because his wife had not been missing long enough.

According to Eddy, Donella Nash had no enemies. He knew of no one who would have wanted to hurt her. He said she had never been in trouble with the law, except for a couple of possession of marijuana arrests, and he was quick to point out that, even then, she was only arrested, never convicted.

Nash's final testimony was a heart-rending story of how they had argued over money and had not made love that last morning.

"I was angry when she left. I didn't even get to tell her I loved her...." He began to cry.

"No further questions, Your Honor," said Conchman.

Defense attorney Hatfield rose from his chair and told the court, "The defense has no questions of this witness." Then he sat down slowly.

The courtroom was quiet except for the sound of Eddy Nash's sobs as Mikel Conchman announced, "Your Honor, the state rests."

It was theatrical, but an excellent trial tactic. It left the jury wanting to convict.

Chapter 13 — Death Defense

THERE WERE ONLY two witnesses for the defense—Fawn Lee and Jon Clayton. I had watched Hatfield try a half a dozen cases. His technique was to simply stand beside the podium and look directly at the witness on the stand. He usually got down to business with almost no introduction.

No one was close enough to smell the scotch on Hatfield's breath as he questioned Fawn Lee. "Ma'am, do you know the defendant, Jon Clayton?"

"Yes, sir, I do. He's the gentleman sitting at your table, the defendant," Fawn answered, smiling.

"Tell the jury how you met the defendant."

"I dance at a club here in town...Delicto's. Jon...Mr. Clayton had been coming in a couple times a week for months. He was always real nice, never got drunk...just sat and watched me dance. Sometimes, when I got off work, we would talk. I guess you could say we were acquaintances."

"Is this club, Delicto's, over near Countryside Boulevard and U.S. 19?" Hatfield asked.

"Yes, sir," answered Fawn, nodding.

"Do you recall seeing the defendant on the night of June the first...of this year?"

"I do."

"Would you tell us about that night? What was so special about it that you would remember seeing him that particular night?"

"It was the only time he ever went home with me," she replied, looking straight at Hatfield.

"Would you care to elaborate on that for the jury? What exactly happened that night...from when you first saw the defendant?"

"All right, sir," she replied. Fawn Lee turned toward the jury and continued, "It was a slow night at the club. Jon came in later than usual. He had told me the night before he was not going to be in. He's normally there when I start my shift."

"When is that usually?"

"I work eight to midnight."

"Okay. So do you recall what time he arrived?" Hatfield steadied himself on the podium, the scotch he drank at lunch affecting his balance.

"It was nine-thirty. He had been going to go to the arena for a football game. He said the ticket lines were too long and that I was...more entertaining," she said, blushing slightly. It was obviously hard for her to talk about her business in front of the jury. She likely felt as though she was also being tried. People who testify on behalf of a criminal defendant often feel that way. They, too, are suspect, guilty by association.

"Can you tell the jury what happened next?" asked Hatfield, his voice without inflection, trying to distance himself from his witness.

"Well, I danced for a couple hours. But I guess a lot of our regular customers must've gone to the arena and gotten in. The club was almost empty. I told Tiny, my manager, I wanted to leave early and he said, 'Yes.'" She looked at the jury, trying to find a kind set of eyes, to no avail.

"Please don't say what other people said. Just tell the jury what happened next," said Hatfield. While it had been hearsay, it was not objectionable, but Hatfield was in his control mode and wanted to score points with the jury.

"I asked Jon if he wanted to go home with me. He did, and we did."

"Exactly what do you mean by 'he did, and we did'?"

"He wanted to go home with me, and he followed me to my place."

"Where do you live?"

"I have a condo off of Philippe Parkway in Safety Harbor."

"Can you tell us what happened when you and Mr. Clayton arrived at your home?"

Fawn took a breath. She could feel the heat as her face flushed a little. She was embarrassed for Jon, not herself. "We went in, we showered, and we went to bed."

"Do you know what time Mr. Clayton left your be...apartment the next morning?" Hatfield's slip echoed the thoughts of the jury.

"It was right around sunrise, about six-thirty."

"No further questions. Answer Mr. Conchman's questions," Hatfield said, as he turned his back on his witness and the jury and walked to his seat.

Prosecutor Mikel Conchman took his time getting up. He made a show of reviewing his notes, taking time to let the witness swing in the wind. He smiled at the jury as he stepped to the podium. Then he turned a cold smile on Fawn Lee.

"Miss...it is *Miss* Lee, isn't it? You're not married?"

"No, sir. I'm single."

Conchman nodded as if in approval and asked, "Miss Lee, your work at the club...you're an exotic dancer, are you not?"

"Sometimes. It depends on what you mean by exotic."

"Do you dance in the nude? You know, naked, no clothing?" he asked, watching the jury as they watched Fawn Lee.

"Yes, sir, I do. Actually, I wear a G-string."

"So basically, you dance in the nude in front of dozens of men?"

"Well, most of the time there are dozens, yes."

"Is that not an unusual occupation? Perhaps a bit, exotic?" asked Conchman, an edge of sarcasm to his voice. Without waiting for her answer, he continued, "When Mr. Clayton spent the night in your bed, did you have sexual intercourse with him?"

"Yes, I did," Fawn answered, looking directly at Conchman. Even though Hatfield had not prepared her, she expected the next question.

"Did he pay you to have sex with him?"

"No. I asked for nothing, and he paid nothing."

"Other men have paid you for sex, though, haven't they?"

"Yes, I've been a prostitute. Is that what you want me to say?" Her voice was clear, no hint of shame.

Conchman turned to look at the jury. Feigning surprise in his voice, he asked, "As a prostitute, don't men normally pay you to have sex with them?"

"Sometimes, but Jon didn't. I haven't—"

"Some do, but Jon Clayton didn't," said Conchman, cutting her off. "Thank you. I have no further questions of this witness, Your Honor."

Hatfield stood at the defense table and asked, "Has Mr. Clayton ever paid you for sexual favors?"

"No, sir."

"Never?"

"Well, he has bought me a drink once or twice...when I was dancing. But, no, he didn't pay me for sex. I don't—"

"No, further questions, Your Honor," he said and sat down.

"But...but...."

Fawn tried to say more, but Judge Harris stopped her, "That will be all, miss. You may step down from the witness stand. Call your next witness, counselor."

Fawn's testimony could have been worse and the state could have done more damage than they did. On the other hand, it was clear Fawn was a hooker and danced naked in front of dozens of men at a club, G-string or not. I felt sure the good citizens of the jury had as little respect for her as the prosecutor did.

When it comes to alibis, few defendants are ever in good company when they need to be. While Fawn Lee's testimony may have not have helped Clayton, it established where he was until six-thirty a.m., more or less. Still, Flynt's testimony indicated Clayton could have been at the right place and time to find Donella Nash needing a ride—with time to kill.

JON CLAYTON TOOK the stand in his own defense, a dangerous thing to do in any trial, much less a murder trial. Again, Hatfield did as little as possible to introduce his witness, who, after all, was the defendant.

"Mr. Clayton, did you know the victim in this case, Donella Nash?" asked Hatfield, eyes on his client, no inflection in his voice, wishing the case were over and he were in a bar.

"No, sir. I never met her in my life."

"Tell the jury, Mr. Clayton…did you rape Donella Nash?"

"No, sir. I did not," answered Clayton, looking at the jury. He felt a little dizzy, the trial seemed as if were a bad dream, and he would wake up...and none of this was really happening.

"Did you kill Donella Nash?" asked Hatfield, emphasizing the word kill.

"No, sir. I did not. I'd never kill anyone," answered Clayton. Though he knew it was coming, the question still stung.

"No further questions, Your Honor. Answer Mr. Conchman's questions," Hatfield said, and sat down.

This time, Conchman was at the podium almost before Hatfield's bottom was in the chair. He placed both hands on the podium, leaned forward, and glared at the defendant.

"Mr. Clayton," he began, "you say you would *never* kill anyone?"

"I'd never intentionally hurt anyone, much less kill them, and I swear I didn't kill Donella Nash."

The bait had worked. It was almost too easy. Conchman prepared to set the hook. "You swear you didn't kill her and you say you would never intentionally hurt anyone. Is that correct? Is that what you're telling this jury under oath?"

"Yes, sir."

"Would you break someone's legs with—"

Hatfield jumped up and said loudly, "Objection, Your Honor. He's not on trial for—"

"Overruled," said Judge Harris leaning forward and smiling. "Your client opened the door. The defendant said he would never hurt anyone. If you don't like it, take it up on appeal. Ask the question, Mr. Prosecutor."

"Mr. Clayton, you say you'd never hurt anyone, but would you break someone's legs?"

"That was self-defense."

"You would, and in fact you did, recently break a man's legs with a wooden two-by-four. Did you not?" asked Conchman, his voice rising in volume and tone.

"Yes, but it was—"

"Let me ask you this, were you arrested with a .38 caliber pistol in your possession?"

"Yes." Clayton could not hide the disgust in his voice, both for the questions, and the answers he had to give.

"The pistol was loaded, was it not?"

"Yes."

"It had five live rounds of ammunition in it?"

"Yes, but—"

"But you wouldn't hurt anyone with a two-by-four or that loaded pistol, would you?"

"I did not kill that girl. I swear it. And I've never even fired that pistol," said Clayton, his voice cracking slightly. Tears welled up in his eyes. He remembered Hatfield's warning about how dangerous it was to testify, a warning Clayton had chosen to ignore. Now it was too late.

Conchman had convinced Clayton to plead guilty on the possession of a firearm charge in return for a two-year prison sentence. That, combined with the biker incident, made Jon Clayton a twice-convicted felon at the time of the trial.

"Have you ever been convicted of a felony?" asked Conchman, preparing one final slash for the jury.

"You know I have."

"Yes, I do, but answer the question for the jury. Have you ever been convicted of a felony?"

"Yes."

"How many times?"

"Once."

"Only once? Maybe once last week!" said Conchman. "How about twice?"

"Yeah, twice," answered Clayton, his voice barely audible, tears streaming down his pale face.

"No further questions," said Conchman, his face red, contempt in his voice.

The jury now saw Clayton as a twice-convicted felon and a whore-monger, who broke someone's legs with a two-by-four and was less than truthful on the witness stand. Clayton looked like a three-time loser and a murderer.

Hatfield, sensing the case was over, asked no other questions, not even bothering to clear up the questions raised by the felony convictions. He simply rose from his seat and announced, "The defense rests, Your Honor."

Chapter 14 — To Die Or Not To Die...

THE JURY WAS allowed an hour-and-a-half to eat lunch—if they could—before they would be instructed and sent out to deliberate. When the jury returned, Harris did his normal housekeeping chores, making sure everyone was present and that the defense and prosecution had reviewed the jury instructions.

Harris, Hatfield, and Conchman had taken the time the evening before to agree on which jury instructions would be given the jury. At Conchman's suggestion, Hatfield had agreed to waive any instructions regarding excusable or justifiable homicide, thus stating on the record there was no evidence to support either defense. When he felt all was in order, Judge Harris began the lecture known as instructing the jury.

"Ladies and gentlemen of the jury, in this case, Jon Clayton is accused of murder in the first degree in the death of Donella Nash. The charge of murder in the first degree includes the lesser crimes of murder in the second degree, murder in the third degree, and manslaughter, all of which are unlawful. If you find Donella Nash was killed by Jon Clayton, you will then consider the circumstances surrounding the killing in deciding if the killing was a murder in the first degree, the second degree, the third degree, or manslaughter..."

Admonishing the jury to listen carefully, Harris began to read the jury instructions which explained the law which they were to apply.

"There are two ways in which a person may be convicted of first degree murder. One is known as premeditated murder and the other is known as felony murder. To prove the crime of first degree, premeditated murder, the state must prove the following three elements beyond a reasonable doubt: first, Donella Nash is dead, second the death was caused by a criminal act of Jon Clayton, and third that there was a premeditated killing of Donella Nash."

Harris hesitated, looked up at the jury to make sure no one seemed to be too lost, and then continued. "These are definitions you need in which to decide if those three elements are proven. An act includes a series of related actions arising from and performed pursuant to a single design or purpose. That is what is meant by the requirement of a criminal act."

"Premeditation…killing with premeditation is killing after consciously deciding to do so. The decision must be present in the mind at the time of the killing. The law does not fix the exact period of time that must pass between the formation of the premeditated intent to kill...and the killing. However, the period of time must be long enough to allow reflection by the defendant, and the intent must be formed before the killing."

"The question of premeditation is a question of fact to be determined by you from the evidence. It will be sufficient proof of premeditation if the circumstances of the killing and the conduct of the accused convince you beyond a reasonable doubt of the existence of premeditation at the time of the killing."

Judge Harris hesitated, looked around the room, took a deep breath and began again, saying, "I will now read the instruction for first degree felony murder.

"Before you can find the defendant guilty of first degree felony murder, the state must prove the following three elements beyond a reasonable doubt: First, Donella Nash is dead; second, her death occurred as a consequence of, and while the defendant, Jon Clayton, was engaged in the commission of a kidnapping or a sexual battery; and third, Jon Clayton was the person who actually killed Donella Nash."

Again Judge Harris hesitated and looked up at the jury. In a slightly deeper voice, he read the defining instruction on first degree felony murder: "In order to convict Jon Clayton of the offense of first degree felony murder, it is *not* necessary for the state to prove Jon Clayton had a premeditated design or intent to kill."

The reading of the instructions to the jury droned on for over forty-five minutes. Instructions were read for each crime, including each element of the crime. Then, there were instructions on the meaning and application of reasonable doubt. Because the victim died of a gunshot wound, instructions were given concerning the use of a firearm in the commission of a felony. The term "firearm" was defined. How the jury was to consider the testimony of expert witnesses and the testimony of the defendant was explained in detail.

Even attorneys, especially the first few times they hear the instructions in a capital case, have become confused. For a juror, a person without legal training, hearing the convoluted legal instructions for the first time had to be a daunting experience. Daunting and deathly boring. Which is why Harris had not told the jurors they would have a copy of the instructions to refer to in the jury room while deliberating.

Finally, Judge Harris reached the last of the instructions. Again he hesitated, looked up at the jury, and sighed deeply. As he began again, the tone of his voice had changed to a gentler baritone, and the cadence of his words slowed.

"Ladies and gentlemen, in just a few moments you'll be taken to the jury room by the deputy. The first thing you should do is elect a foreperson.

The foreperson presides over your deliberations like a chairperson of a meeting. It is the foreperson's job to sign and date the verdict form when all of you have agreed on a verdict in this case. The foreperson will bring the verdict form back to the courtroom when you return."

"Your verdict finding the defendant, Jon Clayton, either guilty or not guilty of each of the crimes charged must be *unanimous*."

Judge Harris looked at the face of each juror for a second, then added, "That verdict must be the verdict of *each juror*, as well as of the jury as a whole."

"Finally, in closing, let me remind you it is important that you follow the law spelled out in these instructions in deciding your verdict. There are no other laws that apply to this case. Even if you do not like the laws that must be applied, you...must...use them. For over two centuries, we have agreed to a constitution and to live by the law. No one of us has the right to violate the rules we all share.

THE RECORD INDICATED that, shortly before midnight of that day, the eight men and four women returned unanimous verdicts of: *guilty* of first degree, premeditated murder, *guilty* of kidnapping, and *guilty* of sexual battery. And in each charge, the jury found that a firearm had been used. Clayton's three convictions were all capital crimes, with the murder conviction being punishable by death.

It was only then that the jury was told it would have to recommend to the trial court whether Clayton should be put to death for his crimes.

Judge Harris allowed the jury to take a three-day weekend. The following Monday, the court reconvened and Judge Harris again addressed the jury. Those who expected to have to listen to a long and confusing set of instructions would be pleased at how short the penalty phase instructions would be.

"Ladies and gentlemen of the jury, you have found the defendant, Jon Clayton, guilty of murder in the first degree. The punishment for this crime is either death...or life imprisonment. *Final* decision as to what punishment shall be imposed rests solely with me as the judge of this court. However, the law requires that *you*, the jury, render to this court an advisory sentence as to what punishment should be imposed upon the defendant."

Nodding toward the attorneys as he spoke, Harris continued, "The state and the defendant may now present evidence relative to the nature of the crime and the character of the defendant. You are instructed that this evidence, when considered with what you have already heard, is presented in order that you might determine, first, whether sufficient aggravating circumstances exist that would justify the imposition of the death penalty and, second, whether there are mitigating circumstances sufficient to outweigh the aggravating circumstances, if any.

"At the conclusion of the taking of the evidence, and after argument of counsel, you will be instructed on the factors you may consider as aggravation and mitigation."

Prosecutor Conchman, called only one witness, Medical Examiner Behrooz Caspari.

"Dr. Caspari, did the position of the body indicate to you how Mrs. Nash was standing at the time she was shot?" asked Conchman.

"Yes. I observed her at the crime scene. From the position of her body and the wound, and from the marks on her knees, I believe that she was not standing. She was kneeling when she was shot. Kneeling as a person would be in prayer."

"That is all I have, Your Honor," said Conchman.

"Defense?" asked the judge.

"No questions, Your Honor," said Hatfield.

"Call your next witness, Mr. Prosecutor."

"Your Honor, the state rests," said Conchman.

"Alright," said Judge Harris. "In that case, we will proceed to the defense. Mr. Hatfield?"

Jon Clayton was the only witness presented by attorney Hatfield in the penalty phase. Unfortunately, for every good thing Clayton could say about himself, there was a "but...."

Clayton told of his parent's untimely death, indicating he was orphaned when he was eighteen. But...on cross examination, he admitted forcing his brother to sell his parent's house and that he squandered the money to go surfing. He told of his brother's murder and trying to help his sister-in-law by living and working at her business. But that hurt him because, as Conchman had argued at trial, "This man *lives* in a bar." Even trying to save his sister-in-law's virtue from a biker worked against him because he had to admit he was convicted of aggravated battery for his actions.

After short arguments by Conchman and Hatfield, Judge Harris instructed the jury for less than five minutes. First as to what specific aggravating items it was allowed to consider. Those aggravating circumstances included such things as Clayton having been previously convicted of a felony and being on probation at the time of this crime.

The jury was also instructed to consider mitigation, such as Clayton having no significant prior criminal history, or the catch-all mitigating factor: any other aspect of the defendant's character, record, or background.

Then came a surprise for the jury.

Judge Harris again addressed the jury with the deep baritone and cadence which came from reading specific instructions. "The sentence you recommend to the court must be based upon the facts as you find them from the evidence and the law. You should weigh the aggravating circumstances against the mitigating circumstances, and your advisory sentence must be based on those considerations.

"In these proceedings, this penalty phase of the trial, it is *not* necessary that the advisory sentence of the jury be unanimous. The fact that the determination of whether you recommend a sentence of death or a sentence of life in this case can be reached by a single ballot should not influence you to act hastily or without due regard to the gravity of these proceedings. Before you vote, you should carefully weigh, sift, and consider the evidence, and all of it, realizing that a human life is at stake, and then bring to bear your best judgment in reaching your advisory sentence. Again, it is *not* necessary that this advisory sentence be unanimous."

The record indicated it took the jury less than an hour to decide Jon Clayton should die. The vote was seven to die—five to live. Had it been a tie, six to six, the recommendation would have been life. One person's vote meant the difference between life and death.

After the jury announced its recommendation, Judge Harris prepared to announce the actual sentence. It was then Hatfield conceded that Clayton had been convicted of a felony involving violence to a person for the biker incident, and that he was on felony probation at the time of the murder. Both concessions were statutory aggravating circumstances—reasons to kill his client. However, both concessions had been proven by the state during the trial and Hatfield knew he wouldn't get in trouble for them. He knew when the case was appealed, his concessions would be considered a reasonable trial tactic.

Additionally, Judge Harris announced he was finding that the murder was committed while Clayton was engaged in the commission of a sexual battery and kidnapping. "Finally, I find, as a fourth statutory aggravation that the murder of Donella Nash was done in a manner which can only be described as cold... calculated...and premeditated. She was a helpless victim, shot in the back of the head...execution style...while she knelt as though in prayer. Murder rarely comes colder than that."

With a deep sigh, Judge Harris leaned back in his chair and looked at Jon Clayton for a long moment then said, "Mr. Clayton, as to mitigation, I find very little in your favor, either statutory or non-statutory. However, in an abundance of caution, and I'm certain over the objection of the state, I will find Mr. Clayton, that you do not have a significant history of prior criminal activity—the key words here being significant history.

"Nonetheless, even if I gave that mitigation great weight, the four aggravating circumstances found in this case far, far outweigh it, and thus I'm in accord with the recommendation of the jury."

"Mr. Prosecutor," said Judge Harris.

Conchman rose to his feet and replied, "Yes, Your Honor?"

"This is the time I reserve for next-of-kin to make a statement to this court, if they so wish. I understand the father of the victim wishes to address this court."

"That is correct, Your Honor."

"Proceed."

Conchman turned toward the jury as he announced, "The State of Florida calls Mr. Fletcher McBeth, father of the murdered victim, Donella Nash."

Fletcher McBeth walked to the witness stand, where he was sworn to tell the truth, and only when he had sat down did he turn his sad eyes toward Jon Clayton.

"Sir, you have my deepest sympathy for your loss," said Judge Harris. "I understand you have requested to address this court."

"Thank you, sir," replied McBeth. "I will be quick."

"We have all the time you might wish, sir," replied Harris. "What is it you would like to say?"

Fletcher McBeth sighed deeply, and placed his huge hands on the rail in front of the witness stand. His head nodded a little, then he began. "Donella was my...our youngest daughter. My wife, Dana, and I had two daughters...once. A few years ago, our oldest daughter died in a tragic accident. Our youngest daughter, Donella, became our...joy, and our worry. Still, we never...we never expected her life to be cut so short...in the manner in which it was."

Tears began to run down McBeth's cheeks as he spoke. "I don't know why this had to happen, or what we could have done to prevent it. But this young man took more than my daughter from me. After her funeral, my wife became very sad. She stopped laughing. She stopped eating. She stopped sleeping. And one day, she stopped breathing.

"The doctor said that she took her own life, and...in truth, she did. She took an entire bottle of a prescription medicine." His breath came in short gasps. Tears dripped from his chin as he continued. "But I truly believe that the man who killed my little girl...killed my wife also. And he may as well have taken my life."

With that, Fletcher McBeth started to get up from the seat. Then he sat down and turned toward Judge Harris, saying, "I must go now, sir. Please...do what you feel you must do."

Judge Harris thanked him for coming, and for addressing the court. He watched the tall man, the widowed father of a dead child, walk out of the courtroom, bent, as though the weight of the world had landed squarely on his strong shoulders—and it was too much to bear. The sound of sniffles echoed in the quiet courtroom. Then Judge Harris turned his attention to Jon Clayton.

"Will the defendant rise?"

Jon Clayton stood, his head bowed.

"Sir, before I pronounce sentence, do you have anything you wish to tell this court?"

Clayton looked at Hatfield standing beside him. Hatfield started to speak for him, but Clayton spoke first. "Your Honor, I am so sorry for that man's loss. I'm sorry he lost his daughters...and his wife. But, sir, I swear before you and God that I had nothing to do with it. Never in my life have I even seen the woman...the woman I am supposed to have killed. I did not do these things," said Clayton, with a sob. Then as the tears rolled down his face he gasped one last time, "I swear to God, I didn't do it."

Judge Harris just sat and stared at Jon Clayton. The only sound in the courtroom was the sound of Clayton's sobs.

Then Harris spoke. "Thank you. I shall now pronounce the sentence. Upon the jury's recommendation of death, and upon my own findings, I have reached the sentence which I feel must be imposed. I want it to be clearly understood I had decided on this sentence before the father of the victim spoke. And I had decided on it before the defendant spoke.

"It is the sentence of this court, that the defendant, Jon Clayton, be incarcerated in Florida State Prison... until such time as he may be executed. Jon Clayton... for the crime of first degree murder...in the death of Donella Nash...you are to die in the electric chair."

Chapter 15 — No Alibis

TINY WAS CORRECT when he said Fawn Lee would return my call. We met at my favorite restaurant, Saffron's at Jungle Prada, in St. Petersburg. Fawn was late, but she was worth the wait, being everything Clayton and Tiny had said and more. She had told me she'd be in a '66 red Mustang rag-top, or I wouldn't have recognized her when she arrived.

Fawn no longer had the long, black hair shown on her billboards. It was now shoulder length, auburn streaked with silver and gold, and turned under at the ends. She wore a long, open white tunic over a white silk blouse and loose white slacks that drifted over her slim hips. While I could not see through the top, it was obvious from the quick jiggle and bounce that she was nicely, but not overly, buxom—and that she was not burdened with a bra. She moved with grace and sensuality. She was the kind of woman women love to hate.

Unlike a lot of women in her profession, the closer Fawn Lee got, the better she looked. She had dark almond eyes, high cheek bones, and full lips which seemed to smile at life. Even her voice was pleasing—low, musical, with just a hint of an accent, melodic and slightly foreign to my ear.

Like all of Tiny's girls, Fawn addressed men as "Honey"—me, the man who took us to the table, even the boy who brought us water and stared at her with his mouth hanging open.

Fawn ordered Rasta Pasta and I ordered jerk chicken with fried plantains. We made small talk until halfway through the meal. I asked a lot of questions and learned a lot about Clayton's lady friend.

The sick friend Tiny had mentioned didn't exist. It was indeed a relative. Fawn had been in Hawaii, helping sell her mother's dance studio and moving her mother into a special assisted-living facility for those with Alzheimer's. The sadness in Fawn's eyes as she spoke of the decisions and loss told me it had been an extremely painful trip.

Fawn Lee was a show name. She had been born Maylea Hoshi Lee on the island of Maui. Her mother was Japanese and Hawaiian. Her father had been a building contractor and surfer named Bobby Lee from Mobile, Alabama. Bobby Lee, who traced his family back to Robert E., went to Hawaii to spend a week in the early 50s, and only returned to the mainland a half-dozen times the rest of his life.

Fawn moved to California after high school, hoping to get into show business. The agency that was supposed to find work for her turned out to be devoted to "modeling" and finding girls to dance at men's clubs. She soon became involved in drugs, ran out of money, was ashamed to go or even call home, and then things got worse.

I watched Fawn's face as she spoke. Her eyes had small laugh lines around them. She sometimes seemed to look through me as she told me of her life, but her voice never wavered.

"I was nineteen years old and living on the street. Some of my friends stole to eat, but I couldn't steal. It was...too dishonest."

"The short story is I was beaten, raped, and I got VD… more than once." She sighed and sipped some Caribbean tea, then continued in a quiet, matter-of-fact manner. "I had a cheap abortion—can't have children anymore. I started selling the only thing of value I had left...but before I had been hooking six months, I was arrested."

"All that in less than six months? And you were only nineteen?" I asked.

"Oh, and another girl tried to cut my throat," she said, touching a thin, faded scar which started below her left ear and nearly crossed her neck.

"My God, I've seen a lot of girls in trouble like that. Most can't break the cycle. How'd you do it?"

"My lawyer," she answered, reaching across the table and touching my law school ring with a long, manicured index fingernail. "He convinced me to call my parents. They were in the courtroom the next day.

"He was a public defender," she said. "Thought he could save the world. He *did* save me, I guess. He got the judge to not convict me. Had me put on probation to be served in Hawaii, and I didn't have to report in. I just got drug treatment, psychological counseling, and stayed out of trouble for a year. I did it. Been a good girl ever since, more or less." She smiled and ate a little more of her vegetarian meal.

"Sounds like a good deal."

"It was. Then I went to college and worked as a bookkeeper for my daddy's construction company for a while. I married a boy from Florida. We moved here, and were divorced within three months—when he found out I couldn't have kids. I ended up dancing again, but actually made some money at it this time."

"So you weren't really hooking at the time you met Jon Clayton?" I asked.

"No," she said. "Not only that, I didn't even have to dance anymore. My daddy's brother died and left me a considerable amount of stock—IBM, Xerox, AT&T, some mutuals. I've been very careful with it."

"I didn't think you could buy the club on the money you'd make dancing or hooking."

"Oh, no," she said and laughed. Her laughter was light, gentle, real. "I was dancing there when the owner got in trouble over gambling debts. He had to sell everything he owned, fast. I looked over his books and realized what he was asking for the club was a steal. I had plenty for a down payment, borrowed the rest, and paid it off in eighteen months."

"So what Tiny said about you having some well-heeled Johns isn't true?" I asked.

"Oh, that," she said, smiling and glancing away. "Well, yes and no. It isn't exactly true." Then she sighed, looked back at me and said, "I met these four guys. Three are widowers, the other's wife doesn't like to socialize. I call them my benefactors. They came into the club together for one of their birthdays, and they liked me. They had a proposition I couldn't refuse."

"Not hooking?"

"Professional escort. All four are involved in politics, and the married one is an ex-judge. They go to a lot of dances, benefits, and shows, and I'm.... Well, as Betty, the judge's wife says, I'm their showpiece. No sex, and we have separate accommodations if it's overnight. Strictly arm candy. They pay me well and I get to have fun, dress up nice, dance, even meet foreign dignitaries."

"You're kidding," I said. "You actually get along with the man's wife that well?"

"Oh, yeah! Betty once told me she didn't even care if I slept with him. I told her I didn't want to sleep with him, and didn't know how she slept with him. She said, 'I don't.' She even chose the name for the club when I bought it: F. Delicto's. The "F" stands for flagrante. Flagrante delicto...as in..."

"Caught in the very act of the crime," I said, and we both laughed. " How did you actually meet Clayton?"

"At the club. Basically what I told the jury. Jon had been coming in for months. He had asked to take me home before, but I had...prior arrangements."

"What kind of...prior arrangements?" I asked.

"I don't date customers. It tends to cause trouble—except for the benefactors—and they only came in once." Fawn sighed, sipped her water and continued. "The night of the murder I was feeling lonely, pushing forty, all that middle-age trauma."

"A beautiful woman like you...lonely?"

"It happens. Probably more than you'd think...and to women who look better than I do," she said, sliding her plate away. "Jon showed up at a weak moment. I asked him if he wanted to...go home with me. Business was slow, and Tiny said I could leave early."

"You had to ask Tiny?"

"Well, I owned the place, but he scheduled the dancers and managed it for me. He's an easy guy to work with, and I try to treat him as I would like to be treated."

"Good rule to live by," I said. "What time did you leave?"

"We switch dancers at eleven-fifteen, so Jon and I left by eleven-twenty.

I live less than ten minutes from the club, so we were home, showered, and in bed before midnight. He was a wonderful, gentle lover. Nothing kinky, just—" She paused. "—a gentle man. You know what I mean?"

I remembered how, even after five years in prison, Jon Clayton was still a gentleman, and a gentle man. He had stood to greet me when I walked into the attorney conference room. Despite his shackles, he shook my hand, and waited for me to be seated. He had a gentle presence, a quiet voice, and eyes that still smiled.

"Yeah. I know what you mean, and he's still a gentleman. You testified you knew exactly what time he left. How did you know?"

"It was light out, but the sun wasn't up when he got up to get dressed. My bedroom opens to the east, and I watch the sunrise every day. The bay haze had not cleared before he left. I'd say he left...maybe five minutes before sunrise."

The state had proven that sunrise was at six-thirty-five the day of the murder. Which meant Clayton left at six-thirty. He still had time to kill. I had one more question. "Fawn, you've told several people you know Jon didn't kill that woman. How do you know that? What makes you so sure he didn't do it?"

"Honey, we had just spent six hours together...and we didn't sleep at all. The cops say the girl was raped, but he couldn't have raped anything, even if he'd wanted to. And he wouldn't have wanted to. I was surprised he could even walk."

Great, just great, I thought. *This was Clayton's big secret, his alibi*. I wondered why he hadn't just come right out and told me. Then I realized, *Perhaps he was just being a gentleman.*

I was glad I had spoken to Fawn, and she was probably as good as she said, but it would be a whole lot better if we could show that Clayton had left her bed after the murder had been committed. She had told me nothing to change my mind, much less a juror's. Clayton may have been a gentleman, but he was probably a murderer and, so far, nothing I had heard would have helped him at trial.

We finished our supper, drank ginger tea, and talked about Hawaii and parents. It was time to go when I remembered to ask about Tiny. "You owned Delicto's back at the time of the trial, right?"

"Yeah. I'd had it for about three years."

"And from what I gathered from Tiny, he became your partner, and now he owns the whole thing. Tell me about him. How come you took him on as a partner?"

"That's the easy part. After the trial, I started being harassed by the local cops, deputies, health department, everyone. Seems they didn't like the fact I stood up for Jon at trial. Tiny was working as my manager. He saw what was happening and said he might be able to help."

"I keep hearing he's a real helpful sort of guy. What'd he do for you?" I asked.

"Well, there is more to it than just what he did. I didn't want to sell off my investments, but I needed some cash to help my parents. Tiny offered to buy me out, but I wanted to keep fifty-one percent of the business. He knew there was good money to be made, and he really liked the club, so he made me an offer. It was too good to refuse. We agreed on the conditions, wrote up a contract, and three days later I received a cashier's check for three times what I had invested...for less than half the business."

"Sounds pretty good to me. That's a big return on your investment, and you kept control. What else did he do?"

"The harassment stopped immediately. He has good connections. Back when they tried to outlaw lap dancing, we were set up by the sheriff and raided, but nothing happened. He said he'd take care of it, and it never even went to court."

"Do you think he was bribing someone?"

"I don't know. Maybe. I was just glad to let him take over the day-to-day operations. I was tired of the management hassle. Then, a couple years ago, I got a call from one of the girls at two a.m. on a Monday morning. She said something was going on at the club, and I might want to drop by.

"I got there at three, and there were two vans outside and a half-dozen men installing video cameras and microphones in the ceiling. They got real upset when I showed up and didn't want to let me in. One guy even flashed a pistol. I had turned around and was headed to my car when Tiny came out and told them to let me in...to let me in my own club!"

"Who were they?"

"Tiny said they were some Navy buddies of his and that they were rigging up a special security system. I was upset. I told him I wanted it taken out. He put his hands on my shoulders, looked me in the eyes, and said, 'How much for your fifty-one percent, cashier's check, tomorrow?'

"I said I'd call him by noon if I wanted to sell. I did and he had the check in my hands by two in the afternoon. He delivered it personally. He asked me if I'd stay on and dance. I said no, but after about a month...well, I guess I'm a little kinky, but I missed it. And not just the exercise." She blushed as she said, "I like showing off."

"So Tiny ended up owning the club, and you became one of his dancers."

"He has a corporation that owns the club. I guess there are others with the money. But, yes, I still dance there."

"Did you ever find out what the cameras were about?"

"No. I've never asked, and he's never told me."

In the parking lot, I asked Fawn if she would like to go out dancing or to dinner again sometime.

"I'd love to, Woody," she replied smiling. Then she closed her eyes, turned away and opened them while looking toward the bay and continued,

"But...I've sold my home and I'm moving back to Hawaii next week. While I was out there I realized how much I missed the islands. Florida is nice, but I'm not coming back."

I mumbled something about it being okay as I felt cold embarrassment and disappointment wash through me. Then she kissed me on the cheek, thanked me for trying to help Jon, and slipped into the white bucket seat of the classic red Mustang.

THE NEXT MORNING found me on my way to find the victim's husband, Eddy Nash. Fawn had suggested I go by Delicto's to see Sharil, the young, coffee-skinned dancer I'd met earlier. Sharil told me that Nash still lived in the little house on Stevenson Creek. She had gone to a party with him recently, and he had been more than she had bargained for.

"That boy is white trash," she said. "He was doing toot, and trying his damnedest to get in my pants, hands all over me. He bruised my breasts. They looked so bad I couldn't work for a week. I don't care if he does have money, I don't need that mess, honey."

"Money?" I asked.

"Yeah," she said. "Tiny was going to help him out. I mean, his wife was working and he wasn't when she got killed. Then he found out the Weasel had a fat insurance policy on her. That boy owns that little house they were living in, and he doesn't work at all nowadays."

"Is Weasel his nickname, or just what you call him?"

"You ain't met the boy, have you?" she asked. "You'll know when you do. We all call him that."

I was in the parking lot, almost to my car, when Sharil yelled to me from the door. Standing in the daylight in her G-string, she looked like a well-tanned, topless beach bunny. I enjoyed the view as I walked back to her. Someone tossed her a white robe from inside the club and she stepped back in the doorway and wrapped it around herself.

"One of the other girls just told me something I thought you ought to know," Sharil said, stepping back into the parking lot. "There were two plainclothes cops by here a couple of hours ago. They were asking about you. Are you in some kind of trouble, honey?"

"I don't think so. At least not that I know of," I answered.

"Well, watch your back, honey. Those boys gotta bad rep, 'specially that Flynt guy."

FROM HATFIELD'S FEW notes, I knew Nash had not been a suspect. As his wife drove off the morning of the murder, he'd joined two of his neighbors to go fishing. The neighbors saw her leave, and they fished together until ten-thirty that morning. Nash first learned something was wrong when he found the message on his answering machine to call Donella's boss.

Word travels fast when you start looking into old murders. An unmarked police car, late model, dark gray, small hub caps, two antennae, was leaving the street where Nash lived as I arrived. The car sat at the intersection and its occupants took a long, good look at me as I turned into the street.

I looked back at them through the car's tinted windows. The driver was lean and gray and the passenger was huge and dark. They looked like cops. I suspected it was Flynt and his partner, and I had a feeling we would meet again. Mr. Nash would probably not be very cooperative. There were only five houses on the street, and I could guess which one the cops had visited.

There was now a new, flame-red, Camaro Z-28 parked behind the house beside the old Cavalier. I now knew what had mashed down the grass I'd noticed on my first visit.

Eddy Nash's face was pale when he finally answered my pounding on the door. Sharil was right. He looked like a weasel. He had narrow-set, dark eyes on a lengthy face with a long, thin nose, a permanent five o'clock shadow, and a little moustache that wiggled when he talked. Nash apparently hadn't used any of the insurance money to have his yellow teeth straightened, and his smoker's breath would peel wallpaper. I couldn't help but wonder how cute, elfish Donella Nash had ended up with this slime bag.

Nash didn't invite me in. Standing on the steps to his little frame house, I told him who I was, and got down to business. "Mr. Nash, did your wife have any enemies?"

"No, none. She was just a sweetie." His voice squeaked, he could not maintain eye contact and his face, at first pale, was becoming redder each second.

"Was she into drugs?"

"Nah. No way, man. Just booze." His voice cracked. He was real nervous.

"What did those cops want?"

"They didn't want nothin'," he said, wiping his nose on the back of his hand.

Right house, wrong answer, I noted. I now knew for sure the police had gotten to him before I did. *Why?* I wondered. *What's he trying to hide? Or perhaps more important—what were they trying to hide?* "Whatcha scared of, Eddy?"

"What're you talking about?" he replied. "I ain't scared of nothin'."

Nash's hands were shaking and he was sweating. I decided to push a little harder. Something was bothering him, and I wanted to know what it was. I felt my old shark reflex kick in. Here was a wounded fish, splashing around, just waiting to get bit. "Were you and Donella having problems? You know, marital stuff? Money problems? I know you didn't have sex the morning she died—or did you?"

Nash finally looked me in the eye and said, "Get off my property. I don't have to answer your damn questions."

He stepped back to close the door. I could see things strewn all over the living room floor. I caught the door with my left foot. It was not a wise move. Canvas deck shoes offer little protection from slamming doors.

"Either you're a messy housekeeper or you've had a party, big boy."

He pushed the door again, hard, but there was a size twelve white canvas deck shoe in it. More to save my foot than to be aggressive, I shoved the door and Nash back into the house. I was pushing my luck. I had no authority to question him, much less to enter the house. I knew Nash could have me arrested, but I sensed he wouldn't. His face was beet red and he looked like he was going to cry...or puke.

"That unmarked car that just left here was visiting you, wasn't it?" I asked from the open door.

"Come on, mister, have a little heart, I can't talk to you. Please, please leave me alone."

He was scared, but it was obvious he was more scared of the cops than of me. I decided I had pushed my luck far enough. The cops might be watching or might return any moment. I tossed Weasel my business card, just in case he had a change of heart. The card landed at his feet. His actions had piqued my interest. I knew I'd be back.

I drove to a place two blocks away where I could park and watch Nash's house for a few minutes. As I suspected, the cops came back. I tried to get a picture of the driver, but the passenger side was toward me, and even my big lens couldn't penetrate the tinted windows.

Nash met them in the street and shook his head no a lot before they left. Someone obviously did not want me to find out something, though who and what were both a mystery.

Chapter 16 — Bridges

I SPENT THE rest of the day doing boat chores, and cleaning and checking all the systems, especially the electrical and air conditioning. Unlike a house, if you fail to do all the little projects on a boat, it can—and eventually will—sink.

A little after eight, at the beginning of another beautiful sunset, I went for the evening version of my twice daily walks. My knees won't let me run, and my heart is probably grateful.

My normal route took me over Clearwater Pass Bridge, a modern concrete sculpture soaring up and over the channel to Clearwater Harbor from the Gulf of Mexico. The high arc has plenty of clearance for a sixty-foot sailboat mast, and is the closest thing to a hill in the area.

On my return, I stopped and stood at the top of the bridge, enjoying the view. The night, dark, hot, and sticky, was much like Southeast Asia, a resemblance which brought a lot of Vietnam veterans to Florida. I thought of 'Nam. I could see the faces of friends I had lost, men whose names were on The Wall. I remembered how some said they knew we couldn't win the war, but they continued to fight. We served because we believed in our country—because it was what we were taught to do. I wondered, *Why did they have to go...and to die...and not I?* I felt a chill and remembered it was often simply that fate was the hunter.

My mind wandered back to Korea in 1968, to the Pueblo, to the war that had never ended. I remembered the heat of summer and the smell of rice paddies fertilized with human excrement. I remembered helping recover the body of a GI, a young American, who had been killed by a sniper on the highway north of Seoul. As I touched the rail of the bridge I could again feel the stickiness of his blood on my hands as I helped lift him...

sss SSS ssssss....

I glanced up and to my right, in the direction of the sound. Something had flown by close and fast. *A bullet? Much too quiet...and where was the muzzle sound?* My mind spun. *Was this some kind of flashback? A bad dream? Had I really heard something? Or was it my imagination?* I decided I was more tired than I realized.

Turning to walk down the bridge, I noticed a can sitting on the concrete barrier about ten feet away. Two steps later I saw a red flash of light, and heard a plink…nnnn nnnnn . The whine was as quiet as the sound I had heard moments before. It seemed to go off to my right forever as the can tumbled to the walk and rolled in front of me.

My mind made a quick reality check—*dreams do not move cans*. It was neither dream nor flashback. Real bullets were coming in my direction. I dropped to the walkway and cuddled up to the concrete barrier. I was running on reflexes honed over thirty years before.

Who the hell is shooting at me? I thought, as I reached for the can.

The entrance hole was punched dead center of the can. The exit hole was higher, deforming the rim. I realized the red flash was probably the momentary reflection of a laser sight. Whoever fired the shot was good. They could have easily hit me.

For a second, I popped my head up, looking in the direction from which the bullet would have come, the Clearwater Point side of the bridge. I saw nothing out of the ordinary, only a hundred motel rooms from which the shot could have been fired. The closest building was less than a hundred yards away. Not far, but still a damn good shot.

I kneeled between the concrete barriers and looked more closely at the can. The hole appeared to be about the same size my .308 caliber hunting rifle made when I shot empty cans. I assumed a silencer had been used, since I'd heard no report from the weapon.

My intuition said the shots were probably fired to intimidate me, and suspected it had something to do with Clayton's case. Somebody wanted my investigation to stop. I had just been given a high-tech message. Whoever fired the shots had the weaponry, the skill, and the guts to kill me whenever they wanted. I had been warned.

I felt a little dizzy as I rose to my feet. My arms were throbbing and a kind of cold chill went through my body—fight or flight. Whoever fired the shots had made a mistake. Instead of intimidating me, they had released my worst demon—anger. *Come on, try it again, bastard!* flashed through my head.

My mind spun out of control, trying to picture the person who'd fired the shot and what I would do to him if I caught him. If the shooter knew how crazy I could be, he would never have crossed me. In the past I'd broken a few faces, arms, and legs. I had thrown things at people. Hell, I had thrown people at things...

I felt the rage build. I hated to lose control to anger, but now the beast was loose. My stomach tightened as my mind played revenge movies. The itty-bitty-shitty committee between my ears brought up every pain I'd ever felt, and every blow I had ever struck. I was building a grade-A, first-class rage. I knew the rage was based in fear that the next shot fired would not miss, but that didn't matter. I crushed the can and tossed it off the bridge. I began walking fast...down the bridge in the direction from which the shots seemed to have been fired.

My heart still pounded as I made my way back toward the condo and *Defender*. The city seemed normal. People talked, walked, and drove by, not noticing me, not knowing the beast of rage was loose in my head. The mind-chatter would not stop.

Then I noticed a hi-rider pickup parked in front of a Vietnamese restaurant three blocks from the bridge. The iridescent colors in the custom paint job were very familiar: poison-green with hot-pink flames streaming back over the hood. Walking close by I couldn't miss Delicto's Gentlemen's Club, Rt. 19 North, Clearwater painted on the door in day-glow pink. I glanced at the tag: "TINYS." I touched the hood—it was warm. My anger suddenly had a focus.

Tiny was sitting in the restaurant with a tall, lean, bearded black man. If I just stormed into the restaurant the odds were two to one against me. I was angry—not stupid. I stayed in the shadows and watched. The black man glanced at the door several times. He was sitting on the edge of his chair. There was no food in front of him. He was talking fast.

Tiny dabbed his brow with his napkin occasionally, but he spoke only a few words. Finally, Tiny said something and nodded, then gestured toward the door with his fork. I hid behind a minivan as the black man stood up and quickly left. Except for the cook, Tiny was alone in the restaurant.

When I walked up to his table and sat down Tiny did not act or look the least bit surprised. He didn't seem to notice I was angry, though I felt barely on the edge of sanity.

"How you doing, bro? I seen you walkin' 'round here a lot…figured we'd bump into each other sometime. I eat here at least once a week. Keeps the pain fresh," he said, waving his fork over the food.

Tiny was halfway through a plate of spicy-hot chicken with lemongrass. I watched as he poured Tiger Sauce on it. Sweat poured from his brow as he ate. His mouth had to burn from the spices and sauce. He either had a cast iron stomach or he liked pain.

My mouth tasted like cold steel, acid, bitter—the taste of exquisite rage. I ordered sweet tea with extra lemon in hopes of washing away the taste and preventing the cotton mouth that would come next. I tried to maintain my composure, but my hands shook and my voice seemed a bit high.

The fact Tiny was half-finished eating indicated he had been there too long to be the shooter. I decided to pretend nothing was wrong, discuss the case, and see if he let anything slip. After all, he might know nothing about the shots on the bridge.

"Tiny, I need to talk to you about the pistol you gave Clayton."

"Damned if that wasn't one of the stupidest things I've ever done," he said, looking straight at me, fork hung in mid-air. "I mean, that was dumber than jumping out of a perfectly good helicopter in the middle of the night. Really dumb. I mean, I never suspected he'd use it. I still don't believe he killed that girl."

"Well, killing's what most guns are for, man. Hell, you know that. Period."

Tiny stared at me a moment and said, "We ain't going there, bro, but either way, Clayton just didn't seem like the kind of guy. Shit, man...you know what I mean. I really feel bad about it. What do you want to know?"

"I've been investigating the case and reading the trial transcript, and I've come up with a couple of problems...questions really. I need to know where you got the pistol."

"I didn't steal it."

"I never said you did." I wondered how he knew it was stolen.

"Somebody stuffed it between the cushion and the wall in one of the booths at the club one night. One of the girls found it and I took it home with me."

"So how did Clayton get it?"

"I'm getting there, man. After the incident with the biker over at Billy Jean's, the biker's buddies said they were going to cap Clayton's ass. Clayton came to me and asked if I had a piece he could borrow or buy cheap. I collect weapons, but this was no collector's item. Still, it was a good piece. It was kinda my fault that the bikers were after him, so...I gave it to him."

"Did he know how to handle a pistol?" I asked.

"Well, he said he did, but I didn't think so. I showed him some safety stuff...got him to promise to go to the range with me. We never made it, though. He got busted first."

"What kind of safety stuff did you show him?"

"Well, basically how to hold the pistol, and I told him to always keep an empty chamber under the hammer. I mean, the piece was old, like about a 1905 S and W, M and P."

"A what?" I asked. Pearson had said it was a Model 10 Smith and Wesson.

Tiny replied, "It was a real old .38 caliber Smith and Wesson, the Military and Police model. The older ones could fire if you hit the hammer or dropped 'em."

"You called it a 1905 M and P model. What's the difference between that and a model 10?"

"Not much. They're basically the same pistol. I may be wrong about it being a 1905, but I remember it being in pretty cherry condition for a really old piece. Still, it wasn't worth much money-wise, and I had no use for it, so I let Clayton have it."

"Did you ever check on the pistol to see if it was stolen or anything?"

"No, man, why would I?" He picked up a forkful of chicken and set it down without taking a bite. "I take it you did."

Tiny rocked back in his chair, taking a long drink of beer. I waited for him to finish, then I said slowly, "Well, yeah, I did...sort of. I talked to Pearson from FDLE, the firearms expert who testified at trial. He ran the serial number on the pistol through NCIC and found it had already been used to murder one person."

"No shit, man. I sure didn't know that or I'd of dumped that piece fast." Eating had ceased, both his hands and his beer were on the table. Tiny was obviously interested in what I had to say. I wished his glasses were not so heavily tinted. I wanted to see his eyes.

"There's more," I said. "The gun was one of a bunch stolen from an evidence locker up in Pasco County." I noticed I had struck a nerve. We were now both tense. Tiny stared right through me for a full ten seconds.

"Shit. Man, I wish I'd of known that," he said. "You ain't shittin' me, are you? I mean, damn. A stolen murder weapon...damn."

"I shit you not. It was stolen. The prosecutor decided not to let the jury know about the theft. He was afraid he'd cause a mistrial."

Tiny seemed to have lost his appetite. He appeared in deep thought, staring at his food. Then he made a show of glancing at his Rolex. "Oh, man...shit. Look at the time, gotta go." Tiny threw a ten and some ones on the table and said, "'Bye, dude."

Before I could react, he was headed out the door. He hollered back, "When you see Clayton, tell him I'm sorry about the pistol." Then he was in the pickup and gone.

I had definitely touched a nerve somewhere deep in the big man. Maybe my stress level had spilled over to him. Maybe he could smell the anger.

I decided to move Tiny's name up to the top of my to-do list. I needed to know more about him.

That night, I slept in the condo, just in case whoever fired the first two shots wanted to finish the job.

I awoke with a headache and cotton mouth, an adrenalin hangover from the anger. The first thing I did was leave a message for Elsa Salvadora. I needed help from inside the system, and she could get it for me.

Jean Clayton called before nine to see how the investigation was going. She was not working until the evening shift, so I invited her to share lunch with me on *Defender*.

Jean arrived before noon in a little green Miata with the top down, and I suggested she park it under the condo so the sun wouldn't cook the seats. She was dressed for Florida in green shorts that matched her car, a white silk blouse, and white sandals.

"Nice boat. You live here?" she asked, nodding toward Noah's condo.

"Nope, 'fraid not," I replied. "I'm just using my friend's dock. I live aboard."

"You're kidding. That's what Bill always wanted to do. He dreamed about getting a sailboat and taking off a couple years to sail the Caribbean."

Jean walked down the narrow finger-pier and stepped aboard *Defender* with confidence—like someone comfortable around boats.

"Have you done much sailing?" I asked.

"No, not really. Bill and I had a little, red day-sailor we took out whenever we could. But I was raised on the water. My uncle was a fisherman. He never could afford his own boat, so he just worked for others. I'd go out with them sometimes. I loved being on the water."

"How'd you end up running a restaurant?"

"You want the whole story?" she asked.

"Yeah," I replied, "I'd like that."

"Well...after Mom died...I never knew my dad...one of the church ladies took me in. I was a live-in babysitter, you might say. She had a Cajun lady named Lynnette from Mobile, Alabama, who cooked for her. Lynnette and I shared a little apartment above the garage for three years and became pretty good friends. I enjoyed helping her in the kitchen. Sometimes the two of us would cook for parties of fifty or more. Lynnette loved to cook, and taught me how to make Cajun dishes and to dance when I was cooking."

Jean sat quietly in the sun for a moment as we watched a pair of pelicans perform a beautifully synchronized dive less than twenty feet from the dock, then she leaned back on the cockpit cushions, smiled, and continued her story.

"A few years later I got a job as specialty cook at one of the hotels on the beach. Bill was managing the bar at the same hotel. We met, fell in love, and were married three months later. Eventually, when Tuna's went bankrupt, we took our savings and the money from the sale of Bill's parents' house and bought it.

"Bill ran the bar, I ran the restaurant, and well...you know the rest of the story." Jean ran her hand over the varnished teak wheel and said, "We used to walk the docks and look at boats. Bill would've liked this one a lot. I'd forgotten how wonderful it is to sit on a boat, or even just on a dock, and watch the birds and the water."

We sat in the shade of the Bimini top and enjoyed a cold fruit salad filled with pineapple and coconut. We talked of boats, places I'd been, and places she and Bill had wanted to go…many were the same. It was obvious she had shared his dream.

Jean joined me in the galley while I put together Greek Scampi. The fragrance of fresh garlic in hot olive oil filed the cabin. The shrimp had only sautéed a minute when I added the lemon juice, feta cheese, tomatoes and spices. Our talk ranged from the weather, to the victim, to Jon, but what she had to say about Tiny interested me most.

"After Jon was jailed on the murder charge, Tiny helped me out at the bar. He sent biker friends over as both customers and bouncers. I thought the bouncers were working real reasonable, until I found out he was paying them, too." She was very matter-of-fact, as if Tiny's actions were normal.

"Tiny seems to be a real nice guy. What do you know about him?" I asked.

"Timothy Jacobs. He was in the Navy, and ended up in the hospital for a while after he got out. He looks and talks a bit rough, but he's just a big teddy bear."

"Did he ever tell you why he was helping you out so much? I mean, what did he want? A piece of the action or something?"

"No. He just wanted to make up for the biker incident…you know, when Jon broke the guy's legs? I think he still feels bad about it." She sounded sincere, as though she believed what she was telling me.

We spent three hours together and I felt very alone when Jean left to go to work. I called Elsa's office again. She was in court, but this time I was able to reach her secretary, Connie.

"I heard you were here a few days ago. You didn't even say 'hey,'" she said. "Why don't you come on down to the courthouse? Elsa's just finishing up a trial. If she can't help you, I will."

"Thanks. I need all the help I can get."

"So I hear. Well, you got it. See you in a bit," she said, hanging up before I could reply.

Chapter 17 — Florida Sunshine

IT WAS AFTER four when I arrived at the Pinellas County Justice Center. Judging from the media vehicles in the parking lot, someone had a high-profile case.

Across the street at the public defender's temporary office, Connie greeted me with a fresh cup of coffee and a smile. "Elsa is on her way back now. She won another big one! Wanna help me hang the flag?"

At Elsa's office, we hung a three-foot by five-foot pirate flag next to the door. My back was to the hall when I heard Elsa yell, "Pirate Defenders to the core! What are you doing here again, Woody?"

"I came to celebrate! I hear you just freed another Florida felon."

Celebrations of trial wins were infrequent, even for the best of us, so we enjoyed them when we could. Connie and a couple of young attorneys brought in pizza and cold sodas. I had forgotten how hard it is to eat when you're doing a trial, and how good pizza tastes afterwards.

Elsa told the story of her win, a capital sexual abuse trial where she was certain the child-victim had been abused, and even more certain that her client was, if not innocent, at least not guilty of this crime. The jury had only been out twenty minutes, returning a not guilty verdict. It was almost an hour before she came down from the adrenalin rush and asked what I really wanted.

"Look, re-tire-ee, you don't come around unless you want something, so what is it this time?" Elsa asked, smiling.

I outlined what I wanted then I asked why the PD had gotten out of Clayton's case. "Just what was the conflict?"

"It was the biker case. You know, the guy with the broken legs. We were already handling the biker on other charges and he was charged with assault on Clayton's sister-in-law. Jon was a witness in that case, so there' would have been a major conflict."

"What happened to the assault charges? I take it that it didn't go to trial."

"Nah. The boy pled out to six months' probation, great deal. Of course, he went up for fifteen years about two years ago. Sold crystal meth to a narc. I couldn't help him out of that one. He'll be out in about twelve years, if he's a good boy."

I told her about Tiny, also known as Timothy Jacobs, and that I knew nothing besides his name, the connection to Delicto's, and the truck license plate. Connie, who had stayed for pizza, started typing on her computer and, within seconds, called us over. She had opened up the city licensing and records files and pulled up Delicto's business license. Flushing Businesses, Incorporated was shown as the owner, not Timothy Jacobs. Jacobs' name was on the liquor license, however, which meant he had no felony convictions.

The license also gave us the key to his other records—his social security number and date of birth. When we ran criminal checks on him we found four arrests, all more than five years old, and none resulting in convictions. There was nothing, not even a traffic ticket for the last five years. A federal arrest was cited, but it was seven years old and none of us recognized the arrest code. Connie promised to try to find out what the federal code meant the next morning.

Next we ran a check on the victim, with quite different results. Donella Nash, whose maiden name was Donella Anne McBeth, had two prior addresses—one in Miami Beach, the other near Savannah, Georgia. I knew from the trial lawyer's file that she and Eddy had moved to Clearwater less than two years before her death. She married Nash just before the move, and as I had found out from Randy James, she had never been employed until two weeks before her death.

Donella Nash had not just one or two arrests, but arrests on seventeen drug charges over two years. Yet she had no convictions. Every charge had been "no info'd" or dropped by the state. Thirteen of the arrests had been for possession of small amounts of marijuana, three were for sale of marijuana, and the last was for possession of cocaine. We did a printout of Donella's record, and Connie promised to have the cases pulled the next day.

Donella's record did clear up one thing. I now knew why Eddy Nash was so nervous when I tried to talk to him. Nash had perjured himself. He lied when he testified that she had no criminal background. I wondered if he also lied about having sex with her the morning of her death.

It was after sunset when Elsa and I walked out of the courthouse. Her eyes still twinkled as we hugged goodbye, but I could feel the tiredness in her body and see it in her walk. I remembered how incredibly hard it was to do trial work, day after day, trial after trial. I was lucky. I had gotten into appeals before trials killed me. One mild stroke had been warning enough.

Back on *Defender*, I perused the trial attorney's file over oatmeal-graham crackers and milk. Hatfield had asked for discovery, specifically asking for information about the criminal record of any witnesses, but not the victim. It was a discovery violation nonetheless. The information should have been released to the defense anyway. Still, I knew the victim's criminal record was not relevant, unless the defendant was claiming self-defense and the victim had a violent record. That was not a problem here.

I went to an AA meeting in the early evening. I needed it. The twelve steps and fellowship helped, but my walk was later than usual that night. Walking past the Clearwater Police station near the condo, I noticed an unmarked police car identical to the one I'd seen at Eddy Nash's house a couple days before. I felt the hair on the back of my neck stand up.

It was almost eleven p.m. when I got back aboard *Defender* and found the message on my answering machine. Angela had called. Victor had flown back that morning to be a witness in a trial. Angela was ready to go back south to Marathon and wanted me to call in the morning to set something up for the coming weekend.

Part of the payment for helping bring *Defender* north was that I would rent a car and the three of us would drive back down to the keys together. It would have been fun, but like a lot of things lately, the trip was not working out exactly as I had expected.

ELSA CALLED SHORTLY after ten the next morning.

"Connie got to work early today and found those seventeen cases on Donella Nash for you," she said. "You aren't going to believe what she found."

"Try me."

"Would you believe all seventeen cases were handled, or rather dropped, by the same prosecutor, all within one or two hours of arrest?"

"I suspected she had a friend in the system, so I'm not surprised."

"Well, you will be when you find out who it was," she teased.

"I'll bite. Who?"

"Does Mikel Conchman ring a bell?"

"No kidding? He prosecuted this case." I felt a rush, a little like a shark sensing blood.

"Yeah, but that's not all, Woody. You know that last arrest, the one two nights before the murder?"

"That was in Tampa, wasn't it?"

"Yeah, Rockpile X, the big drug sweep where they busted a couple of hundred low-level dealers. It looks like Nash was caught holding powder after a buy. The record shows Conchman as the prosecutor who requested the case dropped, even though it's out of his jurisdiction. There's also a note on the second page which says, 'Investigator Flynt from the Pinellas County State Attorney's office' called with the request."

One more thing for my to-do list. Now I wanted to know what the connection was between Conchman and Donella Nash. Judging from what we'd just found, there was one.

"Elsa, can you 119 Conchman's personnel file?"

Florida Statutes Section 119 is called the Sunshine Law. It opens most meetings and almost all state employees' files to anyone who wants to know. Law enforcement officers are protected only to the extent that certain personal information, such as their home address, is not released. I wanted to see prior jobs, colleges, and anything that might give me a clue to how Conchman knew Donella Nash.

"Woody, you're a damn trouble maker, you know that?"

"Yep."

"Last time I 119'ed someone for you I almost got fired. You remember that?"

"Yep, and I said I was sorry, but it did help win—"

"Yeah, yeah," she interrupted. "I know all about it. I thought you'd be asking, so I made a few calls. A civil attorney over in Largo 119'ed Conchman earlier this year in a discrimination suit against Pinellas County. He's making a copy of the file and will personally deliver it to you at your boat."

"Wow! Great service! Thank you!"

"No, problem, big guy. You'll pay for it in the end. He's looking to buy a boat and when I told him that the file was for the Great Captain Woody...well, he'll be calling you any time now. His name is Oscar Ward."

Fast service, free copying, and home delivery, and if the only cost was to talk boats, that was even better. I could talk about boats for days. For most of my fifty years I've loved them, messed with them, owned them, repaired them. I was happy.

"Elsa, thank you. You're a saint," I said.

"Any time, Woody. You've done me a lot of favors."

"There is one more little thing."

"Oh, Lord, no! What is it now?"

"I need everything you can find on Tiny Jacobs, fast."

"We're already checking him out."

"No, Elsa. I need everything now. I didn't tell you about it when I was in your office, but somebody fired a couple of shots at me the other night. I think Jacobs was involved."

"Are you okay?"

"Yeah, whoever it was just tried to scare me."

"Be careful, Woody. Why don't you get out of town for a few days and let me see what I can find on this Jacobs guy, okay?"

"I'm getting ready to drive down to Marathon and pick up the Crown Vicky."

"Good idea. Call me when you get back. And Woody...please, be careful."

Oscar Ward called within the hour. I gave him directions and he said he would be at the dock by three. I spent the rest of the day making travel arrangements and doing laundry. Such is the glamorous life of the Great Captain Woody.

WARD WAS TRUE to his word, arriving about five minutes before three with a half-inch-thick stack of copies. A short man, powerful-looking and tan, Ward had left his jacket and tie in the car, and took off his shoes and socks on the dock without being asked. He then stood on the pier and waited for permission to board. I liked him.

We talked for over two hours and I let him look in every corner of the Gulfstar. He was really impressed at how good a twenty-two-year-old sailboat could look, and how comfortable it could be, especially to someone only five-feet-three. I agreed to call him when I came back to town and take him and his wife for a sail. It was the least I could do in return for the time and trouble he had saved me. When Ward left, I closed the hatch, turned on the air conditioner, and poked into the life of Mikel Conchman. I was impressed.

I already knew some of what I would find. As an assistant state attorney, Mikel Conchman was, by statute, a law enforcement officer. I knew there would have been a serious background check, that he would have access to a state car, and, as with all law enforcement officers, he was permitted to carry a weapon. Since he seemed to specialize in high profile cases—murder and drug-related crimes—he would probably be encouraged to carry a gun.

Conchman was in the top five percent of his class at the University of Miami Law School. He made honors as an undergraduate, and still managed to go out for football.

Other than working as an intern in the Miami-Dade State Attorney's office, the only job he held prior to becoming a lawyer was as a waiter at Tropic Delights in Miami Beach. It was a restaurant with which I was very familiar. I remembered their incredible seafood pasta salad with marinated scallops, conch, and whole baby octopus.

Oh yes, I thought, *I must investigate Conchman's work at Tropic Delights!*

I continued through Conchman's personnel file, and became more impressed with every page. He'd served as an officer in the Army Reserve with a military police unit and had received several commendations. He had received a lot of training in the Reserves, including criminal investigations and special weapons, and was an expert with pistol and rifle. He had taken several seminars each year through the state attorney's office, including training in drug prosecutions, always receiving honors or recommendations.

Conchman was a dedicated law enforcement officer. He had invested a tremendous amount of time in training. He was a true all-American boy. But that left a major question in my mind. With his background, why did he protect Donella Nash from prosecution seventeen times? I wondered if she were an undercover operative, a snitch, or a romantic interest of Conchman's.

I decided to start at the beginning, and enjoy some marinated seafood and pasta when I hit Miami Beach.

Chapter 18 — Tropic Delights

I LEFT A message for Edmundo Chavez, a reporter from the *Miami Herald*. Chavez had introduced me to Tropic Delights during a post-conviction hearing several years before. During the hearing we'd meet there every night, grab a sidewalk table, discuss the law of the day, and watch the entertainment that went by on the street. Edmundo returned my call at midnight, Friday night, and agreed to meet for lunch on Sunday.

I was up and almost ready to go seven hours later when Angela and her mother, Gale, arrived. The two came aboard *Defender* so Gale could, as Angela said, "Get to know the infamous Captain Woody a little better." They took turns telling me stories of how the three of them had cooked and shopped until Angela and Victor were stuffed, exhausted, broke, and ready to leave.

Gale drove us to the car rental lot. She hugged us both farewell, and admonished us to stay out of trouble, and out of each other's bed.

"What did you *tell* your mother?" I asked Angela as we drove away in the rental car.

"Nothing, Woody," she said. "I mean, she knows I sleep in your bed a lot." Then after a pause, she giggled and continued, "But she also knows we don't sleep together."

We rolled into Marathon after a smooth, eight-hour drive, and found both Vicky and Victor were missing. I asked the dock master, Angus, where they were and he said simply to call Victor right away. There had been a couple of problems. Several times he asked if I was in trouble, and seemed concerned both for me and for his business. No one else at the office would tell me anything. They just said, "Call Victor."

Victor's first words when he answered his cell phone troubled me.

"Woody, are you in some kind of trouble with the law? Just answer yes or no."

I assured him I was fine and, as far as I knew, I was not in any trouble with anyone. He wouldn't tell me where my car was and only said he would be at the marina within twenty minutes.

"Lay low," he said as he hung up.

Minutes later the big white-and-green cruiser marked Monroe County Sheriff roared into the marina parking lot and slid to a stop beside me. When

I opened the door, Victor said sharply, "Get in."

It was a command, not a request. I got in with my little duffle bag, without questions. Victor headed out of the marina before I had my seatbelt fastened.

"Now will you tell me what is going on?" I asked, "And where is my car?"

"First, you tell me," he said. "Is there any reason my department would be getting questions about you?"

"Questions? Like what?"

"Well, they tricked me into flying down here for a non-existent trial. Then I was called in and asked about your boat, your habits, and your car, not once but twice."

"No kidding? Weren't you told why?"

"Yeah, sort of," he said. "The captain told me that there were complaints about you over in Clearwater, and some investigator had called him."

"Did you find out his name?" I said, thinking immediately of Flynt.

"No, but that isn't your worst problem. There were two FBI agents here last evening. They were checking out your car and asking questions, like when we expected you back. I didn't tell them you'd be here today. And I didn't tell Angela about what was happening here."

"I appreciate it, but I have no idea what this is about."

We had pulled into the fenced yard of a private residence just north of Marathon, a large house with a two-car garage, three blocks east of A1A. I had been to a party there with Angela and Victor a few months before and knew it belonged to another sailor, a good friend of Victor's.

"Last night Angus and I brought your car over here for safekeeping. I was afraid someone would do something else to it."

"Whoa! Hold it! What do you mean something else?" I asked with a sinking feeling in my gut.

Victor was already out of the cruiser and opening the garage. Vicky looked fine—shiny, burgundy and chrome—just like she always did.

Victor dropped to his knees by the rear bumper, his chrome shades tossed on Vicky's trunk. "Look at this," he said, pointing under the bumper. "I presume this isn't one of your modifications."

Attached inside the rear bumper of my car was a small square black box with a wire hanging out of it and a slide type switch on the side. I was not pleased.

"Well, it doesn't look like a bomb," I said. "You think it's a tracking device?"

"Yeah, it's a bug. I'm sure of it. I saw one of the Feds bend down behind her when they didn't think I was watching. After they left, I found this. I flipped the switch and brought her here. They were back at the marina before I was, but I told them you must've come and gone already. They were very unhappy."

I appreciated the risk he had taken, and told him so. It's not safe to play games with the super cops, even if you're a cop yourself. I pulled the transmitter from under the car.

"What should we do with it?" he asked.

"We should do nothing. I think I should stick it on some tourist's car, say from Montana or Idaho, and you should not be around when I do it."

I unlocked the door and slipped under the wheel. It felt like home. Vicky's split bench seat was like a living room couch. She roared to life with a deep full-throated V-8 sound, dual exhaust all the way back. I belted up, slammed the four hundred- pound door, and eased out of the garage.

Victor grinned and waved as I headed to A1A. I was on my way to Miami, and in search of a car headed somewhere else, preferably far away from Florida.

In Key Largo, I stopped for gas and placed the bug under a camping trailer towed by a Pathfinder filled with tired-looking, sunburned people. Their license plate read Quebec, La Belle Province. I flipped the switch on, hoping the Feds were monitoring the bug again.

One thing about full-size cars, you can sleep in them. Rather than go back to the marina and chance meeting the Feds, I rented a tent space and parked Vicky for the night at John Pennekamp State Park. Weighted mosquito netting from the trunk covered my windows and the night was perfect, quiet and breezy.

The next morning I took my time getting ready. A walk on the nature trail, a swim in the pool, a restaurant breakfast, and I was ready to head into the wildest jungle in North America—Miami, Florida.

Welcome to South Beach, I thought as I walked six blocks from the nearest parking space to Tropic Delights. There were already two empty wine glasses on Edmundo Chavez's table when I arrived. He'd gotten us a prime table with a good umbrella and a great view. It was a warm, breezy Sunday morning, and the people were on the street: women, men, children, and "other" in thongs; bicyclists, skate boarders, joggers, jugglers, and T & A jigglers; Harleys, Rolls Royces, VWs, Ferraris, and Yugos; beggars, kings, and queens...a whole lot of queens. In South Beach, the circus is always in town.

We spent a half hour waiting for our food, watching the show and joking. The fun continued for an hour while we ate. The seafood pasta was delicious and exotic, as spicy and eccentric as the show going by. Finally, over Key lime pie and pink lemonade, I got to the business at hand.

I showed Edmundo a picture of Conchman that I had copied from one of the newspapers found in the prosecutor's file. When I explained he had worked at the restaurant, Edmundo's face suddenly lit up in recognition, then literally darkened as he frowned.

"Tragic what happened," he said. "He was in love with one of the waitresses and one night, she killed herself."

"Tell me more," I said.

"Mikey...we called him Mikey," said Edmundo. "He lived with this beautiful, little gal from Georgia. They were engaged to be married. I think her name was Bonnie, Scottish for beautiful, and she was that. Anyway, they stayed in a little third floor walk-up about four blocks from here. They were both in college, but it was July...I think...let me think. July '86 or '87. Yes, it was '87. Mikey had graduated from law school. One night they threw a party to celebrate his admission to the bar. Later that same night Bonnie fell, or jumped, from the balcony."

Edmundo was in his late seventies, but his memory was as sharp as ever. Conchman's records indicated he was admitted to the bar in July, 1987. *Maybe this tragedy was part of what drove Conchman to succeed,* I thought.

Edmundo rose suddenly and tugged my shirt sleeve. "Come with me," he said, as he headed inside the restaurant. He cornered the head waiter and spoke in his ear, pointing toward the back. The waiter nodded and handed Edmundo a key. In moments we were in a large, bright office. On one wall hung a dozen group pictures, all with dates printed on the bottom of the pictures. Edmundo was peering from one to another.

"Here. Woody, come here." Edmundo liked to illustrate his stories with pictures, and was doing so again. "Leon, the owner, always takes group photographs in August and February. He calls them his family photos, pictures of the kids who work here during the year. This is Mikey and Bonnie in February '87. And look, they're not in the August '87 picture."

Mikel Conchman had not changed much, but what caught my attention was Bonnie. She was not only beautiful, but she looked very familiar.

"Edmundo, you wouldn't happen to remember Bonnie's last name, would you?" I asked.

Edmundo lifted the picture off its hook and flipped it over. On the back, everyone's name was listed, including Bonnie McBeth. My heart skipped a beat. Donella Nash's maiden name was McBeth. She was from Georgia, had lived in Miami, and they looked like sisters.

"Do you know if Bonnie had a sister?" I asked.

"Yes. I think she had come down to visit Bonnie and Mikey for the summer. She shared their apartment. She was fifteen...maybe sixteen. Funny name..."

"Donella?" I asked.

"Yes. Yes! I believe it was. Wait. What is this about, Woody? How do you know Mikey and the sister?"

I told Edmundo about the murder and how Conchman had helped Donella so many times. We sat silent for a while, grieving both for the girls and Conchman. To have lost his love and then her sister, after trying so hard to protect her, had to have hurt him deeply. It had to be what drove him so hard to be a top prosecutor, and to push for the death penalty for Clayton.

"So he turned out good after all," said Edmundo.

"Yeah, he did," I said. "But, what do you mean after all?"

"Mikey...maybe I shouldn't say this, but Mikey was a small-time dealer. Grass, coke, small quantities, good prices. He never used, but he could always get some if you wanted it. He'd go down to Key Largo and come back with stuff any time. Never a problem getting it, and never got caught. I think it's how he paid his way through law school."

"Are you sure we're talking about the same man?" I asked. I was surprised. I had come to respect Conchman, and found it hard to picture him doing anything illegal, much less dealing drugs, even small-time.

"Oh, yes. Trust me. He sold. His prices were good. He always sold high quality stuff. Nice stuff...I know."

Edmundo laughed and took the fifth when I asked if he knew about the drugs from personal knowledge. He was a wonderful source of information, and I always enjoyed his company. I did not pursue the question further.

Edmundo had given me all the help he could, and for now, it was free. I knew someday I probably would be asked to do the same for him. I hoped I would be able to be as useful to him as he had been to me. I paid our lunch bill and was soon headed west on Tamiami Trail in the afternoon sun.

I felt sorry for Conchman. He had apparently suffered a lot over these two young women. I now understood why he would have wanted to prosecute the person who murdered Donella. I could even understand why he might be willing to stretch the evidence to get the conviction and the death sentence. However, he certainly would want the right person to be convicted. Clayton's story of the pistol being switched seemed even less believable now.

I was almost to Clearwater before I remembered what had occurred the day before in Marathon. I wondered if the Feds were still headed toward Canada, and who I had irritated so much that they were willing to send the Feds after me. It wasn't the first time they had investigated me.

The night was crystal clear, breezy, dry and cool—perfect to sleep aboard *Defender* with the hatches open.

I was so tired I didn't hear the car arrive. I didn't hear the footfalls in the parking lot or on the finger pier. But I awoke instantly when the boat rocked lightly, as the intruder stepped aboard.

Chapter 19 — The Visitor

I MOVED WITH the motion of the boat. When the intruder stepped, I stepped. Silently, I pulled my new stainless steel .357 Magnum from its nylon case and crept toward the main hatch. Whoever it was had already stepped into the center cockpit. As I moved through the passageway, I glanced out the four-inch porthole I had installed for viewing the engine gauges from below deck. My heart skipped a beat at the sight of a woman's shapely calf and gold bracelet on her ankle. Then came a tap, tap, tapping on the cabin top and a voice softly calling my name. I recognized the voice. It was Jean Clayton.

"What are you doing sneaking onto my boat this time of night?" I said, as I stepped up to the hatch.

"I'm sorry, but I just got off work, and...I'm sorry," she said, backing away from the hatch and starting to leave.

I apologized for my abrupt greeting and invited her to come below deck. Standing close, in case she slipped on the ladder, I watched as Jean eased down into the main cabin. It may have been the sight of her short skirt sliding up as she climbed down, or it may have been the stench of cigarette smoke in her hair and clothing. Something made me feel light-headed and dizzy.

Jean had closed the bar at two a.m. and decided to just drop in for a visit. From the odor of alcohol on her breath and from her movements, I realized she was drunk, which had probably contributed to her decision. I decided she shouldn't drive, and invited her to stay the night—in the forward cabin—alone.

Jean didn't wake when I left for my morning walk. I glanced in when I returned and she was still asleep, but had rolled over. A small, silver automatic pistol lay beside her on the V-berth.

As I prepared to cook a three-cheese omelet for two, Jean wandered out into the main cabin. Her hair was a tangled mess, her eyes were swollen, and her face was pale white with a green tinge.

"You don't do that often, do you?" I asked.

"Do what?"

"You don't remember last night? You sure enjoyed it at the time," I said with a smile.

"What are you talking about? You didn't...we didn't...did we...?" Jean blushed and her voice went up an octave. She checked to see if any of her clothing were missing, clearly flustered she couldn't remember what may have happened.

"No, we didn't," I said. "Do you always sleep with that little, silver pea-shooter?"

"Yeah, I do. It's the pistol Bill took from the robber, that he killed..." her voice trailed off.

"You don't drink very often, do you?" I asked, as I handed her a hangover remedy from my old drinking days.

"No. Almost never. What's this?"

"A homeopathic remedy. Dissolve three of these little suckers under your tongue," I said. "You must've been lonely last night to come here. Wanna talk about it? I'm a good ear."

Jean admitted she had been depressed ever since she'd told me the story of Bill's death. Last night it had finally gotten to be too painful. It was only the third time in her life she had been drunk.

"Booze doesn't work, you know. It doesn't kill the pain, just makes it worse."

"Yeah, I noticed," she said. "Sounds like you tried before, too."

"Thirty years' worth. Kept doing the same dumb things. They never worked, but I always thought...maybe this time."

"So you don't drink now?" she asked, her complexion returning to normal, despite the smell of the omelet cooking.

"Not for over six years, but before I stopped, it cost me my marriage, my family, my job, and almost my life. I'm one of those who just can't drink…ever."

The second dose of hangover remedy worked. I watched with a true cook's pleasure, as Jean downed her half of the omelet plus toasted English muffins with apple butter.

After breakfast, she showered in the condo. I had about a dozen new women's two-piece swimsuits on board, all different sizes, just in case. Bachelor's dream insurance, my friends called them. Jean put on a conservative swimsuit bottom with one of my XXL, flowered, Hawaiian shirts over it. She looked and smelled a hundred percent better, and the shirt had never looked so good.

Jean's eyes showed a lot of pain, but it was the color of them that caught my attention. I suspected they had once been blue, but now were light gray. There was almost no color left in them. I had seen eyes lose color like that before. First my mother's eyes after my father had died, and later in others who had lost loved ones. While the color eventually returned, for a while it was as though color had simply been drained from their lives.

For the next four hours, we sat in the cockpit, ate fresh fruit that I had purchased on my morning walk, and talked about the murder and its main players. I watched Jean's eyes as I continued to talk about the case and explain my concerns.

I would see those eyes in my sleep for a long time to come.

"Did Jon have any military training?" I asked. "Did he take a martial art, karate, kung fu, or anything?"

"Not that I know of. Why?"

"I've been thinking over the murder itself," I said. "I'm concerned by the way the victim was killed. The prosecutor was right when he argued to the jury that it was execution style, like a professional killing. The shot was extremely well-placed. The bullet entered the base of skull from very close range…maybe one to two inches. It was angled just right, and guaranteed to kill instantly. Whoever fired that shot knew what they were doing. They knew *exactly* what they were doing.

"What I'm wondering is, if Clayton had no training, then who did, and had the opportunity and motive to kill the girl?"

Jean sat up, leaned toward me and said, "Woody, there's no way I'll ever believe Jon killed anyone." Then she sighed and asked, "What about the ballistics test, where the bullet and the gun match?"

"The court records show the murder weapon was signed out by the chief investigator, Clancy Flynt, and the prosecutor, Mikel Conchman. They could've switched weapons for the test, then back again. But why?" I asked. "Unless they made a mistake?"

I told Jean what I had discovered the day before, and how Conchman had protected Donella Nash from the law for so long. "I just can't see how he could make such a mistake. He is a bit co-dependent perhaps, maybe even anal, but lawman to the core and good at his job. Flynt on the other hand, I'm not so sure about.

"Besides that, Tiny gave Jon the murder weapon," I continued, "and Tiny showed him how to use the five round carry. There were only five bullets in the pistol, so it wouldn't accidentally fire."

"Wait a minute," she said. "The prosecutor argued that the missing bullet was the one in the girl's head. Are you saying there were only five bullets in the gun in the first place?" Jean picked up on the problem fast.

"Tiny said there were only five bullets in the gun when he gave it to Jon. And Tiny is a gun collector. He knows weapons. Doesn't it seem strange Tiny has been so friendly toward Jon, and now you, since the murder?"

"I just thought he was being nice. I mean, he admits he was responsible for Jon having the pistol, and takes some responsibility for the assault conviction Jon has."

"What do you really know about him?" I asked.

"Not much really. He isn't much different than anyone else. He showed up in Clearwater a couple of years before the murder. He seemed to have a lot of money. He's gotten better than he was back then."

"What do you mean?" I asked. "What was he like 'back then'?"

"Well, I heard he used to collect kiddy porn and snuff flicks. Paid big money for them. Then he was involved in drugs a little…never sales, just bought stuff. Now he runs an exotic dance club and collects guns." She leaned toward me and asked, "You think Tiny killed that girl?"

"I don't know. But I believe he knows more about this case than he's told anyone," I added. "I've got a friend doing a little research on Tiny. Maybe there's a link between him and the victim or the victim's husband."

"You mean Eddy?"

"Yeah, Nash. You sound like you know him."

"Better than I'd like to," she said. "He asked me out several times that first year after his wife died. I made the mistake of going out with him once, and the bastard tried to rape me. I had to knee him in the nuts to get him off."

"You're kidding." I was surprised. "He seemed like such a scared wimp when I saw him last week. He wouldn't even let me in his house."

"How 'bout taking me along next time?" Jean suggested. "I bet he'll let you in if I'm with you." She grinned an evil grin and winked. "And if he doesn't talk, I'll bust his nuts again."

Once again, I had underestimated someone. There was a down and dirty streak to Jean Clayton that I had not suspected. I agreed to meet her at the restaurant the next afternoon, and we'd visit Eddy Nash together. It could be fun.

Neither of us suspected that it would put our lives in danger.

I WAS AT an AA meeting later that day when Tracey Sanders left a message on my answering machine telling me he was home, and would be available to talk to me any day during the next week.

The following morning, I headed to Tarpon Springs, just north of Clearwater. Tarpon Springs is not just a picturesque Florida town. It is a real Greek fishing community. There I knew I would find a lot of beautiful boats and restaurants which serve some of the best food on God's green Earth. This was a part of the investigation I knew I would enjoy.

Corporal Tracey Daemon Sanders had retired with twenty years' service only a few months after Jon Clayton's conviction. He had only been doing his job, traffic control, when he had arrested Clayton and found the murder weapon. Still, Sanders' retirement made the local section of the *St. Petersburg Times*. As he was quoted in the article, it was "just luck," but it was his "fifteen minutes of fame out of twenty years of work."

The heart-shaped sign in the yard announced I'd found the home of Tracey and Sofi Sanders. Sofi met me at the door and gave me directions to the marina where Tracey was working on her father's boat. Things were looking up again. I suspected I would get to mess around with a boat, and there was little I liked better.

I arrived at the marina in time to see the fishing vessel, *Aristotle*, being raised out of the water by a mobile lift. She was a sixty-foot long, steel vessel, in desperate need of bottom scraping and painting. By the time she was being lowered on the blocks, I had changed into work clothing and grabbed a scraping iron from the trunk where it had been stashed for days.

I scraped away the barnacles and grass from four of the eight places where braces were being placed to hold Aristotle upright before anyone realized I was not a yard worker or relative. I introduced myself to Sanders and his father-in-law.

"You're a lawyer, but you help with my boat? Are you sure you are really a lawyer?" asked Cosmo Cristofides, Sofi's father.

"Yes, sir. I'm a lawyer by trade, but I own a boat and I know every minute she hangs in the lift costs money. It's truly my pleasure to help," I said.

The smiles and thanks were as genuine as my pleasure in helping them, especially after we had spent almost two more hours scraping and shoveling the dying sea life from *Aristotle's* bottom.

At noon, Sofi Sanders brought lunch, including a plate for me. She had made us each a gyro sandwich with lamb, lettuce, tomato, onions, and sanziki sauce. She had also brought one of my favorites—*spanakopita*, a spinach pie in a flaky crust.

We said grace together before we ate, I in English, and the others in Greek. Then, and only then, sitting at a picnic table in the shade, did we discuss my business.

I told Sanders that I was researching Clayton's case, and needed to check and cross-check everything. When I mentioned I knew many officers kept personal files not released to the department or to the prosecutor, he didn't flinch. He just kept eating. However, when I asked him if he had kept such a file in this case, I saw a little red show in his cheek.

Tracey Sanders looked away from me when he told me he had no such file. He lied, and he knew I knew it. If this case were his "fifteen minutes of fame" in twenty years, he had to be lying. I noticed he had suddenly lost his appetite and began to pick at the food. Our conversation stopped.

As I was leaving, I gave Sanders my card and pleaded with him to call me if he remembered anything. I squeezed Sofi's hand and thanked her for the wonderful lunch.

"*Efharisto*," she said. "It is we who thank you for your hard work."

Walking to the Vicky, I could hear harsh-sounding words being spoken softly in Greek by Sofi and Cosmo. Tracey Sanders was an honest man and his wife and his father-in-law were going to keep him that way. I had no idea exactly what was being said, but I had the feeling I'd be hearing from Tracey Sanders again soon.

Chapter 20 — Just A Little Off

JEAN WAS WAITING outside the restaurant when I arrived. She had let her hair down and it flowed in soft waves over her shoulders. She was wearing makeup for the first time since I'd met her. She looked very sexy in her off-white silk blouse and short green skirt, carrying her white, sling-back, high-heeled shoes in her hand. As I walked toward her, I noticed several other men giving her appreciative looks.

"I love the barefoot look," I said.

Jean did a little twist step and a hop as she started toward me in the sand parking lot. Holding up the shoes, she said, "I had to borrow them from one of the girls. I don't even own a pair of these damn things." She fluffed her hair with the other hand. "I even went to the hairdresser for the first time in years!" Then she smiled that slightly evil grin again and sort of purred as she said, "You think Eddy boy will be a little friendlier and maybe invite us in?"

"Oh, yeah. Probably shoot me and keep you there. You certainly know how to get a man's attention," I said, as she hooked her arm on mine. My heart skipped a beat when I caught a whiff of her perfume. It was a fragrance I vaguely remembered from sometime far in my past.

"Let's take the Maz," she said.

I didn't argue, although putting my extra-large self in a Mazda Miata is not the easiest thing in the world. My head stuck up two inches above the windshield. Still, riding around Clearwater Beach on a beautiful June day, in a convertible sports car with the roof down was great. Especially when the car was being driven by a good-looking woman in a real short skirt.

We pulled into the foot-high weeds at Nash's little house before five, just in time to see him going inside. The little Cavalier still sat in back, and parked next to it was the flame-red Camaro Z-28. From marks in the grass, I could tell the Z had been driven up the neighbor's concrete drive and across the back of the yard instead of up Nash's dirt driveway.

"Damn place is still a dump," Jean said, as she leaned on the car and slipped the white heels on her bare feet. She brushed her hair, tossed the brush behind the seat, and walked unsteadily through the weeds in the unfamiliar shoes.

I sat in the car while Jean went to the door. She looked very enticing in her heels and short dress, and Nash was out the door and on the front step the second he saw her. He was so enthralled he didn't notice me until I was within five feet of them. Even from that distance, I could tell Nash needed a shave and a shower.

"What do you want?" Nash demanded, turning his weasel face my way. "I don't have anything to say to you, and I have company, so leave. Leave now or—"

"Eddy, Woody is a friend. May we come in for a while?" Jean said, as she placed her hand on the scrawny punk's waist.

Nash's face flushed, he muttered something to her, and lost the battle. Jean was already herding him into the house as I held the door.

We found few clean spots to sit, Jean next to Nash on the couch, and me in a chair. She did the pleasantries, introducing me as her friend. Jean was like a two-legged truth serum on the boy. Nash calmed down, and when it was my turn to talk, he was very cooperative.

I asked Nash if he knew Tiny, the biker, and he answered he'd never met him. As we talked, I asked the question again in different ways, always getting the same response, with no indication Nash was lying. I couldn't read his expression as he spoke because his eyes were on Jean's blouse and legs. He watched every breath she took, every move she made.

"Eddy, I talked to the medical examiner the other day, and he says he gave you an earring Donella was wearing when she was found. You wouldn't still have it, would you?" I asked.

"Yeah. It's with some of her things."

"Oh, Eddy, can I see it?" asked Jean.

Nash jumped from the couch and removed a box from a table near me, never taking his eyes off Jean. I moved to the other side of Jean on the couch. Nash didn't seem to notice. He opened the box and removed a plastic baggie. I saw at least a dozen letters tied with string and two small, hard-bound white books in the box as he set it on the floor.

"Oh, it's so beautiful!" Jean said, as Nash put the earring in her hand. "Tell me about it."

"Donella's parents gave her this pair of earrings Christmas before she died," Nash said. "They brought 'em back from a trip to Scotland."

"It's beautiful. What kind of stone is it?" Jean asked. "It has all those sparkles in it."

"I don't know, but it was supposed to be from some real old rocks, from some place in Scotland. It's somethin' like Stonehenge, but older." He hesitated then said, "You can have it if you want it."

Jean glanced at me out of the corner of her eye and I nodded. She purred a thank you and slipped the earring into the chest pocket of the silk blouse. Nash was almost drooling as he watched the stone slide down the pocket and stop at the tip of Jean's breast.

"Whatever happened to the car Donella was driving the day she disappeared?" I asked, keeping my voice gentle so as not to break Jean's spell.

"It's out back," Nash mumbled. "I had it fixed and...it still runs."

"What was wrong with it?" Jean asked sensing where I was headed with the first question.

"Some fuc...somebody poked a hole in the radiator."

"How do you know somebody poked a hole in it?" Jean asked. She was good, and I was impressed.

"It was a fresh half-inch hole, all the way through, like made by a tire iron," Nash replied. "The radiator is still out back in the shed."

He had kept the busted radiator for five years. Nash really was an automotive packrat, a "motor head," as Randy James had called him. We had been there for only ten minutes, but it was time to go for the hard questions.

"Eddy, how well do you know Mikel Conchman?" I asked.

"Mikey was a friend of...." Too late, Nash caught himself. "I don't know him."

"Your wife did though, didn't she?" I asked.

Nash locked eyes with me for the first time, and I saw a flash of fear, as though he sensed he was shark bait.

"It's okay, Eddy. Woody really is a friend. He wants to help us," Jean said, her voice a gentle purr.

Nash started to get up, fear in his eyes, but Jean leaned up against him, her breast touching his arm. Nash's eyes lost focus, and his brain did, too.

Too dumb or horny to be afraid, I thought.

"Eddy, we know about the seventeen drug arrests, and that Mikey helped Donella out," I said. "It's okay. And we know he was engaged to Bonnie, and about Bonnie's suicide." I was gambling, showing a lot of cards in this game, but sometimes it's necessary to get a decent discard.

"Yeah...Mikey took care of us," he said with a sigh. Nash had lost his sense of danger, thinking with his crotch instead of his brain.

"Both? You and Donella?" I asked.

"No...just her. But that helped me," he said, beginning to sweat. "I need...How 'bout a drink?" he asked Jean. His hand brushed her breast as he got up from beside her.

"Sure, whatever," she answered as Nash headed toward the kitchen.

I pulled Jean close and whispered, "Keep him out there five minutes, and see if you can find out if he had sex with his wife the day she was murdered. And don't hurt him."

Jean made a gagging sound, pulled herself up, straightened her skirt, and walked slowly into the kitchen as I took the box from the floor.

The envelopes were all letters to Donella, some from Eddy, some from her sister. I decided to go for the little books, both of which appeared to be journals. A quick scan of the last entries in the top book took my breath away.

May 15: Mikey says he won't give me any more money. He doesn't want me anymore. He refuses to answer my calls. He knows I'm afraid to talk....

I heard a sharp smack in the kitchen followed by Jean's muffled voice saying, "Bastard!"

Before I could get to the kitchen, I heard a sound like bread dough being punched, a fist hitting flesh, and the house shook as something hit the floor.

I ran to the kitchen and found Jean on the floor with Eddy on his knees straddling her, his back toward me. He was trying to pin her arms. I knew Nash was no mental giant, but I hadn't realized he'd be so stupid as to try something with me in the house.

Certain things cause attack reflexes to go on automatic. For me, seeing a friend, especially a woman, being hurt is one of those things. I defend my friends, and often, the best defense is a good offense.

In a heartbeat, I was behind Nash, leaning down. My right forearm slammed across his throat, left hand locked to my right hand, my right cheek pressed against his left ear. I pulled back hard with my left arm, and then I stood up. Nash's body was lifted firmly by his neck, the bone of my right wrist cutting off both breath and sound.

Nash struggled like a cat caught by the scruff of the neck, but with my forearm tight over his throat, he was helpless. For a split second my body tensed—I wanted to throw my weight back and break his neck. I knew the move rendered the enemy limp and lifeless as a dishrag—instantly, silently. It was deadly combat training I had never actually used, and would not use now—for this was not war and I needed Nash alive.

I walked back four steps, dragging Nash away from Jean. Suddenly, I released his neck. He fell to the floor hard.

I spun and sat on Nash's diaphragm with my knees on his biceps. My left thumb and forefinger pulled his right ear, ready to tear it from his head. Nash fought to breath, his eyes wide, angry, fearful.

"Jean, are you okay?" I could hear her moving behind me. "Did this little piece of shit hurt you?"

"Bastard hit me. He pawed my tits and ripped my damned blouse. I think he was gonna try and rape me," she said.

I felt Nash's body twitch violently and he screamed. I knew Jean had kicked him, and I was pretty sure where.

"No. Don't...not like that," I said. "You remember what I said about hurting him?"

Jean stood leaning against the sink, her face red, her blouse ripped, the lace of her bra showing. She looked at me and nodded.

"Good. Remember that...and see if you can find a sharp knife. Let's give this boy a Bobbitt special," I said, smiling and winking at her.

Jean's face changed slowly, then she smiled that evil smile again. "You mean like we talked about on the way over?"

Jean had asked whether we would hurt Nash if he wouldn't tell us what we wanted to know. I recalled telling her, "*No, but we can scare him, make him think we are going to. Just leave no marks but psychic marks.*" From her smile she now knew what I meant.

"Yeah, we're just gonna do the Bobbitt thing, if you know what I mean," I said, grinning menacingly at the weasel pinned beneath my legs.

Nash's eyes bugged out as he squirmed to get away. He understood what I meant. Every adult male in the early 90s knew the story of Lorena Bobbitt from Manasas, Virginia. Mrs. Bobbitt cut her abusive husband's penis off and threw it out the car window as she drove away. American males have lived with a new fear ever since.

Nash screamed again, "No! Oh, God. Please, don't hurt me. What do you want, anything. Money? Drugs? What do you want? Oh, God, no!"

Jean stood beside me with a ten-inch butcher knife at her side, its blade black and flecked with rust. Her voice was flat and she smiled as she said, "It's real dull, Woody, but that's even better."

My arm blocked Nash's view of anything but the knife. Jean grinned and winked. I presumed she wasn't really going to use the knife. I hoped not anyway. What we were doing already was illegal. Still, I sensed Nash was more afraid of the law than us and that he was hiding something. I was certain he wouldn't turn us in to the police.

Nash squirmed as Jean knelt behind me. I heard a snick, and felt side to side movement as she unfastened his belt. He began to whimper when she unsnapped his pants.

"Now, Jean, don't be too hasty," I said as I heard a zipper being pulled down.

Jean leaned around my shoulder, looked at Nash, held up the knife, and asked, "So, Eddy, did you lay your ole lady the morning she was murdered?"

"Oh, God," he said, beginning to sob. I felt a violent movement behind me and Nash's body stiffened as he cried out, "Yes!"

"Why'd you lie?" I asked.

Nash sobbed harder and gasped as he spoke. "The cops said...they asked if we'd made love that morning. I told them, yes, but we didn't make love. We didn't...I forced her. They said just answer the question. We didn't make love."

I rose up so he could breath and Nash twisted and almost broke free. Then he screamed again. I felt something hit him in back of me.

"Easy, Jean, just a little off the top for now," I said.

I brought my full weight to bear on Nash's chest again. His forearms made ineffective, little flaying motions toward his crotch. Whatever Jean was doing was certainly having the desired effect.

"Now, boy," I said in my best Cool Hand Luke prison warden accent, "we needs to have us a li'l die-a-log he'a. Yo' understan', boy?"

Nash whimpered and nodded.

I heard Jean giggle behind me. I realized she was just acting in the spirit of the inquisition. Sweet, young women do not usually get to behave this way. Lawyers never should...even though we'd often like to.

I leaned forward so that two hundred of my two-hundred-twenty-five pounds rested squarely on Nash's biceps. "So tell me about Conchman. Why was he giving you money? You blackmailing him?"

Even though the pain, at the word blackmail, Nash's eyes widened in terror.

"I'll take the look on your face as a yes. What were you blackmailing him over?"

Nash's eyes closed, and his breath became short and choppy. Since there was no weight on his chest, I knew it was from fear. Still, he didn't answer. I knew he feared something worse than me. I spoke in a deep, quiet voice, "Jean, filet that thing. Cut it the long way."

From the sound and movement, I knew Jean had ripped Nash's underwear apart with one yank. Then she yanked something else causing Nash to almost sit up with me still on top of him.

"He raped Donella," he screamed.

"Who? Conchman?" I asked, stunned. It was an answer I had not even considered.

Jean knelt beside me, holding the knife so Nash could see it. Dangling from the blade was white cloth with little pink hearts printed on it—a large piece of his underwear.

"When and where? Tell us or I'll cut it off and feed it to you," she said, her voice a cold hiss.

Nash's eyes were on the knife. He sweated, drooled and shook violently as he spoke. "In Miami...the night before his graduation party. He was doing her when her sister walked in."

"Is that why Bonnie killed herself?" I asked.

"I don't know," he said, whimpering, gasping for breath.

"Who killed your wife?" Jean asked.

"I don't know," Nash sobbed. He no longer moved. He just lay there gasping, drooling, and sobbing. "I don't know. Don't hurt me."

We left Nash lying on the floor. Jean had ripped the front out of his boxer shorts and had placed several ice cubes on his penis so he'd think he was cut and bleeding. A large pair of metal tongs lay between his legs. I didn't ask why.

Chapter 21 — Blue Light Special

I PICKED UP the two books, but left the envelopes in the box, placing it back in the end table where Nash had kept it. Jean washed her hands at the kitchen sink and dried them on a paper towel. Muttering, “Bastard,” she threw the used paper towel at Nash and picked up the earring from the floor.

“Let’s get out of here before I puke,” she said, handing me the earring. Jean’s blouse was ripped completely open. She yanked it out of her skirt and tied it in front of her as we walked toward the car. Her hands shook as she handed me the keys and said, “Drive.”

Snatching off the high-heels and throwing them behind the seats, Jean stepped over the door and slid down into the passenger seat. I shoe-horned myself into the driver’s seat, and fired up the little car with a flourish. It slid sideways and dirt flew from the spinning wheels as we left Nash’s yard.

I glanced at Jean and saw tears streaming down her face.

“Are you alright?” I asked.

“Take me to your boat,” she said. “I don’t want anyone to see me like this.”

On board *Defender*, Jean went straight to the forward berth and lay down. She sobbed a few times, and was asleep before I could talk with her.

I read through our latest spoils, now “newly discovered evidence.” In addition to what Nash had told us, the journals indicated that Donella had become a drug user after the incident in Miami. She continued to have sex with Conchman even after she married Nash. Conchman furnished money for two years, and kept her out of trouble. Finally, in the last month of her life, Donella tried to get more money out of Conchman. He refused, cutting off everything, except the legal help. The last entry was Memorial Day, 1991. The last arrest, the one in Hillsborough County just before the murder, was not mentioned in the journal.

I sat back in my computer chair and thought, *Now we have a motive, but Conchman is not the killer type.* I considered another possibility. *Tiny has no record—did he kill her for Conchman in return for legal favors? Perhaps for money and fun.* My mind clouded as the adrenaline rush faded and I dozed off to sleep.

THERE IS NO privacy on a small boat. I awoke to the sound of Jean in the forward head. I was surprised the motion of her walking had not awakened me, but we were at the dock, which is quite different than being at anchor.

"Well?" she asked, pointing at the books.

"We have a motive, but there's still a problem, and it's a serious one."

"I know. The bullet matches the gun. Loan me a shirt. I've got to go." Her voice was hoarse and she still sounded upset. She pulled a T-shirt over her torn blouse, hugged me and asked, "How long have you been doing this crap, Woody? Investigations...murders?"

"Too long, way too long," I replied. "And by the way, thanks. You were great today. What happened in there?"

"Don't ask."

"Did he hurt you?"

She raised the blouse and T-shirt, revealing a bruise the size of a fist on her stomach. "I teased him too much. He grabbed my breasts hard. I kicked and missed, and he punched me. But I'm okay," she said turning to go.

Then she was up the ladder, off the boat and headed to her car. I felt a warm glow deep in my chest as I watched her walk away. It was something I hadn't felt for a very long time.

That night, I took a different route for my nightly walk, partially because I needed to retrieve Vicky from Billy Jean's, and partially because of the danger. I hadn't forgotten the two shots on the bridge, and knew the next ones might not be warnings. I would just be another tourist, shot out of season.

The next morning I wrote a one-page letter explaining the significance of the two journals. I carried the journals and the letter to a print shop where I made three sets of copies and purchased six envelopes. I placed a copy inside each of three smaller envelopes, and wrote on them that they were to be opened unless the person receiving them heard otherwise from me within three weeks. Two envelopes were to go to attorneys in Tallahassee, each of whom had helped me before. The third copy went to Elsa Salvadora. This was life insurance for my client.

On the way back to *Defender,* a marked police cruiser pulled in behind me. Fear started coiling in the pit of my stomach. When I crested the bridge to Memorial Causeway, the blue lights came on and he wasn't passing me. My heart missed a few beats and my throat got very tight. I knew my driving was fine and had recently checked all Vicky's lights, so I suspected the stop was for something else.

I decided Eddy Nash had called the police after all. Most of the time lawyers clean up other person's messes after they occur. Now I tried to figure out how to clean up the mess I had created the afternoon before. My mind spun, wondering how to make bond on assault with a deadly weapon, or aggravated battery, and worrying about Jean. I looked at the three envelopes laying on the seat and wished I had already mailed them. It was too late now.

For just an instant, I considered trying to outrun the cop. Vicky's V-8, tires, and suspension were a match for the patrol car, but this wasn't the farms and woods of my native Eastern Shore of Maryland. This was a major Florida resort in summer filled with tourists, traffic, and cops. There was no chance of escape. I decided to play dumb.

Pulling onto the grass shoulder of the causeway, I stopped at the exact spot where Jon Clayton had probably stopped five years before, the fateful stop which led him to death row. The realization caused a knot to form in my stomach.

A tall, dark Hispanic officer walked to my window and, without ordering me out of the car, asked to see my license and registration. He spoke with professional politeness, but I still told him I would be taking out my wallet and getting the registration out of the glove compartment. I didn't want him to think I was reaching for a weapon and shoot me.

Handing the papers to the officer, I did my best innocent imitation. "What's the problem, officer?"

He glanced at my license and answered, "Just remain in your car, Mr. Thomas. This is for your own safety." Then he was gone, back to the patrol car.

The officer's words, "...for your own safety," caused the short hair on the back of my neck to stand up.

A familiar gray Chevy drove slowly by. It looked like the same unmarked police cruiser I had seen at Nash's on my first visit. Suddenly the officer returned to my window, the sun above his right shoulder shining in my eyes.

"Mr. Thomas, listen to me very carefully, and keep your mouth shut," the officer said. "That was Officers Flynt and Hedeon who just went by. They've been following you."

I was stunned that one officer would break the cover of another as this one had just done, especially with the detectives outranking him. I kept my mouth shut.

"I have an envelope for you from Tracey Sanders. It's under the ticket pad. When I hand this to you, sign the warning, and take the envelope. Do you understand?"

"Yes, sir," I replied meekly as I took the clipboard. I signed a warning for improper lane changing, and slipped the envelope out on the seat.

When I handed the clipboard back to the officer, he took off his dark sunglasses and looked me in the eyes. He was serious. There was no smile on his face, no twinkle in his eyes.

"I know who you are, what you are doing, and where you keep your boat. Here's my card," he said, as he handed me a copy of the warning, and a business card.

"There are two phone numbers on the back. If you need help dealing with Flynt and Hedeon, call me. And...watch your back." He put on his sunglasses, turned sharply and left.

I felt dizzy. The card indicated I had just been warned by Sergeant Lazaro Ramirez, and there were two phone numbers written in pencil on the back. I had a good idea what was in the envelope, and decided to put a copy in the insurance envelopes.

Back at the copy center, I opened Sanders' package and found an original evidence receipt. I scribbled another note that the copy was of the original police evidence receipt in Clayton's case, and that I suspected the serial number did not match the murder weapon. I ripped open all three envelopes and inserted the copies and notes.

Realizing I was probably still under surveillance, I bought three similar envelopes to carry to the car when I left the copy shop and paid one of the men to mail the real packets for me. You have to trust somebody, sometime, and often that means your life is in the hands of a stranger.

Chapter 22 — Storm Sails

I ARRIVED AT *Defender* with the two journals and the envelope from Sanders, and had just unlocked the hatch when I heard a familiar sound in the parking lot. It was Jean's Miata. Jean parked next to the dock and ran toward me. Tears ran down her cheeks.

"What's the matter?" I asked.

"Somebody shot out my windshield."

"When did it happen?" I asked, walking to the car with her.

"About an hour ago. I got in the car to make my noon bank run and it popped. I called the cops, and they wouldn't listen. They said it was probably a rock. Damn it, Woody, I was sitting in the car. I was parked facing the water. If it was a rock it would have been thrown two blocks."

The right side of her windshield had a beautiful spider web of cracks. Several ran the full width of the car. In the center of the web was a hole almost a half-inch in diameter.

"You were in the car when this happened?"

"Yes. It scared the hell out of me. I didn't hear a shot, just a loud pop."

This sounds familiar, I thought as I noticed a matching hole in the center of the passenger's headrest.

"The bullet must've hit something metal inside," I said, pointing to the hole, "because it didn't come out the back. You parked on the north side of the lot again?"

Jean nodded. "I was parked by the dock house."

"There's a county park across the cove from the parking lot. Did you see any cars over there? Anyone leaving after the shot?" I asked as I dug carefully in the headrest with my Swiss Army knife.

"There were a couple, but none left immediately," she said. "Do you think it was a bullet?"

A deformed slug popped out like the core of a zit and plopped on the leather seat. It had mushroomed and twisted from striking the windshield and the headrest, but enough remained intact for me to recognize it.

"Yep. Looks like a .308 rifle slug. I think someone was giving you a message." I sighed and then said, "There's something I haven't told you."

Jean's chin began to quiver as I told her about the two shots that were fired at me on the bridge.

"Woody, do you think someone is trying to kill us?"

"Nah. I think we're making someone real nervous, and they are not happy, so they want to make us even more nervous and unhappy than they are."

"I'm not nervous," she said. "I'm just plain scared. I don't like this, Woody."

We were walking toward *Defender* when I heard the voice coming from the cabin. "Mr. Thomas, this is Layla at Dr. Caspari's office. Please call me as soon as..."

I dove through the hatch and grabbed the phone. "This is Woody Thomas. May I help you?"

"Mr. Thomas, this is Layla, the receptionist at Dr. Caspari's. We spoke last week about a certain file."

"Yes, you were so very kind to me. Thank you again. To what do I owe the pleasure of your call?" I laid it on thick because I suspected she was putting her job in jeopardy by calling me.

"I'm calling from home because...well, I might get fired if Dr. Caspari finds out I called."

"I understand. This call is not happening. What's the matter?"

"Well...yesterday, Dr. Caspari was visited by two police officers—investigators—from the state attorney's office. One was named Flynt and the other was a huge, dark man who just showed his badge. They wanted to see the same file you looked at."

"Oh, I'm glad to know that—"

"Mr. Thomas, that's not all. There was an argument about a missing earring. They got nasty and threw things on the floor. They yelled at Doc. He was really scared. So was I. I called the regular police, but no one would come to help us. What's this about, Mr. Thomas? Am I in trouble for giving you that file?"

"Listen, carefully. First, this call never happened. Second, unless you're in a courtroom, sitting on a witness stand, under oath and being questioned, do not mention anything about this incident or the earring again. Okay?"

"Yes, sir. But did I do anything wrong?"

"No. Absolutely not. But for now, pretend you know nothing. Okay?"

"Yes, sir. I can do that, sir."

When she hung up the phone, I heard the sound of a second and third click. The telephone on Noah's dock was tapped. Someone was listening to my calls, and had just heard that one. Layla's call was bad, but the news got worse. I noticed that the answering machine showed two calls. One would be the beginning of Layla's call that I had just taken. I pushed the button for the first message.

A woman's voice began softly, "Mr. Thomas, this is Sofi Sanders. Tracey doesn't know I am calling you, but I think you need to know...Investigator Flynt was here this morning. Tracey had left copies of the documents you wanted on the table, and Flynt took them. He mentioned your name to his partner. I thought you should know. I hope you are not in trouble. Flynt is why Tracey quit the force. I've got to go now...Good luck."

Click. Click. Click, buzzz."

"Damn," I said.

"Flynt?"

"Worse than that. You heard those clicks? The phone is tapped, which means someone, probably police of some kind, is very interested in us."

"Whadda you mean, 'us?'" Jean asked. "I haven't done anything."

"Well, how about the Bobbitt thing with Nash?" I asked. "Since we've both been shot at, I think we're both in deep shit. How would you like to go for an overnight sail, maybe up toward Tarpon Springs? It should buy us some time so we can decide on our next move. Maybe we can get some help."

There was a storm line on the horizon to the south. The tropical wave I'd worried about when I'd left Marathon had reached tropical storm strength. It was over Cuba and sending bands of bad weather our way. Still, I figured I could make the run quick enough to be safe, and if not, I'd simply run offshore and ride it out. I sensed that staying at the dock would be more dangerous than gale force winds. I also knew the storms hovering over the coast would keep small aircraft from searching for us.

Jean parked her Miata next to the Ford, under the condo. By the time she had her purse and was back at the boat, the diesel was warming up and I had disconnected the shore power, water, and telephone cords. In less than ten minutes from the decision to leave, we were out of the slip and cutting through the harbor traffic, most of which was headed in the opposite direction. When we reached the number five marker at the mouth of Clearwater Pass, we were the only boat on the horizon.

We had worked so fast I'd overlooked an empty soda can caught in the corner of the cockpit. I almost threw it in the trash bin before I saw the note taped to it.

> *Cpt. Woody, I think you're in big trouble. Cops were on you boat last week, and again this morning. They were looking for something, even went up your mast. The two this morning told me to move the* Rambunctious *for my own safety. I think they may be planting, not looking. If they find this note, I suspect my scrawny butt will be in big trouble. You'd do it for me too. Dread*

Dread Smith, my neighbor in the Hatteras sport fisherman, had seen fit to try and warn me of possible trouble. *Bless his powerboat lovin' heart, dreadlocks and all*, I thought.

Jean called J.R., her bartender, from the cockpit on her own cellular phone. I heard her tell him he was in charge, and to have one of the girls pick up her car and get the windshield replaced.

"Where are we going?" She was obviously repeating J.R.'s question to me.

I looked at her and shook my head.

"I'm not sure," she said. "But I'll call you tomorrow." No further explanations were given.

I decided to make a quick check of the boat and see if the visitors Dread had warned of had left any presents. We were two miles into the Gulf, headed west under sail when I found the package in the aft deck locker.

"Jean, look at this!" I said, holding up the pure white brick of plastic wrapped powder.

"Is that what I think it is?"

"Cocaine? We'll never know for sure, and I'm not taking any chances," I said as I walked to the rail and ripped the plastic. The brick hit the water creating a white liquid plume. "Damn, I hate throwing plastic overboard, but I don't want any trace of that shit on board if the cops are after us."

We spent the next few minutes checking every place someone could easily hide drugs above deck, and found another brick of what appeared to be cocaine in the cockpit locker under the spare dock lines. It, too, made the fish happy.

When I went to place the spare dock lines back in the locker, I noticed another new addition to my supplies. It was a little black box with a switch and an antenna wire, similar to the one I had found under Vicky in Marathon.

"That's not yours either?" asked Jean, as I set the box down in the cockpit.

"Nope. I think it's a radio tracking device," I replied. "I should probably toss it overboard, too."

"Who put it there?"

"I don't know for sure, maybe the FBI," I replied, "But I don't want them or anyone else to know where we are."

I told Jean what I had done with the bug I found in Marathon. This one we placed in an old, foam plastic cooler I kept in the dingy for bait. Gray duct tape sealed it, and it would float high enough to be blown by the wind.

"Let 'em track this," I said tossing the newly amphibious bug over the rail.

Lowering the Bimini top onto the coaming and strapping it down, I began to prepare *Defender* for rough weather. Everything loose was tied down or stowed below.

When the storms finally hit, they packed wind gusts of forty-five to fifty knots, blowing the tops off the waves. I reduced sail to a double reefed mainsail. With the main reduced and the jib furled and tied, *Defender* stood up to the winds without any trouble. We were heading west into the Gulf of Mexico, cruising at hull speed.

Ten miles off shore, the squalls passed and the wind died. I checked our position on the GPS, and found we had been blown farther north than I had anticipated. We motor-sailed southeast toward Tarpon Springs, and an hour later rounded the north end of Anclote Key.

The east side of the key, a long, uninhabited island, had long been one of my favorite anchorages. It would be safe enough for the night, squalls or not.

I felt that no one was searching for us. We saw no helicopters, and only one twin-engine private plane. We monitored marine radio channel sixteen, but no one called us or spoke of us. It appeared no one even knew we were gone, except Jean's bartender, J.R.

We had a choice of safe anchorages to ourselves. It was the middle of the week and the squalls had chased the day sailors away. I dropped anchor a quarter mile east of Dutchman Key, a small island protected by the much larger Anclote Key. In the distance, we could see the abandoned lighthouse, the only sign of man's aborted invasion of one of the prettiest islands on the west coast of Florida.

I watched an osprey as he circled low above *Defender*. Suddenly, the fish hawk gave a loud cry of alert and hovered above us. I wondered at the message in his warning. We watched the hawk dive low to the water and glide to Dutchman Key.

Seconds later we heard the sound of a twin-engine aircraft. It was an old red-and-white Piper Apache, the same one we had seen a half hour before. This time it was lower and flying slowly north to south, between us and Tarpon Springs. I waved, like any tourist, and the plane dipped its wings and continued on, south toward Clearwater.

"Do you think he was looking for us?" Jean asked.

"I doubt it. It was a real old, civilian-type aircraft. Just a private pilot out for kicks," I answered. I hoped I was right.

Chapter 23 — Flash

WE ATE PEANUT butter and jelly sandwiches under a pink, gold, and blue sky. Storm clouds in the east reflected the colors from the west. Clouds in the west created huge purple sculptures. A wild sunset, even for Florida. And it got better.

As the sun sank below the horizon beyond Anclote Key, I stood on the cabin top with my arms around Jean, and together we witnessed one of the most elusive phenomena in nature—the green flash. The instant before the last of the sun's circle of light dropped below the horizon, it changed from yellow-red to bright green for a single heartbeat of time.

I had seen the green flash many times and yet, this was one of the few times I had been able to share it with a companion or friend. We raised our coffee cups and toasted the setting sun by making a sizzling sound, pretending the fire of the sun had been quenched by the sea. Then we sat quietly and watched the colors fade slowly to purples, blacks and whites, then to grays, and finally to black.

I left the Bimini top down, both in case of high winds and so we could watch the stars. The gentle offshore breeze kept the bugs at bay and we were comfortably cool. In the light of a small lamp hung from the boom, I opened the packet from Tracey Sanders. Inside was a note.

> *Mr. Thomas,*
>
> *Sofi says that a man who helps without request, who asks no reward, and who says grace over his food, deserves to be treated with respect and not lied to. Here are the papers you wanted, the originals. I didn't treat you right when you asked for them, I'm sorry*
>
> *I hear Clancy Flynt and Nigel Hedeon don't like you. They don't like me either.*
>
> *Good luck,*
> *Tracey S.*

Enclosed were a handwritten police report signed by Tracy Sanders—the first copy of it I had ever seen—and the original evidence slip. The slip was a receipt given to Sanders when he turned in the pistol he had taken from Jon Clayton. I had copied it earlier for my insurance packs.

The handwritten report listed the pistol as a .38 caliber Smith and Wesson, loaded with "five rounds, exposed tip hollow point ammunition." No serial number was recorded for the pistol.

However, the evidence slip not only listed a serial number, it had a rubbing, where the paper had been laid on the barrel of the pistol and a pencil point brushed over it to transfer the serial number to the slip. Sanders was a careful cop.

I read aloud to Jean and told her what each thing meant. We both held our breaths as I pulled out the lab report from Drew Pearson. The serial number of the pistol he tested and the one taken from Jon Clayton were not the same. They were not even close.

"I knew it," said Jean. "Thank God."

"Amen," I said.

I could now prove the guns had been switched. Even the cartridges were different. Clayton was arrested with regular hollow point ammunition. Pearson's report indicated the weapon was loaded with hollow base wad-cutters. The medical examiner's report also indicated the bullet found in Donella Nash's head was a hollow base wad cutter. The bullets were similar, but they could not be mistaken for one another.

I was both happy and sad. The idea of an innocent person in prison or being put to death is frightening enough, but the job of trying to save that innocent life is absolutely terrifying.

I knew that proving a convicted man was actually innocent would not be a first, or even all that unusual. In the prior twenty years, sixty-five persons sentenced to death were completely cleared by the federal system. I wonder how many innocent persons were not so lucky. The federal system had been hogtied by legislation since the early 90s. Were those earlier sixty-five persons still in the system, they would not have been so lucky.

Even with the evidence we had discovered, we still faced a long fight for Jon Clayton's freedom. And he could still be put to death because, after all, he was convicted and sentenced to die.

My thoughts were interrupted by the quiet, "Now what do we do?" asked by Jean.

"We get help," I said. "Right now, we're the only people beside Jon and the real killer who know Jon is innocent. I think we need to insure his life by letting someone else know."

"Someone else does know," said Jean. "That's why they shot at us."

"You're right," I said as I went below for more coffee.

In the dark, I noticed the message light blinking on the answering machine. When we left the dock, I'd disconnected the dock phone line, but left the cellular phone and answering machine turned on. Two calls had come in during the trip north, either during the storm or while we were under power and could not hear the phone. I pressed the new calls button.

"Woody, this is Elsa. Call me when you get the chance. I can hardly wait to tell you about little Timmy and what he's been up to. Oh, yeah, that case you asked me about was Berger vee New York, 388 U.S. 41. It applies to both you and the Clayton woman. Take care, and I'll talk to you later."

The machine added, "Time, 2:45 p.m."

"Thomas, this is Pearson in Tallahassee. What the hell is going on, boy? I get to work this morning and the FBI is waiting to talk to me. They were hot about that gun we talked about. Before they left, an ATF agent showed up asking about the same gun. And now my boss has just finished chewing my ass over it. Thanks a bunch, buddy." A loud click indicated he had slammed the phone down.

The machine added, "Time, 3:05 p.m.."

"What's that first one, a girl friend?" asked Jean as she climbed down the ladder.

"No, another attorney. I don't know a little Timmy. She doesn't have any kid named Timmy, and I didn't ask her about any cases," I said.

I had Florida case law and statutes on CD-ROM for my computer, but not federal cases. My only law books were a couple of old hornbooks, normally more useful as ballast than for research. In the constitutional law hornbook, I found Berger v. New York…a 1967 case cited as the lead case upholding wiretap statutes.

"I think she was trying to tell us our phones are tapped, both mine and yours," I said, showing Jean the book. "The only thing I asked her to do was check on Tiny..."

"Timothy Jacobs," Jean chimed in. "Would he be little Timmy?"

"Yep. And it sounds like she has something for us. We need another way to contact her, though, since this phone may also be tapped."

"Pearson of Tallahassee, isn't he the gun expert, the guy whose report we were just reading?"

"Yeah. He sounds upset, and I'm real concerned about his message." I explained about how I made the copies of the diaries and the evidence receipt, and how I'd tried to prevent them from being intercepted by Flynt and company.

"I guess the Feds got to the kid I paid to mail the stuff before he got rid of it," I said. "And it sounds like the Feds are also interested in Jon's case."

"Why would they care about a Florida murder?"

"They probably don't, but the gun was stolen from a police evidence locker, so the FBI could look into it under the Federal Firearms Act, or maybe as a theft of government property. ATF is the Bureau of Alcohol, Tobacco and Firearms, and stolen weapons fall into their domain, too. That must be why the FBI put the tracking devices on my car and the boat and is probably listening to our phones."

"How is Tiny connected to all of this?"

"Well, he gave the stolen..." Then I realized something. "No, wait a minute. That was a different gun. The one Tiny gave Jon was not the murder weapon. I haven't the foggiest idea, but I bet Elsa knows something that'll help us."

I had a vague sense of uneasiness, as though I were forgetting something, but for now, I decided to do only what was absolutely necessary. Realizing the copies I had tried to mail had been intercepted bothered me. I wanted copies to be in friendly hands, and I had not trusted the Feds since 'Nam.

Defender was outfitted with three of the largest deep cycle marine batteries made. They could run all her systems for two days without recharging, and could be recharged from the engine or my wind generator. I turned on my desktop computer and, as it powered up, bounded to the deck and released the prop-stop on the wind generator. I wanted to make sure I didn't have a power failure.

The next hour was spent typing frantically, laying out all that had occurred and what we had learned. As I scanned the evidence receipt into the PC, I felt a cool wind blow through the cabin.

Jean called to me through the hatch. "Woody, I see a lot of lightning in the distance. Do we need to do anything to the boat?"

"No, but I'm glad you told me. I better try and get this sent. I doubt whoever is tapping our phone is ready to intercept e-mail."

I dialed NOAA weather to see how the cell phone was working and was pleased with the reception. The antenna mounted on the aft rail boosted performance considerably over a regular cell phone, and the storms were not yet causing a problem.

Elsa's computer stayed on night and day, and though it was almost ten in the evening, there was a good chance she'd still be working. I carbon copied the message to my friends in Tallahassee, just in case she didn't receive it.

The transmission was over in seconds. I had hoped for an immediate reply. It came a half hour later, from Elsa.

> *Woody, RE: Tiny the biker. Timothy Jacobs was a SEAL, but died in a training exercise in 1970. No idea who Tiny really is, but be careful.*
>
> *Rumor 1: several people have just plain disappeared after dealing with him. I assume you understood your cell phone, the phone at the dock, and Jean Clayton's phones are all tapped. A warrant was issued at ASA Conchman's request—drug investigation.*
>
> *Rumor 2: A drug strike team tried to raid your boat this PM, presume they missed you. What the hell is going on? Do not answer that. FBI visited boss PD this PM. I am officially not at the office and am not supposed to contact you as per FBI and boss PD.*

Love and prayers.
ES

The news about Tiny was not a surprise. The warrant and raid were to a degree, but they explained the drugs we had found.

It was eleven and time for the television version of the local news and weather. *Defender* was equipped with a small black-and-white TV and a mast mounted, omni-directional antenna for news and weather, emergencies and hurricanes. I liked the radar weather updates, which were often more accurate than NOAA. However, something was wrong with the reception tonight. We had sound, but no picture. While I tried to adjust the picture, the news began. For Jean Clayton and me, a bad day suddenly got worse.

"A tragedy unfolded in Clearwater today where police are investigating an apparent burglary which has left the homeowner near death. The mother of Eddy Nash found him lying unconscious on the floor of his home near Stephenson Creek. Initial reports indicate Nash suffered several knife wounds and severe head injuries, apparently inflicted by one or more intruders. He remains hospitalized in a coma this evening.

"This was not the first tragedy to strike the Nash home. It was five years ago next month that Eddy Nash's wife, Donella Nash, was kidnapped, raped and murdered. The man convicted of her murder, Jon Clayton, was sentenced to death, but five years later, he has yet to be executed.

"In reaction to this latest tragedy, Assistant State Attorney Mikel Conchman has requested the governor to sign Clayton's death warrant immediately. There is no indication from the governor's office as to whether he will comply with the request."

I turned to Jean, who looked as ill as I felt. "Who do you think they're going to name as suspects?" I asked, cutting off the TV.

We climbed back on deck with glasses of lemonade. Silently, we watched the lightning as storms passed offshore to the west of us. Above us the sky cleared and we could see stars. In the east we could see the lights of the huge power plant at the mouth of the Anclote River. From where we sat, it looked as if Old Sparky itself loomed in the night.

"This may move Jon's execution up four or five months," I said. "I'll have thirty days, tops, to try and get him a new trial."

"Is that legal? Can you do what is necessary to stop his execution in thirty days?"

"Yeah, I think so. If we're not in jail or beaten into a coma."

"You mean like Eddy?"

"Yep," I replied. "Ironic that he was beaten right after Flynt and his buddy found out about the earring."

"You think Flynt did that? No way," she said. "Why?"

"Flynt's reputation, for one. For another, I've seen Flynt at Nash's recently. He and his partner were shaking Nash down, scaring him because of me, I think. And, well, I just have a feeling.... You know what I mean? If it looks like a snake and acts like a snake, it's probably a snake."

We spent the next few hours talking, until we ran out of words. Our thoughts kept turning to the power plant in the distance, and what it held for Jon Clayton, an innocent man.

Finally, after the moon rose, we went below to try to rest. As always, when I had guests aboard at night, I turned on the red night-vision lights in the cabin. Jean climbed into the V-berth in the bow as I retired to my queen-sized, and very lonely, berth in the aft cabin.

Chapter 24 — Strangers In The Night

I TRIED TO sleep, but sleep wouldn't come. The aft hatch, partially open, scooped in the cool breeze, bringing hints of distant islands on its breath. The moon, crystal white, near full and high, shone through the hatch. I lay alone, thinking of the woman who slept thirty-five feet away. I decided to try and sleep on deck under the stars.

Gently, so as not to awaken Jean, I walked to the main cabin. She was there, standing in the square of light shining through the main hatch. The moonlight played soft upon her hair, shining black, mixed with silver threads. Softer yet, it lit her face as she looked up at me. Gone were the worry lines from her brow. Her eyes sparkled in the night. I could feel the warmth of her body, though we stood two feet apart.

Jean spoke, her voice soft and husky. "Woody, hold me. Please, just...hold me."

I silently prayed, *Thank You, God*! I had been lonely too long.

I reached my hand out and touched her hair, feeling it flow like liquid through my fingers. My hand, golden tan from the sun, appeared black in the moonlight, a stark contrast to the pale glow of Jean's face. I gently touched her cool, soft cheek. My breathing faltered. My heart pounded in my ears. And then...I felt the world move beneath my feet.

It, too, was soft and quiet, but quite unnatural—a gentle bump in the dark that moved the boat. Jean's eyes opened wide; she felt it too. When you live aboard a boat, you know its every sound, its every motion, and I recognized this one.

I placed a finger over Jean's lips and whispered, "We have visitors—pirates." Then leaning closer I added, "Don't move until they board, then move gently toward..."

Another noise, distinctly harder than the first, and muffled. My guess was a boarding ladder. The boat rocked slightly to port, and Jean and I moved as one toward the navigation table. I reached beside the computer and pulled the .357 Magnum from its holster. Fearing visitors, I had released its cover snap before sunset. I set an HKS Speed Loader with six more rounds next to the hatch, hoping I wouldn't need it.

My senses now ran on high speed. Movement and time slowed to a crawl. I watched Jean place her white purse back on the navigation station, the small, silver .25 caliber semiautomatic pistol now in her hand. Compared to the massive, stainless steel .357 Magnum, it looked pitiful. Still, I knew it had killed once, and could again.

Jean moved toward the main hatch and peeked aft. From the sound, I could tell one pirate had stopped by the aft hatch over my berth. There were two; no more boarded.

I moved forward, following the soft, quick footfalls of the other pirate. Whoever they were, they were very good at stealthy boarding, as though they had practiced this. Had we been asleep, we'd never have heard them and probably not have felt the motion. I glanced back and could see a large shadow on the aft cabin top. I realized they knew where we slept and I guessed what their intentions were. I reached for the switch to light the deck lights. My hand was still inches away when they opened fire.

With shattering blasts and muzzle flashes, semi-automatic weapon fire came through the hatches into the forward and aft cabins. They were trying to kill us in our sleep.

Plastic from the fore hatch flew from the forward cabin striking my legs. I stepped back, lost my balance and fell to the cabin floor on my back.

Lying on the floor, I raised both arms and, aiming through the cabin top toward where I imagined the forward pirate was standing, I fired three rounds from the Magnum. The blasts lit the interior of the boat like flashbulbs. Though I felt the concussion of each shot, I heard nothing.

No more shots came through the forward hatch. No more plastic shrapnel struck me. I heard something heavy hit the forward deck and a metal object rattled through the busted hatch. I recognized the silhouette of an M-16 laying on the V-berth in the moonlight.

Hearing the rapid popping of Jean's little semi-automatic behind me, I pulled myself from the floor and dragged myself the ten feet to her side. Jean stepped to my left to reload her pistol as I reached the hatch, looked out, and faced death.

It was the dream—the dream that had haunted me for weeks—but this time it was real. Against the dark gray of the pre-dawn light, a large, dark shadow on the aft cabin formed the silhouette of a standing man. Death personified turned toward me, and a narrow beam of red light suddenly pierced the night, a laser sighting beam.

Time stopped. I watched in horror as Death swung its deadly light toward me. My hands rose of their own accord to shoot at a black shadow, against a dark sky, with moonlight my only ally. I heard a scream. It was mine.

The red light continued its swing toward me, reflected off the heavy moist air. I held the .357 in both hands and looked over it, aligning it with the center of the shadow. I pulled the trigger. Once, a flash, a blast of fire and sound and the red light jerked skyward. Twice, and the red light beam aimed into the rigging and I heard the distinct rapid crack of an M-16 rifle firing on automatic. I watched as red-hot shell casings being ejected from the rifle arced into the night.

The dark figure, which only seconds ago had appeared huge, seemed to dissolve. The white hull of my dingy appeared behind it. I aimed for the center of the shadow now only three feet off the cabin top and fired my last shot. A white flash of sparks appeared only feet from my face. The white dingy suddenly appeared to have a huge dark hole in it.

Damn, I missed and blew my dingy apart, I thought, as I stepped back down the ladder to the galley floor.

Jean took my place at the hatch, but there was nothing left moving. Even the red beam of light had disappeared behind the cabin.

A step to the navigation station and my spent shells hit the floor. I grabbed the Speed Loader and loaded the next six rounds in the dark. I hit the deck light switch, turning on flood lights mounted high on the mast. Night seemed to turn into day. Jean was out of the hatch before I could stop her. She screamed.

Time returned to normal as I stepped on deck. I glanced toward the bow and saw a leg and an arm hanging over the cabin top. Aft of the cockpit, I saw the cause of Jean's distress. Blood and gore, once the memories, dreams, and the hopes of one pirate, had caused the dark splotch on the dingy.

A .357 Magnum is a powerful weapon. My last shot had struck the binnacle, destroying my compass. The reshaped bullet had continued on apparently catching the pirate on the aft cabin as he fell backwards, striking him below the chin, and exiting out the top rear of his head. His caved-in face looked like a camouflage-painted jack-o-lantern which had rotted in the sun. White showed through two large holes in his black, long-sleeve T-shirt. I reached down and found he was wearing body armor, which even the Magnum could not penetrate. I noticed six more, smaller holes in the side and front of the T-shirt. Jean was a good shot, even in the dark.

Jean stood behind me as I surveyed the damage on the aft deck. I heard a blast and Jean bumped into me then fell to the deck with a gasp. In the few seconds it had taken to check on the pirate on the aft cabin, the pirate on the bow had propped himself up and shot Jean. In the second it took for me to realize what had happened, he fired a second shot. The bullet tugged at my shirt as it passed below my left arm.

With no time to assume a decent firing stance, and nowhere to seek cover, I fired the Magnum freehand, striking his right leg, just below his kneecap. I jumped over Jean's legs and, landing square, assumed a two-handed combat position and fired twice more into the legs and groin of the pirate. His right arm fell back to the deck. The pistol, still in his hand, now touched his head. A red steam of blood flowed down the deck from his legs.

After scrambling along the deck, my bare feet suddenly stuck to the bloody surface as I stood staring down at another man in black. He raised his head. His eyes watched me, and the pistol remained in his hand, its barrel touching his right ear. Even with the camouflage war paint, I recognized my enemy—Clancy Flynt.

"Drop the gun, Flynt! Give it up," I yelled as I aimed directly between his eyes. "Drop it or I'll blow your damned brains out!"

"Fuck you," said Flynt. Then he pulled the trigger. A bang. A flash. A nine-millimeter bullet tore through Flynt's brain, taking his life with it in a crimson spray.

Startled, I jerked the trigger on the Magnum. I missed Flynt and blasted a large section of deck and toe rail from *Defender's* bow.

Flynt lay still. Pieces of fiberglass and wood rained down on the water. Flynt's gun dropped from his hand making a plopping sound as it struck the surface of the water.

"No...fuck you," I replied.

I became dizzy and fell to my knees. I watched Flynt shrink and turn to clay as the pressure of his spirit left his body. It was a sight I had seen too many times in my life. It was a sight I had hoped never to see again.

I have no idea how long I knelt, stunned at Flynt's final act. My mind and ears functioned again only when I heard Jean calling to me, "Woody, please help me...please be alive."

I crawled to Jean's side. She had pulled herself into the cockpit and lay on the floor. Her blood ran across the cockpit to the drain and then into the sea. She squeezed her eyes tight as I lifted her to the cushioned seat.

"It's over. They're both dead," I said, surprised at the hollow, distant sound of my voice. My ears were still ringing from the gunfire in the cabin.

"Was that Tiny on the back cabin?"

"I don't think so," I replied.

"Who?"

"Flynt's partner."

I reached through the hatch and grabbed the first aid kit. In minutes I had pads and gauze on the bullet wounds. One bullet, two wounds. It had passed through her left thigh, about four inches below her crotch. It was a clean wound, bleeding freely, but not spurting. Talking to her constantly, I stuffed an extra cushion under her knees, raising the wound above her heart.

I hadn't realized how loud the Magnum was below deck. As my hearing returned, I heard the bilge alarm. We were sinking.

"Excuse me, but I've got to run below and call for help," I said.

"What's that bell?" Jean asked.

"Must be the phone."

I expected to find the floor boards floating when I went below, but they weren't. I pulled up the main access hatch in the cabin floor and found water running from the bow of the boat.

The shots into the forward cabin must have penetrated the hull, I thought.

Then the alarm stopped.

I was surprised, but yanked the V-berth apart and pulled the access hatches open. Fifty one-gallon plastic jugs of water, my emergency supply, had been shot to pieces. The water had finally washed enough sand and dirt out of the limber holes to flow back to the bilge pump.

The hull of a Gulfstar 41 is thick. That, and firing through the Lexan plastic hatch, the five-inch foam mattress, the three-quarter-inch plywood of the berth, and the water jugs, had prevented any further damage. As the emergency drinking water drained out, no water came in.

I had stowed canned goods under the berth in the aft cabin, and there were also several layers of drawers and clothing to slow the bullets. When I checked the aft bilge I found soup, but no water. From the depths of my heart, I thanked God and the builders of my *Defender*.

We were not sinking, but I still faced two serious problems. Jean needed medical attention, and I had two dead cops on my boat.

Chapter 25 — Hawk Eyes

WE WERE NOT in a mayday situation. That had already passed. Jean was in distress, but there was no imminent loss of life. The urgency call for assistance, "pan-pan," would alert officials to our situation and location. However, I was unsure if I wanted officials alerted.

I saw Sergeant Ramirez's business card as I reached for the radio. His words echoed in my mind. *If you need help dealing with Flynt and Hedeon, call me. And...watch your back.*

He was right, I thought. *Flynt had tried to shoot me in the back and struck Jean instead.*

I called Ramirez on the cell phone. It was our best chance of getting help, yet not alerting too many officials about our situation.

The first number Ramirez had written on the back of the card gave me his answering machine. I left a short message. "This is Woody Thomas. You were right about watching my back."

On the fourth ring of the next number, I heard a friendly voice. "Ramirez."

"Sarge, this is Woody Thomas. You were right about watching my back. There's been a problem."

"Are you all right?" he asked.

"Yeah, but they shot Jean Clayton in the leg. She needs a doctor."

"How bad is she?"

I was pleased with his concern over our well-being, and not where we were.

"She'll be all right. I stopped the bleeding, and the bullet passed completely through."

"Have the, ah...shooters left?" he asked.

"Well, sort of. Let's just say they won't do it again—ever."

"Oh, really. That makes a difference. Call me back at this number in fifteen minutes. I'll see that you get help from a neutral party. Okay?"

"Fifteen minutes, this number. Will do," I answered, and the phone went dead.

Sometimes not wearing a watch can be a problem. I set the stove timer for fifteen minutes before I climbed back into the cockpit with Jean. Her face was even paler than normal, but she was smiling.

"The hawk was back," she said. "He circled twice and then flew off to the south. It was like he was checking to see who won."

"What's your name?" I asked, concerned she might be hallucinating.

Jean turned toward me and smiled again, "I'm okay, Woody. It just burns. I really saw the hawk."

We watched the sun rise over the carnage on the stern of the boat. A brilliant red sunrise—a bad omen for sailors. The red light glowed through a hole the bullet had made in the side of my dingy after it had ended Hedeon's life. It reflected off the blood on the deck. It turned the bay around us red.

My mind replayed the fight, like a movie playing in my head, the "coulda, shoulda dones." I thought of what might have been done to keep Jean from being shot, or to punish Flynt, had he lived. Through it all, I kept remembering what a judge told me years before. "If you kill a cop in Florida, you will die for it." He meant my client, but now I realized it also meant me.

The cell phone, still in my left hand, rang and brought me back to reality.

"Yeah?" I answered with a question, anticipating the call was from Ramirez.

The voice on the other end asked, "Nigel?"

"No." I looked at the bloody mess on the stern of my boat and said quietly, "Nigel's not here." The phone went dead.

"What was that about?" asked Jean.

"Someone just called for Nigel. Nigel Hedeon was the name of the headless wonder on the aft deck." I nodded toward the dead man.

"Oh."

"This means they weren't doing this by themselves," I said.

The timer rang. I punched redial for Ramirez's number. It rang once.

"Thomas, is everything still okay?" he answered, assuming it was me.

"Yeah. Jean's doing good, and the boat and I are fine," I answered. I decided not to mention the call, until I knew for sure who our friends were, if we had any.

"All right, I need to know where you are so I can send help."

"Sarge, do you know this phone has been tapped?"

"Yes. It's okay. There's nothing either of us can do about it. I have some help and a Coast Guard rescue chopper warming up. All I need is your location and they'll fly. Where exactly are you?"

"Up toward the Anclote River off Tarpon Springs. We're anchored behind Anclote Key, about two hundred yards behind Dutchman Key. Large single-mast sailboat, off-white hull, green stripe along the deck, green sail covers. There are no other boats in the area, so she should be easy to find."

"All right. Behind Anclote Key. Got it. The rescue chopper will take both of you off the boat. It should be there in less than fifteen minutes. Good luck, Thomas."

"Wait a minute. What about my boat?"

"There's help coming with the Coast Guard. They'll probably impound it. Nothing I can do about that. Let's just make sure you and the girl are safe."

Fifteen minutes later I heard the roar of the huge rescue chopper, so unlike the Hueys in 'Nam. Then, like a flashback or a bad dream, I heard the sound of a Huey, a wop-wop-wop that was unmistakable. A second Huey chimed in.

I saw them coming, a flock of choppers, fast, low and straight out of the sun. In the lead were two Hueys and behind them, like a giant white grasshopper, roared the Coast Guard helicopter. My chest tightened as I considered the possible occupants of the Hueys.

Within seconds, men were jumping in the water from the rescue chopper and swimming toward *Defender*. I slipped the .357 Magnum into the cockpit locker and helped the rescue team aboard. Appalled at the scene on the boat, the first man on board exclaimed, "My God, man, you've had a friggin' war here!"

I explained we'd been boarded at night and that both men were dead.

"We know. We're here to remove you and her, and to guard the boat until they board," said one of the Coast Guardsmen, pointing toward a Huey which had landed on the beach.

"Who are they?" I asked

"Federal agents," he replied.

The rescuers decided the safest way to transfer Jean to the helicopter was to wait for the four men now paddling toward us in an inflatable boat from the Huey, and use their boat. Whoever the Feds were, they were dressed in black combat fatigues or BDUs and were armed with automatic weapons.

The first man out of the inflatable identified himself as Special Agent Featherstone and told me he and the others were FBI agents. Jean was already being helped into the inflatable before the last two got out. Then the Coast guardsmen, the two last agents and Jean headed toward the rescue chopper, also now on the beach.

I noticed the third chopper remained well aloft, circling much like the hawk. It was not for rescue. There was a machine gun hanging out of the side door. Suddenly, I felt nauseous.

Agent Featherstone started questioning me as the other agent took photographs of the carnage. "Do you know who these men are? What happened? Why?"

I answered his questions as best I could, never thinking I, like my clients, should keep my mouth shut. Then I heard the Coast Guard helicopter increase its rotor speed and begin to lift off.

"Wait a minute. I'm supposed to be on that chopper," I said, my stomach tightening more.

"That's been changed. You'll be flying with us," said Featherstone. Then he started questioning me again.

"No. No more questions. I won't answer any more damn questions. I want a lawyer. I know my rights," I said. I realized I was beginning to sound like my clients.

"You aren't charged with anything. Why do you want a lawyer?" Featherstone asked as the inflatable returned to *Defender*. I had heard that ruse used before on so many of my clients that I immediately decided I was in serious trouble. I refused to speak at all, but it didn't matter.

"Get a life jacket on. It's time for you to go," said Featherstone. "And, hmm. Wait a minute. You'd better put some pants on first. And get another shirt. That one's a bloody mess."

I went below without escort, washed Jean's blood from my hands, and pulled on cargo shorts and a fresh shirt. When I returned on deck, I found four more heavily-armed men had boarded. They made it clear—I was being ordered off.

"Are you impounding my boat?" I asked.

"Yes. It's now evidence of a federal crime," Featherstone replied. Then he smiled and said, "Now, you know Uncle Sam will take good care of it."

"Please...this is my home. She's all I've got. Don't tear her up," I said. "I've seen what happens to confiscated boats—cut up, stripped and sold at auction." *Defender* was more than a boat. She was my friend. She had protected me and kept me safe through more storms than I could remember.

One of the other men spoke up. "She'll be taken care of, sir. I'll personally see to it. I'm in charge of processing her for evidence." He handed me a card. I stuck it in my pocket without looking at it and climbed into the inflatable.

It was only then that I noticed Flynt's boat. He and Hedeon had arrived in a black, semi-rigid inflatable with a fiberglass, vee-shaped bottom, capable of high speed. It had a forty-horsepower motor on the back, and paddles on the floor. Between the paddles sat a pair of two-gallon gasoline tanks. Since the motor was hooked to a six-gallon fuel tank, I suspected the spare tanks were for something else. Plastic explosives and timers in a plastic milk crate in the bow confirmed my suspicions.

Flynt and his buddy planned a serious going away party for us, I thought.

Paddling toward the chopper, I looked back at my *Defender* and was surprised to see one of the agents climbing the mast. He stopped at the spreaders, and appeared to be working on my television antenna.

On the beach, I was ushered quickly into the waiting Huey by another agent. When the helicopter lifted off, there were only the pilot and co-pilot, one agent and me on board. Airborne, I could see several high speed boats, with blue lights flashing, in the distance, their V-shaped wakes pointing in our direction. From Tarpon Springs, I saw a Coast Guard cutter cutting through the river, blue light flashing, also headed toward *Defender*.

I realized the old Huey might not be such a bad place to be after all. The agent sitting beside me wore a pistol, but it was in his shoulder holster, and he seemed unconcerned about me. I wasn't hand-cuffed. I was alive. And the view from that chopper was beautiful. I thought again of the hawk—this was his view of the world. Things could be worse.

AS CLEARWATER/ST. PETE airport came into view, we dropped to less than a hundred feet above the water and followed the canal toward the Coast Guard station. I saw a rescue chopper on the ground, its rotors still moving. I hoped it had brought Jean to safety.

We suddenly banked, hovered and landed in front of a small white hanger. There were no signs on the building, but there was a high fence topped with barbed wire around it, and at least a dozen men in suits carrying M-16 rifles standing near the perimeter.

The skids had hardly touched asphalt before my guard yanked the door open, and motioned for me to take off the hearing protectors and get out. I was less than four steps from the chopper when it lifted off.

I dropped to my knees and closed my eyes against the dust. Seconds later, I was lifted bodily to my feet by two men in light gray suits. We were half-running toward a small office attached to the hanger. I noticed there were at least a dozen white cars and vans, and two more black helicopters in the hanger.

Moments after leaving the chopper, I was in a twelve-by-twelve room with two doors, a table, five chairs, and no windows. My escorts had left their rifles inside the building's main door and now sat across the table from me. We had not spoken.

"Smoke if you want," said the pale blonde. He looked Swedish.

"Don't smoke, but I could sure use a bathroom and a soft drink—sugar and caffeine," I said.

He pointed at the door behind me. It was a bathroom with no window. While there, I took a quick sink bath with paper towels and hand soap, removing the salt spray, sweat, and, hopefully, odor. When I returned to the room, a cold can of soda and a cup of ice awaited me. The two men did not appear to have moved.

"Thank you. And since you are being so kind, will you tell me what the hell is going on?" I said to Blondie.

"Sorry, sir. We aren't authorized to talk to you about anything."

"How about your silent partner?" I turned toward the other man. "Can you speak?"

"Arf, Arf," he barked.

It broke the tension and we all three laughed.

"Look, sir," said the barking agent, "we've been ordered to babysit you until our supervisor arrives. I think he'll answer your questions, but he may be a while getting here. Meanwhile, if you're interested, I have an undercover agent's survival packet," he said, withdrawing a deck of playing cards from his pocket with a flourish. "Do I play solitaire, or shall we play cards?"

"How about you play cards and I walk out that door?" I started to rise.

"I wouldn't do that, sir," said Blondie. "You're safe in here with us, but you might not make it out of the compound alive."

I noticed he wasn't smiling, so I sat back down. "Dealer's choice?" I asked.

We hadn't even dealt the second hand of blackjack before someone knocked at the door. Both officers rose from the table and stepped to opposite sides of the door.

"Yes?" inquired Blondie.

"Sergeant Ramirez, Clearwater Police," said a familiar voice from the other side. "Hinton wants me to stay with Thomas."

Blondie unlocked the door and I saw the first familiar face of the day. Lazaro Ramirez was in uniform, but showed an ID anyway.

"Any weapons?" asked Blondie.

"Already checked them at the door. Some club you guys run. Jeeze." Ramirez walked over to me and stuck out his hand. "You okay, Thomas?"

"Yeah, I'm fine," I replied, shaking his hand. "How about Jean? Do you know if she got to the hospital?"

"She's being treated at a private clinic, courtesy of the government. It's not a bad wound and, until we find out who was involved, we want to keep a low profile."

The agents had moved their chairs to opposite corners of the room near the door. They now sat, watching, saying nothing.

"You want to talk about it?" asked Ramirez.

"Not really. I've been through it all before I left the boat, and until someone tells me what the hell is going on, I'm invoking my right to remain silent." I crossed my arms and tilted my chair back. "Nothing 'til I know what's going on."

"Well, first, you aren't being charged with anything. We already know Flynt and Hedeon were trying to kill you and the girl. Whatever you did was probably in self-defense," said Ramirez.

"How do you know that?"

"There have been several incidents in the past few years where people died in what appeared to be drug deals gone bad. Each time it was the same—case unsolved. We had suspected police involvement and we were closing in on Flynt. Then you showed up and found the link we were looking for."

"And what, pray tell, was that?"

"The gun. The one substituted for Clayton's."

Before he could say more, someone pounded on the door and yelled, "Open the damned door, Swenson!"

Blondie Swenson jumped to the door and unlocked it. A tall, severe-looking man, in his late fifties, with short gray hair and wearing glasses, stomped into the room. In his hand was my Styrofoam ice chest, which I had sealed with duct tape and thrown overboard the day before. The man did not look pleased.

Blondie Swenson made the introductions. “Mr. Thomas, this is Assistant Special Agent-in-Charge, Stan Hinton. You’ve upset him several times this past week.”

Hinton tossed the ice chest on the table, stood with his hands on his hips, and glared at me for several seconds.

Finally, he placed his hands on the table, leaned toward me, and said, “You, sir, have seriously pissed...me...off. You have no idea how pissed off I am. Do you have any idea how much trouble you have caused me?”

Chapter 26 — Bomb!

“THAT DEPENDS. DID you put the bug on my boat?” I said with a smile, nodding toward the ice chest.

“Yes, and the one on your car, too. We followed that damn thing to Philadelphia before we realized what you’d done, and I’ll bet you think it’s funny, don’t you?” he said, frowning.

Noticing that Blondie and the other agent were stifling smiles, I asked, “How far did you chase the cooler?”

“Halfway to Mobile Bay, smart ass.” He flopped into one of the chairs and turned toward the other men. “There’s always a clown, someone who could screw up a wet dream.” Then turning toward me and leaning forward, Hinton continued, “And this time it’s you. Do you have any idea what’s going on here?”

“Well, I was getting ready to enjoy a game of cards with these nice young fellows—”

“Aaaaiieee!” Hinton screamed and started climbing across the table at me, hands out as if to choke me. Inches from my throat he stopped, sat back and grinned. “You’ve got a pretty good sense of humor for a man who just killed two cops.”

“Only one. Flynt killed himself,” I replied.

Hinton leaned back in his chair, his face serious again. “No shit. Wow, he *was* a hard case. I guess you want to know what’s going on and why we’re involved.”

“I wait with bated breath.”

It was a good thing I didn’t hold my breath until the explanation. Before Hinton could say anything, the door flew open and another clean-cut, well-dressed young man stepped in and said, “Hinton, somebody just torched the warehouse.”

Hinton rushed out. He returned in what seemed like seconds and spoke to me. “We’re going to Flynt’s office. If you want, you can ride with us and we’ll talk on the way.”

“Love to, chief, but am I dressed for the occasion?” I asked. I was wearing shorts, a T-shirt and deck shoes.

“Swenson, get this man some BDUs...and a hat.” Then Hinton stopped. “You can stuff all that hair under a baseball cap, can’t you?”

"I'll give her a try." I was, surprised at the offer of a uniform, almost as much as being allowed on what I perceived was a raid. I felt like I was being allowed in the LEO club. LEOs—Law Enforcement Officers—protect their territory and mystique jealously. Feds even more so.

Five of us piled into a white van with dark windows, with Blondie Swenson at the wheel. Ramirez left before us in a marked cruiser. I pulled on lightweight black BDUs over my shorts, and piled my pony tail under a black baseball cap. The clothing was emblazoned with white with "FBI."

As we roared out of the hanger, Hinton turned to me and said, "You found a small piece of a much larger puzzle, and we're trying to solve that larger puzzle." We lurched onto the highway and he glared at Blondie, then continued. "It involves the thefts of thousands of weapons over the past ten years, mostly from government agencies and the military."

"And the one used to kill Donella Nash was stolen from an evidence locker in Pasco County," I said to show I was following the story.

"Right. It was one of over thirty weapons taken in that theft alone, weapons that were to be destroyed a couple of days later. What is special here is that it was one of the few to find its way into our hands here in the U.S. Most have ended up in Ireland and the Caribbean, and the U.S. has been catching a lot of heat from other governments over it."

"So what part did Flynt and Hedeon play in all of this?" I asked.

"A lot of other stolen weapons were traced to the Tampa/St. Pete area, and about three months ago, we got a lead on a warehouse near Clearwater Air Park—"

"The one that just got torched?"

"The same. We were going to raid the place and nail Flynt and Hedeon when you entered the picture, Don Quixote, trying to save the world." Hinton was showing his irritation clearly.

"Not the world," I replied. "Just one life. And why should that stop your investigation? What did I have to do with it?"

"A senior agent made a plea on your behalf. He asked that we give you a couple of weeks to investigate your case before we moved in. He believed you could prove your client's innocence. I agreed to hold off until today...but that may have been twenty-four hours too long." Hinton turned and looked me directly in the eyes. "If you hadn't played games with our tracers, Flynt and Hedeon might be alive, the girl probably wouldn't have been shot, your boat would've been safe, all the evidence in the warehouse might not be burned, and...but, no, you had to be a smart ass."

"Hey, don't lay all that guilt crap on me. What was I supposed to do? You used me as tiger bait, like a tethered goat. You could've let me in on your little game, you know."

"No, we couldn't. You're a loose cannon, always have been," he said. "Some goat…you killed the tigers."

A chuckle from one of the other agents was stifled by a glare from

Hinton.

Then Hinton sighed. “Look, Thomas, I know your record by heart. Raced cars and took flying lessons as a teenager, enlisted for four years in the Army, Military Intelligence, expert with pistol and rifle, went to Korea during the Pueblo mess. But I also know you had to have a waiver to get into MI because you’d gotten two dozen speeding tickets and forty-two points on your license before you were nineteen.

“You skated the law so many times I don’t know how you maintained a clearance for all those years at the Pentagon and with the NASA. You were even in Media, Pennsylvania the night our offices were broken into—.”

“I didn’t have anything to do with that.”

“We know. You were being followed by two agents at the time because of the stuff you *did* do. And then there were the peace demonstrations in Harrisburg.”

“Hey, all I did was march.”

“In uniform, and call attention to the agents you recognized in the crowd. Do you know our file on you is almost two-and-a-half inches thick?” Hinton said, slumping in his seat, seeming to relax a little. “And you became a damn good lawyer...we have yet to dig up any real dirt on you. That’s why I was willing to go along with Murdock’s request.”

“Who’s Murdock?” I asked.

“He’s the agent who spent the last few years putting this case together.”

The conversation ended abruptly as we approached the Justice Center. Fire trucks and police cars blocked the streets, and crowds of people were leaving the area.

“What’s happening?” I asked.

“Bomb scare,” said Hinton. “They had to empty the whole damn courthouse.”

“A false bomb threat? That’s illegal,” I said.

He smiled and turned away.

I remembered why I didn’t trust the alphabet agencies. All the Feds, FBI, ATF, IRS, and INS were much too willing to bend the law to suit their purposes.

We piled out of the van beside the courthouse. “Carry this,” Hinton said, handing me a black cloth briefcase. “Try and look official.”

We scurried into the courthouse, up the fire stairs, and into the state attorney’s office, which I had visited only a few days before. Gone were the scowling faces, and in their places were a half-dozen men in suits and several in BDUs.

“Damn, Hinton, can’t your boys do a better job than this?” I asked, peering through the door around him.

Flynt and Hedeon’s office, a shared space, was a wreck. Drawers were pulled out and things thrown on the floor. A file cabinet lay on the floor on its back, the front showing scars from a fire ax which lay nearby.

"What happened?" Hinton asked one of the men in suits.

"This is how we found it. Someone got here before us."

"What stage are you at?" Hinton asked.

"The team finished processing prints ten minutes ago and we're just waitin' for you."

Hinton stepped inside and introduced me to Larry Farnam, a tall bald-headed agent, head of the crime scene team. I stopped just inside the door and stared at the filing cabinet.

"Somebody wanted to get in that real bad. Maybe you should check it out," I suggested.

"We're way ahead of you," Farnam said, as he picked up a slap hammer from the floor. Within seconds, the lock was ripped out of the filing cabinet.

One of the men in BDUs suggested we leave the room, just in case the cabinet was booby trapped. "After all, they torched the warehouse," he said.

We didn't need extra coaxing.

"YOU NEED TO check out the bottom drawer first, sir." Farnam said, a few minutes later. I noticed beads of sweat on his brow.

Hinton carefully reopened the drawer. I leaned over his shoulder to see in. In the back of the drawer were four automatic pistols, a couple of boxes of ammunition, and several sealed paper bags, one of which caught my eye. The bag had evidence tape on it, dated June 16, 1991, the day after Clayton's arrest. I started to reach for it, but Hinton grabbed my wrist.

"Easy, big boy. I see it, too," he said, pulling me back from the cabinet. Then to the Farnam, "Process this drawer first."

"Sorry, I got carried away," I said, as Hinton ushered me out of the room.

"No problem. You're just trying to do your job, and we're doing ours. Sit a while," he said to me. Then he called to Farnam, "Pull that bag with the evidence tape first. The one that says June '91. When you get done with it, bring it out here."

After what seemed hours to me, the bag was brought to the table where Hinton and I sat. It had undergone ninhydrin development for fingerprints and several purple prints were evident. "Don't touch," the evidence technician said, as he sat the bag on the desk.

"This is not the way it is supposed to be done, but I think we should open the bag for Mr. Thomas," said Ramirez. He'd arrived without my noticing.

"The case number is right, the date is right. It says Jon Clayton, and the unbroken evidence tape is initialed by Flynt and MC," said Hinton, as we were being videotaped.

"I presume MC is Mikel Conchman, the prosecutor," I said.

Hinton nodded and the agent who had delivered the bag laid it on its side and, using a razor knife, made a clean slit across the bottom, then up both sides, carefully avoiding the developed prints. As he gently pulled the bag open, I saw a beautiful sight—a Smith and Wesson .38 caliber revolver. It looked identical to the one introduced as evidence at the trial, but I was sure this was the earlier Military and Police model, not a Model 10. A separate bag was brought out a few minutes later labeled the same as this one, but noting that it contained, "5 unfired cartridges."

"Mr. Thomas, I think you have a case," Hinton said, smiling. "Our office will assist you in any manner we can, including producing this as evidence, and I'll make myself and any of my men available as witnesses. Of course, we expect your cooperation in return."

"Excuse me," said Ramirez, "but Mr. Thomas has another little problem that needs to be addressed. Elwood Thomas, you are under arrest for burglary and the attempted murder of Eddy Nash."

Chapter 27 — Right To Remain Silent

"WHAT ATTEMPTED MURDER? That's bull crap. I didn't do it," I said.

"You're under arrest, Mr. Thomas," said Ramirez. Then he began the litany. "You have the right to remain silent—"

"I know my damn rights," I said, starting to rise from the chair.

Someone behind me placed his hand over my right shoulder. His fingertips slipped behind my collar bone, and I felt intense pain as he forced me back in the chair. The control grip—I'd seen the police grab my clients like it many times before, but had no idea how much it hurt until now. I sat down.

"I didn't hurt Nash," I said as the hand released my shoulder.

"That's not what he says," said Ramirez.

"What *he* says? The news said he was in a coma. Is he out of it?" I asked.

Ramirez smiled. "Nash is going to be fine, but he's really pissed at you and Miss Clayton."

"What did he tell you?" I asked. "And what happened to him? He wasn't actually hurt, was he? I mean...*we* didn't hurt him."

Ramirez pulled a desk chair over and joined Hinton and me at the table. I could tell he was expecting a long explanation.

"We know about you and Jean visiting ol' Eddy boy the night before last. And he told us about the Bobbitt trick you pulled on him." Ramirez smiled as he spoke. "For shame! You know you could both go to jail for that kind of crap."

I cringed and felt a rush of red to my cheeks. "Well, yes, but...it was exigent circumstances, you know, like you guys and the bomb threat."

"That's different," snapped Hinton. "We're the government and you're a civilian. It sounds like you got way out of line."

Ramirez continued, "Anyway...Nash called Flynt after you left, but Flynt was gone and I intercepted his voice mail. So we know he wasn't hurt until after you and Miss Clayton left. He was fine until about one in the morning when we received a 911 call from his address."

"When his mother found him," I said.

"That's what we told the media. We didn't know where you or Flynt were, and we couldn't take any chances spooking either of you," said

Ramirez. "And in answer to your next question, Flynt and Hedeon are the ones who jumped Nash. They beat him unconscious then stuck a knife in his guts a couple times so he'd bleed to death. Somehow he made it to the phone and dialed 911. I heard the call and was among the first on the scene. Nash lost a lot of blood, but he responded well to treatment and was talking yesterday afternoon...right about the time you sailed out of the harbor."

Hinton asked, "By the way, how did you find out about that drug bust?"

"If you mean the one where they tried to raid my boat after I left—I didn't. It was luck. I found out about it after the fact."

"I guess that was the scrambled electronic transmission you received?" asked Hinton.

"Yeah, e-mail. I didn't know who was bugging me, but I doubted they'd be able to decipher that."

"You didn't know your boat was wired, did you?"

"I found the bug—"

"No, *wired*." Hinton said, stressing the word. "Micro TV cameras on the mast and in the cabin, at least five microphones, and a sound-activated recording unit."

"You're shittin' me. No way. When did you do all that? How did you do all that?" I asked.

"When you went to Marathon to pick up your car," Hinton replied. "We wired her up right. Should have a video of the whole thing. Sure hope you're telling us the truth."

"I am, but I've got a question. Did your boys plant the coke on board?" I asked, unable to disguise my irritation at the attempted frame-up.

"No," answered Ramirez. "We think Flynt and Hedeon did that personally, and if the cameras worked, we should have it on video. Flynt got Conchman to have a search warrant issued. They were going to arrest you and the girl, and send you up for big-time possession with intent to sell."

"But it didn't work, and we were prepared to intervene if it had," said Hinton. "As usual, you lucked out and left before they could bust you. By the way, since you obviously found the coke, what did you do with it?"

"I tossed it over the side," I said. "I don't use, I don't sell, and I value life too much to even have that shit near me."

I suddenly realized what had bothered me before about the bug on my car—the timing had been wrong. "Wait a minute," I said, looking at Hinton. "Did you intercept my mail, the packages I mailed?"

"What packages?

"The ones with copies of the diaries and evidence slips in them," I said.

"No, we didn't receive any packages," said Hinton. "Did you?" he asked, looking at Ramirez, who shook his head. "No."

"No...you bugged my car before that. Why did you bug my car in Marathon?" I asked.

"We were told by a confidential informant that you had information about the stolen pistol," Hinton replied. "We acted on that information and got a warrant. But it was actually for your own safety, in case Flynt and Hedeon found out and came after you."

I thought to myself, *Prior to going to Marathon, only three people knew that the murder weapon was stolen— me, Drew Pearson, and Tiny Jacobs.* I decided to push a little and asked, "Is your C.I. a biker, by any chance? Maybe a fake biker who runs a show bar?"

"Sorry, you know I can't tell you that," replied Hinton.

"Sarge, who got the arrest warrant issued against me on this Nash crap?" I asked.

"There's no arrest warrant. I was just yanking your chain for being so damn stupid," Ramirez said. "Although the initial report did mention the little green Miata seen by the neighbors, it was never tied to either of you. By the way, what did you torture out of Nash?"

For an instant, I thought of lying, but they would know soon enough, and besides, the truth was equally important to them.

"Gentlemen, I think there are some things you need to know about Mikel Conchman," I said, and proceeded to tell the two officers all I knew about him. By the time I was done, the criminalist and his crew of two had finished and suggested we seal Flynt's office and allow the workers back in the building.

"Perhaps we should wait for Prosecutor Conchman and talk to him about what Mr. Thomas has shared with us," Hinton said to Ramirez. "Better yet, I'll invite him to my office and talk to him...the home court advantage, you know."

Home court advantage— cops do it all the time, when they ask you to stop by the station house, the jail, or the court house, just to "talk." I had used the trick myself, many times.

It was obvious I was not invited to Conchman's inquisition, and I needed food, rest, and a shower. Hinton told me it would be at least a couple of days before they could release *Defender*. Ramirez offered to take me to the condo since he was on his way to the police station a few blocks past it.

As we got up to leave, I felt a toothache-like pain in my left hip and a stabbing pain in my lower back. The adrenalin had worn off. I remembered the fall I had taken earlier in the day, flat on my back, weapon in hand. I limped to the police cruiser and we left, as the denizens of the courthouse returned to their cubicles, caves, and cubby-holes.

Near the condo, I spotted Tiny's green-and-pink, four-wheel-drive truck, and suddenly my back pain disappeared. "Hey, let me out here," I said. "I want to stop by that Vietnamese restaurant. I think I see a friend."

Chapter 28 — Turn-Key Condo

TINY WAS SITTING alone at the same table we had shared just over a week before. He looked up, grinned and greeted me as I walked in. "Hey, bro, how ya doing?" Then to the counterman he called, "Ho, bring my friend some food. He looks starved!"

"Do you eat here every damn day?" I pulled up a chair. To Ho I said, "Iced tea—no food."

"What's up, man? Great outfit, but you look like death warmed over," Tiny said.

I noted he didn't question the letters FBI emblazoned on my cap, nor did he stop eating.

"I feel like death warmed over. It's been one hell of a day." Then knowing he wouldn't be expecting it I asked him, "So are you the FBI informant?"

Tiny choked on his food and sputtered, "What the hell are you talking about, man? I mean, shit...where would you get an idea like that?"

"Well, a little while back, the FBI started investigating me," I said. "They told me it was because I had information about a stolen gun…the one you and I had discussed about a week ago, sitting right here."

"So?" he said, raising the beer to his lips and looking at me over the bottle.

"So, the only other person who knew about it was a guy from FDLE and they jumped his ass the day after I talked to you. The three of us were the only ones who knew about the pistol at that time. I didn't talk to the Feds, and I don't think he did, so that leaves you."

"Why would I talk to the Feds?"

"Money, for one thing. They told me they got their info from an informant, so I assume you're a paid informant."

"Well, you can un-ass-ume," he said, finally looking me in the eye. "I'm not an informant, FBI or otherwise, paid or otherwise."

"Okay, so you're not an informant. One other question…who the hell are you? I know you aren't Timothy Jacobs."

"The hell you say!" he said, setting his bottle down and leaning his chair back on two legs. "You want to see my driver's license? How 'bout my passport? Birth certificate?" Even through the tint of his glasses, I could see his eyes narrow. “Where the fuck are you getting all this weird bullshit?”

I didn’t get a chance to answer. The tall black man I’d seen with Tiny the first night came in and loudly greeted him, “Hey, my man!” But he stopped in his tracks when I turned to look at him.

"Are you a FBI?" he asked.

I assured him I was not, and realizing I still had on the cap, told him I’d borrowed the clothing.

"Woody Thomas, meet B.K. Washington, better known ’round town as Whopper," said Tiny, as the black man grabbed a spare chair and joined us at the table.

I took my hat off and as my hair fell down around my shoulders, Whopper’s eyes bugged out. "Oh, man…shit!" he said, starting to get out of his seat. "You the dude on the bridge."

I grabbed his skinny wrist, held it to the table, and asked, "What about the bridge?"

"Nothing, man...nothing," Whopper said, half-sitting, half-standing and twitching as he tried to break my grasp. "Oh, man. Shit."

"How do you know about the bridge?" I asked, raising my voice, rising from my seat, and pulling him toward me.

"Sit down, and cool it, asshole," Tiny said to me.

Whopper snatched his hand from mine and knocked over his chair trying to leave, but Tiny grabbed his other wrist and pulled him back to the table. "Tell him about the bridge, Whopper."

"Oh, man, shit.” He looked at Tiny, then at me and said, “You da dude got shot at."

"How do you know? I want to know what happened.”

"Oh maaann, shi...” he said, rolling his eyes.

“Now!" I said

“Okay, man, I’m tellin’ you. I’s buying a rifle for this dude." He nodded toward Tiny. "A sniper gun from a cop named Flynt and his buddy. They set the time for the meet, then they and me stopped over by one of them hotels and went up to a room. He wanted me to see how well it shot."

"Yeah, so...how did I end up getting shot at? And how do you know it was me?"

"I saw you through the scope, man. It was a big scope. Had one of them little red-light-sight things. I saw you on the bridge."

"Tell him the whole thing," said Tiny.

Sweat was dripping from Whopper’s face. "Oh, maaann. Shit. Flynt took the first shot. They gave me binocs so’s I could see. ’Bout scared shit out of me. You looking off the bridge, didn’t even notice the red dot on you ponytail. Then he moved the dot off’n you and pulled the trigger."

"That must be the shot I heard," I said.

"You looked, but I didn’t hear no shot, so I thought the thing wasn’t loaded and they was shittin’ me...said so. And Flynt, he say, 'Okay, smart-ass, you do it.'"

"And?" said Tiny.

"Oh, man, shit. I sorry, but they told me to do it." Whopper was shaking as he continued. "I shot at the can on the bridge-fence 'cause it was away from you. I didn' wanna hit you. They told me to do it, man. I's sorry."

"So you're the one hit the can?" I asked.

"Yes, sir. But it was strange, man. I didn' even think the gun fired—sound like a damn, ole BB gun. Then the can fell and you ducked." Whopper was still half-sitting, half-standing, with no chair under him. "I didn' know..."

Tiny pulled the man toward him until their faces were only inches apart, knuckles white from the grip. "Whopper, you ain't seen either of us tonight, you got it? Lay low a few days and keep your mouth shut, got it? Beat it. I'll get in touch...get you some money in a few days," he said and released the man's wrist.

Whopper almost fell then tripped over his chair in his haste to escape. He stopped and turned toward me when he got to the door. "I sorry, man, really." I gave him a thumbs-up sign, and he added, "You be cool, dude."

Tiny shook his head and took something from his shirt pocket as the door closed. Sliding the object across the table to me, he said, "I collect weapons, but mostly stuff that's...special. Ever see one of these?"

He had given me a cartridge unlike any I'd ever seen before. The brass casing appeared to be for a pistol, but it had a long, pointed bullet, more like that found in rifle ammunition.

"What the hell is this?"

"Suppressed ammo," he replied. "It's called a.300 Whisper cartridge, and it's part of a system developed by a guy at SSK Industries."

I handed the cartridge back as Tiny said, "Basically it's a modified pistol cartridge, fitted with a 7.62-millimetre rifle bullet, accurate for up to three hundred yards, maybe more. The heavy, streamlined rifle bullet doesn't lose velocity like a blunt pistol slug. The rifle was a Thompson Center Contender, rigged with a custom barrel. It's a single-shot rifle, breaks like a shotgun, and when these things are fired in it, it sounds like a low-powered hand gun, and that's without using a silencer for sound suppression."

"I didn't hear a shot, or much anything else, 'cept a whine when they went by."

"Hell, Woody, the rifle was likely also fitted with a big silencer." He held his hands about a foot apart. "With one of those on, the damn thing sounds like a spring-fired air rifle, loudest things are the springs and firing pin...and the bullet hitting the target."

"So why didn't I hear a crack from the bullet going by? All I heard on that first shot was something that sounded like an insect."

"It was firing subsonic ammo—the bullet travels below the speed of sound. It's a wonder you heard anything at all. Unlike those fake silencers from the movies, this stuff works—silent and deadly." Raising his beer as in a toast he said, "It's a whole new ball game."

"Why did you want it?"

"I told you…I'm a collector." He grinned. "And...I like to shoot city rats and weasels. But I didn't get to buy that one—they didn't deliver it last night like they said they would," he said, turning to watch a marked police car lurch to a halt in front of the restaurant.

Ramirez sprung from the car and burst through the door saying, "Thomas, you've got to get off the street and out of sight now!"

I sat in the front of Ramirez' patrol car as he related my latest disaster. Word had gotten back to the local police that a drug-dealing boat freak—me—had gunned down two cops. There was a very good chance I'd be dead by sunrise. There were snipers on the rooftops nearby, watching for me to return to my condo. Roadblocks were being set up all around the county. My life suddenly felt like *The Perils of Pauline.*

"Have you got anywhere else to go?" Ramirez asked.

"No. My boat was my home. It's shot all to hell and the Feds have her. Now you tell me I can't go near my condo, and my car is under the condo."

"How about your friend in there?" Ramirez said, referring to Tiny.

Tiny, a friend? I thought. I replied, "I could go to Billy Jean's..."

"Nope. It's being watched."

"A motel?"

"They have the picture off your driver's license and are combing the area."

"Oh, great. How about you..."

"Sorry. I've got a wife and three small kids. I like them alive."

"Okay, let's ask Tiny," I said with a sigh.

Politics and war make strange bedfellows, but this is ridiculous, I thought, as I waited in the car. Ramirez asked Tiny if I could stay with him. I trusted Ramirez, but I'd have liked to have heard the conversation.

Tiny stuck his head in the car. "I've got a townhouse down toward Indian Rocks Beach. It's clean and empty. If you want, you can stay there."

"Sounds great," I said, starting to get out of the car.

"Don't get out of the car. You can't ride with him," said Ramirez. "I'll take you there."

Ramirez got directions from Tiny. I ducked down in the back seat of the patrol car and we headed south, passing two roadblocks before we pulled into an expensive set of low-rise townhouses, each built over its own two-car garage. *The strip joint must pay well*, I thought.

Ramirez said he'd only told Tiny that this was a police matter, I was in danger, and needed help. "You don't need to tell him anything else."

Tiny showed up five minutes later.

"Damn, boy, you really pissed somebody off!" he said with a laugh.

He gave me a quick tour of my three-bedroom, two-bath prison. If I was going to have to lay low for a few days, this was as good a place as any. Even the refrigerator was well stocked with frozen microwave dinners and diet soda.

"Keep the curtains closed, don't go outside, and don't make any phone calls," said Ramirez as they left.

A bath, a clean jogging suit borrowed from the only room with clothing, a nuked dinner, and I felt human again. If not human, at least not like a hunted animal. Then I made the mistake of turning on the late news.

"More tonight on the tragedy in the waters off Tarpon Springs," began the all-too-pretty, blonde newswoman. The media version of what had occurred less than twenty-four hours before was no longer a reflection of reality.

Officially, two officers from Clearwater had attempted to intercept a drug shipment and boarded the wrong boat. The owner of the boat appeared on deck between the two officers and shot at one of them in self-defense. Thinking he was a dangerous drug dealer, the two officers attempted to catch him in a cross-fire and killed each other. "The owner of the vessel, attorney Elwood Thomas of Marathon, has not been charged in the incident."

I sat stunned, though relieved.

The phone rang and I didn't think before I picked it up and answered, "Woody Thomas."

"Agent Hinton here. Congratulations, you may live through this after all. But what the hell are you doing answering the phone? And using your name?"

"I...ah, what do you mean, live through this?"

"We convinced the local boys to call off the manhunt. You can go home again."

"Except your boys confiscated my home," I replied.

"Oh, the boat. Sorry about that. We've removed the cameras and recorders, and you'll be delighted to know they worked great."

"I'm glad to know that...but when can I have her back?"

"That depends. I've been authorized to have it repaired for you gratis, if that's okay with you."

"Great! Yes! Do it! But where is she? I need to get my stuff off."

"It's on land at a marina in Tarpon Springs. We have a unit that repairs and refurbishes our boats. They say they can do yours, maybe be done in three or four days or less."

"Are they good?"

"The best. And hello! The work will be free."

"Fine, as long as they're good. Thank you...very much. By the way, how did you get this number?"

"Ramirez. And we have a couple guys watching the place, just in case. So, stay inside. Gotta go."

"Wait! What about Jean?" I asked as the line went dead.

I turned back to the TV just in time to see sports file footage of a football game. A huge lineman ran toward the end zone carrying another man high over his head. Once in the end zone, the lineman dropped his burden to the ground and commenced to do a Cossack dance. Across the bottom of the screen scrolled, "Florida mourns FSU's 'Bear' Hedeon."

In a state where college football players are deified, I now faced a more dangerous problem than angry police—enraged football fans.

THREE DAYS AFTER my conversation with Hinton, the phone rang again. I picked it up and a voice said, "Mr. Thomas, this is Special Agent Ray Sailor. We met when the bureau confiscated your Gulfstar 41. I gave you my business card, said I'd take care of her for you, and I'm just calling to let you know she's ready."

I was glad to hear someone speak of *Defender* as more than just a boat and "it." Agent Sailor had stayed with her from the day she was taken. He was in charge of processing her for evidence, which included removing every piece of lead that had entered the hull. He asked if I wanted to inspect her before she was launched. The work would be completed by the next afternoon.

"Oh, by the way," he said, "a lady named Jean called on your cell phone. She said to tell you she's all right, and she'll try to reach you again tomorrow night."

I was so delighted, I hung up before I realized I had no way to get to Tarpon Springs, where *Defender* was being repaired. That night, for the first time in years, I dreamed of sailing. In the dream, I wasn't alone.

I was jarred awake by the ringing of the telephone. Not a good way to start my day. This time I just answered, "Yes."

"Woody Thomas?" asked the familiar voice on the other end.

"Depends…who wants to know?"

"Lazaro Ramirez."

"Okay, you're speaking to him. What's up, Sarge?"

"I heard you might need a ride back to your condo, and I can pick you up in about an hour," he said. "You haven't seen the morning news, have you?"

Chapter 29 — Warranted Fear

THE MORNING SUN burned my right arm and the side of my face as I rode up Gulf Boulevard with Ramirez. The *St. Petersburg Times* and the *Tampa Tribune* both carried the same lead stories. Eddy Nash had died of complications following emergency surgery, a direct result of the beating he had received from the "unknown assailants." And, in response to the request from Mikel Conchman, the governor had signed Jon Clayton's death warrant.

The warrant had not been due for another four months. Now I had only thirty days to get the courts to agree Clayton was not guilty. If I failed, Jon Clayton would die, innocent or not.

Conchman's request of a death warrant was justified retribution in the eyes of society. For the governor, it is just good politics to order executions in Florida. But for Jon Clayton, it couldn't have come at a worse time. His direct appeal had been denied. He had a previous post-conviction motion claiming his trial attorney was ineffective, but Hatfield had been found to have done a sufficient job, and that appeal had been denied. There were no federal claims. Even if there had been, I had to "exhaust all remedies" within the state courts before I could address any federal claims.

My options—Jon Clayton's options—were limited.

I had been investigating the case, but at the time there was no appeal pending—there were no motions pending—there was nothing to slow the system. No grounds existed to request a stay of execution. Filing a second or "successor" post-conviction motion after the warrant was issued would be considered simply as an obstructionist move—some damn liberal trying to fight the system. The system would fight back.

But fighting the system was what I did best.

My first step would be to file a post-conviction motion before the original trial court. Judge Harris would probably come out of retirement for this. And who better? Who knows the case better? Who better to say, "I saw the trial and I don't think what you say now would have made a dime's worth of difference."

I heard Harris say those words before, when someone other than my client had confessed to committing the crime. I remembered how that case ended. In the tornado of activity that death warrants create, it had only taken two days for all my client's appeals to be denied: By the Florida Supreme

Court the next morning, by the Eleventh Circuit Court of Appeals in Atlanta that same afternoon, and by the U.S. Supreme Court the following afternoon. At six in the morning on the third day, less than seventy two hours after Judge Harris turned us away, my client was executed. That day I stood in the rain outside the prison watching believers in retribution have an execution party. They drank champagne, lit off fireworks, and threw eggs at my client's hearse as it passed.

I shivered.

When *Defender* was under attack there'd been no time for fear, only reaction. Now there was time to feel the fear. I prayed that mental paralysis would not prevent me from doing what had to be done, but it was too late.

I felt the symptoms begin. First came hunger, which no amount of food or booze would ever slake. It was true gut-fear. Each time I looked at the headlines, I felt slightly dizzy.

Ramirez drove without speaking as I read through the articles, both of which quoted a "Tallahassee source" as saying, "The governor's action yesterday afternoon was in direct response to Eddy Nash's death early yesterday morning."

"Dead? What's this crap about Nash being dead?" I asked. "I thought you said he was doing fine. Dead is not fine."

"He had a seizure and died. The doctors still aren't sure what happened. I'm sorry. I know you needed his testimony."

By the time we arrived at the Clearwater Pass Bridge, I was staring into space, my mind spinning. He was right. I needed Nash. Without him, I had no way to prove the diaries were what I said they were, and his statement about having sex with his wife was hearsay and not admissible as evidence in any court.

"Are you going to be all right?" asked Ramirez. "You look sick."

"I feel sick. What's happening with the local police? Do I still have to worry about being shot in the back by your buddies?"

"Hey, back off. Just because a couple cops are bad doesn't mean we all are."

"Yeah, sorry. But the question still stands."

"No. You've been cleared of the stuff on the boat, and the FBI has been interviewing a lot of the officers. The word on the street is that you work for the Feds. The way the deaths have been handled will allow the force to save face, and Hedeon's family will get death benefits. Flynt didn't have anyone.

"Also, it seems Flynt provided a lot of throw-down pieces to some of the officers over the past few years. Hinton and his crew are trying to find out how many pieces went out."

Throw-down pieces, I thought. *Spare weapons carried by officers in case they accidentally shoot an unarmed suspect. Some people considered it wise…others, a dirty trick.*

"Are they having much luck?" I asked.

"Yeah. A half-dozen officers turned in weapons already. It's a clemency deal—no questions, no charges. There are also investigations being made into several cases where the suspect died while holding a weapon with no serial number. Funny thing, most were killed by Flynt or Hedeon."

Again I was surprised by Ramirez' candor. "How do you fit in this mess?" I asked. "I notice you get along with the Feds real well and don't seem to have a whole lot of respect for your own."

"How did I get involved in the investigation? Well, I was assigned to a multi-agency task force. This gun-running mess started boiling over almost five years ago. The Feds were the only ones involved, until someone realized cops had to be among the bad guys.

"I'd been doing internal investigations for a couple years when the chief called me in and told me he was assigning me. He said the FBI had called and wanted...Well, his exact words were, 'a cop with a hard-on for justice who doesn't care if he screws his buddies, and that's you.'

"I wasn't flattered, but...I guess I fit the description," Ramirez said as we pulled up to the Raphaels' condo.

Two familiar-looking men wearing sunglasses, flowered shirts, and white slacks stepped out of a car parked next to mine as I got out of the cruiser. "Mr. Thomas? Agent Hinton has asked us to stay with you for the next few days. You may remember me from a few days ago—Ralph Swenson, and this is Agent John Hammer."

It was the blonde agent and his card-playing partner from the airport. "We were told to dress a little more casual for this assignment," Hammer said, pointing at his shirt with a grin.

Swenson stopped me as I started to enter the condo. He insisted on going in first. "Just to make sure." While Swenson checked the condo, Hammer told me that my car had been checked out and was safe. "No bombs and no tracking devices."

I began to realize these men had a more cynical outlook than Ramirez—or they knew something he didn't.

I'd hardly had time to shower and dress when Agent Hinton pounded on the door. He stormed up the stairs and flopped in Noah Raphael's big leather chair with a grunt.

"Before you go outside, there's something you need to know," Hinton began.

I hate conversations that start like that, but it fit the pattern of the day.

Hinton told me that Nigel Hedeon had a seventeen-year-old son, Boris, who had disappeared, but not before he armed himself and swore to avenge his father's death.

"Look, Thomas, you need to take this kid seriously. He not only studied martial arts for several years, he's brilliant...not a good student, but extremely intelligent." Hinton hesitated and added as an afterthought, "And he's armed with at least one semi-automatic weapon."

"Then he can't be so brilliant," I said. "How hard can it be to find a seventeen-year-old? Where can he go?"

"There's a large Russian community in the Tampa Bay area," replied Hinton. "They take care of their own. We expect Boris to find you before we find him."

"Great. Do I get to play the tethered goat again, waiting for Boris the tiger to strike?" I asked, with as much sarcasm as I could muster.

"No. We aren't going to do that to you again. In fact, you aren't going to go anywhere or do anything without an agent beside you...at least not until we get young Master Hedeon off the street." Hinton frowned. His voice had a serious edge to it as he added, "And here's your piece back. We don't need it for evidence, but you might need it for protection."

The pistol he handed me looked like mine. As I pulled it from its nylon holster to see if it was loaded, a piece of paper fell to the floor.

"That's a permit to carry. We found you had taken the concealed weapons course and filled out the paperwork. I took the liberty of arranging the rest for you, just in case...."

The pistol was loaded with Teflon coated, hollow point rounds—serious killer ammo. I checked the serial number against the receipt I still carried in my wallet six months after buying the pistol. It was my pistol, and it was time to clean out my wallet.

Considering what I'd been told, and that I was suddenly licensed to carry a concealed weapon, I realized there must be more involved than a seventeen-year-old-kid.

"Hinton, who was the third person? You know…the one who called my boat after Flynt and Hedeon were dead."

Hinton looked me in the eye. "I wondered when you'd mention that call. We don't know. But we do know the call was made from Flynt's phone at the courthouse."

"How so?"

"We traced that last call to the main line at the courthouse. When the boys processed Flynt's office, they hit re-dial and your answering machine picked up. That call to you was the last call made from his phone. That's all we know."

"Any idea who placed the call?"

"Yes, and no," he said. "You remember the warehouse fire? We'd tapped the warehouse phone also, and a call came in just before the fire. Apparently, the call activated an incendiary device. After the answering machine in the warehouse came on, the caller punched in a six digit code and set the bomb off. That call was also traced to the courthouse system. The only clue we have to who may have made the call was the music in the background."

"Music? It wasn't elevator music, was it?"

"Well, I guess you could call it that, but it was actually classical. One of our agents identified the particular piece as “Autumn” from Vivaldi’s “The Four Seasons.”

“So all we have to do is find a murdering arsonist who listens to popular classics and works at the courthouse, right? Maybe the call was made from the elevator, on the emergency phone,” I said half-joking.

Hinton wasn’t amused.

I told him about Donella Nash’s boss hearing elevator music during her last phone call and he wrote a note in a small spiral pad.

“Was the call to the warehouse before or after the call to my boat?” I asked.

“The caller set the bomb off while we were at the airport, minutes before agents were to kick in the door on the place. That was over an hour after the call to your boat.”

“That’s why the guardians. There’s someone else out there.”

“Correct. We know Flynt and Hedeon were not alone,” said Hinton. “They tried to kill you and failed. We don’t know for sure why they wanted to kill you, but we expect the other person, or persons, to try and finish the job.”

“And the kid Boris?”

“He’s a wild card—and potentially more dangerous. For all we know, he could be involved in the arms ring.”

“Okay, so I’m in deep shit, but I still have a job to do, and I need to get to my computer to do it. When will that happen?”

Hinton replied as he walked to the stairs. “I told you that you’d have our full cooperation and that stands. We’d like you to use our agents and their cars for transportation, at least for a while.”

“No problem. How about my boat? I want to get back on my boat.”

“Your boat will be ready to launch this afternoon, if you approve the repairs. Murdock personally covered any costs the agency wouldn’t.”

“Personally covered the costs? I’d like to meet this Murdock fellow and thank him personally.”

Hinton was headed down the stairs. “Maybe someday you will,” he called back. “Maybe someday, but I doubt it. Murdock’s leaving for Washington early in the fall, and he’s retiring this winter. I’ll tell him thanks for you, though.”

Suddenly, I found myself very alone, looking at the Smith and Wesson Magnum on the coffee table. I felt panic and dizziness wash over me like a wave.

I had only thirty days to take on the entire legal system of Florida to save an innocent man. Win or lose, it was a task I knew would tear me apart physically and emotionally, if the people who were trying to kill me didn’t succeed first.

My mind began to race. The itty-bitty-shitty committee in my head began a meeting—screaming, telling me how bad things were, how weak I was, reminding me of the cases I'd lost. Memories of every mistake I had ever made, every person I'd ever let down, every creature I'd ever hurt, flashed through my mind like a screaming train in the night. Nausea swept over me as all the fear and shame I had ever felt returned and clutched at my throat. I wanted to die. I could taste the cold steel of the Magnum on my tongue...could hear the last thing I'd ever hear, the click....

I shivered as I recognized the symptoms of my disease. My mind was attacking my spirit—my very soul. The dragons of alcoholism and suicide were back clawing at me.

I stared at the Magnum as I ran through my mental check list. *Hungry, Angry, Lonely, Tired—four out of four. No wonder the dragons are back*, I thought. I'd let my guard down. I had eaten very little breakfast. I feared I would not be able to save Clayton, which made me angry about the warrant. I had not slept well last night and was still tired. And I felt alone like a sniper in the jungle—both hunter and hunted.

Having recognized the problems, I could defeat them. I said a prayer for help, and with shaking hands, tossed the pistol into a pillow case with some spare clothing. Walking out into the Florida sunshine, I was greeted by Swenson and Hammer, my guardian agents. I could feel the panic subsiding. I mumbled a prayer of thanks and crawled into the back of the cruiser.

It was a fast trip. We ate tasteless fast food on the way out of town, and Swenson drove fast all the way to Tarpon Springs.

I recognized *Defender's* mast sticking above a tent at the far end of the boat lot as soon as we turned into the marina. I sighed deeply at the sight, and as I sighed, the last of the panic subsided like a wave sliding back from the beach. I had missed her, but now I was home.

Several vans and cars were parked around the tent, and a half-dozen men greeted Swenson and Hammer. Agent Sailor, who had taken responsibility for *Defender*, was dressed in white painter's overalls and covered with dust and paint. He took me on a tour of the repairs.

"There was little damage to the aft sections, but in the bow, a few of the bullets almost passed though the hull just below the waterline. We dug them out for evidence and the holes have been repaired," he said.

The hull, rail and deck had been repaired so well it looked like nothing bad had ever happened. "We checked your maintenance log and tried to use the same or better supplies. The marina that did the Imron job for you last year furnished enough paint from the original job for the repairs." Sailor was grinning. He knew the work his crew had done was impeccable, and that I was pleased. He was correct on both counts.

I caught the sweet chemical odor of fresh bottom paint, a fragrance like freshly-minted money. "Time to clear out of the tent," said Sailor. "They're getting ready to do the bottom. I hope Trinidad red is what you wanted again."

I was amazed. It would have taken a professional yard weeks to do what

Sailor's crew had done in four days, and the job could not have been done better. Best of all, it was free. I gave my approval for launching, and left with Swenson and Hammer for lunch.

By nightfall, *Defender* was moored safely in a slip at the marina where the repairs had been done, and I was sitting at my computer console.

Agent Sailor requested permission to stay on board *Defender* the first night she was back in the water.

"Why?" I asked.

"Just to make sure everything's right."

"Why? Really?"

"It's my job to clean up messes. This time I got to enjoy my passion, messing around in boats."

"Does the agency always do this kind of thing, you know, clean up after its act?"

"No, but Murdock usually does."

"Murdock. I hope I get to see him some day."

"Don't hold your breath. He isn't with the FBI, and some of us think there is no such person. No one has seen him in the eight years I've been with the bureau."

"Now I really want to meet him."

"Hey, you got to meet Hinton. That's a miracle. He's been a desk jockey for fifteen years. Rumor is he and this Murdock used to work together back when they were both new."

Chapter 30 — Extraordinary Relief

EVERYTHING ON BOARD had either been removed and returned, or sealed with plastic during the repairs on *Defender*. Had it not been, fiberglass dust would have destroyed the computer and electronics. All my boxes and floppy disc holders had been sealed with evidence tape. I broke the seal on the first box of documents and began to form the legal motions in my mind.

I read and made notes until Agent Sailor called to me, "Captain, you have company."

Ralph Swenson and his partner John Hammer had been off for the afternoon, and had returned with pizza and sodas. We picnicked in a little gazebo on the dock and passed the time telling war stories of our work.

"Is your life always this exciting?" Swenson asked. "You know, people trying to kill you and all?"

"Sometimes, but it's a living," I replied. "But really, no. Usually, law is boring. I have to deal with twits and assholes, liars and whores. And then there are my clients!" We laughed and I added, "Criminal law is still safer than domestic relations!"

"Speaking of relatives, Ralph told me about the Hedeon kid," said Sailor. "He sounds pretty dangerous."

"Yeah. Sorta like in divorce law—it's the relatives who kill you," I replied.

"What do you plan on doing if you run into him?" asked Swenson.

"I haven't the foggiest idea. What would you do?" I asked.

"I would live," Swenson said, as he nodded and grasped my left shoulder. "No matter what, I'd live."

The other two agents nodded their agreement.

After sundown, I returned to *Defender* and found a phone message from Jean Clayton asking me to return her call immediately, "...no matter what time you get this message." I did an un-lawyer-like thing and I returned her call right away.

"Jean? This is Woody."

"Woody! Are you all right?"

"Sure. How about you? How's the leg? And where are you?"

"The leg's fine. I'm home. Eddy Nash is dead and Jon knows about the warrant. What are we going to do? Can we stop the execution?"

"Of course we can," I said, wanting to believe it myself. "I'm going to the prison tomorrow."

Jean insisted on joining me for the trip to the prison. I had often represented clients under warrant and knew FSP would allow us in, even on short notice. Hammer agreed to pick Jean up at her home and meet Swenson and me at eight a.m. at a restaurant on I-75.

I expected a poor night's sleep, bad dreams and night sweats. However, saying my prayers, I realized that the day had been a mix of terror and joy. Yes, the dragons had returned and several people seemed to be trying to end my life, including the itty-bitty-committee in my head. But I was still alive and I was home on *Defender*, and she had been repaired beautifully. The dragons were gone, and Jean had called. Life was good—very good indeed.

WE WERE AT the prison by ten-thirty. There was very little trouble getting Jean in as my assistant, even though the guards knew she was Jon's sister-in-law. She had visited Jon every other week for five years.

"Mr. Thomas, just get down to business. We don't have time to sweat the small stuff," Jon said. "I just want to know what happens next. What can we do? Do I have a chance? What about my thirty-eight-fifty? Can you still file it?"

"Two short answers," I said. "Yes, there's a good chance we can stop the execution. Second, we can still file a motion to vacate, set aside or correct your sentence. However, it will be under a different section. It's the same thing, just different numbers and handling because of the warrant."

"I wasn't asking about the sentence," he said. "I didn't kill that girl. I'm innocent. Can you get me out of here? That's what I want to know."

Jean slipped her hand over his as he spoke. Her eyes met mine and asked the same question.

I tried to sound more certain than I actually felt. "Yes. I think we have enough to overturn your conviction."

"Think? That's all? You *think* we can overturn it—"

"Jon, let me explain the whole process. First, I write a motion for post-conviction relief. In it I say I have newly-discovered evidence. I argue to the court that, if this evidence had gone to the jury, it would have resulted in a verdict of not guilty."

"That's the gun?" he asked.

"Yes, and the fact yours was in Flynt's possession and he submitted the other pistol in its place."

"Okay, that goes to the Supreme Court, right?" he asked.

"Wrong. Post-conviction motions are filed in the court of original jurisdiction. Basically, I'll be asking your original trial judge to say that the new evidence is so important it would have caused the jury to return a verdict of not guilty."

"You mean Judge Harris has to say he was wrong?" Jon asked.

"Not exactly," I replied. "He just has to say that the verdict was unfair. Whether he was wrong or right at trial no longer really matters. All that should've been raised on direct appeal."

"And I lost that. So Harris has to say he was wrong," Jon said, a disgusted look on his face.

Clayton was correct in one way. I would be asking the judge to overrule the last death penalty he ordered before retirement, and then order a new trial. *Slim chance,* I thought.

"Usually, in order to get the judge to even look at the evidence, we have to show it was available but not presented because your trial attorney was ineffective," I said. "That almost never works, and we can't find Hatfield. He was last seen in Texas over two years ago."

Jon grimaced and started to speak, but I held my hand up to silence him "We don't need him. We'll be arguing the evidence was not known at the time of trial, and that even a good attorney could not have found it because of misconduct by an officer of the state."

"Do you think the judge will listen?" asked Jean.

"Maybe. We have something special. Not only has the evidence just been discovered, but it was intentionally concealed by someone in authority. This is a very unusual situation," I said.

"Not really. Everyone in here says the cops do it all the time," said Jon.

"Maybe so, but they usually don't get caught," I said. "We can prove you were framed by a cop."

"So you file the motion and they have to decide the motion before they can execute me?"

"Not really. I'll also file a motion to stay the execution. In other words, not execute you until we have a hearing on the motion."

"If we lose, I die?"

"If we lose, I appeal to the Florida Supreme Court."

"Not to the U.S. one?" Jon asked.

"No. That might come later, but Jon, don't expect anything out of the federal courts. You had one shot on your regular appeal, and I doubt they'll bother to look at your case again."

"Why not? I'm innocent. Doesn't that count for anything?"

"Short answer—no. Not in the federal courts. Not anymore."

Pain and shock showed in their eyes, as both Jon and Jean sputtered a variation of, "What do you mean, 'No?'"

I leaned back and waited a moment before answering them. I knew they were not going to like what I had to say.

"The problem is called *habeas* reform, which translated loosely means change the laws, to hell with the Constitution, let's kill somebody," I said. "And there is also bad case law. In a 1993 case out of Texas, Rehnquist said that the federal courts should not review 'newly discovered evidence' in capital cases. He said they never should have considered it. But to make it worse, O'Connor said that the standards for a claim of actual innocence are to be extraordinarily high, as in nearly impossible. Her concern was that federal courts would otherwise be... I think her exact words were 'deluged with frivolous claims of actual innocence.'"

"What're we going to do?" asked Jon. "This is not a frivolous claim."

"We are going to win in the state court, or Florida will probably kill another innocent man."

"Oh, my God. You mean it's happened before?" asked Jean.

"Yes. And probably will again. If not Jon, somebody else."

There was little left for us to talk about. Jon no longer looked serene. He seemed to have physically shrunk. His head sank into his shoulders. His face grew dark. He aged before my eyes. Sitting beside him, holding his hand, Jean looked pale and frail, as though she were a frightened child.

"Jon, don't give up," I said. "See yourself a free man, walking in the sand, on a beach in the sun. Visualize it! See yourself...surfing in Hawaii! With someone you love!"

He promised to try, to which I replied, "There is no try. Just do it."

Jean didn't cry until we were in the car. Then she laid her head on my shoulder and sobbed uncontrollably. Swenson stared straight ahead as Hammer drove us swiftly south.

The visit had been hard on all three of us. I knew Jean had visited Jon at the prison at least twice a month. After seeing the way they touched hands and looked at each other, I was glad nothing had happened between Jean and me that night on the boat. I felt loss, but knew I couldn't lose Jean. You can't lose something you never had.

I had a job to do. Shortly after the afternoon thunder storms had passed, I was in shorts and a flowered shirt, at the computer console, typing furiously.

> Motion To Vacate Judgment Of
> Convictions And Sentence, With Leave To Amend
>
> Jon Clayton, Defendant in the above-captioned action, respectfully moves this Court for an order, pursuant to Fla. R. Crim. P. 3.851, vacating and setting aside the judgments of conviction and sentence, including his sentence of death, imposed upon him by this Court. In support thereof, Mr. Clayton, through counsel, respectfully submits as follows:
>
> 1.This motion must be filed at this point in time under Rule 3.851, Fla. R. Crim. P, because a premature death warrant has been....

I SPENT THE next five days researching, writing, and honing the motion. Shaken by Jean's grief, Agent Swenson became my assistant and editor. He had graduated from law school with honors, but had never practiced and wanted to see how it felt.

"Besides, I've got to be with you all the time anyway," he said.

I wanted independent expert witnesses, but now there was no time. I would have to use the FDLE experts who testified at the trial. The FBI had offered help, but I didn't know what kind of help it would be, or when it would arrive. It might be too little too late.

The fact that the guns had been switched was important, but I knew it might not be enough to overturn Jon's conviction. Swapping the guns was state misconduct, and it was egregious, but nothing was guaranteed. If the state could prove that the switching of the weapons *could have been* discovered by a reasonably competent attorney, we might be barred from presenting any evidence regarding it.

Going over the transcripts again, I looked for loopholes—anything I could use to show Jon's other convictions were in error. I was especially concerned about the rape conviction and the life sentence Jon had received for it. Even were the death case overturned, if that or the kidnapping conviction remained….

I realized I was thinking in circles. I had not slept but a few hours a night for days. I lay across the big bed in the aft cabin and napped fitfully for an hour, then picked up my phone list and began making calls.

Pat Hurley, the serology expert, was not happy about returning to the witness stand in this case, but I assured him that I would have a subpoena issued and have the trial judge declare him a hostile witness.

"Hey, in that case, no problem. But make damn sure you have me declared hostile. I don't want to get in trouble with the boss," he said.

I told him what I was going to ask him, and he agreed with my hypothesis that, based on the evidence at trial, any one or more of seventy-five percent of the men on earth could have had sex with the victim.

Drew Pearson was openly hostile when I first called. Once filled in on the details of what had been discovered and what I would be asking, he volunteered to take a leave of absence, if necessary, to testify. I assured him he would get a subpoena. He was still a cop and could get in trouble otherwise.

One morning Swenson arrived with a pack of affidavits sent by Hinton. The affidavits detailed the FBI's involvement in finding the pistol, and included a sworn statement by Conchman concerning his being blackmailed by Donella Nash, and his belief Flynt had murdered her when he learned of the blackmail.

Hinton also sent a list of several witnesses whose names I didn't recognize. I assumed they were the agents who had processed Flynt's office and added their names to the witness list I would soon release to the state. In so doing, I violated one of my cardinal rules: never list witnesses unless you know exactly what they are going to say.

Telling the court the facts of a case is never enough, no matter how compelling the facts appear. It is the argument that tells the court how it must act on those facts. Swenson researched the law while I wrote the arguments. In the end, we had produced a small book of a hundred-thirty-four pages with a sixty-page appendix which included the FBI affidavits.

The finished motion could not just be signed by me as the defendant's attorney, so Swenson and I took a fast afternoon run to FSP. There, Jon Clayton signed the motion before a notary, swearing what was alleged was true.

Finally, at four-ten in the afternoon, ten days after the governor signed Jon Clayton's death warrant, I plopped the 3.851 motion and the motion requesting a stay of Clayton's execution on the court clerk's desk. Copies of the motions and Clayton's court file were forwarded to Judge Harris, the original trial judge. While he was officially retired, he still occasionally heard cases and had agreed in advance to hear this one.

Three days later, I received notice that a hearing was scheduled for the twenty-seventh day of the thirty-day warrant. Harris did not grant the stay of execution. I had two weeks to get the witnesses together and prepare for the hearing.

That evening, for the first time since the shootout, I enjoyed a sunset. I had been so involved in the case I'd forgotten how beautiful life could be. I stood in the heat of an early July evening, the sweat running down my body and, for what seemed like the first time in over ten days, I breathed.

As the sun sank below the horizon and the sundogs faded, I heard the telephone ring.

Chapter 31 — Attorney At War

THE CALL WAS from my friend Bill in Tallahassee. He wanted to know what to do with the documents he had received almost two weeks before. I had forgotten about my client insurance policy—the envelopes I had mailed containing copies of Donella's diaries and the evidence receipt. I assured Bill I was alive and well, and I asked another favor.

"You and I both know Harris is going to deny Clayton a new trial, no matter what," I said. "And he'll do it in such a way the entire thirty days will have been used up."

"You want me to do the Supreme thing, right?" asked Bill with a chuckle.

"Bingo. I'll draft the motion for a stay of execution and leave the date blank for when Harris issues his denial. Can you file it on a moment's notice?"

"But of course, ol' buddy," he said. "Day or night, twenty-four hours a day. I'll beat on them big, steel doors, and personally deliver copies to each of the Supreme Beings. I'll catch 'em in the john and place the papers in their hands, if that's what it takes."

Bill and I often joked about the Florida Supreme Court, and we had our reservations about certain members, but we knew the justices didn't play games. They were not as political as the circuit court judges, who must pander to the electorate. If they thought it should be done, the Supreme Court would stop an execution, and they would actually consider the arguments presented. It was getting to the point this was Jon's best chance for justice.

I made more quick phone calls to my other friend in Tallahassee and to Elsa, telling them all was well and thanking them for being insurance agents for my client. Their offers to help in any way possible made me feel less lonely and vulnerable.

I had good reason to feel alone and at risk. It was never just the defense attorney against the prosecutor. It was always the defense attorney against "The State." Literally every judge and prosecutor, every cop—professional or amateur—could be available to try to keep my client on Death Row. The attorney for Jon Clayton versus the whole State of Florida.

I worked until two in the morning, and when I stopped, Clayton's motion for stay of execution to the Florida Supreme Court was ready to be filed. I had even started writing the appeal from the expected denial of relief by Judge Harris. Positive thinking said we would win, but good lawyering meant being ready to continue the fight if we lost.

Tomorrow, I must check my armor, I thought as I fell into my bunk. I hadn't worn my blue three-piece suit in months.

THE HEARING WAS to begin at ten on Friday morning. When I left *Defender* at six-thirty, I was surprised to find four smiling guardian agents dressed in light-colored suits, waiting to escort me to the justice center. I told Swenson I wanted him to sit with me at the defense table. "You've earned it, and it'll look like I've got help!"

Swenson smiled and replied, "You have more help than you know, counselor."

When we pulled onto U.S. 19, traffic was solid, bumper-to-bumper to the horizon. Hammer did a fine imitation of Moses parting the Red Sea when he turned on the siren and blue flashing lights. Still, the parking lot at the courthouse was almost full when we arrived. Even the local news vans were on the scene.

Sitting in the middle of the backseat, I spotted the three men with rifles on the roof of the building and remarked, "I hope they're yours." Once parked, all four doors opened and all four men stepped out at the same time. For an instant, they stood with their backs to the car, blocking my exit, and any bullet's entrance.

I was whisked into a back entrance where other men in suits joined us, then up to the courtroom where Assistant Special Agent-in-Charge Stan Hinton waited.

"That's fourteen agents, counting you, I've seen this morning. Are we expecting trouble?" I asked.

"As a matter of fact, we are," replied Hinton. "Hedeon's son has been seen in the area several times, and last night he was seen leaving the courthouse parking lot on a white motorcycle."

I was so wired I hardly felt the chill down my back. My guardians really were expecting trouble. "What can be so hard about catching a kid on a white motorcycle? Is he a ghost or something?"

Hinton ignored my question and introduced me to Agent Charlie Kenyon. I recognized his name from the witness list. "Charlie is our serology expert," said Hinton, "and he...Oh hell, you tell him, Charlie."

"Mr. Thomas, when we talked earlier, you said a major part of your case was the blood typing and whether or not your client raped the victim. As I told you, we can't do DNA because the evidence taken from the victim has been contaminated."

"You mean someone smashed the test tubes," I said.

"Matter of fact," he said, "the footprint on the package looked like about a size ten-and-a-half men's dress shoe, but that doesn't matter. A couple days ago, based on what Conchman told us, I decided to try another tactic. I typed Flynt and Hedeon. Flynt was O positive, and he was a secreter. Hedeon was A positive, but he was a non-secreter. Either of them could've had left the semen in the victim, and I'm prepared to testify to that."

Swenson leaned over Agent Kenyon's shoulder and added with a smile, "I told you. You have more friends than you knew."

I now faced an ethical dilemma. Eddy Nash told me he'd had sex with his wife the morning before she died. That meant he was the probable source of the semen, but now I had evidence that two other men could have had sex with her.

"Could more than one man have done the deed? I mean, maybe Flynt or Hedeon *and* someone else?" I asked.

"Sure, as long as they were a non-secretor. Or they could be O positive, secretor or not. It wouldn't matter. In fact, Flynt and Hedeon could both have had sex with her. There's no way to tell."

I decided I could present Kenyon's testimony, and not worry about whether or not Nash had raped his wife. I did, however, have the obligation to tell the state what he was going to say. The state had a duty to investigate, to ask questions, but it hadn't. If I didn't disclose the new evidence to the state, the judge might not consider it when I presented in court.

As I sat and pondered how to handle the situation, a hand touched my shoulder. It was Jean. "Where's Jon?" she asked.

"The judge wouldn't order transportation for him. The rules say he doesn't have to be here."

But even as I spoke Jean called out, "Jon!"

I spun around and was surprised to see my client being escorted into the room by two bailiffs. He was dressed in orange overalls. His hands were cuffed, his legs shackled, and a chain ran from the cuffs to the shackles. Still, he smiled so brightly we could feel his joy.

"A federal judge had him transported last night as a witness in one of my cases," said Hinton with a smile. "It was a mistake, of course, but since he's here anyway, your judge has agreed to let him sit in on the hearing."

I stood and looked around the courtroom as the prosecution arrived. On our side of the room were Jon's few supporters, federal agents, Ramirez and a few court watchers. On the prosecution's side were a dozen police officers, some in uniform, some not, and one old man.

The old man was tall, straight and gray. His face was tan and heavily lined, his steel blue eyes among the saddest I had ever seen. He looked like a man who had lost all hope.

"Fletcher McBeth, the victim's father," a woman whispered from behind me.

I turned to find Elsa Salvadora waiting to give me a hug.

"Need co-counsel?" she asked.

"You can't do this. You're a PD."

"I signed out on annual leave, two days' vacation," she said. "I can second chair, if you need me. The boss already said it was okay."

I smiled and nodded to a chair beside Clayton. "Introduce yourself to Ralph "Blondie" Swenson. He's an Honors grad of American U., and he's been a great help. I'd best go talk to the 'prostitution.'"

"You're going to slip up someday and call them that to their face." Elsa laughed as I walked toward the prosecutor's table.

"Marlene Saint Lucie, how is the execution business these days?" I said, greeting the Senior Assistant Attorney General from Tallahassee. Leggy, tall, and blonde, St. Lucie, a capital crimes specialist, often bragged she had legally killed more men than Bonnie and Clyde. She proudly displayed pictures on her office wall of each man she'd prosecuted to death.

"Well, Mr. Thomas, it goes well…very well indeed," she said, smiling broadly and fluffing her hair. "I'm here today to add yet another picture to my gallery. By the way, how did you get your boy here? Pull strings in Tallahassee?" She was obviously not pleased to see me or my client.

"Nah. I pulled strings in Washington. I guess you and I'll be doing most of this. Is this Mr. Conchman?" I asked, extending my hand to the man beside her. He looked like Conchman, but his face was so pale and drawn I hardly recognized him. He did not shake my hand.

"You gonna prosecute, or be a witness?" I asked Conchman. I was pleased to see his face flush at the question. Now he knew that I knew about his talk with the FBI, and that he was in trouble. *One point for the defense*, I thought.

"Are you going to offer any plea bargains?" I asked Saint Lucie.

"No. Your scum client is gonna die," she replied, loudly enough for Jon to hear. Then she said, "Well, no...wait. How about this? Plea to first, premeditated, and we'll agree to lower the voltage."

"All rise!" called the bailiff as I shook my head, turned and walked away.

Chapter 32 — Hearing The Motion

THE PRESUMPTION OF innocence applies only before conviction. Clayton had been found guilty, and now we had to prove his innocence. To do so, we had to show that the newly-discovered evidence, had it been presented at trial, would have caused the jury to acquit Clayton of murder.

The bailiff sang his song of, "Hear ye," as Judge Harris glared around the room and flopped into his chair, his normal unpleasant self. I decided to get his mood on the record.

"Your Honor, in an abundance of caution, the defense asks that there be nothing off the record. We ask that both the court reporter and tape recorder record everything said here today, including any sidebars."

"What? You afraid someone will…." He stopped. His face turned red. "So ordered. Ms. Court Reporter, did you get that?"

"Also, Your Honor, Mr. Clayton is still in handcuffs and shackles and there is no need for them. I ask this court order them removed."

"No. No way. That man is a convicted murderer. He will be treated as such, and in my courtroom, that means cuffs and shackles. I'd have him chained to the floor like a dog if I could. And just so you'll know, Mr. Clayton, the bailiff with the shotgun has orders to kill you instantly should you so much as think about escape. How or why you were brought here for this hearing, I don't know. But while you are in this courtroom, you're mine. Remember that. Now, counselor," he said, turning toward me, "let's see this important new evidence you say you've got."

"One more thing, Your Honor. This morning I discovered certain new evidence which I need a little more time to investigate—"

"No damn continuance," yelled Harris, cutting me off. "You can present the evidence or not. I will not grant a continuance. And I will not grant a stay of execution. So where does that leave you, counselor?"

"No continuances at all, Your Honor?"

"None! Let's get this dog and pony show on the road."

"Thank you, Your Honor. I just wanted to be clear on that. The defense calls Special Agent Stan Hinton."

Hinton identified himself as a supervisor for the Federal Bureau of Investigation and gave the details about finding the firearm in Clancy Flynt's file cabinet. While referring only to an investigation, he was specific about the bag, the case numbers, and the pistol.

"Well, where the hell is this pistol you found?" interrupted Judge Harris. "Are you going to produce it?"

Swenson handed me two bags and a videotape, all of which I handed to Hinton.

"This is the evidence bag removed from Investigator Flynt's file cabinet," said Hinton. "And this is a video tape of the opening of the evidence bag."

"Agent Hinton, when it was found, did you notice anything special about the bag? That is, anything which may have called it to your attention?"

"Yes, sir," he answered. "The bag was sealed with this evidence tape. It was unbroken at the time and remains so today. You can see here, State v. Clayton, the case number, the date it was sealed, and the initials, C.F. and M.C."

"Was there anything in that bag?"

"Yes sir. There was a .38 caliber pistol in it, which bore an evidence tag."

"And where is that weapon now?"

"I have it in this separate evidence bag."

"Sir, would you remove the weapon from the bag and describe it for the record?"

"Yes, sir," said Hinton. He took the pistol from the bag. "This is an early model Smith and Wesson revolver. It is a Military and Police model, six-shot revolver, with a four-inch barrel. By the prefix to the serial number I'd say it was made before World War I, around 1905 to 1906. It appears to be in excellent condition."

"Sir, are you very familiar with this particular type of weapon?" I asked.

"Yes, I am. Between this and the later versions, including the Model Ten, Smith and Wesson manufactured almost six million pistols like this."

Judge Harris raised the palm of his hand to me, turned toward Hinton and said, "Six million?"

"Yes, Your Honor. This particular pistol has been in production about a hundred years."

Harris muttered something, shrugged his shoulders, and nodding toward me, said, "Continue, counsel."

"Is there any visible difference between the Military and Police version and the Model Ten?" I asked.

"For all intents and purposes, they're the same weapon. It was first made in 1899, and there were few changes in it that you'd notice, at least not until...I believe it was 1968...except the serial number, placement of screws, little things."

"You are certain the pistol in your hand is the pistol found in the bag with Mr. Clayton's name and case number on it?"

"Yes, sir. I am absolutely sure. I personally sealed it in a separate bag, which I had delivered to the Florida Department of Law Enforcement's laboratories in Tallahassee. It was tested there, picked up by one of my agents, and delivered to my office. I opened the returned bag this morning sitting in this courtroom. I have before me my notes from the day we discovered it, and the serial number is the same."

"What is the serial number on that pistol?"

Hinton read the serial number off of the weapon, I sat down, and the state had no questions. I noticed Conchman looking over his shoulder, his hands shaking as he sat beside Saint Lucie.

"The defense calls Tracey Sanders."

Through Sanders, I was able to get the original evidence receipt admitted as evidence. The little slip of paper showed the serial number of the weapon actually taken from Clayton. Sanders said he laid the paper on the pistol over the serial number and rubbed it with a pencil, so there could be no mistake.

He'd been told earlier that the pistol from the original trial was the wrong one—that it had been switched—but I hadn't told him that we had found the right weapon. Sanders thought he would just be testifying that the one in evidence was the wrong one.

"Officer Sanders, I have here defense exhibit one, a pistol. Would you look at the pistol and see if you recognize it?"

"Sir, this is an early model, Smith and Wesson, .38 caliber revolver. It's got a four-inch barrel and looks about like all the rest of this particular model I've seen. It has my initials on the handle, and this appears to be the tag I affixed to the trigger guard."

"Would you compare the serial number on the pistol to the one you recorded on the evidence slip in June, 1991?"

Sanders lay the property receipt next to the pistol and started to read the serial number aloud, "The number is...hey...they match! This is the pistol I took from Jon Clayton the night I arrested him!" He turned to Judge Harris, read the number and said, "This is the pistol I took from the defendant, Your Honor."

"Did that slip with the serial number on it exist at the time of the trial?" asked Harris.

"Yes, Your Honor."

"Then why didn't you testify to it then?" asked the judge.

"No one asked for the serial number. I was shown a pistol, it looked like the same pistol, it had my mark on the handle and a case tag on it. I thought it was the same pistol. I mean, the prosecutor wouldn't give me the wrong pistol...."

"Hummph...continue." The judge sank back into his chair. He stared at Conchman, who stared intently at his shaking hands.

I had no further questions.

Saint Lucie asked Sanders if he withheld the serial number from the defense attorney, Jake Hatfield.

"I gave it to Officer Flynt...and Mr. Conch—"

I rose from my seat and said loudly, "Your Honor, I object to the question. The court records show that the discovery given to the defense attorney did not contain the serial number."

I knew Saint Lucie was trying to show the evidence was available, but that Hatfield had made a tactical decision not to use it. Tactical decisions, dumb or smart, are allowed and do not indicate an attorney was ineffective—a rule many of us considered to be legal fiction.

"Your Honor, the state only asked if this witness gave the serial number of the weapon to the defense. The state will stipulate that the discovery documents say whatever they say," said Saint Lucie.

Harris leaned forward on the bench and looked over his glasses at Saint Lucie. He sighed deeply. "I'm sure they do, counselor." Then sitting up and looking at me, Harris asked, "Do they list a serial number for the pistol?"

"They do not, Your Honor," I replied. "The only items released by the state at trial were the normal, sanitized summaries of the evidence. No serial numbers."

"Move on then," said Harris before Saint Lucie could reply. Saint Lucie had no further questions for Tracey Sanders.

Drew Pearson, the FDLE firearm identification expert, had abandoned his deep Southern drawl. He testified about his original testimony at trial, and that the bullet found in the head of Donella Nash had come from the gun provided to him by the state.

"The state? Any particular person in the state?" I asked.

"Yes, sir," he said. "Investigator Clancy Flynt of the Pinellas County State Attorney's office sent the weapon to me. I received it in sealed condition, and the evidence tape sealing it was initialed C.F. and M.C., which I understood to be Flynt and Mikel Conchman."

I handed Pearson the weapon from the Clerk's evidence file which he identified as the one he'd tested for the trial.

"This is a Smith and Wesson Model Ten, the serial number has an S prefix indicating it was made after World War II, probably around 1946 or early '47, and the serial number matches my records," said Pearson. "This is the weapon I tested prior to Mr. Clayton's trial."

"Mr. Pearson...Officer Pearson, you are actually a law enforcement officer, aren't you?" I asked. I wanted solid credibility, acknowledgment that my witness was one of them. "And you are an expert in firearms identification, qualified by this court?"

"Counsel, the court is quite aware of Mr. Pearson's qualifications," interrupted Harris. "Cut the crap and ask your questions."

"Thank you, Your Honor. I'll be glad to," I said. Then shuffling some papers for effect and picking up the weapon actually found on my client at the time of his arrest, I began. "Officer Pearson, I'm handing you a pistol, marked defense exhibit number one. Do you recognize it?"

"This is a Smith and Wesson, Military and Police model, four-inch barrel, pre-World War I vintage, but in excellent condition."

"Have you seen this weapon before?"

"Yes, I have. It bears my tag, indicating I tested it seven days ago at your request. It was brought to me by an agent of the Federal Bureau of Investigation."

"Are you sure this is the weapon? We wouldn't want a mix-up here." I turned and smiled at the judge. He was leaning back in his chair with his eyes closed. He looked dead.

"Yes, sir. The serial number on my tag and the pistol is the same, and I just compared the serial number with the one in my report which has remained in my personal possession. It is the same pistol."

"You say you tested the pistol. Would you please tell the court what test you are speaking of, and what results you found?"

"I did a comparison firing of this weapon."

"A comparison to what?"

"To the bullet which I was given before Jon Clayton's murder trial in 1991, the one identified as having been found in the victim's head," he said, looking at Conchman. "And I compared it to the bullets fired from the gun I'd tested in 1991."

"A different pistol was given to you to test then, is that what you are saying?"

"Yes. It was a Smith and Wesson Model 10, which looks pretty much the same, but for the serial number," said Pearson.

"Were you able to reach any conclusions concerning the comparisons, the tests of these two pistols and the bullet that killed the victim in State v. Clayton?"

"Yes, sir, I was."

"What were those conclusions and how sure are you about them?"

"Based on my tests, I am of the opinion that the bullet found in the head of Donella Nash was fired from the weapon presented me in 1991."

"The Model 10?

"Yes."

"And?"

"It did not come from the pistol presented here as defense exhibit number one. In fact, there is absolutely no doubt in my mind that the bullet allegedly found in the victim, the one provided by the state as evidence—" Pearson held up the pistol found in Flynt's file cabinet in his right hand, shoulder high, barrel aimed straight up "—did not come from this weapon."

"Your witness, counselor," I said turning to Saint Lucie, with a smile.

"No questions," said Saint Lucie. "But, Your honor, it doesn't matter if the weapons were mixed up. Forensic evidence proved Jon Clayton raped that girl."

"If the state does not wish to cross-examine this witness, we'll address that matter right now, Your Honor," I replied.

Saint Lucie's face was turning red as she said, "No questions, Your Honor."

I had waited a long time for this moment. I had a royal flush, and the state had bet big and bluffed. I felt no pity for Saint Lucie.

Chapter 33 — First Blood

"THE DEFENSE CALLS Special Agent Charlie Kenyon of the Federal Bureau of Investigation."

"Special Agent Kenyon, what are your duties with the FBI?"

"I am one of the regional serology experts."

"Your Honor!" Saint Lucie was on her feet and headed toward the bench at a trot. "Your Honor, the state was unaware of this witness. The defense did not comply with discovery, and we object to this testimony."

"Your Honor, if the court will review the record, it will note Agent Kenyon was named as a witness, and it states specifically, FBI evidence expert. If the state failed to contact him, that's its problem. There's no reason to exclude his testimony."

Harris still leaned back in his chair with his eyes closed, his hand now across his mouth.

"Your Honor, the state requests a continuance to review this evidence."

"Your Honor—" I didn't get my argument out before Judge Harris rocked forward, head low to the bench, looking at Saint Lucie.

"Ms. Prosecutor, no continuances, remember? We talked about this yesterday."

"Excuse me, Your Honor. Did I hear you correctly?" I asked. "You spoke to the state about this case without my being present? That's *ex parte—*"

"Counselor, we discussed procedural matters, nothing more. In particular, the state wanted to make sure there would be no continuances, and there will be none...for either side." Harris rocked back in his chair, ran his hand though what was left of his white hair, smiled, and said, "Proceed, counselor. Ms. Saint Lucie, you will take your seat."

"But, Your Honor...."

"Sit down, counselor. And the next time you wish to approach the bench, *ask* first. The defense may continue."

Kenyon gave his credentials and was declared an expert by the court. That allowed him to give an opinion in the field of serology, and the state still had no idea about what he was going to testify.

"Agent Kenyon, are you familiar with two Clearwater police officers, Clancy Flynt and Nigel Hedeon?"

Saint Lucie sprung to her feet, speaking as she rose. "Objection—relevance, Your Honor. Flynt and Hedeon are not on trial here."

"Your Honor, if I may proceed, I will show the relevance."

"If the state had done its job preparing for this hearing, it would already know the relevance," said Harris, again leaning back in his chair. "Overruled. Proceed, counselor. I suspect this is going to be very interesting."

Kenyon had drawn the blood and extracted serum samples from the bodies of both men himself during the investigation of the shootout on *Defender*. There was no chain of custody to be concerned with. I produced a copy of the transcript of the original trial, and he said he was familiar with the testimony which related to the semen found in the victim.

"Could either Flynt or Hedeon have been the man who deposited the semen found in Donella Nash's body?" I asked.

"Yes. Either could have...and, in fact, both could have. It would've been consistent with what was presented at trial."

"Your Honor, I object. Counsel has no reason to defame these two men," said Saint Lucie.

"Mr. Thomas, I realize you have a weapon and...other evidence, but why, what motive?" asked Harris. His face was deeply lined. He looked like he had just seen the system at its worst, and it hurt him. "Why would two of the state's best investigators commit a crime like this? It just doesn't make sense."

"Your Honor, if I may call Mikel Conchman, I think I can show a motive." I turned toward the state's table, but Mikel Conchman was gone.

Saint Lucie stood and said, "Mr. Conchman had to leave, Your Honor...perhaps the defense wishes to proffer its scandalous accusations, rather than place an officer of the court on the witness stand."

"Counselor, what is this about?" asked Harris.

"Your Honor, I had hoped not to have to get into this, but I have here an affidavit signed by Mr. Conchman and a video of his deposition, both furnished by the FBI." I started toward the bench.

"Just tell me about them first, counselor," said Harris.

"Very well, Your Honor," I said. "Mr. Conchman was once engaged to Donella Nash's sister, Bonnie McBeth. Bonnie died tragically before they could be married. In fact, she died within hours of Mr. Conchman's admission to the bar. Mr. Conchman then appears to have assumed responsibility, so to speak, for Donella McBeth Nash, the victim in this case."

"What do you mean by assumed responsibility? This is the sister of the girl he was going to marry, right?" asked Harris.

"That is correct, Your Honor—her younger sister. Unfortunately, Donella Nash had a drug habit. On at least sixteen occasions, Mikel Conchman personally *nolle prossed* drug charges which had been placed against her. She had no record, or at least no convictions.

"Then, there was a seventeenth time, Your Honor. According to the records I have, Donella Nash was arrested in a drug sweep in Hillsborough County. Her release was signed by Clancy Flynt, less than forty-eight hours prior to her murder. It is the defense's hypothesis that Clancy Flynt killed Ms. Nash."

"Why, if Conchman and Flynt were helping the girl...why would Flynt kill her?" asked Judge Harris.

"According to his affidavit, Mr. Conchman thinks Flynt found out about the blackmail and wanted to punish Nash for it."

"Excuse me...blackmail?" said Saint Lucie, jumping to her feet again. "Your Honor, this has gone much too far."

"At ease, Ms. Prosecutor. Just take a seat and let him finish," said Harris. "Was Mr. Conchman being blackmailed?"

"Yes, Your Honor. Donella Nash was blackmailing Mikel Conchman."

"Your Honor, this is absurd," said Saint Lucie. "How can this court allow Mr. Thomas to stand there and destroy another officer of the court? Mikel Conchman is an honest—"

Holding up the diaries I had taken from Eddy Nash, I interrupted. "These are Donella Nash's diaries, Your Honor. They say when and how much Mr. Conchman paid her, and they indicate it was to keep Ms. Nash from talking about something in Mr. Conchman's past. I believe her father can identify the handwriting," I said, nodding toward the tall, gray man with the sad eyes.

Fletcher McBeth nodded and said aloud, "Yes, sir. I can do that."

"Perhaps Mr. Conchman will enlighten us as to why he was paying her," I continued.

"Where the hell is Conchman?" asked Judge Harris, on his feet and taking charge of his courtroom. "Damn. Where is that motion—the one for the stay?

"Counselor, I'm granting an indefinite stay of your client's execution, and I'm continuing this case for seven days. At that time, I expect the state to have a better grasp of what is going on. Oh, and Mr. Clayton is to remain in this county. Do not return him to Starke."

The hearing was over and the judge gone in seconds. However, the question lingering on everyone's mind was, "Where the hell is Conchman?"

About a dozen of us left the courtroom running. Hinton, Ramirez and I headed for the stairs and Conchman's office. It was lunchtime and most of the state attorney's employees were out of the office, including Conchman's secretary, Red.

Conchman's door was open, so I just walked in.

"Touch nothing. Move nothing," said Hinton, standing outside the doorway.

Easy listening music came from a CD player on Conchman's credenza. The desk held a half-filled coffee cup. Trophies lined the window. On the wall of photographs behind Conchman's desk a pair of eight-by-ten photos caught my attention, and gave me chills.

"Hinton, Sarge, you'd better come look at this," I said. "I don't believe Mr. Conchman is coming back."

Chapter 34 — Runaway

BOTH OFFICERS STEPPED into the room and looked at the two pictures. One was of Clancy Flynt and Mikel Conchman standing beside an old red-and-white, twin engine Piper Apache. The other was of Mikel Conchman and a distinguished looking, older man standing in front of a black Infiniti Q-45. Under the car were the words, Happy Birthday! Love, Dad. February 12, 1991.

"That's Flynt and Conchman," I said. "And I assume the car and plane belong to Conchman."

"Yeah. He's a private pilot. He flies down to the Keys to see his parents a lot," Ramirez answered.

I recounted the story of the plane we had seen the evening before the shootout on *Defender*. "That plane was an old Apache with a short nose, round tail, red-and-white. It sure looked like this one, and I'm willing to bet there are not very many old red-and-white Apaches around here. Conchman was probably searching for me that evening for his buddies, Flynt and Hedeon," I said.

Then pointing to the other picture, I added, "Donella Nash was picked up by someone in a black, four-door car, and it appears Conchman drove a black, four-door car at the time of the murder."

The CD player changed discs, and the lilting strains of Vivaldi filled the room. I looked at Conchman's collection of music, and found an empty CD case labeled, "The Very Best of Vivaldi." The second selection was "Autumn" from "The Four Seasons."

"He's playing your song," I said, handing the case to Hinton. "The one that was playing when the warehouse was torched."

Hinton pulled a cell phone and a radio from his jacket, and started poking buttons and talking to both at once.

Ramirez called me over to the pictures. "That was taken over at Clearwater Airport, a couple blocks from the warehouse that burned. Wanna take a fast ride?" he asked.

We left Hinton to deal with the flurry of gray-jacketed agents running toward him, and were almost out of the office when we met Conchman's red-haired secretary.

"Hold it a minute," I said to Ramirez.

I stepped in front of Red and asked, "Does your boss still keep his airplane at Clearwater Airpark?"

Red ignored my question and tried to push me out of the way. Ramirez grabbed her shoulder, spun her around so that her face was inches from his, and said, "Listen, damn it, your boss is in trouble. His life is in danger. Where the hell is his airplane?"

Red was visibly shaken. She stuttered, "He...he moved it last week. It's right up the road at Clearwater-St. Pete Airport. I think it's near Gate H."

Swenson and Hammer had joined us in the hallway, and told Ramirez they would follow him, and that I should ride with them. They stayed very close to me as we ran out of the building. I realized they were still concerned about Boris Hedeon.

We cut through the noon traffic, Ramirez leading the way, siren wailing and lights ablaze. Gate H was closed and, as the cruisers roared into the airport, I saw a black Q-45 sitting at the far end of the hangers. Someone was face down on the ground next to the car, and a man in white overalls stood next to him waving frantically at us. We slid to a halt at the gate.

Ramirez grabbed the admittance telephone and was speaking to security when we heard a blast. Hammer had used a twelve-gauge pump shotgun to remove the drive chain from the security gate. Shrapnel composed of chain, shot, and concrete clattered on the cars as Hammer grabbed the gate and, with one yank, rolled it back out of the way. Hammer joined Ramirez in the police cruiser and roared into the restricted area ahead of us.

"The guy's gone crazy!" the man in overalls yelled as we jumped out of the cars. "This kid said something to him and he just started shooting."

Boris Hedeon looked like his father. He had dark hair, dark eyes, and was ruggedly handsome. Blood ran from his left shoulder and abdomen. A Mac-10 semi-automatic lay on the ground nearby. The white motorcycle stood next to the hanger. Ramirez called for help on the radio. Hammer laid the shotgun in the trunk of our plain white cruiser and ran to the boy's side with a medical kit.

"Was it Mikel Conchman?" I asked the man in the overalls.

"Yes."

"Where is he now?" asked Swenson.

"Taking off," the man said pointing past the hangers.

"Is he alone?" I asked as I reached in the trunk for the shotgun.

"Yes," yelled the man in overalls as I slammed the trunk.

Swenson slid under the steering wheel as I dove in the passenger door of the big white Chevy. I laid the shotgun across my lap, barrel out the window.

"Get out!" he yelled as we simultaneously latched our seat belts.

"Go, damn it!" I yelled back. "You can't stop him alone."

Swenson screamed, "Arrrggh!" and stomped the gas pedal.

The big Chevy had plenty of acceleration, but slid on the turns. We straightened out on the runway and Swenson aimed the hood ornament directly at the rear of the old twin-engine airplane, never once letting up on the accelerator.

A blast of blue smoke from the engines announced that Conchman had seen us and he was going to try and get airborne before we could stop him. We were driving two tons of steel and he was in two tons of aluminum. If we hit, the odds of survival were on our side, I hoped. But Conchman had two engines and a head start.

The car's engine screamed as Swenson held the pedal to the floor. There was no feeling of movement or covering distance, but the airplane appeared larger every second. The nose wheel of the plane was off the ground. The speed of the car leveled off. I pumped a round into the shotgun and slid the barrel out the window. The buckshot could ruin an engine if we could get close enough.

We were within fifty feet of success when the Apache suddenly became airborne and veered to the left. That's when we saw the jet.

We were approaching each other at a combined speed of what had to be almost three hundred miles-an-hour. From the turned-down nose and huge twin engines, I knew it was a Boeing 757. I could see the landing lights over the nose wheel, the smoke from the tires, and the panic on the faces of the pilots.

We screamed in harmony as Swenson yanked the wheel to the left. The big car responded and we left the runway as the wing of the jet passed overhead. The huge Rolls-Royce fan-jet came so close that the thrust of full reverse rocked the car. I recognized the plane's paint scheme as it shot by; white with a brown stripe. It was a United Parcel Service freighter, heavily laden with packages.

The anti-lock brakes and huge tires did a good job, but not quite good enough. The cruiser went into a spin at over fifty miles-an-hour when it hit the sandy soil beside the runway.

"What the hell!" yelled Swenson, flooring the gas pedal as the body of the car began to rise, tilting toward the passenger side. The engine roared as the rear tires spun in the opposite direction of travel. Then…all movement ceased. The engine stalled. And there was silence.

We watched in the silence as the dust settled and the big jet taxied from the runway.

Swenson asked, "Are we dead?"

"I don't think so, but that sure wasn't like those big FBI chase scenes on TV."

"I think I wet myself," Swenson said weakly. "Wonder if this thing'll start?"

"What happened to Conchman?" I asked as the engine roared to life.

"Don't know," he replied. "Maybe he got sucked into one of those engines. My God, they were big."

"How fast were we going when we came up behind him?" I asked.

"A little over a-hundred-and-thirty."

"I thought so. That bastard sucker-punched us," I said. "He was trying to kill us."

Swenson didn't speak, but the look on his face asked what I meant.

"He must've been holding her on the ground 'til the last second 'cause those old Apaches only have a cruising speed of about one-eighty," I said. "He could've taken off long before he did."

"You mean that wasn't an accident?" asked Swenson.

"Nope," I replied. "He set us up."

That evening Agent Hinton called and told me that Conchman's plane had flown due west for seventy-five miles.

"He flew into a storm front—high wind, lightning, rain. Then he disappeared off radar. We assume he went down in the Gulf...Coast Guard'll search for the wreckage tomorrow."

He started to hang up then said, "Oh, and I guess you didn't hear...it appears that young Master Hedeon got in a few good shots. Turns out he was after Conchman, not you. There was blood on the tarmac from the car to where the plane was parked. It wasn't the kid's—so I doubt Mr. Conchman will be returning."

I wasn't so sure.

Chapter 35 — Justice

ONE WEEK LATER, we were back before Judge Harris. Marlene Saint Lucie had returned to Tallahassee. In her place were two young state attorneys with little experience, but a lot of nerve. One stood before the court and announced the state would accept a plea to second degree murder in exchange for life in prison. Even Judge Harris groaned at the announcement.

To prove Jon's innocence, we put on a mini-trial against Mikel Conchman.

Behrooz Caspari testified about the earring he had given Eddy Nash. He then identified the earring I had gotten back from Nash as being, "virtually identical to the one he had, if not the same."

Conchman had kept his Q-45 just long enough for it to turn against him. The car looked as good as new—shiny and black, with dark-tinted windows. Infiniti was one of the first manufacturers to offer a car phone as an option, and this one had all the options. It even came equipped with a CD player Conchman had stocked with classical music. We were fairly certain Donella Nash had made her last call from the Infiniti.

A search of the car produced an earring matching the one found on the victim after her death. It was firmly snagged in the carpet under the left side of the passenger seat. FBI technicians had to remove the seat to retrieve the earring.

Fletcher McBeth identified the earrings as looking like the ones given his daughter the Christmas before her death. Then he produced an identical pair which had belonged to his wife. The earrings had been purchased at the same time in Scotland.

An FBI expert testified all four earrings were made of the same type of rock—and how rare it is.

"There are a lot of types of rocks. Is there anything that sets this rock apart from the rest of the rocks in the world?" I asked.

"Yes, sir. The stone in these earrings is Lewisian gneiss. It is the oldest crystalline rock on earth and is found only on the Isle of Lewis on the western coast of Scotland. I rarely see any samples of it in the U.S."

FDLE hair and fiber expert, Jane Candy, re-examined the hairs and fibers found on the victim. Unlike at Clayton's trial, this time she was able to testify that she had found matches. Three fibers found on one of the victim's shoes matched the carpet in Conchman's Q-45.

Our final witness was Boris Hedeon. Confined to a wheelchair due to his injuries, and despite objections from the state, he was allowed to testify about certain conversations he had overheard.

"I was twelve years old in June of '91," he said. "It was right after I got out of school. I overheard my father and Mr. Conchman having an argument."

"Can you tell us the essence of that argument?" I asked. "Don't tell us their words, just the essence of the conversations."

"Mr. Conchman wanted my father to kill a young woman."

There was an audible gasp from the spectators. Judge Harris sat stone-faced, listening, but seemingly not really present.

Boris Hedeon continued, "Mr. Conchman said the girl had been blackmailing him and he wanted her dead. My father refused. He told Mr. Conchman if he wanted the girl dead, he'd have to kill her himself."

Realizing the two young prosecutors were probably too stunned to object to even blatant hearsay, I asked, "Was there another similar incident that you wish to tell the court about?"

"Yes, sir. Several weeks ago, Mr. Conchman took my father and Officer Flynt for a plane ride. They came by our house afterwards and talked in the yard."

"And what was the essence of that conversation?"

"Mr. Conchman told my father and Mr. Flynt that they had to kill a man and woman on a boat. It was supposed to look like a botched drug deal."

"Did he name the people he wanted killed?" I asked.

"Yes, sir. You and a Mrs. Clayton."

The state asked no questions. In fact, neither of the two young men seemed capable of speech.

"Your Honor, there's more," I said. "Is the court aware of the federal firearms charges against Mr. Conchman?"

"The court is aware. And...there's no need for any further evidence."

Judge Harris stopped the proceeding. He ordered Jon Clayton's convictions and sentences reversed. As he started to set the case for a new trial date, I interrupted.

"Your Honor, will the court entertain a motion to dismiss the charges under Rule 3.190 C, 3?" I asked, handing a short written motion to the clerk of the court.

I continued talking as I returned to the podium. "The defendant, Jon Clayton, is charged with an offense where there are no material disputed facts and the undisputed facts do not establish a *prima facie* case of guilt against him." I was patterning my argument after the language of the rule.

One of the young prosecutors stood up and said, "Your Honor, the state objects, and will file a traverse to this motion."

"Mr. Prosecutor, what facts can you point to that indicate this man is guilty of anything?" asked Judge Harris loudly.

"Your Honor, the state was able to convict him once, and we can do it again."

I started to speak, but Harris held up his hand to stop me. There was dead silence in the room. It was as though no one breathed. Then the judge spoke.

"This will probably be the last time I ever take the bench, and it is just as well. This case was to be my last capital case, and based on the evidence presented at trial, it looked like a solid conviction. But now...now I find out that the truth was not the whole truth. Now, I find out this man was framed, and framed by an officer of this court."

Judge Harris rose from his seat and continued. "I...I hope and pray...that this sort of thing is very rare. We all suspect it happens occasionally. Once is too often. And now—" He looked at the young prosecutor. "—that all of your evidence has turned to monkey ca-ca, you want me to deny this man his freedom. No! That will not happen. I have heard enough."

The judge took a deep breath. "Having heard the evidence presented at the prior hearing and again here today, this court grants the defendant's motion to dismiss. The state has nothing, absolutely nothing, to link this man to the crimes charged. Therefore, this court orders the indictments for murder, kidnapping and rape dismissed. He is to be released immediately." Then pounding his gavel for each word as punctuation, the judge ended with, "Enough is enough!"

But Jon Clayton was not released. When he was convicted of possession of a firearm by a convicted felon, his new sentence was run consecutive to the sentence for the aggravated battery on the biker. Additionally, the new conviction was a violation of his probation in the aggravated battery, and Judge Harris had sentenced him to five years in prison for the violation of probation. Thus, Jon Clayton was just starting his two year sentence for possession of a firearm when the murder conviction was dismissed.

It wouldn't be death row, but he had two more years to serve in prison.

Chapter 36 — A New Year

LABOR DAY WEEKEND, Tiny Jacobs announced he was selling Delicto's to a national restaurant chain. Three days later, the sale was consummated. Two days after that, Tiny's thirty-foot Scarab sport-boat was found eight miles offshore, going in circles with only one engine running. There was no sign of Tiny.

Tiny never wore a life jacket and he had been out alone at night. Two weeks later, we held a short wake for him at Delicto's. It was the last time the doors of the club were opened. Bulldozers were literally being unloaded in the parking lot as we celebrated the big guy's life.

Noah and Mitzi Raphael decided to winter aboard *The Rx* in Annapolis, Maryland, and offered me free use of their condo for the winter. Although snowbirds were flocking south and I suggested they rent it, they didn't want strangers in their nest.

"Just enjoy it," Mitzi said. "We'll see you in late spring...or maybe next fall!"

Judge Harris refused to grant any motions to reduce Jon's sentence on the weapons charge because it was a bona fide plea bargain.

"Mr. Clayton admitted his crime and agreed to that sentence, and I won't change it," Harris said. "But I'll tell you what I will do. I'll order him kept here in Pinellas County until you can run a pardon by the governor. I'll even recommend the sheriff make him a trustee."

Which is how Jean and Jon got to see a whole lot more of each other. The first week of November, Jon asked me to be his best man at their wedding, to be held sometime after his release. I told them I'd be proud to accept the honor. I was glad they didn't ask me to give away the bride—I felt I'd already done that.

THE TUESDAY BEFORE Thanksgiving, Sergeant Ramirez, Jean Clayton, two prison guards and I went before the governor for a special clemency hearing. Not only did Jon still face almost two more years in prison, but as a convicted felon he could never again vote, have firearms in his possession, or do a lot of other things we take for granted. We were there to ask the governor for a full pardon and restoration of his civil rights.

The two prison guards told the governor what a model prisoner Jon had been, and how he had counseled other prisoners. Then they surprised us all when they presented a sworn, notarized letter from the biker whose legs Jon had broken.

Like a lot of prisoners, the biker had found Jesus and wanted to do the right thing. His letter not only asked the governor to pardon Jon, but in it, the biker admitted the entire incident was his fault. He even thanked Jon for stopping him from raping and possibly killing the barmaid.

Then, the barmaid, Jean Clayton, walked to the podium to speak for Jon. Jean looked radiant as she stood before the governor and his six cabinet members. Her voice was strong and clear as she spoke. "Mr. Governor, I'm the woman who Jon Clayton saved from rape and possibly death."

She went on to tell the story of her husband's death and how Jon had helped her with the restaurant, how he took so little for himself, and how he risked so much for her. She explained the details of the guilty plea, and how it was a plea of convenience, taken so Jon could continue to help her at the restaurant.

Jean ended with her own plea. "Mr. Governor, Jon never would've pled guilty if he'd known how it would hurt not only him, but me and so many others. He should never have been convicted. If you can find it in your heart, please grant him a full pardon and restore his rights as a citizen. We need more men like him. I need him back in my life."

I had prepared a long speech, but Jean's simple honesty was too hard an act to follow. "Mr. Governor," I said, "Jon Clayton started as my client. I do this now out of a deep belief that what we ask is only just. We ask you to do what is right. This is one of those rare cases in which a complete pardon is absolutely proper."

AT EIGHT IN the morning, the first day of December, the phone rang. When I answered, a woman said, "Mr. Thomas, please hold for the governor."

"Woody Thomas? I want you to know I overruled my one cabinet member who was against your boy's pardon. I just signed the papers for complete pardons and restoration of rights in both cases. Wish Mr. Clayton and that sweet young woman a Merry Christmas for me. Okay?...Mr. Thomas?"

I was speechless for a few seconds, but thanked him and hung up knowing I would have the papers in my hands within forty-eight hours.

Jon Clayton was finally released from prison four days before Christmas.

IT WAS A warm day for Christmas, even in Clearwater. A lone figure walked down the dock next to *Defender*. He looked like a snowbird with gray hair, shorts, Hard Rock Café T-shirt, and pasty white skin hanging loose on his arms and legs.

"Captain Thomas, I'm glad to find you home," he said, sticking out his hand. "Stan Hinton…remember me?"

"I didn't recognize you without your suit and tie. You look positively naked! Come aboard and make yourself comfortable? You on vacation or something?"

"I'm retired as of last week," he said. "I just wanted to wish you a Merry Christmas and thank you. You did me a favor this year."

"You mean letting you use me as tiger bait?"

"Nah, that was business," he replied, as we settled into *Defender's* cockpit. "Thirty years ago, I joined the FBI and became close friends with my partner, Kyle Murdock. Then, in the 70s, during all the hoopla about domestic spying, he quit and went with another agency. Your security clearance investigation for the Pentagon was the last case we worked together.

"Then you pop up here and we end up working together again. It was sort of a circle. You brought us back together and made me realize what I got into law enforcement for. You and Murdock still have the fire for justice that I lost years ago."

"I'm glad I could help. Will I ever meet this elusive Mr. Murdock?"

"You may. He wants to talk to you." He started to get up. "Oh, and by the way, we finally found Conchman's plane. Son-of-a-gun made it to Mexico alive. He'll live pretty well, too. Seems before he left, he transferred over two million dollars to some offshore banks." He smiled as he added, "Just thought you'd like to know."

Later Christmas Day, I arrived at Billy Jean's for dinner. Jon and Jean had invited fifty friends to eat and celebrate Jon's first Christmas of freedom. After we had eaten our fill of turkey and dressing, and attacked the desserts, I pinged on my water glass for attention.

"Ladies and gentlemen, Jean and Jon. The Governor of the great State of Florida wishes me to extend to you his warmest wishes for a Merry Christmas. And, folks, just so you know, the governor has granted Jon complete pardons. Now he can serve on a jury again!"

We laughed and cheered. Then Jon and Jean rose to speak. They thanked us all, especially me. I got choked up and teary-eyed.

"We have a couple of announcements, too," said Jean.

I don't know when he'd arrived. I know I'd have noticed him at the dinner—if for no other reason than the fact the tall, smiling man who now stood between Jon and Jean was wearing a blue, red, and green tartan kilt. Suddenly, there was silence in the room as people whispered the question on my mind, "Isn't he the victim's father?"

Jon Clayton answered the question. "Ladies and gentlemen...friends, no doubt some of you recognize this man as Fletcher McBeth. And no doubt you know of the tragedies in his life."

There was silence in the room as we all recognized that something momentous was taking place, but we had no idea how momentous it was.

"Sometimes, horrible things can bring people together in strange ways," said McBeth. "I lost my family, my children and my wife, and fate—" He stopped and looked first at Jean then at Jon and smiled. "—Fate has brought me a new family."

Whispers of confusion began to grow, but stopped when Jon raised his hand. "Friends, many of you know I lost my parents when I was young. And some of you know that Jean...has no parents."

Jon looked toward Jean and nodded. Jean took Fletcher McBeth's huge hand in hers and raised it, then said loudly, "This wonderful man has asked us to be his family."

In the cheering and confusion that followed, we all could see that they were, in fact, family—even though none of us really understood the full implication of the announcement. Finally, Jon and Jean got everyone's attention for the next announcement. We all wondered what it could be after the first.

"Friends, as many of you know, Jon and I have become very close in the years since Bill died," said Jean.

"And we're getting married!" yelled Jon.

Again the shouting broke out and the party continued until late in the evening. Midnight found me sitting with Fletcher McBeth, swapping stories of our past. I was tired and said it was time for me to leave when McBeth asked me to sit another moment more.

"I lost my wife and both my daughters," said McBeth looking down. "I am the last of my branch of the clan." Then he raised his eyes and smiled at me and said, "But since I'm adopting Jean, and since Jon will become my son-in-law, I guess you could become my brother—I never had a brother. What say you, Woody Thomas?"

"Your brother?" I said. "But I'm Irish."

McBeth placed his huge hand on my shoulder, smiled and said, "We can't all be perfect. Irish or not, you'll always be welcome in my home."

That night as I walked home to *Defender*, for the first time in memory, I did not feel alone. But there was more. I felt somehow...different. I felt appreciated. I felt...worthy.

EVERY NEW YEAR'S Day for twenty-five years, I've taken a few special hours to write in my journal. I write about what has happened, what I learned from it all, and what I'd like to see happen in the future. This New Year's Day was to be no different.

At noon I was alone in Sand Key County Park. It was chilly enough for a jacket. I sat in the sun in my old, wooden lounge chair overlooking the beach, in the dunes on the north end of the park for protection from the wind. I listened to the gentle surf as I tried to remember the places and faces from the preceding year.

A red BMW Z-3 eased into the parking lot around one. The entire parking lot was empty, yet it pulled next to Vicky and parked. I was not pleased.

A large man in a white shirt, tan tie, and light tan linen suit got out and walked toward me. There was something familiar about him—something that made me uncomfortable. I became even more uncomfortable when he walked directly to me and stopped.

"Woody Thomas?" he asked. His voice sounded familiar.

The man was clean-shaven. Tan, but not dark. He was handsome with a square, dimpled chin and short, styled hair. Sunglasses hid his eyes. He looked like a cop—a really large cop. I realized he was probably as big as Tiny, but the suit was cut to display a much trimmer waist.

As I struggled to get out of the lounge chair and stand up in the sand, the stranger smiled, and offered me a hand, saying, "I've driven all the way from Washington, D.C. to make you an offer."

I could see the front tag on his car. It was from D.C. all right, a vanity plate which read, "MURDOCK."

"Are you Murdock? With the FBI?"

"Nope. I'm Murdock with ATF, but I'm retiring in forty-four days. I like the way you work. I'm opening an office as a private investigator here in St. Pete, and I'd like to offer you my services.

"My name's Kyle," he said taking off his dark glasses. His eyes twinkled and he smiled as he stuck out his hand and said, "But you can still call me Tiny."

The end

ABOUT THE AUTHOR

As an attorney for the State of Florida, Ray Dix helped provide the last line of defense for men and women sentenced to be executed by the state.

Dix previously had a career in business; designed and built boats; and served in both the Army (Military Intelligence 1966-1970), and the Coast Guard Reserves. He lives on the Gulf Coast with his beautiful wife and two rescue-cats, and is writing the next Woody Thomas novel.

A NOTE FROM THE AUTHOR

If you enjoyed this book, please tell your friends and acquaintances, and if you have time, write a review of it through the on-line sales sites. Only by word-of-mouth from satisfied readers do books truly succeed in finding a wide readership.

Thank you,

Ray Dix

www.raydixbooks.com

19530950R00131

Made in the USA
Charleston, SC
29 May 2013